DON QUIXOTE

VOL. II.

THE
INGENIOUS GENTLEMAN
DON QUIXOTE
OF LA MANCHA
BY
MIGUEL DE CERVANTES SAAVEDRA.

A TRANSLATION
With Introduction and Notes.

BY
JOHN ORMSBY,
Translator of the "Poem of the Cid."

IN FOUR VOLS. — II.

WILDSIDE PRESS

CONTENTS

OF

THE SECOND VOLUME.

———◦◦◦———

PART I.—continued.

CHAPTER XXV.

CHAPTER XXVI.

CHAPTER XXVII.

CHAPTER XXVIII.

DON QUIXOTE

PART I.—continued

CHAPTER XXV.

DON QUIXOTE took leave of the goatherd, and once more mounting Rocinante bade Sancho follow him, which he, having no ass, did very discontentedly. They proceeded slowly, making their way into the most rugged part of the mountain, Sancho all the while dying to have a talk with his master, and longing for him to begin, so that there should be no breach of the injunction laid upon him; but unable to keep silence so long he said to him, 'Señor Don Quixote, give me your worship's blessing and dismissal, for I'd like to go home at once to my wife and children with whom I can at any rate talk and converse as much as I like; for to want me to go through these solitudes day and night and not speak to you when I have a mind is burying me alive. If luck would have it that animals spoke as they did in the days of Guisopete,[1] it would not be so bad, because I could talk to Rocinante about whatever came into my head, and so put up with my ill-fortune; but it is a hard case, and not to be borne with patience, to go seeking adventures all one's life and get nothing but kicks and blanketings, brick-

---

[1] I.e. Æsop.

bats and punches, and with all this to have to sew up one's mouth without daring to say what is in one's heart, just as if one were dumb.'

'I understand thee, Sancho,' replied Don Quixote ; 'thou art dying to have the interdict I placed upon thy tongue removed ; consider it removed, and say what thou wilt, on condition that the removal is not to last longer than while we are wandering in these mountains.'

'So be it,' said Sancho ; 'let me speak now, for God knows what will happen by-and-by ; and to take advantage of the permit at once, I ask, what made your worship stand up so for that Queen Majimasa, or whatever her name is, or what did it matter whether that abbot[1] was a friend of hers or not ? for if your worship had let that pass—and you were not a judge in the matter—it is my belief the madman would have gone on with his story, and the blow of the stone, and the kicks, and more than half a dozen cuffs would have been escaped.'

'In faith, Sancho,' answered Don Quixote, 'if thou knewest as I do what an honourable and illustrious lady Queen Madasima was, I know thou wouldst say I had great patience that I did not break in pieces the mouth that uttered such blasphemies, for a very great blasphemy it is to say or imagine that a queen has made free with a surgeon. The truth of the story is that that Master Elisabad whom the madman mentioned was a man of great prudence and sound judgment, and served as governor and physician to the queen, but to suppose that she was his mistress is nonsense deserving very severe punishment ; and as a proof that

[1] See Note A, p. 25.

Cardenio did not know what he was saying, remember when he said it he was out of his wits.'

'That is what I say,' said Sancho; 'there was no occasion for minding the words of a madman; for if good luck had not helped your worship, and he had sent that stone at your head instead of at your breast, a fine way we should have been in for standing up for my lady yonder, God confound her! And then, would not Cardenio have gone free as a madman?'

'Against men in their senses or against madmen,' said Don Quixote, 'every knight-errant is bound to stand up for the honour of women, whoever they may be, much more for queens of such high degree and dignity as Queen Madasima, for whom I have a particular regard on account of her amiable qualities; for, besides being extremely beautiful, she was very wise, and very patient under her misfortunes, of which she had many; and the counsel and society of the Master Elisabad were a great help and support to her in enduring her afflictions with wisdom and resignation; hence the ignorant and ill-disposed vulgar took occasion to say and think that she was his mistress; and they lie, I say it once more, and will lie two hundred times more, all who think and say so.'

'I neither say nor think so,' said Sancho; 'let them look to it; with their bread let them eat it;[1] they have rendered account to God whether they misbehaved or not; I come from my vineyard, I know nothing;[2] I am not fond of prying into other men's lives; he who buys and lies feels

---

[1] Prov. 170. This is the first of Sancho's frequent volleys of random proverbs.   [2] Prov. 247.

it in his purse;[1] moreover, naked was I born, naked I find myself, I neither lose nor gain;[2] but if they did, what is that to me? many think there are flitches where there are no hooks;[3] but who can put gates to the open plain?[4] moreover they said of God—'

'God bless me,' said Don Quixote, 'what a set of absurdities thou art stringing together! What has what we are talking about got to do with the proverbs thou art threading one after the other? For God's sake hold thy tongue, Sancho, and henceforward keep to prodding thy ass and don't meddle in what does not concern thee; and understand with all thy five senses that everything I have done, am doing, or shall do, is well founded on reason and in conformity with the rules of chivalry, for I understand them better than all the knights in the world that profess them.'

'Señor,' replied Sancho, 'is it a good rule of chivalry that we should go astray through these mountains without path or road, looking for a madman who when he is found will perhaps take a fancy to finish what he began, not his story, but your worship's head and my ribs, and end by breaking them altogether for us?'

'Peace, I say again, Sancho,' said Don Quixote, 'for let me tell thee it is not so much the desire of finding that madman that leads me into these regions as that which I have of performing among them an achievement wherewith I shall win eternal name and fame throughout the known world; and it shall be such that I shall thereby set the

[1] Prov. 55.   [2] Prov. 73.

[3] Prov. 226: *estacas*—literally, stakes or pegs on which to hang them; expressive of unreasonable expectations.

[4] Prov. 195.

seal on all that can make a knight-errant perfect and famous.'

'And is it very perilous, this achievement?' asked Sancho.

'No,' replied he of the Rueful Countenance; 'though it may be in the dice that we may throw deuce-ace instead of sixes; but all will depend on thy diligence.'

'On my diligence!' said Sancho.

'Yes,' said Don Quixote, 'for if thou dost return soon from the place where I mean to send thee, my penance will be soon over, and my glory will soon begin. But as it is not right to keep thee any longer in suspense, waiting to see what comes of my words, I would have thee know, Sancho, that the famous Amadis of Gaul was one of the most perfect knights-errant—I am wrong to say he was one; he stood alone, the first, the only one, the lord of all that were in the world in his time. A fig for Don Belianis, and for all who say he equalled him in any respect, for, my oath upon it, they are deceiving themselves! I say, too, that when a painter desires to become famous in his art he endeavours to copy the originals of the rarest painters that he knows; and the same rule holds good for all the most important crafts and callings that serve to adorn a state; thus will he who would be esteemed prudent and patient imitate Ulysses, in whose person and labours Homer presents to us a lively picture of prudence and patience; as Virgil, too, shows us in the person of Æneas the virtue of a pious son and the sagacity of a brave and skilful captain; not representing or describing them as they were, but as they ought to be, so as to leave the example of their virtues to posterity. In the same way Amadis was the pole-star, day-star, sun of valiant and devoted knights, whom all we who fight under the banner of love and chivalry are bound to imitate. This, then, being so, I consider, friend Sancho, that the knight-errant who shall imitate him most closely will come nearest to reaching the perfection of chivalry. Now one of the instances in which this knight most conspicuously showed his prudence, worth, valour, patience, fortitude, and love, was when he withdrew, rejected by the Lady Oriana, to do penance upon the Peña Pobre, changing his name into that of Beltenebros,[1] a name assuredly significant and appropriate to the life which he had voluntarily adopted. So, as it is easier for me to imitate him in this than in cleaving giants asunder, cutting off serpents' heads, slaying dragons, routing armies, destroying fleets, and breaking enchantments, and as this place is so well suited for a similar purpose, I must not allow the opportunity to escape which now so conveniently offers me its forelock.'

'What is it in reality,' said Sancho, ' that your worship means to do in such an out-of-the-way place as this ? '

'Have I not told thee,' answered Don Quixote, ' that I mean to imitate Amadis here, playing the victim of despair, the madman, the maniac, so as at the same time to imitate the valiant Roland, when at the fountain he had evidence of the fair Angelica having disgraced herself with Medoro and through grief thereat went mad, and plucked up trees, troubled the waters of the clear springs, slew shepherds, destroyed flocks, burned down huts, levelled houses, dragged

[1] See Note B, p. 26.

mares after him, and perpetrated a hundred thousand other outrages worthy of everlasting renown and record? And though I have no intention of imitating Roland, or Orlando, or Rotolando (for he went by all these names), step by step in all the mad things he did, said, and thought, I will make a rough copy to the best of my power of all that seems to me most essential; but perhaps I shall content myself with the simple imitation of Amadis, who, without giving way to any mischievous madness but merely to tears and sorrow, gained as much fame as the most famous.'

'It seems to me,' said Sancho, 'that the knights who behaved in this way had provocation and cause for those follies and penances; but what cause has your worship for going mad? What lady has rejected you, or what evidence have you found to prove that the lady Dulcinea del Toboso has been trifling with Moor or Christian?'

'There is the point,' replied Don Quixote, 'and that is the beauty of this business of mine; no thanks to a knight-errant for going mad when he has cause; the thing is to turn crazy without any provocation, and to let my lady know, if I do this in the dry, what I would do in the moist;[1] moreover I have abundant cause in the long separation I have endured from my lady till death, Dulcinea del Toboso; for as thou didst hear that shepherd Ambrosio say the other day, in absence all ills are felt and feared; and so, friend Sancho, waste no time in advising me against so rare, so happy, and so unheard-of an imitation; mad I am, and mad I must be until thou returnest with the answer to a letter that I mean to send by thee to my lady Dulcinea; and if it be

[1] Probably an allusion to the 'green tree' and the 'dry.'

such as my constancy deserves, my insanity and penance
will come to an end; and if it be to the opposite effect, I
shall become mad in earnest, and, being so, I shall suffer
no more; thus in whatever way she may answer I shall
escape from the struggle and affliction in which thou wilt
leave me, enjoying in my senses the boon thou bearest me,
or as a madman not feeling the evil thou bringest me.
But tell me, Sancho, hast thou got Mambrino's helmet
safe; for I saw thee take it up from the ground when that
wretch tried to break it in pieces but could not, by which
the fineness of its temper may be séen?'

To which Sancho made answer, 'By the living God, Sir
Knight of the Rueful Countenance, I cannot endure or bear
with patience some of the things that your worship says;
and from them I begin to suspect that all you tell me about
chivalry, and winning kingdoms and empires, and giving
islands, and bestowing other rewards and dignities after
the custom of knights-errant, must be all made up of wind
and lies, and all pigments or figments, or whatever we may
call them; for what would anyone think that heard your
worship calling a barber's basin Mambrino's helmet without ever seeing the mistake all this time,[1] but that one
who says and maintains such things must have his brains
addled?   I have the basin in my sack all dinted, and I am
taking it home to have it mended, to trim my beard in it,
if, by God's grace, I am allowed to see my wife and children
some day or other.'

'Look here, Sancho,' said Don Quixote, 'by him thou
didst swear by just now I swear thou hast the most limited

[1] See Note C, p. 26.

understanding that any squire in the world has or ever had. Is it possible that all this time thou hast been going about with me thou hast never found out that all things belonging to knights-errant seem to be illusions and nonsense and ravings, and to go always by contraries? And not because it really is so, but because there is always a swarm of enchanters in attendance upon us that change and alter everything with us, and turn things as they please, and according as they are disposed to aid or destroy us; thus what seems to thee a barber's basin seems to me Mambrino's helmet, and to another it will seem something else; and rare foresight it was in the sage who is on my side to make what is really and truly Mambrino's helmet seem a basin to everybody, for, being held in such estimation as it is, all the world would pursue me to rob me of it; but when they see it is only a barber's basin they do not take the trouble to obtain it; as was plainly shown by him who tried to break it, and left it on the ground without taking it, for, by my faith, had he known it he would never have left it behind. Keep it safe, my friend, for just now I have no need of it; indeed, I shall have to take off all this armour and remain as naked as I was born, if I have a mind to follow Roland rather than Amadis in my penance.'[1]

Thus talking they reached the foot of a high mountain which stood like an isolated peak among the others that surrounded it. Past its base there flowed a gentle brook, all around it spread a meadow so green and luxuriant that

[1] For the character of Orlando's insanity, see the *Orlando Furioso,* canto xxiii. st. 130 *et seq.*

it was a delight to the eyes to look upon it, and forest trees in abundance, and shrubs and flowers, added to the charms of the spot. Upon this place the Knight of the Rueful Countenance fixed his choice for the performance of his penance, and as he beheld it exclaimed in a loud voice as though he were out of his senses, ' This is the place, oh, ye heavens, that I select and choose for bewailing the misfortune in which ye yourselves have plunged me : this is the spot where the overflowings of mine eyes shall swell the waters of yon little brook, and my deep and endless sighs shall stir unceasingly the leaves of these mountain trees, in testimony and token of the pain my persecuted heart is suffering. Oh, ye rural deities, whoever ye be that haunt this lone spot, give ear to the complaint of a wretched lover whom long absence and brooding jealousy have driven to bewail his fate among these wilds and complain of the hard heart of that fair and ungrateful one, the end and limit of all human beauty ! Oh, ye wood nymphs and dryads, that dwell in the thickets of the forest, so may the nimble wanton satyrs by whom ye are vainly wooed never disturb your sweet repose, help me to lament my hard fate or at least weary not at listening to it ! Oh, Dulcinea del Toboso, day of my night, glory of my pain, guide of my path, star of my fortune, so may Heaven grant thee in full all thou seekest of it, bethink thee of the place and condition to which absence from thee has brought me, and make that return in kindness that is due to my fidelity ! Oh, lonely trees, that from this day forward shall bear me company in my solitude, give me some sign by the gentle movement of your boughs that my presence is not distasteful to you ! Oh' thou, my squire, pleasant companion in my prosperous and adverse fortunes, fix well in thy memory what thou shalt see me do here, so that thou mayest relate and report it to the sole cause of all,' and so saying he dismounted from Rocinante, and in an instant relieved him of saddle and bridle, and giving him a slap on the croup, said, 'He gives thee freedom who is bereft of it himself, oh steed as excellent in deed as thou art unfortunate in thy lot; begone where thou wilt, for thou bearest written on thy forehead that neither Astolfo's hippogriff, nor the famed Frontino that cost Bradamante so dear, could equal thee in speed.'[1]

Seeing this Sancho said, 'Good luck to him who has saved us the trouble of stripping the pack-saddle off Dapple! By my faith he would not have gone without a slap on the croup and something said in his praise; though if he were here I would not let anyone strip him, for there would be no occasion, as he had nothing of the lover or victim of despair about him, inasmuch as his master, which I was while it was God's pleasure, was nothing of the sort; and indeed, Sir Knight of the Rueful Countenance, if my departure and your worship's madness are to come off in earnest, it will be as well to saddle Rocinante again in order that he may supply the want of Dapple, because it will save me time in going and returning; for if I go on foot I don't know when I shall get there or when I shall get back, as I am, in truth, a bad walker.'

'I declare, Sancho,' returned Don Quixote, 'it shall be as thou wilt, for thy plan does not seem to me a bad

[1] The hippogriff was the winged horse on which Astolfo went in quest of information about Orlando. Frontino was the name of the destrier of Ruggiero, Bradamante's lover.

one, and three days hence thou wilt depart, for I wish thee to observe in the meantime what I do and say for her sake, that thou mayest be able to tell it.'

'But what more have I to see besides what I have seen?' said Sancho.

'Much thou knowest about it!' said Don Quixote. 'I have now got to tear up my garments, to scatter about my armour, knock my head against these rocks, and more of the same sort of thing, which thou must witness.'

'For the love of God,' said Sancho, 'be careful, your worship, how you give yourself those knocks on the head, for you may come across such a rock, and in such a way, that the very first may put an end to the whole contrivance of this penance; and I should think, if indeed knocks on the head seem necessary to you, and this business cannot be done without them, you might be content—as the whole thing is feigned, and counterfeit, and in joke—you might be content, I say, with giving them to yourself in the water, or against something soft, like cotton; and leave it all to me; for I'll tell my lady that your worship knocked your head against a point of rock harder than a diamond.'

'I thank thee for thy good intentions, friend Sancho,' answered Don Quixote, 'but I would have thee know that all these things I am doing are not in joke, but very much in earnest, for anything else would be a transgression of the ordinances of chivalry, which forbid us to tell any lie whatever under the penalties due to apostasy; and to do one thing instead of another is just the same as lying; so my knocks on the head must be real, solid, and valid, without anything sophisticated or fanciful about them, and it will be needful to leave me some lint to dress my wounds, since fortune has compelled us to do without the balsam we lost.'

'It was worse losing the ass,' replied Sancho, 'for with him lint and all were lost; but I beg of your worship not to remind me again of that accursed liquor, for my soul, not to say my stomach, turns at hearing the very name of it; and I beg of you, too, to reckon as past the three days you allowed me for seeing the mad things you do, for I take them as seen already and pronounced upon, and I will tell wonderful stories to my lady; so write the letter and send me off at once, for I long to return and take your worship out of this purgatory where I am leaving you.'

'Purgatory dost thou call it, Sancho?' said Don Quixote, 'rather call it hell, or even worse if there be anything worse.'

'For one who is in hell,' said Sancho, '*nulla est retentio*, as I have heard say.'

'I do not understand what *retentio* means,' said Don Quixote.

'*Retentio*,' answered Sancho, 'means that whoever is in hell never comes nor can come out of it, which will be the opposite case with your worship or my legs will be idle, that is if I have spurs to enliven Rocinante: let me once get to El Toboso and into the presence of my lady Dulcinea, and I will tell her such things of the follies and madnesses (for it is all one) that your worship has done and is still doing, that I will manage to make her softer than a glove though I find her harder than a cork tree; and with her sweet and honeyed answer I will come back through the air like a witch, and take your worship out of this purgatory

that seems to be hell but is not, as there is hope of getting
out of it; which, as I have said, those in hell have not, and
I believe your worship will not say anything to the contrary.'

'That is true,' said he of the Rueful Countenance, 'but
how shall we manage to write the letter?'

'And the ass-colt order too,' added Sancho.

'All shall be included,' said Don Quixote; 'and as there
is no paper, it would be well done to write it on the leaves
of trees, as the ancients did, or on tablets of wax; though
that would be as hard to find just now as paper. But it has
just occurred to me how it may be conveniently and even
more than conveniently written, and that is in the note-
book that belonged to Cardenio, and thou wilt take care to
have it copied on paper, in a good hand, at the first village
thou comest to where there is a schoolmaster, or if not, any
sacristan will copy it; but see thou give it not to any
notary to copy, for they write a law hand that Satan could
not make out.'

'But what is to be done about the signature?' said
Sancho.

'The letters of Amadis were never signed,' said Don
Quixote.

'That is all very well,' said Sancho, 'but the order must
needs be signed, and if it is copied they will say the signature is false, and I shall be left without ass-colts.'

'The order shall go signed in the same book,' said Don
Quixote, 'and on seeing it my niece will make no difficulty
about obeying it; as to the love-letter thou canst put by
way of signature, " *Yours till death, the Knight of the Rueful
Countenance.*" And it will be no great matter if it is in

some other person's hand, for as well as I recollect Dulcinea can neither read nor write, nor in the whole course of her life has she seen handwriting or letter of mine, for my love and hers have been always platonic, not going beyond a modest look, and even that so seldom that I can safely swear I have not seen her four times in all these twelve years I have been loving her more than the light of these eyes that the earth will one day devour; and perhaps even of those four times she has not once perceived that I was looking at her: such is the retirement and seclusion in which her father Lorenzo Corchuelo and her mother Aldonza Nogales have brought her up.'

'So, so!' said Sancho; 'Lorenzo Corchuelo's daughter is the lady Dulcinea del Toboso, otherwise called Aldonza Lorenzo?'

'She it is,' said Don Quixote, 'and she it is that is worthy to be lady of the universe.'

'I know her well,' said Sancho, 'and let me tell you she can fling a crowbar as well as the lustiest lad in all the town. Giver of all good! but she is a brave lass, and a right and stout one, and fit to be helpmate to any knight-errant that is or is to be, who may make her his lady: the whoreson wench, what pith she has and what a voice! I can tell you one day she posted herself on the top of the belfry of the village to call some labourers of theirs that were in a ploughed field of her father's, and though they were better than half a league off they heard her as well as if they were at the foot of the tower; and the best of her is that she is not a bit prudish, for she has plenty of affability, and jokes with everybody, and has a grin and a jest for everything.

So, Sir Knight of the Rueful Countenance, I say you not
only may and ought to do mad freaks for her sake, but you
have a good right to give way to despair and hang yourself;
and no one who knows of it but will say you did well,
though the devil should take you; and I wish I were on my
road already, simply to see her, for it is many a day since I
saw her, and she must be altered by this time, for going
about the fields always, and the sun and the air spoil
women's looks greatly.   But I must own the truth to your
worship, Señor Don Quixote; until now I have been under a
great mistake, for I believed truly and honestly that the
lady Dulcinea must be some princess your worship was
in love with, or some person great enough to deserve
the rich presents you have sent her, such as the Biscayan
and the galley slaves, and many more no doubt, for your
worship must have won many victories in the time when I
was not yet your squire.   But all things considered, what
good can it do the lady Aldonza Lorenzo (I mean the lady
Dulcinea del Toboso) to have the vanquished your worship
sends or will send coming to her and going down on their
knees before her ?   Because maybe when they came she'd
be hackling flax or threshing on the threshing floor,[1] and
they'd be ashamed to see her, and she'd laugh, or resent
the present.'

    ' I have before now told thee many times, Sancho,' said
Don Quixote, ' that thou art a mighty great chatterer, and
that with a blunt wit thou art always striving at sharpness;

----

[1] Corn in Spain is not threshed, as we understand the word, but separated from the ear by means of the trilla, a sort of toothless harrow, which
is dragged over it as it lies on the era or threshing floor.

but to show thee what a fool thou art and how rational I am, I would have thee listen to a short story. Thou must know that a certain widow, fair, young, independent, and rich, and above all free and easy, fell in love with a sturdy strapping young lay-brother; his superior came to know of it, and one day said to the worthy widow by way of brotherly remonstrance, "I am surprised, señora, and not without good reason, that a woman of such high standing, so fair, and so rich as you are, should have fallen in love with such a mean, low, stupid fellow as So-and-so, when in this house there are so many masters, graduates, and divinity students from among whom you might choose as if they were a lot of pears, saying this one I'll take, that I won't take;" but she replied to him with great sprightliness and candour, "My dear sir, you are very much mistaken, and your ideas are very old-fashioned, if you think that I have made a bad choice in So-and-so, fool as he seems; because for all I want with him he knows as much and more philosophy than Aristotle." In the same way, Sancho, for all I want with Dulcinea del Toboso she is just as good as the most exalted princess on earth. It is not to be supposed that all those poets who sang the praises of ladies under the fancy names they give them, had any such mistresses. Thinkest thou that the Amarillises, the Phillises, the Sylvias, the Dianas, the Galateas, the Filidas, and all the rest of them, that the books, the ballads, the barbers' shops, the theatres are full of, were really and truly ladies of flesh and blood, and mistresses of those that glorify and have glorified them?[1] Nothing of the kind; they only invent them

[1] See Note D, p. 26.

for the most part to furnish a subject for their verses, and
that they may pass for lovers, or for men who have some
pretensions to be so ; and so it is enough for me to think
and believe that the good Aldonza Lorenzo is fair and
virtuous ; and as to her pedigree it is very little matter, for
no one will examine into it for the purpose of conferring
any order upon her,[1] and I, for my part, reckon her the
most exalted princess in the world. For thou shouldst know,
Sancho, if thou dost not know, that two things alone beyond
all others are incentives to love, and these are great beauty
and a good name, and these two things are to be found in
Dulcinea in the highest degree, for in beauty no one equals
her and in good name few approach her ; and to put the
whole thing in a nutshell, I persuade myself that all I say
is as I say, neither more nor less, and I picture her in my
imagination as I would have her to be, as well in beauty as in
condition ; Helen approaches her not nor does Lucretia come
up to her, nor any other of the famous women of times past,
Greek, Barbarian, or Latin ; and let each say what he will,
for if in this I am taken to task by the ignorant, I shall not
be censured by the critical.'

'I say that your worship is entirely right,' said Sancho,
'and that I am an ass. But I know not how the name of
ass came into my mouth, for a rope is not to be mentioned
in the house of him who has been hanged ;[2] but now for
the letter, and then, God be with you, I am off.'

---

[1] Proof of hidalguia was necessary before some orders, that of Santiago
for instance, could be conferred.

[2] Prov. 219.

Don Quixote took out the note-book, and, retiring to one side, very deliberately began to write the letter, and when he had finished it he called to Sancho, saying he wished to read it to him, so that he might commit it to memory, in case of losing it on the road; for with evil fortune like his anything might be apprehended. To which Sancho replied, 'Write it two or three times there in the book and give it to me, and I will carry it very carefully, because to expect me to keep it in my memory is all nonsense, for I have such a bad one that I often forget my own name; but for all that repeat it to me, as I shall like to hear it, for surely it will run as if it was in print.'

'Listen,' said Don Quixote, 'this is what it says:

'*Don Quixote's Letter to Dulcinea del Toboso.*

'Sovereign and exalted Lady,—The pierced by the point of absence, the wounded to the heart's core, sends thee, sweetest Dulcinea del Toboso, the health that he himself enjoys not. If thy beauty despises me, if thy worth is not for me, if thy scorn is my affliction, though I be sufficiently long-suffering, hardly shall I endure this anxiety, which, besides being oppressive, is protracted. My good squire Sancho will relate to thee in full, fair ingrate, dear enemy, the condition to which I am reduced on thy account: if it be thy pleasure to give me relief, I am thine; if not, do as may be pleasing to thee; for by ending my life I shall satisfy thy cruelty and my desire.

'Thine till death,

'THE KNIGHT OF THE RUEFUL COUNTENANCE.'

'By the life of my father,' said Sancho, when he heard the letter, 'it is the loftiest thing I ever heard. Body of me! how your worship says everything as you like in it! And how well you fit in "The Knight of the Rueful Countenance" into the signature. I declare your worship is indeed the very devil, and there is nothing you don't know.'

'Everything is needed for the calling I follow,' said Don Quixote.

'Now then,' said Sancho, 'let your worship put the order for the three ass-colts on the other side, and sign it very plainly, that they may recognise it at first sight.'

'With all my heart,' said Don Quixote, and as soon as he had written it he read it to this effect:

'Mistress Niece,—By this first of ass-colts please pay to Sancho Panza, my squire, three of the five I left at home in your charge: said three ass-colts to be paid and delivered for the same number received here in hand, which upon this and upon his receipt shall be duly paid. Done in the heart of the Sierra Morena, the twenty-seventh of August of this present year.'

'That will do,' said Sancho; 'now let your worship sign it.'

'There is no need to sign it,' said Don Quixote, 'but merely to put my flourish,[1] which is the same as a signature, and enough for three asses, or even three hundred.'

'I can trust your worship,' returned Sancho; 'let me

[1] The *rubrica*, or flourish, which is always a part of a Spanish signature.

go and saddle Rocinante, and be ready to give me your blessing, for I mean to go at once without seeing the fooleries your worship is going to do; I'll say I saw you do so many that she will not want any more.'

'At any rate, Sancho,' said Don Quixote, 'I should like —and there is reason for it—I should like thee, I say, to see me stripped to the skin and performing a dozen or two of insanities, which I can get done in less than half an hour; for having seen them with thine own eyes, thou canst then safely swear to the rest that thou wouldst add; and I promise thee thou wilt not tell of as many as I mean to perform.'

'For the love of God, master mine,' said Sancho, 'let me not see your worship stripped, for it will sorely grieve me, and I shall not be able to keep from tears, and my head aches so with all I shed last night for Dapple, that I am not fit to begin any fresh weeping; but if it is your worship's pleasure that I should see some insanities, do them in your clothes, short ones, and such as come readiest to hand; for I myself want nothing of the sort, and, as I have said, it will be a saving of time for my return, which will be with the news your worship desires and deserves. If not, let the lady Dulcinea look to it; if she does not answer reasonably, I swear as solemnly as I can that I will fetch a fair answer out of her stomach with kicks and cuffs; for why should it be borne that a knight-errant as famous as your worship should go mad without rhyme or reason for a—? her ladyship had best not drive me to say it, for by God I will speak out and have done with it, though it stop the sale: I am pretty good at that! she little knows me; faith, if she knew me she'd be afraid of me.'

'In faith, Sancho,' said Don Quixote, 'to all appearance thou art not sounder in thy wits than I am.'

'I am not so mad,' answered Sancho, 'but I am more peppery; but apart from all this, what has your worship to eat until I come back? Will you sally out on the road like Cardenio to force it from the shepherds?'

'Let not that anxiety trouble thee,' replied Don Quixote, 'for even if I had it I should not eat anything but the herbs and the fruits which this meadow and these trees may yield me; the beauty of this business of mine lies in not eating, and in performing other mortifications.'

'Do you know what I am afraid of?' said Sancho upon this; 'that I shall not be able to find my way back to this spot where I am leaving you, it is such an out-of-the-way place.'

'Observe the landmarks well,' said Don Quixote, 'for I will try not to go far from this neighbourhood, and I will even take care to mount the highest of these rocks to see if I can discover thee returning; however, not to miss me and lose thyself, the best plan will be to cut some branches of the broom that is so abundant about here, and as thou goest to lay them at intervals until thou hast come out upon the plain; these will serve thee, after the fashion of the clue in the labyrinth of Theseus, as marks and signs for finding me on thy return.'

'So I will,' said Sancho Panza, and having cut some, he asked his master's blessing, and not without many tears on both sides took his leave of him, and mounting Rocinante, of whom Don Quixote charged him earnestly to have as much care as of his own person, he set out for the plain, strewing at intervals the branches of broom as his master had recommended him; and so he went his way, though Don Quixote still entreated him to see him do were it only a couple of mad acts. He had not gone a hundred paces, however, when he returned and said, 'I must say, señor, your worship said quite right, that in order to be able to swear without a weight on my conscience that I had seen you do mad things, it would be well for me to see if it were only one; though in your worship's remaining here I have seen a very great one.'

'Did I not tell thee so?' said Don Quixote. 'Wait, Sancho, and I will do them in the saying of a credo,' and pulling off his breeches in all haste he stripped himself to his skin and his shirt, and then, without more ado, he cut a couple of gambados[1] in the air, and a couple of somer-saults, heels over head, making such a display that, not to see it a second time, Sancho wheeled Rocinante round, and felt easy, and satisfied in his mind that he could swear he had left his master mad; and so we will leave him to follow his road until his return, which was a quick one.

[1] *Zapatetas*, capers in which the sole of the shoe is struck with the hand.

Note A (*page* 4).

Sancho in his aptitude for blunders takes 'Elisabad' to be the name of some *abad* or abbot. There are three Madasimas mentioned in the *Amadis*, but not one of them is a queen, nor has Master Elisabad anything to do with any of them. He was in the service of the lady Grasinda, and by her orders attended Amadis when wounded. Scott, in the article on the *Amadis* in the *Edinburgh Review*, suggests that Cervantes must have meant Queen Brio-lania, apparently confounding her also with Grasinda.

Note B (*page* 8).

Beltenebros, i.e. ' fair-obscure.' Clemencin suggests that the Peña Pobre (so called because those who sojourned there had to live in extreme poverty) was Mont St. Michel, but Jersey would suit the description better, as it is said to be seven leagues from the coast of the Insula Firme, which was clearly the mainland of Brittany or Normandy.

Note C (*page* 10).

In the original it is ' for more than four days,' to which some commentators, Hartzenbusch among them, object, as not more than one day had passed since the encounter with the barber. But ' more than four' is a very common phrase to express indefinitely a considerable number, and it is more probably used here vaguely by Sancho in the sense in which I have rendered it.

Note D (*page* 19).

The introduction here of the name of his own heroine, Galatea, may be taken for what it is worth as a contradiction of the story that by Galatea he meant the mother of his daughter Isabel. An ingenious speculator might suggest that his object was to soothe the susceptibilities of his wife Doña Catalina, but it is clear that there were no heartburnings on that score in the household of Cervantes.

CHAPTER XXVI.

IN WHICH ARE CONTINUED THE REFINEMENTS WHEREWITH DON QUIXOTE PLAYED THE PART OF A LOVER IN THE SIERRA MORENA.

RETURNING to the proceedings of him of the Rueful Countenance when he found himself alone, the history says that when Don Quixote had completed the performance of the somersaults or capers, naked from the waist down and clothed from the waist up, and saw that Sancho had gone off without waiting to see any more crazy feats, he climbed up to the top of a high rock, and there set himself to consider what he had several times before considered without ever coming to any conclusion on the point, namely whether it would be better and more to his purpose to imitate the outrageous madness of Roland, or the melancholy madness of Amadis; and communing with himself he said, 'What wonder is it if Roland was so good a knight and so valiant as everyone says he was, when, after all, he was enchanted, and nobody could kill him save by thrusting a corking pin [1] into the sole of his foot, and he always wore shoes with seven iron soles? Though cunning devices did not avail him against Bernardo del Carpio, who knew all about them, and strangled him in his arms at Roncesvalles. But putting the question of his valour aside, let us come to his losing his wits, for certain it is that he did lose them in consequence

[1] See Note A, p. 38.

of the proofs he discovered at the fountain, and the intelligence the shepherd gave him of Angelica having slept more
than two afternoons with Medoro, a little curly-headed
Moor, and page to Agramante.[1] If he was persuaded
that this was true, and that his lady had wronged him,
it is no wonder that he should have gone mad; but I,
how am I to imitate him in his madness, unless I can imitate him in the cause of it? For my Dulcinea, I will
venture to swear, never saw a Moor, as he is in his proper
costume, in her life, and is this day as the mother that bore
her, and I should plainly be doing her a wrong if, fancying
anything else, I were to go mad with the same kind of madness as "Roland the Furious." On the other hand, I see
that Amadis of Gaul, without losing his senses and without
doing anything mad, acquired as a lover as much fame as
the most famous; for, according to his history, on finding
himself rejected by his lady Oriana, who had ordered him
not to appear in her presence until it should be her pleasure,
all he did was to retire to the Peña Pobre in company with
a hermit, and there he took his fill of weeping until Heaven
sent him relief in the midst of his great grief and need.
And if this be true, as it is, why should I now take the
trouble to strip stark naked, or do mischief to these trees
which have done me no harm, or why am I to disturb the
clear waters of these brooks which will give me to drink
whenever I have a mind? Long live the memory of
Amadis, and let him be imitated so far as is possible by
Don Quixote of La Mancha, of whom it will be said, as was
said of the other, that if he did not achieve great things, he

---

[1] See Note B, p. 38.

died in attempting them; and if I am not repulsed or rejected by my Dulcinea, it is enough for me, as I have said,
to be absent from her. And so, now to business; come to
my memory ye deeds of Amadis, and show me how I am to
begin to imitate you. I know already that what he chiefly
did was to pray and commend himself to God; but what am
I to do for a rosary, for I have not got one?' And then it
occurred to him how he might make one, and that was by
tearing a great strip off the tail of his shirt which hung
down, and making eleven knots on it, one bigger than the
rest, and this served him for a rosary all the time he was
there, during which he repeated countless ave-marias.[2] But
what distressed him greatly was not having another hermit
there to confess him and receive consolation from; and so he
solaced himself with pacing up and down the little meadow,
and writing and carving on the bark of the trees and on
the fine sand a multitude of verses all in harmony with his
sadness, and some in praise of Dulcinea; but, when he was
found there afterwards, the only ones completely legible
that could be discovered were those that follow here:

> Ye on the mountain side that grow,
>   Ye green things all, trees, shrubs, and bushes,
> Are ye aweary of the woe
>   That this poor aching bosom crushes?
> If it disturb you, and I owe
>   Some reparation, it may be a
> Defence for me to let you know
> Don Quixote's tears are on the flow,
>   And all for distant Dulcinea
>   Del Toboso.

[1] See Note C, p. 38.

The lealest lover time can show,
　Doomed for a lady-love to languish,
Among these solitudes doth go,
　A prey to every kind of anguish.
Why Love should like a spiteful foe
　Thus use him, he hath no idea,
But hogsheads full—this doth he know—
Don Quixote's tears are on the flow,
　And all for distant Dulcinea
　　　　Del Toboso.

Adventure-seeking doth he go
　Up rugged heights, down rocky valleys,
But hill or dale, or high or low,
　Mishap attendeth all his sallies :
Love still pursues him to and fro,
　And plies his cruel scourge—ah me ! a
Relentless fate, an endless woe ;
Don Quixote's tears are on the flow,
　And all for distant Dulcinea
　　　　Del Toboso.[1]

The addition of ' Del Toboso ' to Dulcinea's name gave
rise to no little laughter among those who found the above
lines, for they suspected Don Quixote must have fancied
that unless he added ' del Toboso ' when he introduced the
name of Dulcinea the verse would be unintelligible ; which
was indeed the fact, as he himself afterwards admitted.　He
wrote many more, but, as has been said, these three verses
were all that could be plainly and perfectly deciphered.　In
this way, and in sighing and calling on the fauns and satyrs
of the woods and the nymphs of the streams, and Echo,

[1] See Note D, p. 38.

moist and mournful, to answer, console, and hear him, as well as in looking for herbs to sustain him, he passed his time until Sancho's return; and had that been delayed three weeks, as it was three days, the Knight of the Rueful Countenance would have worn such an altered countenance that the mother that bore him would not have known him: and here it will be well to leave him, wrapped up in sighs and verses, to relate how Sancho Panza fared on his mission.

As for him, coming out upon the high road, he made for El Toboso, and the next day reached the inn where the mishap of the blanket had befallen him. As soon as he recognised it he felt as if he were once more flying through the air, and he could not bring himself to enter it though it was an hour when he might well have done so, for it was dinner-time, and he longed to taste something hot as it had been all cold fare with him for many days past. This craving drove him to draw near to the inn, still undecided whether to go in or not, and as he was hesitating there came out two persons who at once recognised him, and said one to the other, 'Señor licentiate, is not he on the horse there Sancho Panza who, our adventurer's housekeeper told us, went off with her master as esquire?'

'So it is,' said the licentiate, 'and that is our friend Don Quixote's horse;' and if they knew him so well it was because they were the curate and the barber of his own village, the same who had carried out the scrutiny and sentence upon the books; and as soon as they recognised Sancho Panza and Rocinante, being anxious to hear of Don Quixote, they approached, and calling him by his name the curate said, ' Friend Sancho Panza, where is your master ? '

Sancho recognised them at once, and determined to keep secret the place and circumstances where and under which he had left his master, so he replied that his master was engaged in a certain quarter on a certain matter of great importance to him which he could not disclose for the eyes in his head.

' Nay, nay,' said the barber, ' if you don't tell us where he is, Sancho Panza, we will suspect, as we suspect already, that you have murdered and robbed him, for here you are mounted on his horse ; in fact, you must produce the master of the hack, or else take the consequences.'

' There is no need of threats with me,' said Sancho, ' for I am not a man to rob or murder anybody ; let his own fate, or God who made him, kill each one ; my master is engaged very much to his taste doing penance in the midst of these mountains ; ' and then, offhand and without stopping, he told them how he had left him, what adventures had befallen him, and how he was carrying a letter to the lady Dulcinea del Toboso, the daughter of Lorenzo Corchuelo, with whom he was over head and ears in love.[1] They were both amazed at what Sancho Panza told them ; for though they were aware of Don Quixote's madness and the nature of it, each time they heard of it they were filled with fresh wonder. They then asked Sancho Panza to show them the letter he was carrying to the lady Dulcinea del Toboso. He said it was written in a note-book, and

---

[1] The Spanish phrase is stronger— *hasta los higados*—' down to the liver.'

that his master's directions were that he should have it copied on paper at the first village he came to. On this the curate said if he showed it to him, he himself would make a fair copy of it. Sancho put his hand into his bosom in search of the note-book but could not find it, nor, if he had been searching until now, could he have found it, for Don Quixote had kept it, and had never given it to him, nor had he himself thought of asking for it. When Sancho discovered he could not find the book his face grew deadly pale, and in great haste he again felt his body all over, and seeing plainly it was not to be found, without more ado he seized his beard with both hands and plucked away half of it, and then, as quick as he could and without stopping, gave himself half a dozen cuffs on the face and nose till they were bathed in blood.

Seeing this, the curate and the barber asked him what had happened him that he gave himself such rough treatment.

'What should happen me?' replied Sancho, 'but to have lost from one hand to the other, in a moment, three ass-colts, each of them like a castle?'

'How is that?' said the barber.

'I have lost the note-book,' said Sancho, 'that contained the letter to Dulcinea, and an order signed by my master in which he directed his niece to give me three ass-colts out of four or five he had at home;' and he then told them about the loss of Dapple.

The curate consoled him, telling him that when his master was found he would get him to renew the order, and make a fresh draft on paper, as was usual and customary ; for those made in note-books were never accepted or honoured.

Sancho comforted himself with this, and said if that were so the loss of Dulcinea's letter did not trouble him much, for he had it almost by heart, and it could be taken down from him wherever and whenever they liked.

'Repeat it then, Sancho,' said the barber, 'and we will write it down afterwards.'

Sancho Panza stopped to scratch his head to bring back the letter to his memory, and balanced himself now on one foot, now the other, one moment staring at the ground, the next at the sky, and after having half gnawed off the end of a finger and kept them in suspense waiting for him to begin, he said, after a long pause, 'By God, señor licentiate, devil a thing can I recollect of the letter ; but it said at the beginning, "Exalted and scrubbing Lady." '

'It cannot have said "scrubbing," ' said the barber, 'but "superhuman" or "sovereign." '

'That is it,' said Sancho ; 'then, as well as I remember, it went on, "The wounded, and wanting of sleep, and the pierced, kisses your worship's hands, ungrateful and very unrecognised fair one ; " and it said something or other about health and sickness that he was sending her ; and from that it went tailing off until it ended with "Yours till death, the Knight of the Rueful Countenance." '

It gave them no little amusement, both of them, to see what a good memory Sancho had, and they complimented him greatly upon it, and begged him to repeat the letter a couple of times more, so that they too might get it by heart to write it out by-and-by. Sancho repeated it three times, and as he did, uttered three thousand more absurdities; then he told them more about his master; but he never said a word about the blanketing that had befallen himself in that inn, into which he refused to enter. He told them, moreover, how his lord, if he brought him a favourable answer from the lady Dulcinea del Toboso, was to put himself in the way of endeavouring to become an emperor, or at least a monarch; for it had been so settled between them, and with his personal worth and the might of his arm it was an easy matter to come to be one: and how on becoming one his lord was to make a marriage for him (for he would be a widower by that time, as a matter of course) and was to give him as a wife one of the damsels of the empress, the heiress of some rich and grand state on the mainland, having nothing to do with islands of any sort, for he did not care for them now. All this Sancho delivered with so much composure—wiping his nose from time to time—and with so little common-sense that his two hearers were again filled with wonder at the force of Don Quixote's madness that could run away with this poor man's reason. They did not care to take the trouble of disabusing him of his error, as they considered that since it did not in any way hurt his conscience it would be better to leave him in it, and they would have all the more amusement in listening to his simplicities; and so they bade him pray to God for his lord's health, as it was a very likely and a very feasible thing for him in course of time to come to be an emperor, as he said, or at least an archbishop or some other dignitary of equal rank.

To which Sancho made answer, 'If fortune, sirs, should bring things about in such a way that my master should have a mind, instead of being an emperor, to be an arch-bishop, I should like to know what archbishops-errant commonly give their squires?'

'They commonly give them,' said the curate, 'some simple benefice or cure, or some place as sacristan which brings them a good fixed income, not counting the altar fees, which may be reckoned at as much more.'

'But for that,' said Sancho, 'the squire must be un-married, and must know, at any rate, how to help at mass, and if that be so, woe is me, for I am married already and I don't know the first letter of the A B C. What will become of me if my master takes a fancy to be an archbishop and not an emperor, as is usual and customary with knights-errant?'

'Be not uneasy, friend Sancho,' said the barber, 'for we will entreat your master, and advise him, even urging it upon him as a case of conscience, to become an emperor and not an archbishop, because it will be easier for him as he is more valiant than lettered.'

'So I have thought,' said Sancho; 'though I can tell you he is fit for anything: what I mean to do for my part is to pray to our Lord to place him where it may be best for him, and where he may be able to bestow most favours upon me.'

'You speak like a man of sense,' said the curate, 'and you will be acting like a good Christian; but what must now be done is to take steps to coax your master out of that useless penance you say he is performing; and we had best

turn into this inn to consider what plan to adopt, and also
to dine, for it is now time.'

Sancho said they might go in, but that he would wait
there outside, and that he would tell them afterwards the
reason why he was unwilling, and why it did not suit him
to enter it ; but he begged them to bring him out something
to eat, and to let it be hot, and also to bring barley for
Rocinante. They left him and went in, and presently the
barber brought him out something to eat. By-and-by, after
they had between them carefully thought over what they
should do to carry out their object, the curate hit upon an
idea very well adapted to humour Don Quixote, and effect
their purpose; and his notion, which he explained to the
barber, was that he himself should assume the disguise of a
wandering damsel, while the other should try as best he could
to pass for a squire, and that they should thus proceed to
where Don Quixote was, and he, pretending to be an aggrieved
and distressed damsel, should ask a favour of him, which
as a valiant knight-errant he could not refuse to grant; and
the favour he meant to ask him was that he should accompany her whither she would conduct him, in order to redress
a wrong which a wicked knight had done her, while at the
same time she should entreat him not to require her to
remove her mask, nor ask her any question touching her
circumstances until he had righted her with the wicked
knight. And he had no doubt that Don Quixote would
comply with any request made in these terms, and that in
this way they might remove him and take him to his own
village, where they would endeavour to find out if his extraordinary madness admitted of any kind of remedy.

Note A (*page* 27).

Properly a '*blanca* pin,' i.e. of the size sold for a blanca, or half a maravedi, as we say a 'tenpenny nail.' Viardot, strangely misinterpreting the very common idiom *de á*, indicating the price of an article, and fancying the *á* to have a negative power as in Greek, explains it as 'a pin made of some substance not white.'

Note B (*page* 28).

'Occhi avea neri, e chioma crespa d' oro :
Angel parea di quei del sommo coro.'
Orlando Furioso, c. xviii. st. 166.

But Medoro was not in the service of Agramante, but in that of Dardinel; and a little higher up Cervantes has made another slip of memory, for it was not Orlando, but Ferrau who wore the

'sette piastre fatte a buone tempre.'
Orlando Furioso, c. xii. st. 48.

Note C (*page* 29).

It is thus the passage stands in the first edition ; in the second Don Quixote makes his rosary with oak galls off a cork tree. The alteration was made, no doubt, at the suggestion of some critics who thought the passage indecorous, but Cervantes had nothing to do with it.

Note D (*page* 30).

In its ingenuity of rhyme and versification and its transcendent absurdity this is the best piece of humorous verse in *Don Quixote*. Even Clemencin, who generally grumbles at the verses of Cervantes, cannot help giving it a word of praise. It is, of course, impossible in an English translation to do more than suggest the character of the original, for anything like close imitation is unattainable.

CHAPTER XXVII.

OF HOW THE CURATE AND THE BARBER PROCEEDED WITH THEIR
SCHEME; TOGETHER WITH OTHER MATTERS WORTHY OF
RECORD IN THIS GREAT HISTORY.

THE curate's plan did not seem a bad one to the barber,
but on the contrary so good that they immediately set about
putting it in execution. They begged a petticoat and
hood of the landlady, leaving her in pledge a new cassock of
the curate's; and the barber made a beard out of a grey or red
ox-tail in which the landlord used to stick his comb. The
landlady asked them what they wanted these things for, and
the curate told her in a few words about the madness of
Don Quixote, and how this disguise was intended to get him
away from the mountain where he then was. The landlord
and landlady immediately came to the conclusion that the
madman was their guest, the balsam man and master of
the blanketed squire, and they told the curate all that had
passed between him and them, not omitting what Sancho
had been so silent about. Finally the landlady dressed up
the curate in a style that left nothing to be desired; she
put on him a cloth petticoat with black velvet stripes a palm
broad, all slashed, and a bodice of green velvet set off by a
binding of white satin, which as well as the petticoat must

have been made in the time of king Wamba.[1] The curate
would not let them cover him with the hood, but put on his
head a little quilted linen cap which he used for a night-cap,
and bound his forehead with a strip of black silk, while
with another he made a mask with which he concealed his
beard and face very well. He then put on his hat, which
was broad enough to serve him for an umbrella, and
enveloping himself in his cloak seated himself woman-
fashion on his mule, while the barber mounted his with
a beard down to the waist of mingled red and white, for
it was, as has been said, the tail of a red ox. They took
leave of all, and of the good Maritornes, who, sinner as
she was, promised to pray a rosary of prayers that God
might grant them success in such an arduous and Christian
undertaking as that they had in hand. But hardly had he
sallied forth from the inn when it struck the curate that he
was doing wrong in rigging himself out in that fashion, as
it was an indecorous thing for a priest to dress himself that
way even though much might depend upon it ; and saying
so to the barber he begged him to change dresses, as it was
fitter he should be the distressed damsel, while he himself
would play the squire's part, which would be less derogatory
to his dignity ; otherwise he was resolved to have nothing
more to do with the matter, and let the devil take Don
Quixote. Just at this moment Sancho came up, and on
seeing the pair in such a costume he was unable to restrain his laughter ; the barber, however, agreed to do as
the curate wished, and, altering their plan, the curate went

---

[1] Wamba, a king of the Gothic line who reigned from 672 to 680.

on to instruct him how to play his part and what to say to
Don Quixote to induce and compel him to come with them
and give up his fancy for the place he had chosen for his
idle penance. The barber told him he could manage it
properly without any instruction, and as he did not care
to dress himself up until they were near where Don
Quixote was, he folded up the garments, and the curate
adjusted his beard, and they set out under the guidance of
Sancho Panza, who went along telling them of the encounter
with the madman they met in the Sierra, saying nothing,
however, about the finding of the valise and its contents;
for with all his simplicity the lad was a trifle covetous.

The next day they reached the place where Sancho had
laid the broom-branches as marks to direct him to where
he had left his master, and recognising it he told them that
here was the entrance, and that they would do well to dress
themselves, if that was required to deliver his master; for
they had already told him that going in this guise and
dressing in this way were of the highest importance in
order to rescue his master from the pernicious life he had
adopted; and they charged him strictly not to tell his
master who they were, or that he knew them, and should he
ask, as ask he would, if he had given the letter to Dulcinea,
to say that he had, and that, as she did not know how to
read,[1] she had given an answer by word of mouth, saying
that she commanded him, on pain of her displeasure, to
come and see her at once; and it was a very important
matter for himself, because in this way and with what they

---

[1] A curious reason for giving a verbal answer; but if she did not know
how to read, *à fortiori* she could not write.

meant to say to him they felt sure of bringing him back to
a better mode of life and inducing him to take immediate
steps to become an emperor or monarch, for there was no
fear of his becoming an archbishop. All this Sancho
listened to and fixed it well in his memory, and thanked
them heartily for intending to recommend his master to
be an emperor instead of an archbishop, for he felt sure
that in the way of bestowing rewards on their squires
emperors could do more than archbishops-errant. He
said, too, that it would be as well for him to go on before
them to find him, and give him his lady's answer; for that
perhaps might be enough to bring him away from the place
without putting them to all this trouble. They approved
of what Sancho proposed, and resolved to wait for him
until he brought back word of having found his master.

Sancho pushed on into the glens of the Sierra, leaving
them in one through which there flowed a little gentle
rivulet, and where the rocks and trees afforded a cool
and grateful shade. It was an August day with all the
heat of one, and the heat in those parts is intense, and the
hour was three in the afternoon, all which made the spot the
more inviting and tempted them to wait there for Sancho's
return, which they did. They were reposing, then, in the
shade, when a voice unaccompanied by the notes of any
instrument, but sweet and pleasing in its tone, reached their
ears, at which they were not a little astonished, as the place
did not seem to them likely quarters for one who sang so
well; for though it is often said that shepherds of rare voice
are to be found in the woods and fields, this is rather a
flight of the poet's fancy than the truth. And still more

surprised were they when they perceived that what they heard sung were the verses not of rustic shepherds, but of the polished wits of the city;[1] and so it proved, for the verses they heard were these:[2]

What makes my quest of happiness seem vain?
Disdain.
What bids me to abandon hope of ease?
Jealousies.
What holds my heart in anguish of suspense?
Absence.
If that be so, then for my grief
Where shall I turn to seek relief,
When hope on every side lies slain
By Absence, Jealousies, Disdain?

What the prime cause of all my woe doth prove?
Love.
What at my glory ever looks askance?
Chance.
Whence is permission to afflict me given?
Heaven.
If that be so, I but await
The stroke of a resistless fate,
Since, working for my woe, these three,
Love, Chance, and Heaven, in league I see.

[1] *Cortesanos*, not courtiers, but persons who have caught the tone, tastes, and culture of *La Corte*, 'the Court,' as the capital was always called.

[2] These are intended to be echo verses; but, as Clemencin has pointed out, the echoes are nothing but rhymes. In the novel of the *Ilustre Fregona*, Cervantes introduced similar verses, which Lope de Vega turned into ridicule in a parody.

What must I do to find a remedy?
          Die.
What is the lure for love when coy and strange?
          Change.
What, if all fail, will cure the heart of sadness?
          Madness.
   If that be so, it is but folly
   To seek a cure for melancholy:
   Ask where it lies; the answer saith
   In Change, in Madness, or in Death.

The hour, the summer season, the solitary place, the voice and skill of the singer, all contributed to the wonder and delight of the two listeners, who remained still waiting to hear something more; finding, however, that the silence continued some little time, they resolved to go in search of the musician who sang with so fine a voice; but just as they were about to do so they were checked by the same voice, which once more fell upon their ears, singing this

SONNET.[1]

When heavenward, holy Friendship, thou didst go
   Soaring to seek thy home beyond the sky,
   And take thy seat among the saints on high,
It was thy will to leave on earth below
Thy semblance, and upon it to bestow
   Thy veil, wherewith at times hypocrisy,
   Parading in thy shape, deceives the eye,
And makes its vileness bright as virtue show.

[1] See Note A, p. 58.

Friendship, return to us, or force the cheat
   That wears it now, thy livery to restore,
     By aid whereof sincerity is slain.
If thou wilt not unmask thy counterfeit,
   This earth will be the prey of strife once more,
     As when primæval discord held its reign.

The song ended with a deep sigh, and again the listeners remained waiting attentively for the singer to resume ; but perceiving that the music had now turned to sobs and heart-rending moans they determined to find out who the unhappy being could be whose voice was as rare as his sighs were piteous, and they had not proceeded far when on turning the corner of a rock they discovered a man of the same aspect and appearance as Sancho had described to them when he told them the story of Cardenio. He, showing no astonishment when he saw them, stood still with his head bent down upon his breast like one in deep thought, without raising his eyes to look at them after the first glance when they suddenly came upon him. The curate, who was aware of his misfortune and recognised him by the description, being a man of good address, approached him and in a few sensible words entreated and urged him to quit a life of such misery, lest he should end it there, which would be the greatest of all misfortunes. Cardenio was then in his right mind, free from any attack of that madness which so frequently carried him away, and seeing them dressed in a fashion so unusual among the frequenters of those wilds, could not help showing some surprise, especially when he heard them speak of his case as if it were a

well-known matter (for the curate's words gave him to
understand as much); so he replied to them thus, ' I
see plainly, sirs, whoever you may be, that Heaven, whose
care it is to succour the good, and even the wicked very
often, here, in this remote spot, cut off from human intercourse, sends me, though I deserve it not, those who seek
to draw me away from this to some better retreat, showing
me by many and forcible arguments how unreasonably I
act in leading the life I do; but as they know not what I
know, that if I escape from this evil I shall fall into another
still greater, perhaps they will set me down as a weak-
minded man, or, what is worse, one devoid of reason; nor
would it be any wonder, for I myself can perceive that the
effect of the recollection of my misfortunes is so great and
works so powerfully to my ruin, that in spite of myself I
become at times like a stone, without feeling or consciousness; and I come to feel the truth of it when they tell me
and show me proofs of the things I have done when the
terrible fit overmasters me; and all I can do is bewail my
lot in vain, and idly curse my destiny, and plead for my
madness by telling how it was caused, to any that care to
hear it; for no reasonable beings on learning the cause will
wonder at the effects; and if they cannot help me at least
they will not blame me, and the repugnance they feel at my
wild ways will turn into pity for my woes. If it be, sirs,
that you are here with the same design as others have come
with, before you proceed with your wise arguments, I entreat
you to hear the story of my countless misfortunes, for perhaps when you have heard it you will spare yourselves the

trouble you would take in offering consolation to grief that is beyond the reach of it.'

As they, both of them, desired nothing more than to hear from his own lips the cause of his suffering, they entreated him to tell it, promising not to do anything for his relief or comfort that he did not wish; and thereupon the unhappy gentleman began his sad story in nearly the same words and manner in which he had related it to Don Quixote and the goatherd a few days before, when, through Master Elisabad, and Don Quixote's scrupulous observance of what was due to chivalry, the tale was left unfinished, as this history has already recorded; but now fortunately the mad fit kept off, and allowed him to tell it to the end; and so, coming to the incident of the note which Don Fernando had found in the volume of 'Amadis of Gaul,' Cardenio said that he remembered it perfectly and that it was in these words:

' Luscinda to Cardenio.

' Every day I discover merits in you that oblige and compel me to hold you in higher estimation; so if you desire to relieve me of this obligation without cost to my honour, you may easily do so. I have a father who knows you and loves me dearly, who without putting any constraint on my inclination will grant what will be reasonable for you to have, if it be that you value me as you say and as I believe you do.'

By this letter I was induced, as I told you, to demand Luscinda for my wife, and it was through it that Luscinda came to be regarded by Don Fernando as one of the most discreet and prudent women of the day, and this letter it was that suggested his design of ruining me before mine could be carried into effect.

I told Don Fernando that all Luscinda's father was waiting for
was that mine should ask her of him, which I did not dare to
suggest to him, fearing that he would not consent to do so; not
because he did not know perfectly well the rank, goodness, virtue,
and beauty of Luscinda, and that she had qualities that would do
honour to any family in Spain, but because I was aware that he
did not wish me to marry so soon, before seeing what the duke
Ricardo would do for me. In short, I told him I did not venture
to mention it to my father, as well on account of that difficulty,
as of many others that discouraged me, though I knew not
well what they were, only that it seemed to me that what I
desired was never to come to pass. To all this Don Fernando
answered that he would take it upon himself to speak to my
father, and persuade him to speak to Luscinda's father. O, am-
bitious Marius! O, cruel Catiline! O, wicked Sylla! O, perfidious Ganelon! O, treacherous Vellido! O, vindictive Julian![1]
O, covetous Judas! Traitor, cruel, vindictive, and perfidious,
wherein had this poor wretch failed in his fidelity, who with such
frankness showed thee the secrets and the joys of his heart?
What offence did I commit? What words did I utter, or what
counsels did I give that had not the furtherance of thy honour
and welfare for their aim? But, woe is me, wherefore do I
complain? for sure it is that when misfortunes spring from the
stars, descending from on high they fall upon us with such fury
and violence that no power on earth can check their course nor
human device stay their coming. Who could have thought that
Don Fernando, a high-born gentleman, intelligent, bound to me
by gratitude for my services, one that could win the object of his
love wherever he might set his affections, could have become so
morbid, as they say, as to rob me of my one ewe lamb that was
not even yet in my possession? But laying aside these useless

---

[1] Ganelon or Galalon, who betrayed Roland and the Peers at Roncesvalles; Vellido Dolfos, who treacherously slew Sancho II. at the siege of
Zamora in 1072; and Count Julian, who admitted the Arabs into Spain to
revenge himself upon Roderic.

and unavailing reflections, let us take up the broken thread of my
unhappy story.

To proceed, then : Don Fernando finding my presence an
obstacle to the execution of his treacherous and wicked design,
resolved to send me to his elder brother under the pretext of
asking money from him to pay for six horses which, purposely,
and with the sole object of sending me away that he might the
better carry out his infernal scheme, he had purchased the very
day he offered to speak to my father, and the price of which he
now desired me to fetch. Could I have anticipated this treachery ?
Could I by any chance have suspected it ? Nay; so far from that,
I offered with the greatest pleasure to go at once, in my satisfaction
at the good bargain that had been made. That night I spoke
with Luscinda, and told her what had been agreed upon with Don
Fernando, and how I had strong hopes of our fair and reasonable
wishes being realised. She, as unsuspicious as I was of the
treachery of Don Fernando, bade me try to return speedily,
as she believed the fulfilment of our desires would be delayed only
so long as my father put off speaking to hers. I know not why it
was that on saying this to me her eyes filled with tears, and there
came a lump in her throat that prevented her from uttering a word
of many more that it seemed to me she was striving to say to
me. I was astonished at this unusual turn, which I never before
observed in her, for we always conversed, whenever good fortune
and my ingenuity gave us the chance, with the greatest gaiety
and cheerfulness, without mingling tears, sighs, jealousies, doubts,
or fears with our words ; it was all on my part a eulogy of my
good fortune that Heaven should have given her to me for my
mistress ; I glorified her beauty, I extolled her worth and her
understanding ; and she paid me back by praising in me what in
her love for me she thought worthy of praise ; and besides we
had a hundred thousand trifles and doings of our neighbours and
acquaintances to talk about, and the utmost extent of my boldness
was to take, almost by force, one of her fair white hands and carry
it to my lips, as well as the closeness of the low grating that separated us allowed me. But the night before the unhappy day of my

departure she wept, she moaned, she sighed, and she withdrew leaving me filled with perplexity and amazement, overwhelmed at the sight of such strange and affecting signs of grief and sorrow in Luscinda; but not to dash my hopes I ascribed it all to the depth of her love for me and the pain that separation gives those who love tenderly. At last I took my departure, sad and dejected, my heart filled with fancies and suspicions, but not knowing well what it was I suspected or fancied; plain omens pointing to the sad event and misfortune that was awaiting me.

I reached the place whither I had been sent, gave the letter to Don Fernando's brother, and was kindly received but not promptly dismissed, for he desired me to wait, very much against my will, eight days in some place where the duke his father was not likely to see me, as his brother wrote that the money was to be sent without his knowledge; all of which was a scheme of the treacherous Don Fernando, for his brother had no want of money to enable him to despatch me at once.

The command was one that exposed me to the temptation of disobeying it, as it seemed to me impossible to endure life for so many days separated from Luscinda, especially after leaving her in the sorrowful mood I have described to you; nevertheless as a dutiful servant I obeyed, though I felt it would be at the cost of my well-being. But four days later there came a man in quest of me with a letter which he gave me, and which by the address I perceived to be from Luscinda, as the writing was hers. I opened it with fear and trepidation, persuaded that it must be something serious that had impelled her to write to me when at a distance, as she seldom did so when I was near. Before reading it I asked the man who it was that had given it to him, and how long he had been upon the road; he told me that as he happened to be passing through one of the streets of the city at the hour of noon, a very beautiful lady called to him from a window, and with tears in her eyes said to him hurriedly, ' Brother, if you are, as you seem to be, a Christian, for the love of God I entreat you to have this letter despatched without a moment's delay to the person named in the address, all which is well known, and by this you

will render a great service to our Lord ; and that you may be at
no inconvenience in doing so take what is in this handkerchief ; '
and said he, ' with this she threw me a handkerchief out of the
window in which were tied up a hundred reals and this gold ring
which I bring here together with the letter I have given you.   And
then without waiting for any answer she left the window, though
not before she saw me take the letter and the handkerchief, and
I had by signs let her know that I would do as she bade me ;
and so, seeing myself so well paid for the trouble I would have in
bringing it to you, and knowing by the address that it was to you
it was sent (for, señor, I know you very well), and also unable to
resist that beautiful lady's tears, I resolved to trust no one else,
but to come myself and give it to you, and in sixteen hours from
the time when it was given me I have made the journey, which,
as you know, is eighteen leagues.'

All the while the good-natured improvised courier was telling
me this, I hung upon his words, my legs trembling under me
so that I could scarcely stand.   However, I opened the⸱letter and
read these words :

' The promise Don Fernando gave you to urge your father to
speak to mine, he has fulfilled much more to his own satisfaction
than to your advantage.   I have to tell you, señor, that he has
demanded me for a wife, and my father, led away by what he considers Don Fernando's superiority over you, has favoured his
suit so cordially, that in two days hence the betrothal is to take
place with such secrecy and so privately that the only witnesses
are to be the heavens above and a few of the household.
Picture to yourself the state I am in ; judge if it be urgent for you
to come ; the issue of the affair will show you whether I love
you or not.   God grant this may come to your hand before mine
shall be forced to link itself with his who keeps so ill the faith
that he has pledged.'

Such, in brief, were the words of the letter, words that made
me set out at once without waiting any longer for reply or money ;

for I now saw clearly that it was not the purchase of horses but
of his own pleasure that had made Don Fernando send me to his
brother. The exasperation I felt against Don Fernando, joined
with the fear of losing the prize I had won by so many years of
love and devotion, lent me wings; so that almost flying I reached
home the same day, by the hour which served for speaking with
Luscinda. I arrived unobserved, and left the mule on which I had
come at the house of the worthy man who had brought me the
letter, and fortune was pleased to be for once so kind that I found
Luscinda at the grating that was the witness of our loves. She
recognised me at once, and I her, but not as she ought to have
recognised me, or I her. But who is there in the world that can
boast of having fathomed or understood the wavering mind and
unstable nature of a woman ? Of a truth no one. To proceed :
as soon as Luscinda saw me she said, ' Cardenio, I am in my
bridal dress, and the treacherous Don Fernando and my covetous
father are waiting for me in the hall with the other witnesses,
who shall be the witnesses of my death before they witness my
betrothal. Be not distressed, my friend, but contrive to be present
at this sacrifice, and if that cannot be prevented by my words,
I have a dagger concealed which will prevent more deliberate
violence, putting an end to my life and giving thee a first proof
of the love I have borne and bear thee.' I replied to her distrac-
tedly and hastily, in fear lest I should not have time to reply,
' May thy words be verified by thy deeds, lady ; and if thou hast a
dagger to save thy honour, I have a sword to defend thee or kill
myself if fortune be against us.'

I think she could not have heard all these words, for I perceived that they called her away in haste, as the bridegroom was
waiting. Now the night of my sorrow set in, the sun of my
happiness went down, I felt my eyes bereft of sight, my mind of
reason. I could not enter the house, nor was I capable of any
movement ; but reflecting how important it was that I should be
present at what might take place on the occasion, I nerved myself
as best I could and went in, for I well knew all the entrances and
outlets ; and besides, with the confusion that in secret pervaded

the house, no one perceived me, so, without being seen, I found an opportunity of placing myself in the recess formed by a window of the hall itself, and concealed by the ends and borders of two tapestries, from between which I could, without being seen, see all that took place in the room. Who could describe the agitation of heart I suffered as I stood there—the thoughts that came to me—the reflections that passed through my mind? They were such as cannot be, nor were it well they should be, told. Suffice it to say that the bridegroom entered the hall in his usual dress, without ornament of any kind; as groomsman he had with him a cousin of Luscinda's, and except the servants of the house there was no one else in the chamber. Soon afterwards Luscinda came out from an ante-chamber, attended by her mother and two of her damsels, arrayed and adorned as became her rank and beauty, and in full festival and ceremonial attire. My anxiety and distraction did not allow me to observe or notice particularly what she wore; I could only perceive the colours, which were crimson and white, and the glitter of the gems and jewels on her head-dress and apparel, surpassed by the rare beauty of her lovely auburn hair that vying with the precious stones and the light of the four torches that stood in the hall shone with a brighter gleam than all. Oh memory, mortal foe of my peace! why bring before me now the incomparable beauty of that adored enemy of mine? Were it not better, cruel memory, to remind me and recall what she then did, that stirred by a wrong so glaring I may seek, if not vengeance now, at least to rid myself of life? Be not weary, sirs, of listening to these digressions; my sorrow is not one of those that can or should be told tersely and briefly, for to me each incident seems to call for many words.

To this the curate replied that not only were they not weary of listening to him, but that the details he mentioned interested them greatly, being of a kind by no means to be omitted and deserving of the same attention as the main story.

To proceed, then (continued Cardenio): all being assembled
in the hall, the priest of the parish came in, and as he took the
pair by the hand to perform the requisite ceremony, at the words,
'Will you, Señora Luscinda, take Señor Don Fernando, here
present, for your lawful husband, as the holy Mother Church
ordains?' I thrust my head and neck out from between the
tapestries, and with eager ears and throbbing heart set myself to
listen to Luscinda's answer, awaiting in her reply the sentence
of death or the grant of life. Oh, that I had but dared at that
moment to rush forward crying aloud, 'Luscinda, Luscinda!
have a care what thou dost; remember what thou owest me;
bethink thee thou art mine and canst not be another's; reflect
that thy utterance of 'Yes' and the end of my life will come at
the same instant. O, treacherous Don Fernando! robber of my
glory, death of my life! what wouldst thou? What seekest
thou? Remember that thou canst not as a Christian attain the
object of thy wishes, for Luscinda is my bride, and I am her
husband!' Fool that I am! now that I am far away, and out
of danger, I say I should have done what I did not do: now
that I have allowed my precious treasure to be robbed from me,
I curse the robber, on whom I might have taken vengeance had
I as much heart for it as I have for bewailing my fate; in short,
as I was then a coward and a fool, little wonder is it if I am now
dying shame-stricken, remorseful, and mad.

The priest stood waiting for the answer of Luscinda, who for
a long time withheld it; and just as I thought she was taking
out the dagger to save her honour, or struggling for words to
make some declaration of the truth on my behalf, I heard her
say in a faint and feeble voice, 'I will:' Don Fernando said the
same, and giving her the ring they stood linked by a knot that
could never be loosed. The bridegroom then approached to
embrace his bride; and she, pressing her hand upon her heart,
fell fainting in her mother's arms. It only remains now for me
to tell you the state I was in when in that consent that I heard
I saw all my hopes mocked, the words and promises of Luscinda
proved falsehoods, and the recovery of the prize I had that

instant lost rendered impossible for ever. I stood stupefied, wholly abandoned, it seemed, by Heaven, declared the enemy of the earth that bore me, the air refusing me breath for my sighs, the water moisture for my tears; it was only the fire that gathered strength so that my whole frame glowed with rage and jealousy. They were all thrown into confusion by Luscinda's fainting, and as her mother was unlacing her to give her air a sealed paper was discovered in her bosom which Don Fernando seized at once and began to read by the light of one of the torches. As soon as he had read it he seated himself in a chair leaning his cheek on his hand in the attitude of one deep in thought, without taking any part in the efforts that were being made to recover his bride from her fainting fit.

Seeing all the household in confusion, I ventured to come out regardless whether I were seen or not, and determined if I were, to do some frenzied deed that would prove to all the world the righteous indignation of my breast in the punishment of the treacherous Don Fernando, and even in that of the fickle fainting traitress. But my fate, doubtless reserving me for greater sorrows, if such there be, so ordered it that just then I had enough and to spare of that reason which has since been wanting to me; and so, without seeking to take vengeance on my greatest enemies (which might have been easily taken, as all thought of me was so far from their minds), I resolved to take it upon myself, and on myself to inflict the pain they deserved, perhaps with even greater severity than I should have dealt out to them had I then slain them; for sudden pain is soon over, but that which is protracted by tortures is ever slaying without ending life. In a word, I quitted the house and reached that of the man with whom I had left my mule; I made him saddle it for me, mounted without bidding him farewell, and rode out of the city, like another Lot, not daring to turn my head to look back upon it; and when I found myself alone in the open country, screened by the darkness of the night, and tempted by the stillness to give vent to my grief without apprehension or fear of being heard or seen, then I broke silence and lifted up my voice in maledictions

upon Luscinda and Don Fernando, as if I could thus avenge the
wrong they had done me. I called her cruel, ungrateful, false,
thankless, but above all covetous, since the wealth of my enemy
had blinded the eyes of her affection, and turned it from me to
transfer it to one to whom fortune had been more generous and
liberal. And yet, in the midst of this outburst of execration
and upbraiding, I found excuses for her, saying it was no wonder
that a young girl in the seclusion of her parents' house, trained
and schooled to obey them always, should have been ready to yield
to their wishes when they offered her for a husband a gentleman
of such distinction, wealth, and noble birth, that if she had
refused to accept him she would have been thought out of her
senses, or to have set her affection elsewhere, a suspicion injurious
to her fair name and fame. But then again, I said, had she
declared I was her husband, they would have seen that in choosing
me she had not chosen so ill but that they might excuse her, for
before Don Fernando had made his offer, they themselves could
not have desired, if their desires had been ruled by reason, a
more eligible husband for their daughter than I was; and she,
before taking the last fatal step of giving her hand, might easily
have said that I had already given her mine, for I should have
come forward to support any assertion of hers to that effect. In
short, I came to the conclusion that feeble love, little reflection,
great ambition, and a craving for rank, had made her forget
the words with which she had deceived me, encouraged and
supported by my firm hopes and honourable passion.

Thus soliloquising and agitated, I journeyed onward for the
remainder of the night, and by daybreak I reached one of the
passes of these mountains, among which I wandered for three
days more without taking any path or road, until I came to some
meadows lying on I know not which side of the mountains, and
there I inquired of some herdsmen in what direction the most
rugged part of the range lay. They told me that it was in this
quarter, and I at once directed my course hither, intending to
end my life here; but as I was making my way among these
crags, my mule dropped dead through fatigue and hunger, or, as

I think more likely, in order to have done with such a worthless
burden as it bore in me. I was left on foot, worn out, famishing,
without anyone to help me or any thought of seeking help ; and
so thus I lay stretched on the ground, how long I know not, after
which I rose up free from hunger, and found beside me some
goatherds, who no doubt were the persons who had relieved me
in my need, for they told me how they had found me, and how I
had been uttering ravings that showed plainly I had lost my
reason ; and since then I am conscious that I am not always in
full possession of it, but at times so deranged and crazed that I
do a thousand mad things, tearing my clothes, crying aloud in
these solitudes, cursing my fate, and idly calling on the dear name
of her who is my enemy, and only seeking to end my life in
lamentation ; and when I recover my senses I find myself so ex-
hausted and weary that I can scarcely move. Most commonly
my dwelling is the hollow of a cork tree large enough to shelter
this miserable body ; the herdsmen and goatherds who frequent
these mountains, moved by compassion, furnish me with food,
leaving it by the wayside or on the rocks, where they think I may
perhaps pass and find it ; and so, even though I may be then out
of my senses, the wants of nature teach me what is required to
sustain me, and make me crave it and eager to take it. At other
times, so they tell me when they find me in a rational mood, I sally
out upon the road, and though they would gladly give it me, I
snatch food by force from the shepherds bringing it from the
village to their huts. Thus do I pass the wretched life that
remains to me, until it be Heaven's will to bring it to a close,
or so to order my memory that I no longer recollect the beauty
and treachery of Luscinda, or the wrong done me by Don
Fernando ; for if it will do this without depriving me of life, I
will turn my thoughts into some better channel ; if not, I can
only implore it to have full mercy on my soul, for in myself I
feel no power or strength to release my body from this strait in
which I have of my own accord chosen to place it.

Such, sirs, is the dismal story of my misfortune : say if it be
one that can be told with less emotion than you have seen in me ;

and do not trouble yourselves with urging or pressing upon me what reason suggests as likely to serve for my relief, for it will avail me as much as the medicine prescribed by a wise physician avails the sick man who will not take it. I have no wish for health without Luscinda; and since it is her pleasure to be another's, when she is or should be mine, let it be mine to be a prey to misery when I might have enjoyed happiness. She by her fickleness strove to make my ruin irretrievable; I will strive to gratify her wishes by seeking destruction; and it will show generations to come that I alone was deprived of that of which all others in misfortune have a superabundance, for to them the impossibility of being consoled is itself a consolation, while to me it is the cause of greater sorrows and sufferings, for I think that even in death there will not be an end of them.

Here Cardenio brought to a close his long discourse and story, as full of misfortune as it was of love; but just as the curate was going to address some words of comfort to him, he was stopped by a voice that reached his ear, saying in melancholy tones what will be told in the Fourth Part of this narrative: for at this point the sage and sagacious historian, Cid Hamet Benengeli, brought the Third to a conclusion.[1]

[1] See the note to chapter viii. on the original division into parts.

Note A (page 44).

Notwithstanding Clemencin's disparaging remark that this is 'of the same stuff' as Cervantes' sonnets are commonly composed of, it will be seen, even in translation, that there is at least a backbone here, while the serious sonnets of Cervantes are only too often little better than invertebrate twaddle. Translation, however, cannot reproduce the exquisite melody of the original, and, had it no other merit, this alone would, *pace* Clemencin, entitle the sonnet to a place among the best in the Spanish language.

CHAPTER XXVIII.

WHICH TREATS OF THE STRANGE AND DELIGHTFUL ADVENTURE
THAT BEFELL THE CURATE AND THE BARBER IN THE SAME
SIERRA.

HAPPY and fortunate were the times when that most daring
knight Don Quixote of La Mancha was sent into the world ;
for by reason of his having formed a resolution so honourable as that of seeking to revive and restore to the world the
long-lost and almost defunct order of knight-errantry, we
now enjoy in this age of ours, so poor in light entertainment,
not only the charm of his veracious history, but also of the
tales and episodes contained in it, which are, in a measure,
no less pleasing, ingenious, and truthful, than the history
itself ; [1] which, resuming its thread, carded, spun, and wound,
relates that just as the curate was going to offer consolation
to Cardenio, he was interrupted by a voice that fell upon
his ear saying in plaintive tones :

'O God ! is it possible I have found a place that may
serve as a secret grave for the weary load of this body that I
support so unwillingly ? If the solitude these mountains
promise deceive me not, it is so ; ah ! woe is me ! how
much more grateful to my mind will be the society of these

---

[1] This looks as if some doubt had crossed the mind of Cervantes as to the
propriety of introducing these tales and episodes.

rocks and brakes that permit me to complain of my misfortune to Heaven, than that of any human being, for there
is none on earth to look to for counsel in doubt, comfort in
sorrow, or relief in distress ! '

All this was heard distinctly by the curate and those
with him, and as it seemed to them to be uttered close by,
as indeed it was, they got up to look for the speaker, and
before they had gone twenty paces they discovered behind
a rock, seated at the foot of an ash tree, a youth in the
dress of a peasant, whose face they were unable at the
moment to see as he was leaning forward, bathing his feet
in the brook that flowed past.   They approached so silently
that he did not perceive them, being fully occupied in
bathing his feet, which were so fair that they looked like two
pieces of shining crystal embedded among the stones of the
brook.   The whiteness and beauty of these feet struck them
with surprise, for they did not seem to have been made to
crush clods or to follow the plough and the oxen as their
owner's dress suggested ; and so, finding they had not been
noticed, the curate, who was in front, made a sign to the
other two to conceal themselves behind some fragments of
rock that lay there ; which they did, observing closely what
the youth was about.   He had on a loose double-skirted
grey jacket bound tight to his body with a white cloth ; he
wore besides breeches and gaiters of grey cloth, and on his
head a grey montera ; [1] and he had the gaiters turned up as
far as the middle of the leg, which verily seemed to be of
pure alabaster.

----

[1] A cloth cap, something like a travelling cap in make, worn by the
peasants of Central Spain.

As soon as he had done bathing his beautiful feet, he wiped them with a towel he took from under the montera, on taking off which he raised his face, and those who were watching him had an opportunity of seeing a beauty so exquisite that Cardenio said to the curate in a whisper, ' As this is not Luscinda, it is no human creature but a divine being.'

The youth then took off the montera, and shaking his head from side to side there broke loose and spread out a mass of hair that the beams of the sun might have envied ; by this they knew that what had seemed a peasant was a lovely woman, nay the most beautiful the eyes of two of them had ever beheld, or even Cardenio's if they had not seen and known Luscinda, for he afterwards declared that only the beauty of Luscinda could compare with this. The long auburn tresses not only covered her shoulders, but, such was their length and abundance, concealed her all round beneath their masses, so that except the feet nothing of her form was visible. She now used her hands as a comb, and if her feet had seemed like bits of crystal in the water, her hands looked like pieces of driven snow among her locks ; all which increased not only the admiration of the three beholders, but their anxiety to learn who she was. With this object they resolved to show themselves, and at the stir they made in getting upon their feet the fair damsel raised her head, and parting her hair from before her eyes with both hands, she looked to see who had made the noise, and the instant she perceived them she started to her feet, and without waiting to put on her shoes or gather up her hair, hastily snatched up a bundle as though of clothes that

she had beside her, and, scared and alarmed, endeavoured
to take flight ; but before she had gone six paces she fell to
the ground, her delicate feet being unable to bear the roughness of the stones ; seeing which, the three hastened towards
her, and the curate addressing her first said, ' Stay, señora,
whoever you may be, for those whom you see here only
desire to be of service to you ; you have no need to attempt
a flight so heedless, for neither can your feet bear it, nor
we allow it.'

Taken by surprise and bewildered, she made no reply
to these words. They, however, came towards her, and
the curate taking her hand went on to say, ' What your
dress would hide, señora, is made known to us by your hair ;
a clear proof that it can be no trifling cause that has disguised your beauty in a garb so unworthy of it, and sent it
into solitudes like these where we have had the good fortune
to find you, if not to relieve your distress, at least to offer
you comfort ; for no distress, so long as life lasts, can be so
oppressive or reach such a height as to make the sufferer
refuse to listen to comfort offered with good intention. And
so, señora, or señor, or whatever you prefer to be, dismiss
the fears that our appearance has caused you and make us
acquainted with your good or evil fortunes, for from all of
us together, or from each one of us, you will receive
sympathy in your trouble.'

While the curate was speaking, the disguised damsel
stood as if spell-bound, looking at them without opening
her lips or uttering a word, just like a village rustic to
whom something strange that he has never seen before has
been suddenly shown ; but on the curate addressing some

further words to the same effect to her, sighing deeply she broke silence and said, ' Since the solitude of these mountains has been unable to conceal me, and the escape of my dishevelled tresses will not allow my tongue to deal in falsehoods, it would be idle for me now to make any further pretence of what, if you were to believe me, you would believe more out of courtesy than for any other reason. This being so, I say I thank you, sirs, for the offer you have made me, which places me under the obligation of complying with the request you have made of me; though I fear the account I shall give you of my misfortunes will excite in you as much concern as compassion, for you will be unable to suggest anything to remedy them or any consolation to alleviate them. However, that my honour may not be left a matter of doubt in your minds, now that you have discovered me to be a woman, and see that I am young, alone, and in this dress, things that taken together or separately would be enough to destroy any good name, I feel bound to tell what I would willingly keep secret if I could.'

All this she who was now seen to be a lovely woman delivered without any hesitation, with so much ease and in so sweet a voice that they were not less charmed by her intelligence than by her beauty, and as they again repeated their offers and entreaties to her to fulfil her promise, she without further pressing, first modestly covering her feet and gathering up her hair, seated herself on a stone with the three placed around her, and, after an effort to restrain some tears that came to her eyes, in a clear and steady voice began her story thus:

In this Andalusia there is a town from which a duke takes a title which makes him one of those that are called Grandees of Spain. This nobleman has two sons, the elder heir to his dignity and apparently to his good qualities ; the younger heir to I know not what, unless it be the treachery of Vellido and the falsehood of Ganelon.[1] My parents are this lord's vassals, lowly in origin, but so wealthy that if birth had conferred as much on them as fortune, they would have had nothing left to desire, nor should I have had reason to fear trouble like that in which I find myself now ; for it may be that my ill fortune came of theirs in not having been nobly born. It is true they are not so low that they have any reason to be ashamed of their condition, but neither are they so high as to remove from my mind the impression that my mishap comes of their humble birth. They are, in short, peasants, plain homely people, without any taint of disreputable blood, and, as the saying is, old rusty Christians,[2] but so rich that by their wealth and free-handed way of life they are coming by degrees to be considered gentlefolk by birth, and even by position ;[3] though the wealth and nobility they thought most of was having me for their daughter; and as they have no other child to make their heir, and are affectionate parents, I was one of the most indulged daughters that ever parents indulged.

I was the mirror in which they beheld themselves, the staff of their old age, and the object in which, with submission to Heaven, all their wishes centred, and mine were in accordance with theirs, for I knew their worth ; and as I was mistress of their hearts, so was I also of their possessions. Through me they engaged or dismissed their servants ; through my hands passed the accounts and returns of what was sown and reaped ; the oil-mills, the wine-presses, the count of the flocks and herds, the beehives,

---

[1] See Note [1], p. 48.

[2] *Cristianos viejos rancios : rancio* is applied to anything, like bacon or wine, that has acquired a peculiar flavour from long keeping.

[3] Literally, 'hidalgos and even caballeros : ' 'hidalgo' being a gentleman by birth, 'caballero' one by social position or standing.

all in short that a rich farmer like my father has or can have, I
had under my care, and I acted as steward and mistress with an
assiduity on my part and satisfaction on theirs that I cannot well
describe to you. The leisure hours left to me after I had given
the requisite orders to the shepherds, head-men, and labourers, I
passed in such employments as are not only allowable but necessary for young girls, those that the needle, embroidery cushion,
and spinning wheel usually afford, and if to refresh my mind I
quitted them for a while, I found recreation in reading some
devotional book or playing the harp, for experience taught me
that music soothes the troubled mind and relieves weariness of
spirit. Such was the life I led in my parents' house, and if I
have depicted it thus minutely, it is not out of ostentation, or to
let you know that I am rich, but that you may see how, without
any fault of mine, I have fallen from the happy condition I have
described, to the misery I am in at present. The truth is, that
while I was leading this busy life, in a retirement that might
compare with that of a monastery, and unseen as I thought by
any except the servants of the house (for when I went to Mass
it was so early in the morning, and I was so closely attended by
my mother and the women of the household, and so thickly veiled
and so shy, that my eyes scarcely saw more ground than I trod
on), in spite of all this, the eyes of love, or idleness, more properly
speaking, that the lynx's cannot rival, discovered me, with the
help of the assiduity of Don Fernando; for that is the name of
the younger son of the duke I told you of.

The moment the speaker mentioned the name of Don
Fernando, Cardenio changed colour and broke into a
sweat, with such signs of emotion that the curate and
the barber, who observed it, feared that one of the mad
fits which they heard attacked him sometimes was coming
upon him; but Cardenio showed no further agitation
and remained quiet, regarding the peasant girl with fixed

attention, for he began to suspect who she was. She, however, without noticing the excitement of Cardenio, continuing
her story, went on to say:

And they had hardly discovered me, when, as he owned
afterwards, he was smitten with a violent love for me, as the
manner in which it displayed itself plainly showed. But to
shorten the long recital of my woes, I will pass over in silence
all the artifices employed by Don Fernando for declaring his
passion for me. He bribed all the household, he gave and offered
gifts and presents to my parents; every day was like a holiday
or a merry-making in our street; by night no one could sleep
for the music; the love letters that used to come to my hand, no
one knew how, were innumerable, full of tender pleadings and
pledges, containing more promises and oaths than there were
letters in them; all which not only did not soften me, but hard-
ened my heart against him, as if he had been my mortal enemy,
and as if everything he did to make me yield were done with the
opposite intention. Not that the high-bred bearing of Don Fernando was disagreeable to me, or that I found his importunities
wearisome; for it gave me a certain sort of satisfaction to find
myself so sought and prized by a gentleman of such distinction,
and I was not displeased at seeing my praises in his letters (for however ugly we women may be, it seems to me it always pleases us to
hear ourselves called beautiful); but that my own sense of right
was opposed to all this, as well as the repeated advice of my parents,
who now very plainly perceived Don Fernando's purpose, for he
cared very little if all the world knew it. They told me they trusted
and confided their honour and good name to my virtue and rectitude
alone, and bade me consider the disparity between Don Fernando
and myself, from which I might conclude that his intentions, whatever he might say to the contrary, had for their aim his own
pleasure rather than my advantage; and if I were at all desirous
of opposing an obstacle to his unreasonable suit, they were ready,
they said, to marry me at once to anyone I preferred, either
among the leading people of our own town, or of any of those in

the neighbourhood; for with their wealth and my good name, a match might be looked for in any quarter. This offer, and their sound advice, strengthened my resolution, and I never gave Don Fernando a word in reply that could hold out to him any hope of success, however remote.

All this caution of mine, which he must have taken for coyness, had apparently the effect of increasing his wanton appetite—for that is the name I give to his passion for me; had it been what he declared it to be, you would not know of it now, because there would have been no occasion to tell you of it. At length he learned that my parents were contemplating marriage for me in order to put an end to his hopes of obtaining possession of me, or at least to secure additional protectors to watch over me, and this intelligence or suspicion made him act as you shall hear. One night, as I was in my chamber with no other companion than a damsel who waited on me, with the doors carefully locked lest my honour should be imperilled through any carelessness, I know not nor can I conceive how it happened, but, with all this seclusion and these precautions, and in the solitude and silence of my retirement, I found him standing before me, a vision that so astounded me that it deprived my eyes of sight, and my tongue of speech. I had no power to utter a cry, nor, I think, did he give me time to utter one, as he immediately approached me, and taking me in his arms (for, overwhelmed as I was, I was powerless, I say, to help myself), he began to make such professions to me that I know not how falsehood could have had the power of dressing them up to seem so like truth; and the traitor contrived that his tears should vouch for his words, and his sighs for his sincerity.

I, a poor young creature, the only daughter of the house, ill versed in such things, began, I know not how, to think all these lying protestations true, though without being moved by his sighs and tears to anything more than pure compassion; and so, as the first feeling of bewilderment passed away, and I began in some degree to recover myself, I said to him with more courage than I thought I could have possessed, ' If, as I am now in your arms,

señor, I were in the claws of a fierce lion, and my deliverance
could be procured by doing or saying anything to the prejudice of
my honour, it would no more be in my power to do it or say it,
than it would be possible that what was should not have been;
so then, if you hold my body clasped in your arms, I hold my
soul secured by virtuous intentions, very different from yours, as
you will see if you attempt to carry them into effect by force. I
am your vassal, but I am not your slave; your nobility neither
has nor should have any right to dishonour or degrade my humble
birth; and low-born peasant as I am, I have my self-respect as
much as you, a lord and gentleman: with me your violence
will be to no purpose, your wealth will have no weight, your
words will have no power to deceive me, nor your sighs or tears
to soften me: were I to see any of the things I speak of in him
whom my parents gave me as a husband, his will should be mine,
and mine should be bounded by his; and my honour being preserved even though my inclinations were not gratified, I would
willingly yield him what you, señor, would now obtain by force;
and this I say lest you should suppose that any but my lawful husband shall ever win anything of me.' 'If that,' said this
disloyal gentleman, 'be the only scruple you feel, fairest Dorothea'
(for that is the name of this unhappy being), 'see here I give you
my hand to be yours, and let Heaven, from which nothing is hid,
and this image of Our Lady you have here, be witnesses of this
pledge.'

When Cardenio heard her say she was called Dorothea,
he showed fresh agitation and felt convinced of the truth
of his former suspicion, but he was unwilling to interrupt
the story, and wished to hear the end of what he already
all but knew, so he merely said, 'What! is Dorothea
your name, señora? I have heard of another of the
same name who can perhaps match your misfortunes.
But proceed; by-and-by I may tell you something that

will astonish you as much as it will excite your compassion.'

Dorothea was struck by Cardenio's words as well as by his strange and miserable attire, and begged him if he knew anything concerning her to tell it to her at once, for if fortune had left her any blessing it was courage to bear whatever calamity might fall upon her, as she felt sure in her own mind that none could reach her capable of increasing in any degree what she endured already.

'I would not let the occasion pass, señora,' replied Cardenio, ' of telling you what I think, if what I suspect were the truth, but so far there has been no opportunity, nor is it of any importance to you to know it.'

' Be it as it may,' replied Dorothea, ' to go on with my story : '

Don Fernando, taking an image that stood in the chamber, placed it as a witness of our betrothal, and with the most binding words and extravagant oaths gave me his promise to become my husband; though before he had made an end of pledging himself I bade him consider well what he was doing, and think of the anger his father would feel at seeing him married to a peasant girl and one of his vassals ; I told him not to let my beauty, such as it was, blind him, for that was not enough to furnish an excuse for his transgression; and if in the love he bore me he wished to do me any kindness, it would be to leave my lot to follow its course at the level my condition required ; for marriages so unequal never brought happiness, nor did they continue long to afford the enjoyment they began with.

All this that I have now repeated I said to him, and much more which I cannot recollect; but it had no effect in inducing him to forego his purpose ; he who has no intention of paying does not trouble himself about difficulties when he is striking the bargain. At the same time I argued the matter briefly in

my own mind, saying to myself, ' I shall not be the first who
has risen through marriage from a lowly to a lofty station, nor
will Don Fernando be the first whom beauty or, as is more likely,
a blind attachment, has led to mate himself below his rank.
Then, since I am introducing no new usage or practice, I may as
well avail myself of the honour that chance offers me, for even
though his inclination for me should not outlast the attainment
of his wishes, I shall be, after all, his wife before God. And
if I strive to repel him by scorn, I can see that, fair means
failing, he is in a mood to use force, and I shall be left dishonoured and without any means of proving my innocence to
those who cannot know how innocently I have come to be in
this position; for what arguments would persuade my parents
and others that this gentleman entered my chamber without
my consent ? '

All these questions and answers passed through my mind in a
moment; but the oaths of Don Fernando, the witnesses he
appealed to, the tears he shed, and lastly the charms of his person and his high-bred grace, which, accompanied by such signs
of genuine love, might well have conquered a heart even more
free and coy than mine—these were the things that more than
all began to influence me and lead me unawares to my ruin. I
called my waiting-maid to me, that there might be a witness on
earth besides those in heaven, and again Don Fernando renewed
and repeated his oaths, invoked as witnesses fresh saints in addition to the former ones, called down upon himself a thousand
curses hereafter should he fail to keep his promise, shed more
tears, redoubled his sighs and pressed me closer in his arms, from
which he had never allowed me to escape ; and so I was left by
my maid, and ceased to be one, and he became a traitor and a
perjured man.

The day which followed the night of my misfortune did not come
so quickly, I imagine, as Don Fernando wished, for when desire has
attained its object, the greatest pleasure is to fly from the scene of
pleasure. I say so because Don Fernando made all haste to leave
me, and by the adroitness of my maid, who was indeed the one who

had admitted him, gained the street before daybreak; but on taking leave of me he told me, though not with as much earnestness and fervour as when he came, that I might rest assured of his faith and of the sanctity and sincerity of his oaths; and to confirm his words he drew a rich ring off his finger and placed it upon mine. He then took his departure and I was left, I know not whether sorrowful or happy; all I can say is, I was left agitated and troubled in mind and almost bewildered by what had taken place, and I had not the spirit, or else it did not occur to me, to chide my maid for the treachery she had been guilty of in concealing Don Fernando in my chamber; for as yet I was unable to make up my mind whether what had befallen me was for good or evil. I told Don Fernando at parting, that as I was now his, he might see me on other nights in the same way, until it should be his pleasure to let the matter become known; but, except the following night, he came no more, nor for more than a month could I catch a glimpse of him in the street or in church, while I wearied myself with watching for one; although I knew he was in the town, and almost every day went out hunting, a pastime he was very fond of. I remember well how sad and dreary those days and hours were to me; I remember well how I began to doubt as they went by, and even to lose confidence in the faith of Don Fernando; and I remember, too, how my maid heard those words in reproof of her audacity that she had not heard before, and how I was forced to put a constraint on my tears and on the expression of my countenance, not to give my parents cause to ask me why I was so melancholy, and drive me to invent falsehoods in reply. But all this was suddenly brought to an end, for the time came when all such considerations were disregarded, and there was no further question of honour, when my patience gave way and the secret of my heart became known abroad. The reason was, that a few days later it was reported in the town that Don Fernando had been married in a neighbouring city to a maiden of rare beauty, the daughter of parents of distinguished position, though not so rich that her portion would entitle her to look for so brilliant a match; it was said, too, that her name

was Luscinda, and that at the betrothal some strange things
had happened.

Cardenio heard the name of Luscinda, but he only
shrugged his shoulders, bit his lips, bent his brows, and
before long two streams of tears escaped from his eyes.
Dorothea, however, did not interrupt her story, but went on
in these words :

This sad intelligence reached my ears, and, instead of being
struck with a chill, with such wrath and fury did my heart burn
that I scarcely restrained myself from rushing out into the
streets, crying aloud and proclaiming openly the perfidy and
treachery of which I was the victim ; but this transport of rage
was for the time checked by a resolution I formed, to be carried
out the same night, and that was to assume this dress, which I
got from a servant of my father's, one of the zagals, as they are
called in farmhouses, to whom I confided the whole of my misfortune, and whom I entreated to accompany me to the city where
I heard my enemy was.   He, though he remonstrated with me
for my boldness, and condemned my resolution, when he saw
me bent upon my purpose, offered to bear me company, as he
said, to the end of the world.   I at once packed up in a linen
pillow-case a woman's dress, and some jewels and money to provide for emergencies, and in the silence of the night, without
letting my treacherous maid know, I sallied forth from the house,
accompanied by my servant and abundant anxieties, and on foot
set out for the city, but borne as it were on wings by my eagerness to reach it, if not to prevent what I presumed to be already
done, at least to call upon Don Fernando to tell me with what
conscience he had done it.   I reached my destination in two days
and a half, and on entering the city inquired for the house of
Luscinda's parents.   The first person I asked gave me more in
reply than I sought to know ; he showed me the house, and told
me all that had occurred at the betrothal of the daughter of the

family, an affair of such notoriety in the city that it was the talk
of every knot of idlers in the street. He said that on the night
of Don Fernando's betrothal with Luscinda, as soon as she had
consented to be his bride by saying ' Yes,' she was taken with a
sudden fainting fit, and that on the bridegroom approaching to
unlace the bosom of her dress to give her air, he found a paper
in her own handwriting, in which she said and declared that she
could not be Don Fernando's bride, because she was already
Cardenio's, who, according to the man's account, was a gentleman of distinction of the same city; and that if she had accepted Don Fernando, it was only in obedience to her parents.
In short, he said, the words of the paper made it clear she meant
to kill herself on the completion of the betrothal, and gave her
reasons for putting an end to herself; all which was confirmed,
it was said, by a dagger they found somewhere in her clothes. On
seeing this, Don Fernando, persuaded that Luscinda had befooled,
slighted, and trifled with him, assailed her before she had recovered from her swoon, and tried to stab her with the dagger
that had been found, and would have succeeded had not her
parents and those who were present prevented him. It was
said, moreover, that Don Fernando went away at once, and that
Luscinda did not recover from her prostration until the next day,
when she told her parents how she was really the bride of that
Cardenio I have mentioned. I learned besides that Cardenio,
according to report, had been present at the betrothal; and that
upon seeing her betrothed contrary to his expectation, he had
quitted the city in despair, leaving behind him a letter declaring
the wrong Luscinda had done him, and his intention of going
where no one should ever see him again. All this was a matter of
notoriety in the city, and everyone spoke of it; especially when
it became known that Luscinda was missing from her father's
house and from the city, for she was not to be found anywhere,
to the distraction of her parents, who knew not what steps to
take to recover her. What I learned revived my hopes, and I
was better pleased not to have found Don Fernando than to
find him married, for it seemed to me that the door was not yet

entirely shut upon relief in my case, and I thought that perhaps
Heaven had put this impediment in the way of the second
marriage, to lead him to recognise his obligations under the
former one, and reflect that as a Christian he was bound to consider his soul above all human objects. All this passed through
my mind, and I strove to comfort myself without comfort, in-
dulging in faint and distant hopes of cherishing that life that I
now abhor.

But while I was in the city, uncertain what to do, as I could
not find Don Fernando, I heard notice given by the public crier
offering a great reward to anyone who should find me, and giving
the particulars of my age and of the very dress I wore ; and I
heard it said that the lad who came with me had taken me away
from my father's house ; a thing that cut me to the heart, showing
how low my good name had fallen, since it was not enough that I
should lose it by my flight, but they must add with whom I had
fled, and that one so much beneath me and so unworthy of my consideration. The instant I heard the notice I quitted the city with
my servant, who now began to show signs of wavering in his fidelity
to me, and the same night, for fear of discovery, we entered the
most thickly wooded part of these mountains. But, as is commonly said, one evil calls up another,[1] and the end of one misfortune is apt to be the beginning of one still greater, and so it
proved in my case ; for my worthy servant, until then so faithful
and trusty, when he found me in this lonely spot, moved more by
his own villany than by my beauty, sought to take advantage of
the opportunity which these solitudes seemed to present him,
and with little shame and less fear of God and respect for me,
began to make overtures to me ; and finding that I replied to the
effrontery of his proposals with justly severe language, he laid
aside the entreaties which he had employed at first, and began to
use violence. But just Heaven, that seldom fails to watch over
and aid good intentions, so aided mine that with my slight
strength and with little exertion I pushed him over a precipice,
where I left him, whether dead or alive I know not ; and then,

[1] Prov. 133.

with greater speed than seemed possible in my terror and fatigue, I made my way into the mountains, without any other thought or purpose save that of hiding myself among them, and escaping my father and those despatched in search of me by his orders It is now I know not how many months since with this object I came here, where I met a herdsman who engaged me as his servant at a place in the heart of this Sierra, and all this time I have been serving him as herd, striving to keep always afield to hide these locks which have now unexpectedly betrayed me. But all my care and pains were unavailing, for my master made the discovery that I was not a man, and harboured the same base designs as my servant ; and as fortune does not always supply a remedy in cases of difficulty, and I had no precipice or ravine at hand down which to fling the master and cure his passion, as I had in the servant's case, I thought it a lesser evil to leave him and again conceal myself among these crags, than make trial of my strength and argument with him. So, as I say, once more I went into hiding to seek for some place where I might with sighs and tears implore Heaven to have pity on my misery, and grant me help and strength to escape from it, or let me die among the solitudes, leaving no trace of an unhappy being who, by no fault of hers, has furnished matter for talk and scandal at home and abroad.

CHAPTER XXIX.

WHICH TREATS OF THE DROLL DEVICE AND METHOD ADOPTED
TO EXTRICATE OUR LOVE-STRICKEN KNIGHT FROM THE
SEVERE PENANCE HE HAD IMPOSED UPON HIMSELF.

' SUCH, sirs, is the true story of my sad adventures ; judge
for yourselves now whether the sighs and lamentations you
heard, and the tears that flowed from my eyes, had not
sufficient cause even if I had indulged in them more freely ;
and if you consider the nature of my misfortune you will see
that consolation is idle, as there is no possible remedy for it.
All I ask of you is, what you may easily and reasonably do,
to show me where I may pass my life unharassed by the
fear and dread of discovery by those who are in search of
me ; for though the great love my parents bear me makes
me feel sure of being kindly received by them, so great is
my feeling of shame at the mere thought that I cannot
present myself before them as they expect, that I had rather
banish myself from their sight for ever than look them in
the face with the reflection that they beheld mine stripped
of that purity they had a right to expect in me.'

With these words she became silent, and the colour that
overspread her face showed plainly the pain and shame she
was suffering at heart. In theirs the listeners felt as much

pity as wonder at her misfortunes ; but as the curate was just about to offer her some consolation and advice Cardenio forestalled him, saying, ' So then, señora, you are the fair Dorothea, the only daughter of the rich Clenardo ? ' Dorothea was astonished at hearing her father's name, and at the miserable appearance of him who mentioned it, for it has been already said how wretchedly clad Cardenio was ; so she said to him, ' And who may you be, brother, who seem to know my father's name so well ? For so far, if I remember rightly, I have not mentioned it in the whole story of my misfortunes.'

' I am that unhappy being, señora,' replied Cardenio, ' whom, as you have said, Luscinda declared to be her husband ; I am the unfortunate Cardenio, whom the wrong-doing of him who has brought you to your present condition has reduced to the state you see me in, bare, ragged, bereft of all human comfort, and what is worse, of reason, for I only possess it when Heaven is pleased for some short space to restore it to me. I, Dorothea, am he who witnessed the wrong done by Don Fernando, and waited to hear the " Yes " uttered by which Luscinda owned herself his betrothed : I am he who had not courage enough to see how her fainting fit ended, or what came of the paper that was found in her bosom, because my heart had not the fortitude to endure so many strokes of ill-fortune at once ; and so losing patience I quitted the house, and leaving a letter with my host, which I entreated him to place in Luscinda's hands, I betook myself to these solitudes, resolved to end here the life I hated as if it were my mortal enemy. But fate would not rid me of it, contenting itself

with robbing me of my reason, perhaps to preserve me for
the good fortune I have had in meeting you; for if that
which you have just told us be true, as I believe it to be, it
may be that Heaven has yet in store for both of us a
happier termination to our misfortunes than we look for ;
because, seeing that Luscinda cannot marry Don Fernando,
being mine, as she has herself so openly declared, and that
Don Fernando cannot marry her as he is yours, we may
reasonably hope that Heaven will restore to us what is ours,
as it is still in existence and not yet alienated or destroyed.
And as we have this consolation springing from no very
visionary hope or wild fancy, I entreat you, señora, to form
new resolutions in your better mind, as I mean to do in
mine, preparing yourself to look forward to happier fortunes ; for I swear to you by the faith of a gentleman and a
Christian not to desert you until I see you in possession of
Don Fernando, and if I cannot by words induce him to
recognise his obligation to you, in that case to avail myself
of the right which my rank as a gentleman gives me, and
with just cause challenge him on account of the injury he
has done you, not regarding my own wrongs, which I shall
leave to Heaven to avenge, while I on earth devote myself
to yours.'

Cardenio's words completed the astonishment of Dorothea, and not knowing how to return thanks for such an
offer, she attempted to kiss his feet; but Cardenio would
not permit it, and the licentiate replied for both, commended the sound reasoning of Cardenio, and lastly, begged,
advised, and urged them to come with him to his village,
where they might furnish themselves with what they needed,

and take measures to discover Don Fernando, or restore Dorothea to her parents, or do what seemed to them most advisable. Cardenio and Dorothea thanked him, and accepted the kind offer he made them; and the barber, who had been listening to all attentively and in silence, on his part said some kindly words also, and with no less good-will than the curate offered his services in any way that might be of use to them. He also explained to them in a few words the object that had brought them there, and the strange nature of Don Quixote's madness, and how they were waiting for his squire, who had gone in search of him. Like the recollection of a dream, the quarrel he had had with Don Quixote came back to Cardenio's memory, and he described it to the others; but he was unable to say what the dispute was about.

At this moment they heard a shout, and recognised it as coming from Sancho Panza, who, not finding them where he had left them, was calling aloud to them. They went to meet him, and in answer to their inquiries about Don Quixote, he told them how he had found him stripped to his shirt, lank, yellow, half dead with hunger, and sighing for his lady Dulcinea; and although he had told him that she commanded him to quit that place and come to El Toboso, where she was expecting him, he had answered that he was determined not to appear in the presence of her beauty until he had done deeds to make him worthy of her favour; and if this went on, Sancho said, he ran the risk of not becoming an emperor as in duty bound, or even an archbishop, which was the least he could be; for which reason they ought to consider what was to be done to get

him away from there. The licentiate in reply told him not
to be uneasy, for they would fetch him away in spite of
himself. He then told Cardenio and Dorothea what they
had proposed to do to cure Don Quixote, or at any rate take
him home; upon which Dorothea said that she could play
the distressed damsel better than the barber; especially
as she had there the dress in which to do it to the life, and
that they might trust to her acting the part in every particular requisite for carrying out their scheme, for she had
read a great many books of chivalry, and knew exactly the
style in which afflicted damsels begged boons of knights-
errant.

'In that case,' said the curate, 'there is nothing more
required than to set about it at once, for beyond a doubt
fortune is declaring itself in our favour, since it has so
unexpectedly begun to open a door for your relief, and
smoothed the way for us to our object.'

Dorothea then took out of her pillow-case a complete
petticoat of some rich stuff, and a green mantle of some
other fine material, and a necklace and other ornaments
out of a little box, and with these in an instant she so
arrayed herself that she looked like a great and rich lady.
All this, and more, she said, she had taken from home in
case of need, but that until then she had had no occasion
to make use of it. They were all highly delighted with her
grace, air, and beauty, and declared Don Fernando to be a
man of very little taste when he rejected such charms.
But the one who admired her most was Sancho Panza, for
it seemed to him (what indeed was true) that in all the
days of his life he had never seen such a lovely creature;

and he asked the curate with great eagerness who this beautiful lady was, and what she wanted in these out-of-the-way quarters.

'This fair lady, brother Sancho,' replied the curate, 'is no less a personage than the heiress in the direct male line of the great kingdom of Micomicon, who has come in search of your master to beg a boon of him, which is that he redress a wrong or injury that a wicked giant has done her; and from the fame as a good knight which your master has acquired far and wide, this princess has come from Guinea to seek him.'

'A lucky seeking and a lucky finding!' said Sancho Panza at this; 'especially if my master has the good fortune to redress that injury, and right that wrong, and kill that son of a bitch of a giant your worship speaks of; as kill him he will if he meets him, unless, indeed, he happens to be a phantom; for my master has no power at all against phantoms. But one thing among others I would beg of you, señor licentiate, which is, that, to prevent my master taking a fancy to be an archbishop, for that is what I'm afraid of, your worship would recommend him to marry this princess at once; for in this way he will be disabled from taking archbishop's orders, and will easily come into his empire, and I to the end of my desires; I have been thinking over the matter carefully, and by what I can make out I find it will not do for me that my master should become an archbishop, because I am no good for the Church, as I am married; and for me now, having as I have a wife and children, to set about obtaining dispensations to enable me to hold a place of profit under the Church, would be endless work; so that, señor, it all turns on my master marrying this lady at once—for as yet I do not know her grace, and so I cannot call her by her name.'

'She is called the Princess Micomicona,' said the curate; 'for as her kingdom is Micomicon, it is clear that must be her name.'

'There's no doubt of that,' replied Sancho, 'for I have known many to take their name and title from the place where they were born and call themselves Pedro of Alcalá, Juan of Úbeda, and Diego of Valladolid; and it may be that over there in Guinea queens have the same way of taking the names of their kingdoms.'

'So it may,' said the curate; 'and as for your master's marrying, I will do all in my power towards it:' with which Sancho was as much pleased as the curate was amazed at his simplicity and at seeing what a hold the absurdities of his master had taken of his fancy, for he had evidently persuaded himself that he was going to be an emperor.

By this time Dorothea had seated herself upon the curate's mule, and the barber had fitted the ox-tail beard to his face, and they now told Sancho to conduct them to where Don Quixote was, warning him not to say that he knew either the licentiate or the barber, as his master's becoming an emperor entirely depended on his not recognising them; neither the curate nor Cardenio, however, thought fit to go with them; Cardenio lest he should remind Don Quixote of the quarrel he had with him, and the curate as there was no necessity for his presence just yet, so they allowed the others to go on before them, while they themselves followed slowly on foot. The curate did not forget to instruct Dorothea how to act, but she said they might make their minds easy, as everything would be done exactly as the books of chivalry required and described.

They had gone about three-quarters of a league when they discovered Don Quixote in a wilderness of rocks, by this time clothed, but without his armour; and as soon as Dorothea saw him and was told by Sancho that that was Don Quixote, she whipped her palfrey, the well-bearded barber following her, and on coming up to him her squire sprang from his mule and came forward to receive her in his arms, and she dismounting with great ease of manner advanced to kneel before the feet of Don Quixote; and though he strove to raise her up, she without rising addressed him in this fashion, 'From this spot I will not rise, O valiant and doughty knight, until your goodness and courtesy grant me a boon, which will redound to the honour and renown of your person and render a service to the most disconsolate and afflicted damsel the sun has seen; and if the might of your strong arm corresponds to the repute of your immortal fame, you are bound to aid the helpless being who, led by the savour of your renowned name, hath come from far distant lands to seek your aid in her misfortunes.'

'I will not answer a word, beauteous lady,' replied Don Quixote, 'nor will I listen to anything further concerning you, until you rise from the earth.'

'I will not rise, señor,' answered the afflicted damsel, 'unless of your courtesy the boon I ask is first granted me.'

'I grant and accord it,' said Don Quixote, 'provided without detriment or prejudice to my king, my country, or her who holds the key of my heart and freedom, it may be complied with.'

'It will not be to the detriment or prejudice of any of them, my worthy lord,' said the afflicted damsel; and here Sancho Panza drew close to his master's ear and said to him very softly, 'Your worship may very safely grant the boon she asks; it's nothing at all; only to kill a big giant; and she who asks it is the exalted princess Micomicona, queen of the great kingdom of Micomicon of Ethiopia.'

'Let her be who she may,' replied Don Quixote, 'I will do what is my bounden duty, and what my conscience bids me, in conformity with what I have professed;' and turning to the damsel he said, 'Let your great beauty rise, for I grant the boon which you would ask of me.'

'Then what I ask,' said the damsel, 'is that your magnanimous person accompany me at once whither I will conduct you, and that you promise not to engage in any other adventure or quest until you have avenged me of a traitor who, against all human and divine law, has usurped my kingdom.'

'I repeat that I grant it,' replied Don Quixote; 'and so, lady, you may from this day forth lay aside the melancholy that distresses you, and let your failing hopes gather new life and strength, for with the help of God and of my arm you will soon see yourself restored to your kingdom, and seated upon the throne of your ancient and mighty realm, notwithstanding and despite of the felons who would gainsay it; and now hands to the work, for, as they say, in delay there is apt to be danger.'[1]

[1] Prov. 222.

The distressed damsel strove with much pertinacity to kiss his hands; but Don Quixote, who was in all things a polished and courteous knight, would by no means allow it, but made her rise and embraced her with great courtesy and politeness, and ordered Sancho to look to Rocinante's girths, and to arm him without a moment's delay. Sancho took down the armour, which was hung up on a tree like a trophy, and having seen to the girths armed his master in a trice, who as soon as he found himself in his armour exclaimed, 'Let us be gone in the name of God to bring aid to this great lady.'

The barber was all this time on his knees at great pains to hide his laughter and not let his beard fall, for had it fallen maybe their fine scheme would have come to nothing; but now seeing the boon granted, and the promptitude with which Don Quixote prepared to set out in compliance with it, he rose and took his lady's hand, and between them they placed her upon the mule. Don Quixote then mounted Rocinante, and the barber settled himself on his beast, Sancho being left to go on foot, which made him feel anew the loss of his Dapple, finding the want of him now. But he bore all with cheerfulness, being persuaded that his master had now fairly started and was just on the point of becoming an emperor; for he felt no doubt at all that he would marry this princess, and be king of Micomicon at least. The only thing that troubled him was the reflection that this kingdom was in the land of the blacks, and that the people they would give him for vassals would be all black; but for this he soon found a remedy in his fancy, and said he to himself, 'What is it to me if my vassals are blacks? What

more have I to do than make a cargo of them and carry
them to Spain, where I can sell them and get ready money
for them, and with it buy some title or some office in which
to live at ease all the days of my life? Not unless you go to
sleep and haven't the wit or skill to turn things to account
and sell three, six, or ten thousand vassals while you would be
talking about it! By God I will stir them up, big and little,
or as best I can, and let them be ever so black I'll turn them
into white or yellow. Come, come, what a fool I am!'[1] And
so he jogged on, so occupied with his thoughts and easy in
his mind that he forgot all about the hardship of travelling
on foot.

Cardenio and the curate were watching all this from
among some bushes, not knowing how to join company with
the others; but the curate, who was very fertile in devices,
soon hit upon a way of effecting their purpose, and with a
pair of scissors that he had in a case he quickly cut off
Cardenio's beard, and putting on him a grey jerkin of his
own he gave him a black cloak, leaving himself in his
breeches and doublet, while Cardenio's appearance was so
different from what it had been that he would not have
known himself had he seen himself in a mirror. Having
effected this, although the others had gone on ahead while
they were disguising themselves, they easily came out on
the high road before them, for the brambles and awkward
places they encountered did not allow those on horseback
to go as fast as those on foot. They then posted themselves
on the level ground at the outlet of the Sierra, and as soon

---

[1] Literally, 'I am sucking my fingers.' Shelton and Jervas translate
literally, and so miss the meaning.

as Don Quixote and his companions emerged from it the curate began to examine him very deliberately, as though he were striving to recognise him, and after having stared at him for some time he hastened towards him with open arms exclaiming, 'A happy meeting with the mirror of chivalry, my worthy compatriot Don Quixote of La Mancha, the flower and cream of high breeding, the protection and relief of the distressed, the quintessence of knights-errant!' And so saying he clasped in his arms the knee of Don Quixote's left leg. He, astonished at the stranger's words and behaviour, looked at him attentively, and at length recognised him, very much surprised to see him there, and made great efforts to dismount. This, however, the curate would not allow, on which Don Quixote said, 'Permit me, señor licentiate, for it is not fitting that I should be on horseback and so reverend a person as your worship on foot.'

'On no account will I allow it,' said the curate; 'your mightiness must remain on horseback, for it is on horseback you achieve the greatest deeds and adventures that have been beheld in our age; as for me, an unworthy priest, it will serve me well enough to mount on the haunches of one of the mules of these gentlefolk who accompany your worship, if they have no objection, and I will fancy I am mounted on the steed Pegasus, or on the zebra or charger that bore the famous Moor, Muzaraque, who to this day lies enchanted in the great hill of Zulema, a little distance from the great Complutum.'[1]

---

[1] In the immediate neighbourhood of Alcalá de Henares.

'Nor even that will I consent to,'[1] señor licentiate,' answered Don Quixote, 'and I know it will be the good pleasure of my lady the princess, out of love for me, to order her squire to give up the saddle of his mule to your worship, and he can sit behind if the beast will bear it.'

'It will, I am sure,' said the princess, 'and I am sure, too, that I need not order my squire, for he is too courteous and too good a Christian to allow a Churchman to go on foot when he might be mounted.'

'That he is,' said the barber, and at once alighting, he offered his saddle to the curate, who accepted it without much entreaty; but unfortunately as the barber was mounting behind, the mule, being as it happened a hired one, which is the same thing as saying ill-conditioned, lifted its hind hoofs and let fly a couple of kicks in the air, which would have made Master Nicholas wish his expedition in quest of Don Quixote at the devil had they caught him on the breast or head. As it was, they so took him by surprise that he came to the ground, giving so little heed to his beard that it fell off, and all he could do when he found himself without it was to cover his face hastily with both his hands and moan that his teeth were knocked out. Don Quixote when he saw all that bundle of beard detached, without jaws or blood, from the face of the fallen squire, exclaimed, 'By the living God, but this is a great miracle! it has knocked off and plucked away the beard from his face as if it had been shaved off designedly.'

The curate, seeing the danger of discovery that threat-

---

[1] I have followed here the suggestion of Fernandez Cuesta, for the reading in the original edition is obviously corrupt.

ened his scheme, at once pounced upon the beard and
hastened with it to where Master Nicholas lay, still uttering
moans, and drawing his head to his breast had it on in an
instant, muttering over him some words which he said were
a certain special charm for sticking on beards, as they would
see; and as soon as he had it fixed he left him, and the
squire appeared well bearded and whole as before, whereat
Don Quixote was beyond measure astonished, and begged
the curate to teach him that charm when he had an opportunity, as he was persuaded its virtue must extend beyond
the sticking on of beards, for it was clear that where the
beard had been stripped off the flesh must have remained
torn and lacerated, and when it could heal all that it must
be good for more than beards.

'And so it is,' said the curate, and he promised to teach
it to him on the first opportunity. They then agreed that
for the present the curate should mount, and that the three
should ride by turns until they reached the inn, which
might be about six leagues from where they were.[1]

Three then being mounted, that is to say, Don Quixote,
the princess, and the curate, and three on foot, Cardenio,
the barber, and Sancho Panza, Don Quixote said to the
damsel, 'Let your highness, lady, lead on whithersoever
is most pleasing to you;' but before she could answer the
licentiate said, 'Towards what kingdom would your ladyship
direct our course? Is it perchance towards that of Micomicon? It must be, or else I know little about kingdoms.'

She, being ready on all points, understood that

---

[1] The original says 'two leagues,' but the context shows it must have
been at least thrice as far.

she was to answer 'Yes,' so she said 'Yes, señor, my way lies towards that kingdom.'

'In that case,' said the curate, 'we must pass right through my village, and there your worship will take the road to Cartagena, where you will be able to embark, fortune favouring; and if the wind be fair and the sea smooth and tranquil, in somewhat less than nine years you may come in sight of the great lake Meona, I mean Meotides, which is little more than a hundred days' journey this side of your highness's kingdom.'

'Your worship is mistaken, señor,' said she; 'for it is not two years since I set out from it, and though I never had good weather, nevertheless I am here to behold what I so longed for, and that is my lord Don Quixote of La Mancha, whose fame came to my ears as soon as I set foot in Spain and impelled me to go in search of him, to commend myself to his courtesy, and entrust the justice of my cause to the might of his invincible arm.'

'Enough; no more praise,' said Don Quixote at this, 'for I hate all flattery; and though this may not be so, still language of the kind is offensive to my chaste ears. I will only say, señora, that whether it has might or not, that which it may or may not have shall be devoted to your service even to death; and now, leaving this to its proper season, I would ask the señor licentiate to tell me what it is that has brought him into these parts, alone, unattended, and so lightly clad that I am filled with amazement.'

'I will answer that briefly,' replied the curate; 'you must know then, Señor Don Quixote, that Master Nicholas, our friend and barber, and I were going to Seville to receive some money that a relative of mine who went to the Indies many years ago had sent me, and not such a small sum but that it was over sixty thousand pieces of eight, full weight, which is something; and passing by this place yesterday we were attacked by four footpads, who stripped us even to our beards, and them they stripped off so that the barber found it necessary to put on a false one, and even this young man here'—pointing to Cardenio—'they completely transformed. But the best of it is, the story goes in the neighbourhood that those who attacked us belong to a number of galley slaves who, they say, were set free almost on the very same spot by a man of such valour that, in spite of the commissary and of the guards, he released the whole of them; and beyond all doubt he must have been out of his senses, or he must be as great a scoundrel as they, or some man without heart or conscience to let the wolf loose among the sheep, the fox among the hens, the fly among the honey.[1] He has defrauded justice, and opposed his king and lawful master, for he opposed his just commands; he has, I say, robbed the galleys of their feet, stirred up the Holy Brotherhood which for many years past has been quiet, and, lastly, has done a deed by which his soul may be lost without any gain to his body.' Sancho had told the curate and the barber of the adventure of the galley slaves, which, so much to his glory, his master had achieved, and hence the curate in alluding to it made the most of it to see what would be said or done by Don

---

[1] Clemencin and Hartzenbusch point out that to let the fly loose 'among the honey' would be worse for him than for it, and the latter, giving a quotation in point from Francisco de Rojas, substitutes 'the bear.'

Quixote; who changed colour at every word, not daring to say that it was he who had been the liberator of those worthy people. 'These, then,' said the curate, 'were they who robbed us; and God in his mercy pardon him who would not let them go to the punishment they deserved.'

CHAPTER XXX.

WHICH TREATS OF THE ADDRESS DISPLAYED BY THE FAIR
DOROTHEA, WITH OTHER MATTERS PLEASANT AND AMUSING.

THE curate had hardly ceased speaking, when Sancho said,
'In faith, then, señor licentiate, he who did that deed was
my master; and it was not for want of my telling him
beforehand and warning him to mind what he was about,
and that it was a sin to set them at liberty, as they were all
on the march there because they were special scoundrels.'

'Blockhead!' said Don Quixote at this, 'it is no business
or concern of knights-errant to inquire whether any persons
in affliction, in chains, or oppressed that they may meet on
the high roads go that way and suffer as they do because of
their faults or because of their misfortunes. It only concerns them to aid them as persons in need of help, having
regard to their sufferings and not to their rascalities. I
encountered a chaplet or string of miserable and unfortunate
people, and did for them what my sense of duty demands of
me, and as for the rest be that as it may; and whoever
takes objection to it, saving the sacred dignity of the señor
licentiate and his honoured person, I say he knows little
about chivalry and lies like a whoreson villain, and this I
will give him to know to the fullest extent with my sword;'

and so saying he settled himself in his stirrups and pressed down his morion ; for the barber's basin, which according to him was Mambrino's helmet, he carried hanging at the saddle-bow until he could repair the damage done to it by the galley slaves.

Dorothea, who was shrewd and sprightly, and by this time thoroughly understood Don Quixote's crazy turn, and that all except Sancho Panza were making game of him, not to be behind the rest said to him, on observing his irritation, ' Sir Knight, remember the boon you have promised me, and that in accordance with it you must not engage in any other adventure, be it ever so pressing ; calm yourself, for if the licentiate had known that the galley slaves had been set free by that unconquered arm he would have stopped his mouth thrice over, or even bitten his tongue three times before he would have said a word that tended towards disrespect of your worship.'

' That I swear heartily,' said the curate, ' and I would have even plucked off a moustache.'

' I will hold my peace, señora,' said Don Quixote, ' and I will curb the natural anger that had arisen in my breast, and will proceed in peace and quietness until I have fulfilled my promise ; but in return for this consideration I entreat you to tell me, if you have no objection to do so, what is the nature of your trouble, and how many, who, and what are the persons of whom I am to require due satisfaction, and on whom I am to take vengeance on your behalf ? '

' That I will do with all my heart,' replied Dorothea, ' if it will not be wearisome to you to hear of miseries and misfortunes.'

'It will not be wearisome, señora,' said Don Quixote; to which Dorothea replied, 'Well, if that be so, give me your attention.' As soon as she said this, Cardenio and the barber drew close to her side, eager to hear what sort of story the quick-witted Dorothea would invent for herself; and Sancho did the same, for he was as much taken in by her as his master; and she having settled herself comfortably in the saddle, and with the help of coughing and other preliminaries taken time to think, began with great sprightliness of manner in this fashion.

'First of all, I would have you know, sirs, that my name is—' and here she stopped for a moment, for she forgot the name the curate had given her; but he came to her relief, seeing what her difficulty was, and said, 'It is no wonder, señora, that your highness should be confused and embarrassed in telling the tale of your misfortunes; for such afflictions often have the effect of depriving the sufferers of memory, so that they do not even remember their own names, as is the case now with your ladyship, who has forgotten that she is called the Princess Micomicona, lawful heiress of the great kingdom of Micomicon; and with this cue your highness may now recall to your sorrowful recollection all you may wish to tell us.'

'That is the truth,' said the damsel; 'but I think from this on I shall have no need of any prompting, and I shall bring my true story safe into port, and here it is. The king my father, who was called Tinacrio the Sapient, was very learned in what they call magic arts, and became aware by his craft that my mother, who was called Queen Jaramilla, was to die before he did, and that soon after he too

was to depart this life, and I was to be left an orphan without father or mother.   But all this, he declared, did not so
much grieve or distress him as his certain knowledge that
a prodigious giant, the lord of a great island close to our
kingdom, Pandafilando of the Scowl by name—for it is
averred that, though his eyes are properly placed and straight,
he always looks askew as if he squinted, and this he does
out of malignity, to strike fear and terror into those he
looks at—that he knew, I say, that this giant on becoming
aware of my orphan condition would overrun my kingdom
with a mighty force and strip me of all, not leaving me even
a small village to shelter me ; but that I could avoid all this
ruin and misfortune if I were willing to marry him ; however, as far as he could see, he never expected that I would
consent to a marriage so unequal; and he said no more
than the truth in this, for it has never entered my mind to
marry that giant, or any other, let him be ever so great or
enormous.   My father said, too, that when he was dead, and
I saw Pandafilando about to invade my kingdom, I was not
to wait and attempt to defend myself, for that would be
destructive to me, but that I should leave the kingdom
entirely open to him if I wished to avoid the death and
total destruction of my good and loyal vassals, for there
would be no possibility of defending myself against the
giant's devilish power ; and that I should at once with some
of my followers set out for Spain, where I should obtain
relief in my distress on finding a certain knight-errant
whose fame by that time would extend over the whole kingdom, and who would be called, if I remember rightly, Don
Azote or Don Gigote.'

' " Don Quixote," he must have said, señora,' observed Sancho at this, ' otherwise called the Knight of the Rueful Countenance.'

' That is it,' said Dorothea ; ' he said, moreover, that he would be tall of stature and lank featured ; and that on his right side under the left shoulder, or thereabouts, he would have a grey mole with hairs like bristles.' [1]

On hearing this, Don Quixote said to his squire, ' Here, Sancho my son, bear a hand and help me to strip, for I want to see if I am the knight that sage king foretold.'

' What does your worship want to strip for ? ' said Dorothea.

' To see if I have that mole your father spoke of,' answered Don Quixote.

' There is no occasion to strip,' said Sancho ; ' for I know your worship has just such a mole on the middle of your backbone, which is the mark of a strong man.'

' That is enough,' said Dorothea, ' for with friends we must not look too closely into trifles ; and whether it be on the shoulder or on the backbone matters little ; it is enough if there is a mole, be it where it may, for it is all the same flesh ; no doubt my good father hit the truth in every particular, and I have made a lucky hit in commending myself to Don Quixote ; for he is the one my father spoke of, as the features of his countenance correspond with those assigned to this knight by that wide fame he has acquired not only in Spain but in all La Mancha ; for I had scarcely landed at Osuna when I heard such accounts of his achievements,

---

[1] This was the mark from which the ancestor of the Dukes of Medinaceli, Fernando de la Cerda, took his name.

that at once my heart told me he was the very one I had come in search of.'

'But how did you land at Osuna, señora,' asked Don Quixote, 'when it is not a seaport?'[1]

But before Dorothea could reply the curate anticipated her, saying, 'The princess meant to say that after she had landed at Malaga the first place where she heard of your worship was Osuna.'

'That is what I meant to say,' said Dorothea.

'And that would be only natural,' said the curate. 'Will your majesty please proceed?'

'There is no more to add,' said Dorothea, 'save that in finding Don Quixote I have had such good fortune, that I already reckon and regard myself queen and mistress of my entire dominions, since of his courtesy and magnanimity he has granted me the boon of accompanying me whithersoever I may conduct him, which will be only to bring him face to face with Pandafilando of the Scowl, that he may slay him and restore to me what has been unjustly usurped by him : for all this must come to pass satisfactorily since my good father Tinacrio the Sapient foretold it, who likewise left it declared in writing in Chaldee or Greek characters (for I cannot read them), that if this predicted knight, after having cut the giant's throat, should be disposed to marry me I was to offer myself at once without demur as his lawful wife, and yield him possession of my kingdom together with my person.'

'What thinkest thou now, friend Sancho?' said Don

---

[1] This is a sly hit of Cervantes at Mariana the historian, who makes the troops despatched against Viriatus land at Orsuna, now Osuna.

Quixote at this. 'Hearest thou that? Did I not tell thee so? See how we have already got a kingdom to govern and a queen to marry!'

'On my oath it is so,' said Sancho; 'and foul fortune to him who won't marry after slitting Señor Pandahilado's windpipe! And then, how ill-favoured the queen is! I wish the fleas in my bed were that sort!' and so saying he cut a couple of capers in the air with every sign of extreme satisfaction, and then ran to seize the bridle of Dorothea's mule, and checking it fell on his knees before her, begging her to give him her hand to kiss in token of his acknowledgment of her as his queen and mistress. Which of the bystanders could have helped laughing to see the madness of the master and the simplicity of the servant? Dorothea therefore gave her hand, and promised to make him a great lord in her kingdom, when Heaven should be so good as to permit her to recover and enjoy it, for which Sancho returned thanks in words that set them all laughing again.

'This, sirs,' continued Dorothea, 'is my story; it only remains to tell you that of all the attendants I took with me from my kingdom I have none left except this well-bearded squire, for all were drowned in a great tempest we encountered when in sight of port; and he and I came to land on a couple of planks as if by a miracle; and indeed the whole course of my life is a miracle and a mystery as you may have observed; and if I have been over minute in any respect or not as precise as I ought, let it be accounted for by what the licentiate said at the beginning of my tale, that constant and excessive troubles deprive the sufferers of their memory.'

H 2

' They shall not deprive me of mine, exalted and worthy princess,' said Don Quixote, ' however great and unexampled those which I shall endure in your service may be; and here I confirm anew the boon I have promised you, and I swear to go with you to the end of the world until I find myself in the presence of your fierce enemy, whose haughty head I trust by the aid of God and of my arm to cut off with the edge of this—I will not say good sword, thanks to Gines de Pasamonte who carried away mine '—(this he said between his teeth, and then continued),[1] ' and when it has been cut off and you have been put in peaceful possession of your realm it shall be left to your own decision to dispose of your person as may be most pleasing to you; for so long as my memory is occupied, my will enslaved, and my understanding enthralled by her—I say no more—it is impossible for me for a moment to contemplate marriage, even with a Phœnix.'

The last words of his master about not wanting to marry were so disagreeable to Sancho that raising his voice he exclaimed with great irritation, ' By my oath, Señor Don Quixote, you are not in your right senses; for how can your worship possibly object to marrying such an exalted princess as this? Do you think Fortune will offer you behind every stone such a piece of luck as is offered you now? Is my lady Dulcinea fairer, perchance? Not she; nor half as fair; and I will even go so far as to say she does not come up to the shoe of this one here. A poor chance I

[1] Cervantes seems to have intended that Gines de Pasamonte should carry off Don Quixote's sword, as Brunello did Marfisa's at the siege of Albracca.

have of getting that county I am waiting for if your
worship goes looking for dainties in the bottom of the sea.[1]
In the devil's name, marry, marry, and take this kingdom
that comes to hand without any trouble, and when you are
king make me a marquis or governor of a province, and for
the rest let the devil take it all.'

Don Quixote, when he heard such blasphemies uttered
against his lady Dulcinea, could not endure it, and lifting
his pike, without saying anything to Sancho or uttering a
word, he gave him two such thwacks that he brought him to
the ground; and had it not been that Dorothea cried out to
him to spare him he would have no doubt taken his life on
the spot. 'Do you think,' he said to him after a pause, 'you
scurvy clown, that you are to be always interfering with
me, and that you are to be always offending and I always
pardoning? Don't fancy it, impious scoundrel, for that
beyond a doubt thou art, since thou hast set thy tongue
going against the peerless Dulcinea. Know you not, lout,
vagabond, beggar, that were it not for the might that she
infuses into my arm I should not have strength enough to
kill a flea? Say, O scoffer with a viper's tongue, what think
you has won this kingdom and cut off this giant's head
and made you a marquis (for all this I count as already
accomplished and decided), but the might of Dulcinea, employing my arm as the instrument of her achievements?
She fights in me and conquers in me, and I live and breathe
in her, and owe my life and being to her. O whoreson
scoundrel, how ungrateful you are, you see yourself raised
from the dust of the earth to be a titled lord, and the return

[1] See Note A, p. 107.

you make for so great a benefit is to speak evil of her who·
has conferred it upon you ! '

Sancho was not so stunned but that he heard all his
master said, and rising with some degree of nimbleness he
ran to place himself behind Dorothea's palfrey, and from
that position he said to his master, ' Tell me, señor ; if your
worship is resolved not to marry this great princess, it is
plain the kingdom will not be yours ; and not being so, how
can you bestow favours upon me ?   That is what I complain of.   Let your worship at any rate marry this queen,
now that we have got her here as if showered down from
heaven, and afterwards you may go back to my lady
Dulcinea ; for there must have been kings in the world who
kept mistresses.   As to beauty, I have nothing to do with it ;
and if the truth is to be told, I like them both ; though I
have never seen the lady Dulcinea.'

' How ! never seen her, blasphemous traitor ! ' exclaimed
Don Quixote ; ' hast thou not just now brought me a message from her ? '

' I mean,' said Sancho, ' that I did not see her so much
at my leisure that I could take particular notice of her
beauty, or of her charms piecemeal ; but taken in the lump
I like her.'

' Now I forgive thee,' said Don Quixote ; ' and do thou
forgive me the injury I have done thee ; for our first im-
pulses are not in our control.'

' That I see,' replied Sancho, ' and with me the wish
to speak is always the first impulse, and I cannot help saying, once at any rate, what 1 have on the tip of my tongue.'

' For all that, Sancho,' said Don Quixote, ' take heed of

what thou sayest, for the pitcher goes so often to the well [1]
—I need say no more to thee.'

'Well, well,' said Sancho, 'God is in heaven, and sees
all tricks, and will judge who does most harm, I in not
speaking right, or your worship in doing it.'

'That is enough,' said Dorothea; 'run, Sancho, and kiss
your lord's hand and beg his pardon, and henceforward
be more circumspect with your praise and abuse; and say
nothing in disparagement of that lady Tobosa, of whom
I know nothing save that I am her servant; and put your
trust in God, for you will not fail to obtain some dignity so
as to live like a prince.'

Sancho advanced hanging his head and begged his
master's hand, which Don Quixote with dignity presented to
him, giving him his blessing as soon as he had kissed it;
he then bade him go on ahead a little, as he had questions
to ask him and matters of great importance to discuss with
him. Sancho obeyed, and when the two had gone some distance in advance Don Quixote said to him, 'Since thy
return I have had no opportunity or time to ask thee many
particulars touching thy mission and the answer thou hast
brought back, and now that chance has granted us the time
and opportunity, deny me not the happiness thou canst
give me by such good news.'

'Let your worship ask what you will,' answered Sancho,
'for I shall find a way out of all as easily as I found a way
in; but I implore you, señor, not to be so revengeful in
future.'

---

[1] Prov. 33. In full it is, 'The pitcher that goes often to the well
leaves behind either the handle or the spout.'

'Why dost thou say that, Sancho?' said Don Quixote.

'I say it,' he returned, 'because those blows just now were more because of the quarrel the devil stirred up between us both the other night, than for what I said against my lady Dulcinea, whom I love and reverence as I would a relic—though there is nothing of that about her—merely as something belonging to your worship.'

'Say no more on that subject for thy life, Sancho,' said Don Quixote, 'for it is displeasing to me; I have already pardoned thee for that, and thou knowest the common saying, "For a fresh sin a fresh penance."'[1]

While this was going on they saw coming along the road they were following a man mounted on an ass, who when he came close seemed to be a gipsy; but Sancho Panza, whose eyes and heart were there wherever he saw asses, no sooner beheld the man than he knew him to be Gines de Pasamonte; and by the thread of the gipsy he got at the ball, his ass,[2] for it was, in fact, Dapple that carried Pasamonte, who to escape recognition and to sell the ass had disguised himself as a gipsy, being able to speak the gipsy language, and many more, as well as if they were his own. Sancho saw him and recognised him, and the instant he did so he shouted to him, 'Ginesillo, you thief, give up my treasure, release my life, embarrass thyself not with my repose, quit my ass, leave my delight, be off, rip, get thee gone, thief, and give up what is not thine.'

There was no necessity for so many words or objurgations, for at the first one Gines jumped down, and at a trot like racing speed made off and got clear of them all.

[1] Prov. 177.   [2] See Note B, p. 107.

Sancho hastened to his Dapple, and embracing him he said, 'How hast thou fared, my blessing, Dapple of my eyes, my comrade?' all the while kissing him and caressing him as if he were a human being. The ass held his peace, and let himself be kissed and caressed by Sancho without answering a single word. They all came up and congratulated him on having found Dapple, Don Quixote especially, who told him that notwithstanding this he would not cancel the order for the three ass-colts, for which Sancho thanked him.

While the two had been going along conversing in this fashion, the curate observed to Dorothea that she had shown great cleverness, as well in the story itself as in its conciseness, and the resemblance it bore to those of the books of chivalry. She said that she had many times amused herself reading them; but that she did not know the situation of the provinces or seaports, and so she had said at haphazard that she had landed at Osuna.

'So I saw,' said the curate, 'and for that reason I made haste to say what I did, by which it was all set right. But is it not a strange thing to see how readily this unhappy gentleman believes all these figments and lies, simply because they are in the style and manner of the absurdities of his books?'

'So it is,' said Cardenio; 'and so uncommon and unexampled, that were one to attempt to invent and concoct it in fiction, I doubt if there be any wit keen enough to imagine it.'

'But another strange thing about it,' said the curate, 'is that, apart from the silly things which this worthy gentleman says in connection with his craze, when other subjects are dealt with, he can discuss them in a perfectly rational manner, showing that his mind is quite clear and composed; so that, provided his chivalry is not touched upon, no one would take him to be anything but a man of thoroughly sound understanding.'

While they were holding this conversation Don Quixote continued his with Sancho, saying, 'Friend Panza, let us forgive and forget as to our quarrels, and tell me now, dismissing anger and irritation, where, how, and when didst thou find Dulcinea? What was she doing? What didst thou say to her? What did she answer? How did she look when she was reading my letter? Who copied it out for thee? and everything in the matter that seems to thee worth knowing, asking, and learning; neither adding nor falsifying to give me pleasure, nor yet curtailing lest you should deprive me of it.'

'Señor,' replied Sancho, 'if the truth is to be told, nobody copied out the letter for me, for I carried no letter at all.'

'It is as thou sayest,' said Don Quixote, 'for the notebook in which I wrote it I found in my own possession two days after thy departure, which gave me very great vexation, as I knew not what thou wouldst do on finding thyself without any letter; and I made sure thou wouldst return from the place where thou didst first miss it.'

'So I should have done,' said Sancho, 'if I had not got it by heart when your worship read it to me, so that I repeated it to a sacristan, who copied it out for me from hearing it, so exactly that he said in all the days of his life, though he had read many a letter of excommunication, he had never seen or read so pretty a letter as that.'

'And hast thou got it still in thy memory, Sancho?' said Don Quixote.

'No, señor,' replied Sancho, 'for as soon as I had repeated it, seeing there was no further use for it, I set about forgetting it; and if I recollect any of it, it is that about " Scrubbing," I mean to say " Sovereign Lady," and the end " Yours till death, the Knight of the Rueful Countenance ; " and between these two I put into it more than three hundred " my souls " and " my life's " and " my eyes." '

Note A (*page* 101).

Prov. 60. *Pedir cotufas en el golfo*—a proverbial expression for seeking impossibilities. *Cotufa*, according to Salvá, is equivalent to *golosina*—a dainty : Clemencin says it is the same as *Chufa*, the tuber of the *Cyparus esculentus*, used as an ingredient in *horchata*, and in other ways.

Note B (*page* 104).

A reference to the proverb *Por el hilo se saca el ovillo* (114). This passage down to ' Sancho thanked him,' like that describing the theft of the ass, was first inserted in Juan de la Cuesta's second edition. This, however, seems to be Cervantes' own work, as it agrees with c. iv. Pt. II. The printer, no doubt, did not see its relevancy, and therefore omitted it in the first edition.

CHAPTER XXXI.[1]

OF THE DELECTABLE DISCUSSION BETWEEN DON QUIXOTE
AND SANCHO PANZA, HIS SQUIRE, TOGETHER WITH OTHER
INCIDENTS.

'ALL that is not unsatisfactory to me,' said Don Quixote.
'Go on; thou didst reach her; and what was that queen of
beauty doing? Surely thou didst find her stringing pearls,
or embroidering some device in gold thread for this her
enslaved knight.'

'I did not,' said Sancho, 'but I found her winnowing
two bushels of wheat in the yard of her house.'

'Then depend upon it,' said Don Quixote, 'the grains
of that wheat were pearls when touched by her hands; and
didst thou look, friend? was it white wheat or brown?'

'It was neither, but red,' said Sancho.

'Then I promise thee,' said Don Quixote, 'that, win-
nowed by her hands, beyond a doubt the bread it made was
of the whitest; but go on; when thou gavest her my letter,
did she kiss it? Did she place it on her head? Did she
perform any ceremony befitting such a letter, or what did
she do?'

'When I went to give it to her,' replied Sancho, 'she

---

[1] The division here is very awkwardly managed: chapter xxxi. ought to
have commenced at 'While they were holding this conversation,' in the
preceding chapter.

was hard at it swaying from side to side with a lot of wheat she had in the sieve, and she said to me, " Lay the letter, friend, on the top of that sack, for I cannot read it until I have done sifting all this." '

' Discreet lady ! ' said Don Quixote ; ' that was in order to read it at her leisure and enjoy it ; proceed, Sancho ; while she was engaged in her occupation what converse did she hold with thee ?   What did she ask about me, and what answer didst thou give ?   Make haste ; tell me all, and let not an atom be left behind in the ink-bottle.'

' She asked me nothing,' said Sancho ; ' but I told her how your worship was left doing penance in her service, naked from the waist up, in among these mountains like a savage, sleeping on the ground, not eating bread off a table-cloth nor combing your beard, weeping and cursing your fortune.'

' In saying I cursed my fortune thou saidst wrong,' said Don Quixote ; ' for rather do I bless it and shall bless it all the days of my life for having made me worthy of aspiring to love so lofty a lady as Dulcinea del Toboso.'

' And so lofty she is,' said Sancho, ' that she overtops me by more than a hand's-breadth.'

' What ! Sancho,' said Don Quixote, ' didst thou measure with her ? '

' I measured in this way,' said Sancho ; ' going to help her to put a sack of wheat on the back of an ass, we came so close together that I could see she stood more than a good palm over me.'

' Well ! ' said Don Quixote, ' and doth she not of a truth accompany and adorn this greatness with a thousand million charms of mind ! But one thing thou wilt not deny, Sancho; when thou camest close to her didst thou not perceive a Sabæan odour, an aromatic fragrance, a, I know not what, delicious, that I cannot find a name for ; I mean a redolence, an exhalation, as if thou wert in the shop of some dainty glover ? '

'All I can say is,' said Sancho, 'that I did perceive a little odour, something goaty ; it must have been that she was all in a sweat with hard work.'

'It could not be that,' said Don Quixote, 'but thou must have been suffering from cold in the head, or must have smelt thyself; for I know well what would be the scent of that rose among thorns, that lily of the field, that dissolved amber.'

'Maybe so,' replied Sancho; 'there often comes from myself that same odour which then seemed to me to come from her grace the lady Dulcinea; but that's no wonder, for one devil is like another.' [1]

'Well then,' continued Don Quixote, 'now she has done sifting the corn and sent it to the mill; [2] what did she do when she read the letter ? '

'As for the letter,' said Sancho, 'she did not read it, for she said she could neither read nor write; instead of that she tore it up into small pieces, saying that she did not want to let anyone read it lest her secrets should become known in the village, and that what I had told her by word of mouth about the love your worship bore her, and the extraordinary penance you were doing for her sake, was enough; and, to make an end of it, she told me to tell

[1] Prov. 176.   [2] A popular phrase like ' Well, that's settled.'

your worship that she kissed your hands, and that she had a greater desire to see you than to write to you; and that therefore she entreated and commanded you, on sight of this present, to come out of these thickets, and to have done with carrying on absurdities, and to set out at once for El Toboso, unless something else of greater importance should happen, for she had a great desire to see your worship. She laughed greatly when I told her how your worship was called The Knight of the Rueful Countenance; I asked her if that Biscayan the other day had been there; and she told me he had, and that he was a very honest fellow; I asked her too about the galley slaves, but she said she had not seen any as yet.'

'So far all goes well,' said Don Quixote; 'but tell me what jewel was it that she gave thee on taking thy leave, in return for thy tidings of me? For it is a usual and ancient custom with knights and ladies errant to give the squires, damsels, or dwarfs who bring tidings of their ladies to the knights, or of their knights to the ladies, some rich jewel as a guerdon for good news,[1] and acknowledgment of the message.'

'That is very likely,' said Sancho, 'and a good custom it was, to my mind; but that must have been in days gone by, for now it would seem to be the custom only to give a piece of bread and cheese; because that was what my lady Dulcinea gave me over the top of the yard-wall when I took leave of her; and more by token it was sheep's-milk cheese.'

'She is generous in the extreme,' said Don Quixote,

---

[1] *Albricias,* from the Arabic *al bashara,* a reward given to the bearer of good news.

' and if she did not give thee a jewel of gold, no doubt it must have been because she had not one to hand there to give thee; but sleeves are good after Easter;[1] I shall see her and all shall be made right. But knowest thou what amazes me, Sancho? It seems to me thou must have gone and come through the air, for thou hast taken but little more than three days to go to El Toboso and return, though it is more than thirty leagues from here to there. From which I am inclined to think that the sage magician who is my friend, and watches over my interests (for of necessity there is and must be one, or else I should not be a right knight-errant), that this same, I say, must have helped thee to travel without thy knowledge; for some of these sages will catch up a knight-errant sleeping in his bed, and without his knowing how or in what way it happened, he wakes up the next day more than a thousand leagues away from the place where he went to sleep. And if it were not for this, knights-errant would not be able to give aid to one another in peril, as they do at every turn. For a knight, maybe, is fighting in the mountains of Armenia with some dragon, or fierce serpent, or another knight, and gets the worst of the battle, and is at the point of death; but when he least looks for it, there appears over against him on a cloud, or chariot of fire, another knight, a friend of his, who just before had been in England, and who takes his part, and delivers him from death; and at night he finds himself in his own quarters supping very much to his satis-

[1] Prov. 135, i.e. a good thing may be acceptable even out of its proper season, as after Easter the weather may be still cold enough to make sleeves comfortable. Cf. the Scotch proverb, 'A Yule feast may be done at Pasch.'

faction; and yet from one place to the other will have been two or three thousand leagues. And all this is done by the craft and skill of the sage enchanters who take care of those valiant knights; so that, friend Sancho, I find no difficulty in believing that thou mayest have gone from this place to El Toboso and returned in such a short time, since, as I have said, some friendly sage must have carried thee through the air without thee perceiving it.'

'That must have been it,' said Sancho, 'for indeed Rocinante went like a gipsy's ass with quicksilver in his ears.' [1]

'Quicksilver!' said Don Quixote, 'aye, and what is more, a legion of devils, folk that can travel and make others travel without being weary, exactly as the whim seizes them. But putting this aside, what thinkest thou I ought to do about my lady's command to go and see her? For though I feel that I am bound to obey her mandate, I feel too that I am debarred by the boon I have accorded to the princess that accompanies us, and the law of chivalry compels me to have regard for my word in preference to my inclination; on the one hand the desire to see my lady pursues and harasses me, on the other my solemn promise and the glory I shall win in this enterprise urge and call me; but what I think I shall do is to travel with all speed and reach quickly the place where this giant is, and on my arrival I shall cut off his head, and establish the princess peacefully in her realm, and forthwith I shall return to behold the light that lightens my

---

[1] Alluding to a common device of the gipsy dealers to improve the pace of a beast for sale.

senses, to whom I shall make such excuses that she will be
led to approve of my delay, for she will see that it entirely
tends to increase her glory and fame; for all that I have
won, am winning, or shall win by arms in this life, comes
to me of the favour she extends to me, and because I am
hers.'

'Ah! what a sad state your worship's brains are in!'
said Sancho. 'Tell me, señor, do you mean to travel all
that way for nothing, and to let slip and lose so rich and
great a match as this where they give as a portion a kingdom that in sober truth I have heard say is more than
twenty thousand leagues round about, and abounds with
all things necessary to support human life, and is bigger
than Portugal and Castile put together? Peace, for the
love of God! Blush for what you have said, and take my
advice, and forgive me, and marry at once in the first
village where there is a curate; if not, here is our licentiate
who will do the business beautifully; remember, I am old
enough to give advice, and this I am giving comes pat to
the purpose; for a sparrow in the hand is better than a
vulture on the wing,[1] and he who has the good to his hand
and chooses the bad, that the good he complains of may not
come to him.'[2]

'Look here, Sancho,' said Don Quixote. 'If thou art
advising me to marry, in order that immediately on slaying
the giant I may become king, and be able to confer favours
on thee, and give thee what I have promised, let me tell thee

[1] Prov. 167.

[2] Prov. 21. Sancho, as he almost always does when it is long, makes
a muddle of the proverb: the correct form is, 'Who has good and chooses
evil, let him not complain of the evil that comes to him.'

I shall be able very easily to satisfy thy desires without marrying; for before going into battle I will make it a stipulation that, if I come out of it victorious, even if I do not marry, they shall give me a portion of the kingdom, that I may bestow it upon whomsoever I choose, and when they give it to me upon whom wouldst thou have me bestow it but upon thee?'

'That is plain speaking,' said Sancho; 'but let your worship take care to choose it on the sea-coast, so that if I don't like the life, I may be able to ship off my black vassals and deal with them as I have said; don't mind going to see my lady Dulcinea now, but go and kill this giant and let us finish off this business; for by God it strikes me it will be one of great honour and great profit.'

'I hold thou art in the right of it, Sancho,' said Don Quixote, 'and I will take thy advice as to accompanying the princess before going to see Dulcinea; but I counsel thee not to say anything to anyone, or to those who are with us, about what we have considered and discussed, for as Dulcinea is so decorous that she does not wish her thoughts to be known it is not right that I or anyone for me should disclose them.'

'Well then, if that be so,' said Sancho, 'how is it that your worship makes all those you overcome by your arm go to present themselves before my lady Dulcinea, this being the same thing as signing your name to it that you love her and are her lover? And as those who go must perforce kneel before her and say they come from your worship to submit themselves to her, how can the thoughts of both of you be hid?'

'O, how silly and simple thou art!' said Don Quixote; 'seest thou not, Sancho, that this tends to her greater exaltation? For thou must know that according to our way of thinking in chivalry, it is a high honour to a lady to have many knights-errant in her service, whose thoughts never go beyond serving her for her own sake, and who look for no other reward for their great and true devotion than that she should be willing to accept them as her knights.'

'It is with that kind of love,' said Sancho, 'I have heard preachers say we ought to love our Lord, for himself alone, without being moved by the hope of glory or the fear of punishment; though for my part, I would rather love and serve him for what he could do.'

'The devil take thee for a clown!' said Don Quixote, ' and what shrewd things thou sayest at times! One would think thou hadst studied.'

'In faith, then, I cannot even read,' answered Sancho.

Master Nicholas here called out to them to wait a while, as they wanted to halt and drink at a little spring there was there. Don Quixote drew up, not a little to the satisfaction of Sancho, for he was by this time weary of telling so many lies, and in dread of his master catching him tripping, for though he knew that Dulcinea was a peasant girl of El Toboso, he had never seen her in all his life. Cardenio had now put on the clothes which Dorothea was wearing when they found her, and though they were not very good, they were far better than those he put off. They dismounted together by the side of the spring, and with what the curate had provided himself with at the inn they appeased, though not very well, the keen appetite they all of them brought with them.

While they were so employed there happened to come by a youth passing on his way, who stopping to examine the party at the spring, the next moment ran to Don Quixote and clasping him round the legs, began to weep freely, saying, ' O, señor, do you not know me ? Look at me well ; I am that lad Andres that your worship released from the oak-tree where I was tied.'

Don Quixote recognised him, and taking his hand he turned to those present and said : ' That your worships may see how important it is to have knights-errant to redress the wrongs and injuries done by tyrannical and wicked men in this world, I may tell you that some days ago passing through a wood, I heard cries and piteous complaints as of a person in pain and distress ; I immediately hastened, impelled by my bounden duty, to the quarter whence the plaintive accents seemed to me to proceed, and I found tied to an oak this lad who now stands before you, which in my heart I rejoice at, for his testimony will not permit me to depart from the truth in any particular. He was, I say, tied to an oak, naked from the waist up, and a clown, whom I afterwards found to be his master, was scarifying him by lashes with the reins of his mare. As soon as I saw him I asked the reason of so cruel a flagellation. The boor replied that he was flogging him because he was his servant and because of carelessness that proceeded rather from dishonesty than stupidity ; on which this boy said, " Señor, he flogs me only because I ask for my wages." The master made I know not what speeches and explanations, which, though I listened to them, I did not accept. In short, I compelled the clown to unbind him, and to swear he would take him with him, and pay him real by real, and perfumed into the bargain.[1] Is not all this true, Andres my son? Didst thou not mark with what authority I commanded him, and with what humility he promised to do all I enjoined, specified, and required of him? Answer without confusion or hesitation; tell these gentlemen what took place, that they may see and observe that it is as great an advantage as I say to have knights-errant abroad.'

'All that your worship has said is quite true,' answered the lad; 'but the end of the business turned out just the opposite of what your worship supposes.'

'How! the opposite?' said Don Quixote; 'did not the clown pay thee then?'

'Not only did he not pay me,' replied the lad, 'but as soon as your worship had passed out of the wood and we were alone, he tied me up again to the same oak and gave me a fresh flogging, that left me like a flayed Saint Bartholomew; and every stroke he gave me he followed up with some jest or gibe about having made a fool of your worship, and but for the pain I was suffering I should have laughed at the things he said. In short he left me in such a condition that I have been until now in a hospital getting cured of the injuries which that rascally clown inflicted on me then; for all which your worship is to blame; for if you had gone your own way and not come where there was no call for you, nor meddled in other people's affairs, my master

[1] See chapter iv., Note 3, p. 137.

would have been content with giving me one or two dozen lashes, and would have then loosed me and paid me what he owed me; but when your worship abused him so out of measure, and gave him so many hard words, his anger was kindled; and as he could not revenge himself on you, as soon as he saw you had left him the storm burst upon me in such a way, that I feel as if I should never be a man again as long as I live.'

'The mischief,' said Don Quixote, 'lay in my going away; for I should not have gone until I had seen thee paid; because I ought to have known well by long experience that there is no clown who will keep his word if he finds it will not suit him to keep it; but thou rememberest, Andres, that I swore if he did not pay thee I would go and seek him, and find him though he were to hide himself in the whale's belly.'

'That is true,' said Andres; 'but it was of no use.'

'Thou shalt see now whether it is of use or not,' said Don Quixote; and so saying, he got up hastily and bade Sancho bridle Rocinante, who was browsing while they were eating. Dorothea asked him what he meant to do. He replied that he meant to go in search of this clown and chastise him for such iniquitous conduct, and see Andres paid to the last maravedi, despite and in the teeth of all the clowns in the world. To which she replied that he must remember that in accordance with his promise he could not engage in any enterprise until he had brought hers to a conclusion; and that as he knew this better than anyone, he should restrain his ardour until his return from her kingdom.

'That is true,' said Don Quixote, 'and Andres must have patience until my return as you say, señora; but I once more swear and promise afresh not to stop until I have seen him avenged and paid.'

'I have no faith in those oaths,' said Andres; 'I would rather have now something to help me to get to Seville than all the revenges in the world: if you have here anything to eat that I can take with me, give it me, and God be with your worship and all knights-errant; and may their errands turn out as well for themselves as they have for me.'

Sancho took out from his store a piece of bread and another of cheese, and giving them to the lad he said, 'Here, take this, brother Andres, for we have all of us a share in your misfortune.'

'Why, what share have you got?' asked Andres.

'This share of bread and cheese I am giving you,' answered Sancho; 'and God knows whether I shall feel the want of it myself or not; for I would have you know, friend, that we squires to knights errant have to bear a great deal of hunger and hard fortune, and even other things more easily felt than told.'

Andres seized his bread and cheese, and seeing that nobody gave him anything more, bent his head, and took hold of the road, as the saying is. However, before leaving he said to Don Quixote, 'For the love of God, sir knight-errant, if you ever meet me again, though you may see them cutting me to pieces, give me no aid or succour, but leave me to my misfortune, which will not be so great but that a greater will come to me by being helped by your worship, on whom and all the knights-errant that have ever been born God send his curse.'

Don Quixote was getting up to chastise him, but he took to his heels at such a pace that no one attempted to follow him; and mightily chapfallen was Don Quixote at the story of Andres, and the others had to take great care to restrain their laughter so as not to put him entirely out of countenance.

CHAPTER XXXII.

THEIR dainty repast being finished, they saddled at once, and without any adventure worth mentioning they reached next day the inn, the object of Sancho Panza's fear and dread ; but though he would have rather not entered it, there was no help for it.   The landlady, the landlord, their daughter, and Maritornes, when they saw Don Quixote and Sancho coming, went out to welcome them with signs of hearty satisfaction, which Don Quixote received with dignity and gravity, and bade them make up a better bed for him than the last time : to which the landlady replied that if he paid better than he did the last time she would give him one fit for a prince.   Don Quixote said he would, so they made up a tolerable one for him in the same garret as before ; and he lay down at once, being sorely shaken and in want of sleep.

No sooner was the door shut upon him than the landlady made at the barber, and seizing him by the beard, said, ' By my faith you are not going to make a beard of my tail any longer ; you must give me back my tail, for it is a shame the way that thing of my husband's goes tossing about on the floor ; I mean the comb that I used to stick in my good tail.' But for all she tugged at it the barber would not give it up until the licentiate told him to let her have it, as there was now no further occasion for that stratagem, because he might declare himself and appear in his own character, and tell Don Quixote that he had fled to this inn when those thieves the galley slaves robbed him; and should he ask for the princess's squire, they could tell him that she had sent him on before her to give notice to the people of her kingdom that she was coming, and bringing with her the deliverer of them all. On this the barber cheerfully restored the tail to the landlady, and at the same time they returned all the accessories they had borrowed to effect Don Quixote's deliverance. All the people of the inn were struck with astonishment at the beauty of Dorothea, and even at the comely figure of the shepherd Cardenio. The curate made them get ready such fare as there was in the inn, and the landlord, in hope of better payment, served them up a tolerably good dinner. All this time Don Quixote was asleep, and they thought it best not to waken him, as sleeping would now do him more good than eating.

While at dinner, the company consisting of the landlord, his wife, their daughter, Maritornes, and all the travellers, they discussed the strange craze of Don Quixote and the manner in which he had been found; and the landlady told them what had taken place between him and the carrier; and then, looking round to see if Sancho was there, when she saw he was not, she gave them the whole story of his blanketing, which they received with no little amusement. But on the curate observing that it was the books of chivalry which Don Quixote had read that had turned his brain, the landlord said, ' I cannot understand how that can be, for in truth to my mind there is no better reading in the world, and I have here two or three of them, with other writings that are the very life, not only of myself but of plenty more ; for when it is harvest-time, the reapers flock here on holidays, and there is always one among them who can read and who takes up one of these books, and we gather round him, thirty or more of us, and stay listening to him with a delight that makes our grey hairs grow young again.[1]   At least I can say for myself that when I hear of what furious and terrible blows the knights deliver, I am seized with the longing to do the same, and I would like to be hearing about them night and day.'

'And I just as much,' said the landlady, ' because I never have a quiet moment in my house except when you are listening to some one reading ; for then you are so taken up that for the time being you forget to scold.'

'That is true,' said Maritornes ; ' and, faith, I relish hearing these things greatly too, for they are very pretty ; especially when they describe some lady or another in the arms of her knight under the orange trees, and the duenna who is keeping watch for them half dead with envy and fright ; all this I say is as good as honey.'

'And you, what do you think, young lady ? ' said the curate turning to the landlord's daughter.

'I don't know indeed, señor,' said she ; ' I listen too, and to tell the truth, though I do not understand it, I like hearing it ; but it is not the blows that my father likes that I like, but the laments the knights utter when

---

[1] Literally, ' Rids us of a thousand grey hairs.'

they are separated from their ladies ; and indeed they sometimes make me weep with the compassion I feel for them.'

'Then you would console them if it was for you they
wept, young lady ? ' said Dorothea.

'I don't know what I should do,' said the girl ; 'I only
know that there are some of those ladies so cruel that they
call their knights tigers and lions and a thousand other foul
names : and, Jesus ! I don't know what sort of folk they
can be, so unfeeling and heartless, that rather than bestow a
glance upon a worthy man they leave him to die or go mad.
I don't know what is the good of such prudery ; if it is for
honour's sake, why not marry them ? That's all they want.'

' Hush, child,' said the landlady ; 'it seems to me thou
knowest a great deal about these things, and it is not fit for
girls to know or talk so much.'

' As the gentleman asked me, I could not help answering
him,' said the girl.

' Well then,' said the curate, ' bring me these books,
señor landlord, for I should like to see them.'

' With all my heart,' said he, and going into his own
room he brought out an old valise secured with a little
chain, on opening which the curate found in it three large
books and some manuscripts written in a very good hand.
The first that he opened he found to be ' Don Cirongilio
of Thrace,' and the second ' Don Felixmarte of Hircania,'
and the other the ' History of the Great Captain Gonzalo
Hernandez de Cordova, with the Life of Diego García de
Paredes.' [1]

When the curate read the two first titles he looked over

[1] See Note A, p. 131.

at the barber and said, 'We want my friend's housekeeper
and niece here now.'

'Nay,' said the barber, 'I can do just as well to carry
them to the yard or to the hearth, and there is a very good
fire there.'

'What! your worship would burn my books!' said the
landlord.

'Only these two,' said the curate, 'Don Cirongilio and
Felixmarte.'

'Are my books, then, heretics or phlegmatics that you
want to burn them?' said the landlord.

'Schismatics you mean, friend,' said the barber, 'not
phlegmatics.'

'That's it,' said the landlord; 'but if you want to burn
any, let it be that about the Great Captain and that Diego
Garcia; for I would rather have a child of mine burnt than
either of the others.'

'Brother,' said the curate, 'those two books are made
up of lies, and are full of folly and nonsense; but this of
the Great Captain is a true history, and contains the deeds
of Gonzalo Hernandez of Cordova, who by his many and
great achievements earned the title all over the world of
the Great Captain, a famous and illustrious name, and
deserved by him alone; and this Diego García de Paredes
was a distinguished knight of the city of Trujillo in Estremadura, a most gallant soldier, and of such bodily strength
that with one finger he stopped a mill-wheel in full motion;
and posted with a two-handed sword [1] at the foot of a bridge

---

[1] I.e. the *montante*, marvellous specimens of which may be seen in
the Armería at Madrid.

he kept the whole of an immense army from passing over it, and achieved such other exploits that if, instead of his relating them himself with the modesty of a knight and of one writing his own history, some free and unbiassed writer had recorded them, they would have thrown into the shade all the deeds of the Hectors, Achilleses, and Rolands.' [1]

'Tell that to my father,' said the landlord. 'There's a thing to be astonished at! Stopping a mill-wheel! By God your worship should read what I have read of Felixmarte of Hircania, how with one single backstroke he cleft five giants asunder through the middle as if they had been made of bean-pods like the little friars the children make; [2] and another time he attacked a very great and powerful army, in which there were more than a million six hundred thousand soldiers, all armed from head to foot, and he routed them all as if they had been flocks of sheep. And then, what do you say to the good Cirongilio of Thrace, that was so stout and bold; as may be seen in the book, where it is related that as he was sailing along a river there came up out of the midst of the water against him a fiery serpent, and he, as soon as he saw it, flung himself upon it and got astride of its scaly shoulders, and squeezed its throat with both hands with such force that the serpent, finding he was throttling it, had nothing for it but to let itself sink to the bottom of the river, carrying with it the knight who would not let go his hold; and when they got down there he found himself among palaces and gardens so

---

[1] Neither of these feats is mentioned in the memoir of García de Paredes appended to the life of the Great Captain.

[2] Made by cutting away part of the pod so as to expose the upper bean, which looks something like a friar's head in the recess of his cowl.

pretty that it was a wonder to see; and then the serpent changed itself into an old ancient man, who told him such things as were never heard. Hold your peace, señor; for if you were to hear this you would go mad with delight. A couple of figs for your Great Captain and your Diego García!'

Hearing this Dorothea said in a whisper to Cardenio, 'Our landlord is almost fit to play a second part to Don Quixote.'

'I think so,' said Cardenio, 'for, as he shows, he accepts it as a certainty that everything those books relate took place exactly as it is written down; and the barefooted friars themselves would not persuade him to the contrary.'

'But consider, brother,' said the curate once more, 'there never was any Felixmarte of Hircania in the world, nor any Cirongilio of Thrace, or any of the other knights of the same sort, that the books of chivalry talk of; the whole thing is the fabrication and invention of idle wits, devised by them for the purpose you describe of beguiling the time, as your reapers do when they read; for I swear to you in all seriousness there never were any such knights in the world, and no such exploits or nonsense ever happened anywhere.'

'Try that bone on another dog,' [1] said the landlord; 'as if I did not know how many make five, and where my shoe pinches me; [2] don't think to feed me with pap, for by God I am no fool. It is a good joke for your worship to try and persuade me that everything these good books say is nonsense and lies, and they printed by the licence of the Lords of the

---

[1] Prov. 181.   [2] Prov. 252.

Royal Council, as if they were people who would allow such a lot of lies to be printed all together, and so many battles and enchantments that they take away one's senses.'

'I have told you, friend,' said the curate, 'that this is done to divert our idle thoughts; and as in well-ordered states games of chess, fives, and billiards are allowed for the diversion of those who do not care, or are not obliged, or are unable to work, so books of this kind are allowed to be printed, on the supposition that, what indeed is the truth, there can be nobody so ignorant as to take any of them for true stories; and if it were permitted me now, and the present company desired it, I could say something about the qualities books of chivalry should possess to be good ones, that would be to the advantage and even to the taste of some; but I hope the time will come when I can communicate my ideas to some one who may be able to mend matters ; and in the meantime, señor landlord, believe what I have said, and take your books, and make up your mind about their truth or falsehood, and much good may they do you; and God grant you may not fall lame of the same foot your guest Don Quixote halts on.'

'No fear of that,' returned the landlord ; 'I shall not be so mad as to make a knight-errant of myself; for I see well enough that things are not now as they used to be in those days, when they say those famous knights roamed about the world.'

Sancho had made his appearance in the middle of this conversation, and he was very much troubled and cast down by what he heard said about knights-errant being now no longer in vogue, and all books of chivalry being folly and lies; and he resolved in his heart to wait and see what came of this journey of his master's, and if it did not turn out as happily as his master expected, he determined to leave him and go back to his wife and children and his ordinary labour.

The landlord was carrying away the valise and the books, but the curate said to him, 'Wait; I want to see what those papers are that are written in such a good hand.' The landlord taking them out handed them to him to read, and he perceived they were a work of about eight sheets of manuscript, with, in large letters at the beginning, the title of 'Novel of the Ill-advised Curiosity.' [1] The curate read three or four lines to himself, and said, 'I must say the title of this novel does not seem to me a bad one, and I feel an inclination to read it all.' To which the landlord replied, 'Then your reverence will do well to read it, for I can tell you that some guests who have read it here have been much pleased with it, and have begged it of me very earnestly; but I would not give it, meaning to return it to the person who forgot the valise, books, and papers here, for maybe he will return here some time or other; and though I know I shall miss the books, faith I mean to return them; for though I am an innkeeper, still I am a Christian.'

'You are very right, friend,' said the curate; 'but for all that, if the novel pleases me you must let me copy it.'

'With all my heart,' replied the host.

While they were talking Cardenio had taken up the novel and begun to read it, and forming the same opinion

[1] See Note B, p. 131.

of it as the curate, he begged him to read it so that they might all hear it.

'I would read it,' said the curate, 'if the time would not be better spent in sleeping than in reading.'

'It will be rest enough for me,' said Dorothea, 'to while away the time by listening to some tale, for my spirits are not yet tranquil enough to let me sleep when it would be seasonable.'

'Well then, in that case,' said the curate, 'I will read it, if it were only out of curiosity; perhaps it may contain something pleasant.'

Master Nicholas added his entreaties to the same effect, and Sancho too; seeing which, and considering that he would give pleasure to all, and receive it himself, the curate said, 'Well then, attend to me everyone, for the novel begins thus.'

Note A (*page* 125).

Don Cirongilio de Tracia was by Bernardo de Vargas and appeared at Seville in 1545: for *Felixmarte de Hircania* see chap. vi., Note[1], p. 155. The title of the third is *Cronica del Gran Capitan Gonzalo Hernandez de Cordoba y Aguilar*, to which is added the life of Diego García de Paredes, written by himself. It appeared at Saragossa in 1559. Gonzalo, the reader need hardly be reminded, was the brilliant general whose services against the Moors at Granada and the French in Naples were so ungratefully repaid by Ferdinand. García de Paredes was Gonzalo's companion-in-arms in both campaigns. His battered corselet in the Armería at Madrid is as good as a ballad.

Note B (*page* 130).

Curious Impertinent, Shelton's barbarous translation of *Curioso Impertinente*, is something worse than nonsense, for *Curioso* is here a substantive. There is, of course, no concise English translation for the title; the nearest approach to one would be, perhaps, *The inquisitive man who had no business to be so.*

CHAPTER XXXIII.

In Florence, a rich and famous city of Italy in the province called Tuscany, there lived two gentlemen of wealth and quality, Anselmo and Lothario, such great friends that by way of distinction they were called by all that knew them 'The two Friends.' They were unmarried, young, of the same age and of the same tastes, which was enough to account for the reciprocal friendship between them. Anselmo, it is true, was somewhat more inclined to seek pleasure in love than Lothario, for whom the pleasures of the chase had more attraction ; but on occasion Anselmo would forego his own tastes to yield to those of Lothario, and Lothario would surrender his to fall in with those of Anselmo, and in this way their inclinations kept pace one with the other with a concord so perfect that the best regulated clock could not surpass it.

Anselmo was deep in love with a high-born and beautiful maiden of the same city, the daughter of parents so estimable, and so estimable herself, that he resolved, with the approval of his friend Lothario, without whom he did nothing, to ask her of them in marriage, and did so, Lothario being the bearer of the demand, and conducting the negotiation so much to the satisfaction of his friend that in a short time he was in possession of the object of his desires, and Camilla so happy in having won Anselmo for her husband, that she gave thanks unceasingly to heaven and to Lothario, by whose means such good fortune had fallen to her. The first few days, those of a wedding being usually days of merry-making, Lothario frequented his friend Anselmo's house as he had been wont, striving to do honour to him and to the occasion, and to gratify him in every way he could ; but when the wedding days were over and the succession of visits and congratulations had slackened, he began purposely to leave off going to the house of Anselmo, for it seemed to him, as it naturally would to all men of sense, that friends' houses ought not to be visited after marriage with the same frequency as in their masters' bachelor days : because, though true and genuine friendship cannot and should not be in any way suspicious, still a married man's honour is a thing of such delicacy that it is held liable to injury from brothers, much more from friends. Anselmo remarked the cessation of Lothario's visits, and complained of it to him, saying that if he had known that marriage was to keep him from enjoying his society as he used, he would have never married ; and that, if by the thorough harmony that subsisted between them while he was a bachelor they had earned such a sweet name as that of ' The two Friends,' he should not allow a title so rare and so delightful to be lost through a needless anxiety to act circumspectly ; and so he entreated him, if such a phrase was allowable between them, to be once more master of his house and to come in and go out as formerly, assuring him that his wife Camilla had no other desire or inclination than that which he would wish her to have, and that knowing how sincerely they loved one another she was grieved to see such coldness in him.

To all this and much more that Anselmo said to Lothario to persuade him to come to his house as he had been in the habit of doing, Lothario replied with so much prudence, sense, and judgment, that Anselmo was satisfied of his friend's good intentions, and it was agreed that on two days in the week, and on holidays, Lothario should come to dine with him ; but though this arrangement was made between them Lothario resolved to observe it no further than he considered to be in accordance with the honour of his friend, whose good name was more to him than his own. He said, and justly, that a married man upon whom heaven had bestowed a beautiful wife should consider as carefully what friends he brought to his house as what female friends his wife associated with, for what cannot be done or arranged in the market-place, in church, at public festivals or at stations [1] (opportunities that husbands cannot always deny their wives), may be easily managed in the house of the female friend or relative in whom most confidence is reposed. Lothario said, too, that every married man should have some friend who would point out to him any negligence he might be guilty of in his conduct, for it will sometimes happen that owing to the deep affection the husband bears his wife either he does not caution her, or, not to vex her, refrains from telling her to do or not to do certain things, doing or avoiding which may be a matter of honour or reproach to him; and errors of this kind he could easily correct if warned by a friend. But where is such a friend to be found as Lothario would have, so judicious, so loyal, and so true?

Of a truth I know not; Lothario alone was such a one, for with the utmost care and vigilance he watched over the honour of his friend, and strove to diminish, cut down, and reduce the number of days for going to his house according to their agreement, lest the visits of a young man, wealthy, high-born, and with the attractions he was conscious of possessing, at the house of a woman so beautiful as Camilla, should be regarded with suspicion by the inquisitive and malicious eyes of the idle public. For though his integrity and reputation might bridle slanderous tongues, still he was unwilling to hazard either his own good name or that of his friend; and for this reason most of the days agreed upon he devoted to some other business which he pretended was unavoidable; so that a great portion of the day was taken up with complaints on one side and excuses on the other. It happened, however, that on one occasion when the two were strolling together through a meadow outside the city, Anselmo addressed the following words to Lothario.

'Thou mayest suppose, Lothario my friend, that I am unable

---

[1] *Estaciones*--attendances at church for private devotion at other hours than those of the celebration of the Mass. Among the scenes of the italian and Spanish tales of intrigue the church plays a leading part.

to give sufficient thanks for the favours God has rendered me in making me the son of such parents as mine were, and bestowing upon me with no niggard hand what are called the gifts of nature as well as those of fortune, and above all for what he has done in giving me thee for a friend and Camilla for a wife—two treasures that I value, if not as highly as I ought, at least as highly as I am able. And yet, with all these good things, which are commonly all that men need to enable them to live happily, I am the most discontented and dissatisfied man in the whole world ; for, I know not how long since, I have been harassed and oppressed by a desire so strange and so unusual, that I wonder at myself and blame and chide myself when I am alone, and strive to stifle it and hide it from my own thoughts, and with no better success than if I were endeavouring deliberately to publish it to all the world ; and as, in short, it must come out, I would confide it to thy safe keeping, feeling sure that by this means, and by thy readiness as a true friend to afford me relief, I shall soon find myself freed from the distress it causes me, and that thy care will give me happiness in the same degree as my own folly has caused me misery.'

The words of Anselmo struck Lothario with astonishment, unable as he was to conjecture the purport of such a lengthy prelude and preamble ; and though he strove to imagine what desire it could be that so troubled his friend, his conjectures were all far from the truth, and to relieve the anxiety which this perplexity was causing him, he told him he was doing a flagrant injustice to their great friendship in seeking circuitous methods of confiding to him his most hidden thoughts, for he well knew he might reckon upon his counsel in diverting them, or his help in carrying them into effect.

'That is the truth,' replied Anselmo, 'and relying upon that I will tell thee, friend Lothario, that the desire which harasses me is that of knowing whether my wife Camilla is as good and as perfect as I think her to be ; and I cannot satisfy myself of the truth on this point except by testing her in such a way that the trial may prove the purity of her virtue as the fire proves that of gold; because I am persuaded, my friend, that a woman is virtuous only in proportion as she is or is not tempted; and that she alone is strong who does not yield to the promises, gifts, tears, and importunities of earnest lovers; for what thanks does a woman deserve for being good if no one urges her to be bad, and what wonder is it that she is reserved and circumspect to whom no opportunity is given of going wrong, and who knows she has a husband that will take her life the first time he detects her in an impropriety? I do not therefore hold her who is virtuous through fear or want of opportunity in the same estimation as her who comes out of temptation and trial with a crown of victory; and so, for these reasons and many others that I could give thee to justify and support the opinion I hold, I am desirous that my wife Camilla should pass this crisis, and be refined and tested by the fire of finding herself wooed and solicited, and by one worthy to set his affections upon her; and if she comes out, as I know she will, victorious from this struggle, I shall look upon my good fortune as unequalled, I shall be able to say that the cup of my desire is full, and that the virtuous woman of whom the sage says " Who shall find her ? " [1] has fallen to my lot. And if the result be the contrary of what I expect, in the satisfaction of knowing that I have been right in my opinion, I shall bear without complaint the pain which my so dearly bought experience will naturally cause me. And, as nothing of all thou wilt urge in opposition to my wish will avail to keep me from carrying it into effect, it is my desire, friend Lothario, that thou shouldst consent to become the instrument for effecting this purpose that I am bent upon, for I will afford thee opportunities to that end, and nothing shall be wanting that I may think necessary for the pursuit of a virtuous, honourable, modest and high-minded woman. And among other reasons, I am induced to entrust this arduous task to thee by the consideration that if Camilla be conquered by thee the conquest will not be pushed to extremes, but only far enough to account that accomplished which from a sense of honour will

---

[1] ' Who can find a virtuous woman ? for her price is far above rubies.' Proverbs xxxi. 10.

be left undone; thus I shall not be wronged in anything more than intention, and my wrong will remain buried in the integrity of thy silence, which I know well will be as lasting as that of death in what concerns me. If, therefore, thou wouldst have me enjoy what can be called life, thou wilt at once engage in this love struggle, not lukewarmly nor slothfully, but with the energy and zeal that my desire demands, and with the loyalty our friendship assures me of.'

Such were the words Anselmo addressed to Lothario, who listened to them with such attention that, except to say what has been already mentioned, he did not open his lips until the other had finished. Then perceiving that he had no more to say, after regarding him for awhile, as one would regard something never before seen that excited wonder and amazement, he said to him, ' I cannot persuade myself, Anselmo my friend, that what thou hast said to me is not in jest; if I thought that thou wert speaking seriously I would not have allowed thee to go so far; so as to put a stop to thy long harangue by not listening to thee. I verily suspect that either thou dost not know me, or I do not know thee; but no, I know well thou art Anselmo, and thou knowest that I am Lothario; the misfortune is, it seems to me, that thou art not the Anselmo thou wert, and must have thought that I am not the Lothario I should be; for the things that thou hast said to me are not those of that Anselmo who was my friend, nor are those that thou demandest of me what should be asked of the Lothario thou knowest. True friends will prove their friends and make use of them, as a poet has said, *usque ad aras*; whereby he meant that they will not make use of their friendship in things that are contrary to God's will. If this, then, was a heathen's [1] feeling about friendship, how much more should it be a Christian's, who knows that the divine must not be forfeited for the sake of any human friendship? And if a friend should go so far as to put aside his duty to Heaven to fulfil his duty to his friend, it should not be in matters that are trifling or of little moment, but in such as affect

---

[1] I.e. Pericles, in Plutarch on 'False Shame.'

the friend's life and honour. Now tell me, Anselmo, in which of these two art thou imperilled, that I should hazard myself to gratify thee, and do a thing so detestable as that thou seekest of me? Neither forsooth; on the contrary, thou dost ask of me, so far as I understand, to strive and labour to rob thee of honour and life, and to rob myself of them at the same time; for if I take away thy honour it is plain I take away thy life, as a man without honour is worse than dead; and being the instrument, as thou wilt have it so, of so much wrong to thee, shall not I, too, be left without honour, and consequently without life? Listen to me, Anselmo my friend, and be not impatient to answer me until I have said what occurs to me touching the object of thy desire, for there will be time enough left for thee to reply and for me to hear.'

'Be it so,' said Anselmo, 'say what thou wilt.'

Lothario then went on to say, 'It seems to me, Anselmo, that thine is just now the temper of mind which is always that of the Moors, who can never be brought to see the error of their creed by quotations from the Holy Scriptures, or by reasons which depend upon the examination of the understanding or are founded upon the articles of faith, but must have examples that are palpable, easy, intelligible, capable of proof, not admitting of doubt, with mathematical demonstrations that cannot be denied, like, " *If equals be taken from equals, the remainders are equal:* " and if they do not understand this in words, and indeed they do not, it has to be shown to them with the hands, and put before their eyes, and even with all this no one succeeds in convincing them of the truth of our holy religion. This same mode of proceeding I shall have to adopt with thee, for the desire which has sprung up in thee is so absurd and remote from everything that has a semblance of reason, that I feel it would be a waste of time to employ it in reasoning with thy simplicity, for at present I will call it by no other name; and I am even tempted to leave thee in thy folly as a punishment for thy pernicious desire; but the friendship I bear thee, which will not allow me to desert thee in such manifest danger of destruction, keeps me from dealing so harshly by thee. And that thou mayest clearly see this, say, Anselmo, hast thou not told me that I must force my suit upon a modest woman, decoy one that is virtuous, make overtures to one that is pure-minded, pay court to one that is prudent? Yes, thou hast told me so. Then, if thou knowest that thou hast a wife, modest, virtuous, pure-minded and prudent, what is it that thou seekest? And if thou believest that she will come forth victorious from all my attacks—as doubtless she would—what higher titles than those she possesses now dost thou think thou canst bestow upon her then, or in what will she be better then than she is now? Either thou dost not hold her to be what thou sayest, or thou knowest not what thou dost demand. If thou dost not hold her to be what thou sayest, why dost thou seek to prove her instead of treating her as guilty in the way that may seem best to thee? but if she be as virtuous as thou believest, it is an uncalled-for proceeding to make trial of truth itself, for, after trial, it will but be in the same estimation as before. Thus, then, it is conclusive that to attempt things from which harm rather than advantage may come to us is the part of unreasoning and reckless minds, more especially when they are things which we are not forced or compelled to attempt, and which show from afar that it is plainly madness to attempt them.

'Difficulties are attempted either for the sake of God or for the sake of the world, or for both; those undertaken for God's sake are those which the saints undertake when they attempt to live the lives of angels in human bodies; those undertaken for the sake of the world are those of the men who traverse such a vast expanse of water, such a variety of climates, so many strange countries, to acquire what are called the blessings of fortune; and those undertaken for the sake of God and the world together are those of brave soldiers, who no sooner do they see in the enemy's wall a breach as wide as a cannon ball could make, than, casting aside all fear, without hesitating, or heeding the manifest peril that threatens them, borne onward by the desire of defending their faith, their country, and their king, they fling

themselves dauntlessly into the midst of the thousand opposing
deaths that await them.   Such are the things that men are wont
to attempt, and there is honour, glory, gain, in attempting them,
however full of difficulty and peril they may be ; but that which
thou sayest it is thy wish to attempt and carry out will not win
thee the glory of God nor the blessings of fortune nor fame
among men ; for even if the issue be as thou wouldst have it,
thou wilt be no happier, richer, or more honoured than thou art
this moment ; and if it be otherwise thou wilt be reduced to
misery greater than can be imagined, for then it will avail thee
nothing to reflect that no one is aware of the misfortune that
has befallen thee ; it will suffice to torture and crush thee that
thou knowest it thyself.   And in confirmation of the truth of
what I say, let me repeat to thee a stanza made by the famous
poet Luigi Tansillo at the end of the first part of his " Tears
of Saint Peter," which says thus :

> The anguish and the shame but greater grew
>   In Peter's heart as morning slowly came ;
> No eye was there to see him, well he knew,
>   Yet he himself was to himself a shame ;
> Exposed to all men's gaze, or screened from view,
>   A noble heart will feel the pang the same ;
> A prey to shame the sinning soul will be,
> Though none but heaven and earth its shame can see.

Thus by keeping it secret thou wilt not escape thy sorrow, but
rather thou wilt shed tears unceasingly, if not tears of the eyes,
tears of blood from the heart, like those shed by that simple
doctor our poet tells us of, that tried the test of the cup, which
the wise Rinaldo, better advised, refused to do ; [1] for though this
may be a poetic fiction it contains a moral lesson worthy of
attention and study and imitation.   Moreover by what I am about
to say to thee thou wilt be led to see the great error thou wouldst
commit.

' Tell me, Anselmo, if Heaven or good fortune had made thee
master and lawful owner of a diamond of the finest quality, with

----

[1] See Note A, p. 152.

the excellence and purity of which all the lapidaries that had seen it had been satisfied, saying with one voice and common consent that in purity, quality, and fineness, it was all that a stone of the kind could possibly be, thou thyself too being of the same belief, as knowing nothing to the contrary; would it be reasonable in thee to desire to take that diamond and place it between an anvil and a hammer, and by mere force of blows and strength of arm try if it were as hard and as fine as they said? And if thou didst, and if the stone should resist so silly a test, that would add nothing to its value or reputation; and if it were broken, as it might be, would not all be lost? Undoubtedly it would, leaving its owner to be rated as a fool in the opinion of all. Consider, then, Anselmo my friend, that Camilla is a diamond of the finest quality as well in thy estimation as in that of others, and that it is contrary to reason to expose her to the risk of being broken; for if she remain intact she cannot rise to a higher value than she now possesses; and if she give way and be unable to resist, bethink thee now how thou wilt be deprived of her, and with what good reason thou wilt complain of thyself for having been the cause of her ruin and thine own. Remember there is no jewel in the world so precious as a chaste and virtuous woman, and that the whole honour of women consists in reputation; and since thy wife's is of that high excellence that thou knowest, wherefore shouldst thou seek to call that truth in question? Remember, my friend, that woman is an imperfect animal, and that impediments are not to be placed in her way to make her trip and fall, but that they should be removed, and her path left clear of all obstacles, so that without hindrance she may run her course freely to attain the desired perfection, which consists in being virtuous. Naturalists tell us that the ermine is a little animal which has a fur of purest white, and that when the hunters wish to take it, they make use of this artifice. Having ascertained the places which it frequents and passes, they stop the way to them with mud, and then rousing it, drive it towards the spot, and as soon as the ermine comes to the mud it halts, and allows itself to be taken captive rather than pass through the mire, and spoil and sully its whiteness, which it values more than life and liberty. The virtuous and chaste woman is an ermine, and whiter and purer than snow is the virtue of modesty; and he who wishes her not to lose it, but to keep and preserve it, must adopt a course different from that employed with the ermine; he must not put before her the mire of the gifts and attentions of persevering lovers, because perhaps—and even without a perhaps—she may not have sufficient virtue and natural strength in herself to pass through and tread under foot these impediments; they must be removed, and the brightness of virtue and the beauty of a fair fame must be put before her. A virtuous woman, too, is like a mirror of clear shining crystal, liable to be tarnished and dimmed by every breath that touches it. She must be treated as relics are; adored, not touched. She must be protected and prized as one protects and prizes a fair garden full of roses and flowers, the owner of which allows no one to trespass or pluck a blossom; enough for others that from afar and through the iron grating they may enjoy its fragrance and its beauty. Finally let me repeat to thee some verses that come to my mind; I heard them in a modern comedy, and it seems to me they bear upon the point we are discussing. A prudent old man was giving advice to another, the father of a young girl, to lock her up, watch over her and keep her in seclusion, and among other arguments he used these:

> Woman is a thing of glass;
>   But her brittleness 'tis best
>   Not too curiously to test:
> Who knows what may come to pass?
>
> Breaking is an easy matter,
>   And it's folly to expose
>   What you cannot mend to blows;
> What you can't make whole to shatter.
>
> This, then, all may hold as true,
>   And the reason's plain to see;
>   For if Danaës there be,
> There are golden showers too.

' All that I have said to thee so far, Anselmo, has had reference to what concerns thee; now it is right that I should say something of what regards myself; and if I be prolix, pardon me, for the labyrinth into which thou hast entered and from which thou wouldst have me extricate thee makes it necessary.

' Thou dost reckon me thy friend, and thou wouldst rob me of honour, a thing wholly inconsistent with friendship; and not only dost thou aim at this, but thou wouldst have me rob thee of it also. That thou wouldst rob me of it is clear, for when Camilla sees that I pay court to her as thou requirest, she will certainly regard me as a man without honour or right feeling, since I attempt and do a thing so much opposed to what I owe to my own position and thy friendship. That thou wouldst have me rob thee of it is beyond a doubt, for Camilla, seeing that I press my suit upon her, will suppose that I have perceived in her something light that has encouraged me to make known to her my base desire; and if she holds herself dishonoured, her dishonour touches thee as belonging to her; and hence arises what so commonly takes place, that the husband of the adulterous woman, though he may not be aware of or have given any cause for his wife's failure in her duty, or (being careless or negligent) have had it in his power to prevent his dishonour, nevertheless is stigmatised by a vile and reproachful name, and in a manner regarded with eyes of contempt instead of pity by all who know of his wife's guilt, though they see that he is unfortunate not by his own fault, but by the lust of a vicious consort. But I will thee why with good reason dishonour attaches to the husband of the unchaste wife, though he know not that she is so, nor be to blame, nor have done anything, or given any provocation to make her so; and be not weary with listening to me, for it will be all for thy good.

' When God created our first parent in the earthly paradise, the Holy Scripture says that he infused sleep into Adam and while he slept took a rib from his left side of which he formed our mother Eve, and when Adam awoke and beheld her he said, " This is flesh of my flesh, and bone of my bone." And God said

" For this shall a man leave his father and his mother, and they shall be two in one flesh ; " and then was instituted the divine sacrament of marriage, with such ties that death alone can loose them. And such is the force and virtue of this miraculous sacrament that it makes two different persons one and the same flesh ; and even more than this when the virtuous are married ; for though they have two souls they have but one will. And hence it follows that as the flesh of the wife is one and the same with that of her husband, the stains that may come upon it, or the injuries it incurs fall upon the husband's flesh, though he, as has been said, may have given no cause for them ; for as the pain of the foot or any member of the body is felt by the whole body, because all is one flesh, as the head feels the hurt to the ankle without having caused it, so the husband, being one with her, shares the dishonour of the wife ; and as all worldly honour or dishonour comes of flesh and blood, and the erring wife's is of that kind, the husband must needs bear his part of it and be held dishonoured without knowing it. See, then, Anselmo, the peril thou art encountering in seeking to disturb the peace of thy virtuous consort ; see for what an empty and ill-advised curiosity thou wouldst rouse up passions that now repose in quiet in the breast of thy chaste wife ; reflect that what thou art staking all to win is little, and what thou wilt lose so much that I leave it undescribed, not having the words to express it. But if all I have said be not enough to turn thee from thy vile purpose, thou must seek some other instrument for thy dishonour and misfortune ; for such I will not consent to be, though by this I lose thy friendship, the greatest loss that I can conceive.'

Having said this, the wise and virtuous Lothario was silent, and Anselmo, troubled in mind and deep in thought, was unable for a while to utter a word in reply ; but at length he said, ' I have listened, Lothario my friend, attentively, as thou hast seen, to what thou hast chosen to say to me, and in thy arguments, examples, and comparisons I have seen that high intelligence thou dost possess, and the perfection of true friendship thou hast reached ; and likewise I see and confess that if I am not guided by thy opinion, but follow my own, I am flying from the good and pursuing the evil. This being so, thou must remember that I am now labouring under that infirmity which women sometimes suffer from, when the craving seizes them to eat clay, plaster, charcoal, and things even worse, disgusting to look at, much more to eat; so that it will be necessary to have recourse to some artifice to cure me; and this can be easily effected if only thou wilt make a beginning, even though it be in a lukewarm and make-believe fashion, to pay court to Camilla, who will not be so yielding that her virtue will give way at the first attack : with this mere attempt I shall rest satisfied, and thou wilt have done what our friendship binds thee to do, not only in giving me life, but in persuading me not to discard my honour. And this thou art bound to do for one reason alone, that, being, as I am, resolved to apply this test, it is not for thee to permit me to reveal my weakness to another, and so imperil that honour thou art striving to keep me from losing ; and if thine may not stand as high as it ought in the estimation of Camilla while thou art paying court to her, that is of little or no importance, because ere long, on finding in her that constancy which we expect, thou canst tell her the plain truth as regards our stratagem, and so regain thy place in her esteem ; and as thou art venturing so little, and by the venture canst afford me so much satisfaction, refuse not to undertake it, even if further difficulties present themselves to thee ; for, as I have said, if thou wilt only make a beginning I will acknowledge the issue decided.'

Lothario seeing the fixed determination of Anselmo, and not knowing what further examples to offer or arguments to urge in order to dissuade him from it, and perceiving that he threatened to confide his pernicious scheme to some one else, to avoid a greater evil resolved to gratify him and do what he asked, intending to manage the business so as to satisfy Anselmo without corrupting the mind of Camilla ; so in reply he told him not to communicate his purpose to any other, for he would undertake the task himself, and would begin it as soon as he pleased.

Anselmo embraced him warmly and affectionately, and thanked him for his offer as if he had bestowed some great favour upon him; and it was agreed between them to set about it the next day, Anselmo affording opportunity and time to Lothario to converse alone with Camilla, and furnishing him with money and jewels to offer and present to her. He suggested, too, that he should treat her to music, and write verses in her praise, and if he was unwilling to take the trouble of composing them, he offered to do it himself. Lothario agreed to all with an intention very different from what Anselmo supposed, and with this understanding they returned to Anselmo's house, where they found Camilla awaiting her husband anxiously and uneasily, for he was later than usual in returning that day. Lothario repaired to his own house, and Anselmo remained in his, as well satisfied as Lothario was troubled in mind; for he could see no satisfactory way out of this ill-advised business. That night, however, he thought of a plan by which he might deceive Anselmo without any injury to Camilla. The next day he went to dine with his friend, and was welcomed by Camilla, who received and treated him with great cordiality, knowing the affection her husband felt for him. When dinner was over and the cloth removed, Anselmo told Lothario to stay there with Camilla while he attended to some pressing business, as he would return in an hour and a half. Camilla begged him not to go, and Lothario offered to accompany him, but nothing could persuade Anselmo, who on the contrary pressed Lothario to remain waiting for him as he had a matter of great importance to discuss with him. At the same time he bade Camilla not to leave Lothario alone until he came back. In short he contrived to put so good a face on the reason, or the folly, of his absence that no one could have suspected it was a pretence.

Anselmo took his departure, and Camilla and Lothario were left alone at the table, for the rest of the household had gone to dinner. Lothario saw himself in the lists according to his friend's wish, and facing an enemy that could by her beauty alone vanquish a squadron of armed knights; judge whether he had good reason to fear ; but what he did was to lean his elbow on the arm of the chair, and his cheek upon his hand, and, asking Camilla's pardon for his ill manners, he said he wished to take a little sleep until Anselmo returned. Camilla in reply said he could repose more at his ease in the reception-room than in his chair, and begged of him to go in and sleep there ; but Lothario declined, and there he remained asleep until the return of Anselmo, who finding Camilla in her own room, and Lothario asleep, imagined that he had stayed away so long as to have afforded them time enough for conversation and even for sleep, and was all impatience until Lothario should wake up, that he might go out with him and question him as to his success. Everything fell out as he wished ; Lothario awoke, and the two at once left the house, and Anselmo asked what he was anxious to know, and Lothario in answer told him that he had not thought it advisable to declare himself entirely the first time, and therefore had only extolled the charms of Camilla, telling her that all the city spoke of nothing else but her beauty and wit, for this seemed to him an excellent way of beginning to gain her good will and render her disposed to listen to him with pleasure the next time, thus availing himself of the device the devil has recourse to when he would deceive one who is on the watch ; for he being the angel of darkness transforms himself into an angel of light, and, under cover of a fair seeming, discloses himself at length, and effects his purpose if at the beginning his wiles are not discovered. All this gave great satisfaction to Anselmo, and he said he would afford the same opportunity every day, but without leaving the house, for he would find things to do at home so that Camilla should not detect the plot.

Thus, then, several days went by, and Lothario, without uttering a word to Camilla, reported to Anselmo that he had talked with her and that he had never been able to draw from her the slightest indication of consent to anything dishonourable, nor even a sign or shadow of hope ; on the contrary, he said she threatened that if he did not abandon such a wicked idea she would inform her husband of it.

'So far well,' said Anselmo ; 'Camilla has thus far resisted words ; we must now see how she will resist deeds. I will give you to-morrow two thousand crowns in gold for you to offer or even present, and as many more to buy jewels to lure her, for women are fond of being becomingly attired and going gaily dressed, and all the more so if they are beautiful, however chaste they may be ; and if she resists this temptation, I will rest satisfied and will give you no more trouble.'

Lothario replied that now he had begun he would carry on the undertaking to the end, though he perceived he was to come out of it wearied and vanquished. The next day he received the four thousand crowns, and with them four thousand perplexities, for he knew not what to say by way of a new falsehood ; but in the end he made up his mind to tell him that Camilla stood as firm against gifts and promises as against words, and that there was no use in taking any further trouble, for the time was all spent to no purpose.

But chance, directing things in a different manner, so ordered it that Anselmo, having left Lothario and Camilla alone as on other occasions, shut himself into a chamber and posted himself to watch and listen through the keyhole to what passed between them, and perceived that for more than half an hour Lothario did not utter a word to Camilla, nor would utter a word though he were to be there for an age ; and he came to the conclusion that what his friend had told him about the replies of Camilla was all invention and falsehood, and to ascertain if it were so, he came out, and calling Lothario aside asked him what news he had and in what humour Camilla was. Lothario replied that he was not disposed to go on with the business, for she had answered him so angrily and harshly that he had no heart to say anything more to her.

'Ah, Lothario, Lothario,' said Anselmo, 'how ill dost thou meet thy obligations to me, and the great confidence I repose in thee ! I have been just now watching through this keyhole, and I have seen that thou hast not said a word to Camilla, whence I conclude that on the former occasions thou hast not spoken to her either, and if this be so, as no doubt it is, why dost thou deceive me, or wherefore seekest thou by craft to deprive me of the means I might find of attaining my desire ? '

Anselmo said no more, but he had said enough to cover Lothario with shame and confusion, and he, feeling as it were his honour touched by having been detected in a lie, swore to Anselmo that he would from that moment devote himself to satisfying him without any deception, as he would see if he had the curiosity to watch ; though he need not take the trouble, for the pains he would take to satisfy him would remove all suspicions from his mind. Anselmo believed him, and to afford him an opportunity more free and less liable to surprise, he resolved to absent himself from his house for eight days, betaking himself to that of a friend of his who lived in a village not far from the city ; and, the better to account for his departure to Camilla, he so arranged it that the friend should send him a very pressing invitation.

Unhappy, shortsighted Anselmo, what art thou doing, what art thou plotting, what art thou devising ? Bethink thee thou art working against thyself, plotting thine own dishonour, devising thine own ruin. Thy wife Camilla is virtuous, thou dost possess her in peace and quietness, no one assails thy happiness, her thoughts wander not beyond the walls of thy house, thou art her heaven on earth, the object of her wishes, the fulfilment of her desires, the measure wherewith she measures her will, making it conform in all things to thine and Heaven's. If, then, the mine of her honour, beauty, virtue, and modesty yields thee without labour all the wealth it contains and thou canst wish for, why wilt thou dig the earth in search of fresh veins, of new unknown treasure, risking the collapse of all, since it but rests on the feeble props of her weak nature ? Bethink thee that from him who seeks impossibilities that which is possible may with justice be withheld, as was better expressed by a poet who said :

'Tis mine to seek for life in death,
　　Health in disease seek I,
I seek in prison freedom's breath,
　　In traitors loyalty.

So Fate that ever scorns to grant
　　Or grace or boon to me,
Since what can never be I want,
　　Denies me what might be.

The next day Anselmo took his departure for the village, leaving instructions with Camilla that during his absence Lothario
would come to look after his house and to dine with her, and
that she was to treat him as she would himself. Camilla was
distressed, as a discreet and right-minded woman would be, at the
orders her husband left her, and bade him remember that it was
not becoming that anyone should occupy his seat at the table
during his absence, and if he acted thus from not feeling confidence that she would be able to manage his house, let him try
her this time, and he would find by experience that she was
equal to greater responsibilities. Anselmo replied that it was his
pleasure to have it so, and that she had only to submit and obey.
Camilla said she would do so, though against her will.

Anselmo went, and the next day Lothario came to his house,
where he was received by Camilla with a friendly and modest
welcome ; but she never suffered Lothario to see her alone, for
she was always attended by her men and woman servants, especially by a handmaid of hers, Leonela by name, to whom she
was much attached (for they had been brought up together from
childhood in her father's house), and whom she had kept with her
after her marriage with Anselmo. The first three days Lothario
did not speak to her, though he might have done so when they
removed the cloth and the servants retired to dine hastily ; for
such were Camilla's orders ; nay more, Leonela had directions to
dine earlier than Camilla and never to leave her side. She, however, having her thoughts fixed upon other things more to her taste,
and wanting that time and opportunity for her own pleasures,

·did not always obey her mistress's commands, but on the contrary left them alone, as if they had ordered her to do so ; but
the modest bearing of Camilla, the calmness of her countenance,
the composure of her aspect were enough to bridle the tongue of
Lothario. But the influence which the many virtues of Camilla
exerted in imposing silence on Lothario's tongue proved mis-
·chievous for both of them, for if his tongue was silent his thoughts
were busy, and could dwell at leisure upon the perfections of
·Camilla's goodness and beauty one by one, charms enough to
warm with love a marble statue, not to say a heart of flesh.
Lothario gazed upon her when he might have been speaking to
her, and thought how worthy of being loved she was ; and thus
reflection began little by little to assail his allegiance to Anselmo,
·and a thousand times he thought of withdrawing from the city
and going where Anselmo should never see him nor he see
Camilla. But already the delight he found in gazing on her in-
terposed and held him fast. He put a constraint upon himself,
and struggled to repel and repress the pleasure he found in contemplating Camilla ; when alone he blamed himself for his weakness, called himself a bad friend, nay a bad Christian ; then he
·argued the matter and compared himself with Anselmo; always
coming to the conclusion that the folly and rashness of Anselmo
had been worse than his faithlessness, and that if he could excuse his intentions as easily before God as with man, he need
fear no punishment for his offence.

In short the beauty and goodness of Camilla, joined with the
·opportunity which the blind husband had placed in his hands,
overthrew the loyalty of Lothario; and giving heed to nothing
save the object towards which his inclinations led him, after
Anselmo had been three days absent, during which he had been
·carrying on a continual struggle with his passion, he began to
make love to Camilla with so much vehemence and warmth of
language that she was overwhelmed with amazement, and could
only rise from her place and retire to her room without answering him a word. But the hope which always springs up with love
was not weakened in Lothario by this repelling demeanour ; on

the contrary his passion for Camilla increased, and she discovering in him what she had never expected, knew not what to do ; and considering it neither safe nor right to give him the chance or opportunity of speaking to her again, she resolved to send, as she did that very night, one of her servants with a letter to Anselmo, in which she addressed the following words to him.

Note A (*page* 140).

'Our poet' was, of course, Ariosto ; but Cervantes has confounded two different stories in Canto 43. It was not the doctor but a cavalier, Rinaldo's host, who tried the test of the cup. The magic cup, of which no husband of a faithless wife could drink without spilling, figures frequently in old romance. It appears in the ballad of 'The Boy and the Mantle,' and also in another of the King Arthur ballads.

CHAPTER XXXIV.

IN WHICH IS CONTINUED THE NOVEL OF ' THE ILL-ADVISED
CURIOSITY.'

' IT is commonly said that an army looks ill without its general
and a castle without its castellan, and I say that a young married
woman looks still worse without her husband unless there are
very good reasons for it. I find myself so ill at ease without you,
and so incapable of enduring this separation, that unless you
return quickly I shall have to go for relief to my parents' house,
even if I leave yours without a protector ; for the one you left me,
if indeed he deserved that title, has, I think, more regard to his
own pleasure than to what concerns you ; as you are possessed
of discernment I need say no more to you, nor is it fitting I
should say more.'

Anselmo received this letter, and from it he gathered that
Lothario had already begun his task and that Camilla must have
replied to him as he would have wished ; and delighted beyond
measure at such intelligence he sent word to her not to leave his
house on any account, as he would very shortly return. Camilla
was astonished at Anselmo's reply, which placed her in greater
perplexity than before, for she neither dared to remain in her own
house, nor yet to go to her parents' ; for in remaining her virtue
was imperilled, and in going she was opposing her husband's
commands. Finally she decided upon what was the worse course
for her, to remain, resolving not to fly from the presence of
Lothario, that she might not give food for gossip to her servants ;
and she now began to regret having written as she had to her
husband, fearing he might imagine that Lothario had perceived

in her some lightness which had impelled him to lay aside the
respect he owed her; but confident of her rectitude she put her
trust in God and in her own virtuous intentions, with which she
hoped to resist in silence all the solicitations of Lothario, without
saying anything to her husband so as not to involve him in any
quarrel or trouble; and she even began to consider how to
excuse Lothario to Anselmo when he should ask her what it was
that induced her to write that letter. With these resolutions,
more honourable than judicious or effectual, she remained the
next day listening to Lothario, who pressed his suit so strenu-
ously that Camilla's firmness began to waver, and her virtue had
enough to do to come to the rescue of her eyes and keep them
from showing signs of a certain tender compassion which the
tears and appeals of Lothario had awakened in her bosom.
Lothario observed all this, and it inflamed him all the more. In
short he felt that while Anselmo's absence afforded time and
opportunity he must press the siege of the fortress, and so he
assailed her self-esteem with praises of her beauty, for there is
nothing that more quickly reduces and levels the castle towers of
fair women's vanity than vanity itself upon the tongue of flattery.
In fact with the utmost assiduity he undermined the rock of her
purity with such engines that had Camilla been of brass she
must have fallen. He wept, he entreated, he promised, he
flattered, he importuned, he pretended with so much feeling and
apparent sincerity, that he overthrew the virtuous resolves of
Camilla and won the triumph he least expected and most longed
for. Camilla yielded, Camilla fell; but what wonder if the friendship of Lothario could not stand firm? A clear proof to us that
the passion of love is to be conquered only by flying from it,
and that no one should engage in a struggle with an enemy so
mighty; for divine strength is needed to overcome his human
power. Leonela alone knew of her mistress's weakness, for
the two false friends and new lovers were unable to conceal it.
Lothario did not care to tell Camilla the object Anselmo had in
view, nor that he had afforded him the opportunity of attaining
such a result, lest she should undervalue his love and think that

it was by chance and without intending it and not of his own accord that he had made love to her.

A few days later Anselmo returned to his house and did not perceive what it had lost, that which he so lightly treated and so highly prized. He went at once to see Lothario, and found him at home ; they embraced each other, and Anselmo asked for the tidings of his life or his death.

' The tidings I have to give thee, Anselmo my friend,' said Lothario, ' are that thou dost possess a wife that is worthy to be the pattern and crown of all good wives. The words that I have addressed to her were borne away on the wind, my promises have been despised, my presents have been refused, such feigned tears as I shed have been turned into open ridicule. In short, as Camilla is the essence of all beauty, so is she the treasure-house where purity dwells, and gentleness and modesty abide with all the virtues that can confer praise, honour, and happiness upon a woman. Take back thy money, my friend ; here it is, and I have had no need to touch it, for the chastity of Camilla yields not to things so base as gifts or promises. Be content, Anselmo, and refrain from making further proof ; and as thou hast passed dryshod through the sea of those doubts and suspicions that are and may be entertained of women, seek not to plunge again into the deep ocean of new embarrassments, or with another pilot make trial of the goodness and strength of the bark that Heaven has granted thee for thy passage across the sea of this world ; but reckon thyself now safe in port, moor thyself with the anchor of sound reflection, and rest in peace until thou art called upon to pay that debt which no nobility on earth can escape paying.'

Anselmo was completely satisfied by the words of Lothario, and believed them as fully as if they had been spoken by an oracle ; nevertheless he begged of him not to relinquish the undertaking, were it but for the sake of curiosity and amusement ; though thenceforward he need not make use of the same earnest endeavours as before ; all he wished him to do was to write some verses to her, praising her under the name of Chloris, for he himself would give her to understand that he was in love with a

lady to whom he had given that name to enable him to sing her
praises with the decorum due to her modesty; and if Lothario
were unwilling to take the trouble of writing the verses he would
compose them himself.

'That will not be necessary,' said Lothario, 'for the muses
are not such enemies of mine but that they visit me now and
then in the course of the year. Do thou tell Camilla what thou
hast proposed about a pretended amour of mine; as for the
verses I will make them, and if not as good as the subject
deserves, they shall be at least the best I can produce.' An
agreement to this effect was made between the friends, the
ill-advised one and the treacherous, and Anselmo returning to
his house asked Camilla the question she already wondered he
had not asked before—what it was that had caused her to
write the letter she had sent him. Camilla replied that it had
seemed to her that Lothario looked at her somewhat more freely
than when he had been at home; but that now she was un-
deceived and believed it to have been only her own imagination,
for Lothario now avoided seeing her, or being alone with her.
Anselmo told her she might be quite easy on the score of that
suspicion, for he knew that Lothario was in love with a damsel
of rank in the city whom he celebrated under the name of
Chloris, and that even if he were not, his fidelity and their
great friendship left no room for fear. Had not Camilla, however, been informed beforehand by Lothario that this love for
Chloris was a pretence, and that he himself had told Anselmo
of it in order to be able sometimes to give utterance to
the praises of Camilla herself, no doubt she would have fallen
into the despairing toils of jealousy; but being forewarned she
received the startling news without uneasiness.

The next day as the three were at table Anselmo asked
Lothario to recite something of what he had composed for his
mistress Chloris; for, as Camilla did not know her, he might
safely say what he liked.

'Even did she know her,' returned Lothario, 'I would hide
nothing, for when a lover praises his lady's beauty, and charges

her with cruelty, he casts no imputation upon her fair name ; at any rate, all I can say is that yesterday I made a sonnet on the ingratitude of this Chloris, which goes thus :

SONNET.[1]

At midnight, in the silence, when the eyes
   Of happier mortals balmy slumbers close,
   The weary tale of my unnumbered woes
To Chloris and to Heaven is wont to rise.
And when the light of day returning dyes
   The portals of the east with tints of rose,
   With undiminished force my sorrow flows
In broken accents and in burning sighs.
And when the sun ascends his star-girt throne,
   And on the earth pours down his midday beams,
     Noon but renews my wailing and my tears ;
And with the night again goes up my moan.
   Yet ever in my agony it seems
     To me that neither Heaven nor Chloris hears.'

The sonnet pleased Camilla, and still more Anselmo, for he praised it and said the lady was excessively cruel who made no return for sincerity so manifest. On which Camilla said, ' Then all that love-smitten poets say is true ? '

' As poets they do not tell the truth,' replied Lothario ; ' but as lovers they are not more defective in expression than they are truthful.'

' There is no doubt of that,' observed Anselmo, anxious to support and uphold Lothario's ideas with Camilla, who was as regardless of his design as she was deep in love with Lothario ; and so taking delight in anything that was his, and knowing that his thoughts and writings had her for their object, and that she

---

[1] This sonnet, like that in chapter xxiii., was repeated by Cervantes in the play of the *Casa de los Zelos*—Jornada 2.

herself was the real Chloris, she asked him to repeat some other
sonnet or verses if he recollected any.

' I do,' replied Lothario, ' but I do not think it as good as the
first one, or, more correctly speaking, less bad ; but you can
easily judge, for it is this.

SONNET.

> I know that I am doomed ; death is to me
>   As certain as that thou, ungrateful fair,
>   Dead at thy feet shouldst see me lying, ere
> My heart repented of its love for thee.
> If buried in oblivion I should be,
>   Bereft of life, fame, favour, even there
>   It would be found that I thy image bear
> Deep graven in my breast for all to see.
> This like some holy relic do I prize
>   To save me from the fate my truth entails,
>   Truth that to thy hard heart its vigour owes.
> Alas for him that under lowering skies,
>   In peril o'er a trackless ocean sails,
>   Where neither friendly port nor pole-star shows.

Anselmo praised this second sonnet too, as he had praised the
first ; and so he went on adding link after link to the chain with
which he was binding himself and making his dishonour secure ;
for when Lothario was doing most to dishonour him he told him
he was most honoured ; and thus each step that Camilla de-
scended towards the depths of her abasement, she mounted, in
the opinion of her husband, towards the summit of virtue and
fair fame.

' It so happened that finding herself on one occasion alone
with her maid, Camilla said to her, ' I am ashamed to think, my
dear Leonela, how lightly I have valued myself that I did not
compel Lothario to purchase by at least some expenditure of time
that full possession of me that I so quickly yielded him of my own
free will. I fear that he will think ill of my pliancy or lightness,

not considering the irresistible influence he brought to bear upon me.'

' Let not that trouble you, my lady,' said Leonela, ' for it does not take away the value of the thing given or make it the less precious to give it quickly if it be really valuable and worthy of being prized ; nay, they are wont to say that he who gives quickly gives twice.' [1]

' They say also,' said Camilla, ' that what costs little is valued less.' [2]

' That saying does not hold good in your case,' replied Leonela, ' for love, as I have heard say, sometimes flies and sometimes walks ; with this one it runs, with that it moves slowly, some it cools, others it burns ; some it wounds, others it slays ; it begins the course of its desires, and at the same moment completes and ends it ; in the morning it will lay siege to a fortress and by night will have taken it, for there is no power that can resist it; so what are you in dread of, what do you fear, when the same must have befallen Lothario, love having chosen the absence of my lord as the instrument for subduing you ? and it was absolutely necessary to complete then what love had resolved upon, without affording the time to let Anselmo return and by his presence compel the work to be left unfinished ; for love has no better agent for carrying out his designs than opportunity ; and of opportunity he avails himself in all his feats, especially at the outset. All this I know well myself, more by experience than by hearsay, and some day, señora, I will enlighten you on the subject, for I am of young flesh and blood too. Moreover, lady Camilla, you did not surrender yourself or yield so quickly but that first you saw Lothario's whole soul in his eyes, in his sighs, in his words, his promises and his gifts, and by it and his good qualities perceived how worthy he was of your love. This, then, being the case, let not these scrupulous and prudish ideas trouble your imagination, but be assured that Lothario prizes you as you do him, and rest content and satisfied that as you are caught in the noose of love it is one of worth and merit that has taken you, and one that has not,

[1] Prov. 67.　　　　[2] Prov. 190.

only the four S's that they say true lovers ought to have,[1] but a complete alphabet; only listen to me and you will see how I can repeat it by rote. He is, to my eyes and thinking, Amiable, Brave, Courteous, Distinguished, Elegant, Fond, Gay, Honourable, Illustrious, Loyal, Manly, Noble, Open, Polite, Quickwitted, Rich, and the S's according to the saying, and then Tender, Veracious : X does not suit him, for it is a rough letter ; Y has been given already ; and Z Zealous for your honour.'

Camilla laughed at her maid's alphabet, and perceived her to be more experienced in love affairs than she said, which she admitted, confessing to Camilla that she had love passages with a young man of good birth of the same city. Camilla was uneasy at this, dreading lest it might prove the means of endangering her honour, and asked whether her intrigue had gone beyond words, and she with little shame and much effrontery said it had ; for certain it is that ladies' imprudences make servants shameless, who, when they see their mistresses make a false step, think nothing of going astray themselves, or of its being known. All that Camilla could do was to entreat Leonela to say nothing about her doings to him whom she called her lover, and to conduct her own affairs secretly lest they should come to the knowledge of Anselmo or of Lothario. Leonela said she would, but kept her word in such a way that she confirmed Camilla's apprehension of losing her reputation through her means ; for this abandoned and bold Leonela, as soon as she perceived that her mistress's demeanour was not what it was wont to be, had the audacity to introduce her lover into the house, confident that even if her mistress saw him she would not dare to expose him ; for the sins of mistresses entail this mischief among others ; they make themselves the slaves of their own servants, and are obliged to hide their laxities and depravities ; as was the case with Camilla, who though she perceived, not once but many times, that Leonela was with her lover in some room of the house, not only did not

---

[1] The four S's that should qualify a lover were *sabio, solo, solicito, secreto*. It is needless to say that Leonela's alphabet cannot be literally translated.

dare to chide her, but afforded her opportunities for concealing him and removed all difficulties, lest he should be seen by her husband. She was unable, however, to prevent him from being seen on one occasion, as he sallied forth at daybreak, by Lothario, who, not knowing who he was, at first took him for a spectre; but, as soon as he saw him hasten away, muffling his face with his cloak and concealing himself carefully and cautiously, he rejected this foolish idea, and adopted another, which would have been the ruin of all had not Camilla found a remedy. It did not occur to Lothario that this man he had seen issuing at such an untimely hour from Anselmo's house could have entered it on Leonela's account, nor did he even remember there was such a person as Leonela; all he thought was that as Camilla had been light and yielding with him, so she had been with another; for this further penalty the erring woman's sin brings with it, that her honour is distrusted even by him to whose overtures and persuasions she has yielded; and he believes her to have surrendered more easily to others, and gives implicit credence to every suspicion that comes into his mind. All Lothario's good sense seems to have failed him at this juncture; all his prudent maxims escaped his memory; for without once reflecting rationally, and without more ado, in his impatience and in the blindness of the jealous rage that gnawed his heart, and dying to revenge himself upon Camilla, who had done him no wrong, before Anselmo had risen he hastened to him and said to him, 'Know, Anselmo, that for several days past I have been struggling with myself, striving to withhold from thee what it is no longer possible or right that I should conceal from thee. Know that Camilla's fortress has surrendered and is ready to submit to my will; and if I have been slow to reveal this fact to thee, it was in order to see if it were some light caprice of hers, or if she sought to try me and ascertain if the love I began to make to her with thy permission was made with a serious intention. I thought, too, that she, if she were what she ought to be, and what we both believed her, would have ere this given thee information of my addresses; but seeing that she delays, I believe the truth of the promise she has given me that the next time thou art absent from the house she will grant me an interview in the closet where thy jewels are kept (and it was true that Camilla used to meet him there) ; but I do not wish thee to rush precipitately to take vengeance, for the sin is as yet only committed in intention, and Camilla's may change perhaps between this and the appointed time, and repentance spring up in its place. As hitherto thou hast always followed my advice wholly or in part, follow and observe this that I will give thee now, so that, without mistake, and with mature deliberation, thou mayest satisfy thyself as to what may seem the best course ; pretend to absent thyself for two or three days as thou hast been wont to do on other occasions, and contrive to hide thyself in the closet ; for the tapestries and other things there afford great facilities for thy concealment, and then thou wilt see with thine own eyes and I with mine what Camilla's purpose may be. And if it be a guilty one, which may be feared rather than expected, with silence, prudence, and discretion thou canst thyself become the instrument of punishment for the wrong done thee.'

Anselmo was amazed, overwhelmed, and astounded at the words of Lothario, which came upon him at a time when he least expected to hear them, for he now looked upon Camilla as having triumphed over the pretended attacks of Lothario, and was beginning to enjoy the glory of her victory. He remained silent for a considerable time, looking on the ground with fixed gaze, and at length said, ' Thou hast behaved, Lothario, as I expected of thy friendship : I will follow thy advice in everything ; do as thou wilt, and keep this secret as thou seest it should be kept in circumstances so unlooked for.'

Lothario gave him his word, but after leaving him he repented altogether of what he had said to him, perceiving how foolishly he had acted, as he might have revenged himself upon Camilla in some less cruel and degrading way. He cursed his want of sense, condemned his hasty resolution, and knew not what course to take to undo the mischief or find some ready escape from it. At last he decided upon revealing all to Camilla, and, as there was no want of opportunity for doing so, he found her alone the same day; but she, as soon as she had the chance of speaking to him, said, 'Lothario my friend, I must tell thee I have a sorrow in my heart which fills it so that it seems ready to burst; and it will be a wonder if it does not; for the audacity of Leonela has now reached such a pitch that every night she conceals a gallant of hers in this house and remains with him till morning, at the expense of my reputation; inasmuch as it is open to anyone to question it who may see him quitting my house at such unseasonable hours; but what distresses me is that I cannot punish or chide her, for her privity to our intrigue bridles my mouth and keeps me silent about hers, while I am dreading that some catastrophe will come of it.'

As Camilla said this Lothario at first imagined it was some device to delude him into the idea that the man he had seen going out was Leonela's lover and not hers; but when he saw how she wept and suffered, and begged him to help her, he became convinced of the truth, and the conviction completed his confusion and remorse; however, he told Camilla not to distress herself, as he would take measures to put a stop to the insolence of Leonela. At the same time he told her what, driven by the fierce rage of jealousy, he had said to Anselmo, and how he had arranged to hide himself in the closet that he might there see plainly how little she preserved her fidelity to him; and he entreated her pardon for this madness, and her advice as to how to repair it, and escape safely from the intricate labyrinth in which his imprudence had involved him. Camilla was struck with alarm at hearing what Lothario said, and with much anger, and great good sense, she reproved him and rebuked his base design and the foolish and mischievous resolution he had made; but as woman has by nature a nimbler wit than man for good and for evil, though it is apt to fail when she sets herself deliberately to reason, Camilla on the spur of the moment thought of a way to remedy what was to all appearance irremediable, and told Lothario to contrive that the next day Anselmo should conceal himself in the place he mentioned, for she hoped from

his concealment to obtain the means of their enjoying themselves for the future without any apprehension; and without
revealing her purpose to him entirely she charged him to be
careful, as soon as Anselmo was concealed, to come to her when
Leonela should call him, and to all she said to him to answer as
he would have answered had he not known that Anselmo was
listening. Lothario pressed her to explain her intention fully,
so that he might with more certainty and precaution take care to
do what he saw to be needful.

'I tell you,' said Camilla, 'there is nothing to take care of
except to answer me what I shall ask you;' for she did not wish
to explain to him beforehand what she meant to do, fearing lest
he should be unwilling to follow out an idea which seemed to her
such a good one, and should try or devise some other less prac-
ticable plan.

Lothario then retired, and the next day Anselmo, under pretence of going to his friend's country house, took his departure,
and then returned to conceal himself, which he was able to do
easily, as Camilla and Leonela took care to give him the opportunity; and so he placed himself in hiding in the state of agitation
that it may be imagined he would feel who expected to see the
vitals of his honour laid bare before his eyes, and found himself
on the point of losing the supreme blessing he thought he
possessed in his beloved Camilla. Having made sure of Anselmo's being in his hiding-place, Camilla and Leonela entered
the closet, and the instant she set foot within it Camilla said,
with a deep sigh, ' Ah! dear Leonela, would it not be better,
before I do what I am unwilling you should know lest you should
seek to prevent it, that you should take Anselmo's dagger that I
have asked of you and with it pierce this vile heart of mine?
But no; there is no reason why I should suffer the punishment
of another's fault. I will first know what it is that the bold
licentious eyes of Lothario have seen in me that could have
encouraged him to reveal to me a design so base as that which
he has disclosed regardless of his friend and of my honour. Go
to the window, Leonela, and call him, for no doubt he is in the

street waiting to carry out his vile project; but mine, cruel it may be, but honourable, shall be carried out first.'

' Ah, señora,' said the crafty Leonela, who knew her part, ' what is it you want to do with this dagger? Can it be that you mean to take your own life, or Lothario's? for whichever you mean to do, it will lead to the loss of your reputation and good name. It is better to dissemble your wrong and not give this wicked man the chance of entering the house now and finding us alone; consider, señora, we are weak women and he is a man, and determined, and as he comes with such a base purpose, blind and urged by passion, perhaps before you can put yours into execution he may do what will be worse for you than taking your life. Ill betide my master, Anselmo, for giving such authority in his house to this shameless fellow! And supposing you kill him, señora, as I suspect you mean to do, what shall we do with him when he is dead? '

' What, my friend? ' replied Camilla, ' we shall leave him for Anselmo to bury him; for in reason it will be to him a light labour to hide his own infamy under ground. Summon him, make haste, for all the time I delay in taking vengeance for my wrong seems to me an offence against the loyalty I owe my husband.'

Anselmo was listening to all this, and every word that Camilla uttered made him change his mind; but when he heard that it was resolved to kill Lothario his first impulse was to come out and show himself to avert such a disaster; but in his anxiety to see the issue of a resolution so bold and virtuous he restrained himself, intending to come forth in time to prevent the deed. At this moment Camilla, throwing herself upon a bed that was close by, swooned away, and Leonela began to weep bitterly, exclaiming, ' Woe is me! that I should be fated to have dying here in my arms the flower of virtue upon earth, the crown of true wives, the pattern of chastity! ' with more to the same effect, so that anyone who heard her would have taken her for the most tender-hearted and faithful handmaid in the world, and her mistress for another persecuted Penelope.

Camilla was not long in recovering from her fainting fit, and on coming to herself she said, ' Why do you not go, Leonela, to call hither that friend, the falsest to his friend the sun ever shone upon or night concealed ? Away, run, haste, speed ! lest the fire of my wrath burn itself out with delay, and the righteous vengeance that I hope for melt away in menaces and maledictions.'

' I am just going to call him, señora,' said Leonela ; ' but you must first give me that dagger, lest while I am gone you should by means of it give cause to all who love you to weep all their lives.'

' Go in peace, dear Leonela, I will not do so,' said Camilla, ' for rash and foolish as I may be, to your mind, in defending my honour, I am not going to be so much so as that Lucretia who they say killed herself without having done anything wrong, and without having first killed him on whom the guilt of her misfortune lay. I shall die, if I am to die ; but it must be after full vengeance upon him who has brought me here to weep over audacity that no fault of mine gave birth to.'

Leonela required much pressing before she would go to summon Lothario, but at last she went, and while awaiting her return Camilla continued, as if speaking to herself, ' Good God ! would it not have been more prudent to have repulsed Lothario, as I have done many a time before, than to allow him, as I am now doing, to think me unchaste and vile, even for the short time I must wait until I undeceive him ? No doubt it would have been better ; but I should not be avenged, nor the honour of my husband vindicated, should he find so clear and easy an escape from the strait into which his depravity has led him. Let the traitor pay with his life for the temerity of his wanton wishes, and let the world know (if haply it shall ever come to know) that Camilla not only preserved her allegiance to her husband, but avenged him of the man who dared to wrong him. Still, I think it might be better to disclose this to Anselmo. But then I have called his attention to it in the letter I wrote to him in the country, and, if he did nothing to prevent the mischief

I there pointed out to him, I suppose it was that from pure goodness of heart and trustfulness he would not and could not believe that any thought against his honour could harbour in the breast of so stanch a friend; nor indeed did I myself believe it for many days, nor should I have ever believed it if his insolence had not gone so far as to make it manifest by open presents, lavish promises, and ceaseless tears. But why do I argue thus? Does a bold determination stand in need of arguments? Surely not. Then fears avaunt! Vengeance to my aid! Let the false one come, approach, advance, die, yield up his life, and then befall what may. Pure I came to him whom Heaven bestowed upon me, pure I shall leave him; and at the worst bathed in my own chaste blood and in the foul blood of the falsest friend that friendship ever saw;' and as she uttered these words she paced the room holding the unsheathed dagger, with such irregular and disordered steps, and such gestures that one would have supposed her to have lost her senses, and taken her for some violent desperado instead of a delicate woman.

Anselmo, concealed behind some tapestries where he had hidden himself, beheld and was amazed at all, and already felt that what he had seen and heard was a sufficient answer to even greater suspicions; and he would have been now well pleased if the proof afforded by Lothario's coming were dispensed with, as he feared some sudden mishap; but as he was on the point of showing himself and coming forth to embrace and undeceive his wife he paused as he saw Leonela returning, leading Lothario. Camilla when she saw him, drawing a long line in front of her on the floor with the dagger, said to him, ' Lothario, pay attention to what I say to thee: if by any chance thou darest to cross this line thou seest, or even approach it, the instant I see thee attempt it that same instant will I pierce my bosom with this dagger that I hold in my hand; and before thou answerest me a word I desire thee to listen to a few from me, and afterwards thou shalt reply as may please thee. First, I desire thee to tell me, Lothario, if thou knowest my husband Anselmo, and in what light thou regardest him; and secondly I

desire to know if thou knowest me too. Answer me this, without embarrassment or reflecting deeply what thou wilt answer,
for they are no riddles I put to thee.'

Lothario was not so dull but that from the first moment
when Camilla directed him to make Anselmo hide himself he
understood what she intended to do, and therefore he fell in with
her idea so readily and promptly that between them they made
the imposture look more true than truth ; so he answered her
thus : ' I did not think, fair Camilla, that thou wert calling me
to ask questions so remote from the object with which I come ;
but if it is to defer the promised reward thou art doing so, thou
mightst have put it off still longer, for the longing for happiness
gives the more distress the nearer comes the hope of gaining it ;
but lest thou shouldst say that I do not answer thy questions, I
say that I know thy husband Anselmo, and that we have known
each other from our earliest years ; I will not speak of what thou
too knowest, of our friendship, that I may not compel myself to
testify against the wrong that love, the mighty excuse for greater
errors, makes me inflict upon him. Thee I know and hold in
the same estimation as he does, for were it not so I had not for
a lesser prize acted in opposition to what I owe to my station
and the holy laws of true friendship, now broken and violated by
me through that powerful enemy, love.'

' If thou dost confess that,' returned Camilla, ' mortal enemy
of all that rightly deserves to be loved, with what face dost thou
dare to come before one whom thou knowest to be the mirror
wherein he is reflected on whom thou shouldst look to see how
unworthily thou wrongest him ? But, woe is me, I now comprehend what has made thee give so little heed to what thou
owest to thyself ; it must have been some freedom of mine, for I
will not call it immodesty, as it did not proceed from any deliberate intention, but from some heedlessness such as women
are guilty of through inadvertence when they think they have no
occasion for reserve. But tell me, traitor, when did I by word
or sign give a reply to thy prayers that could awaken in thee a
shadow of hope of attaining thy base wishes ? When were not thy

professions of love sternly and scornfully rejected and rebuked? When were thy frequent pledges and still more frequent gifts believed or accepted? But as I am persuaded that no one can long persevere in the attempt to win love unsustained by some hope, I am willing to attribute to myself the blame of thy assurance, for no doubt some thoughtlessness of mine has all this time fostered thy hopes; and therefore will I punish myself and inflict upon myself the penalty thy guilt deserves. And that thou mayest see that being so relentless to myself I cannot possibly be otherwise to thee, I have summoned thee to be a witness of the sacrifice I mean to offer to the injured honour of my honoured husband, wronged by thee with all the assiduity thou wert capable of, and by me too through want of caution in avoiding every occasion, if I have given any, of encouraging and sanctioning thy base designs. Once more I say the suspicion in my mind that some imprudence of mine has engendered these lawless thoughts in thee, is what causes me most distress and what I desire most to punish with my own hands, for were any other instrument of punishment employed my error might become perhaps more widely known; but before I do so, in my death I mean to inflict death, and take with me one that will fully satisfy my longing for the revenge I hope for and have; for I shall see, wheresoever it may be that I go, the penalty awarded by inflexible, unswerving justice on him who has placed me in a position so desperate.'

As she uttered these words, with incredible energy and swiftness she flew upon Lothario with the naked dagger, so manifestly bent on burying it in his breast that he was almost uncertain whether these demonstrations were real or feigned, for he was obliged to have recourse to all his skill and strength to prevent her from striking him; and with such reality did she act this strange farce and mystification that, to give it a colour of truth, she determined to stain it with her own blood; for perceiving, or pretending, that she could not wound Lothario, she said, 'Fate, it seems, will not grant my just desire complete satisfaction, but it will not be able to keep me from satisfying it partially at least ; ' and making an effort to free the hand with the dagger which Lothario held in his grasp, she released it, and directing the point to a place where it could not inflict a deep wound, she plunged it into her left side high up close to the shoulder, and then allowed herself to fall to the ground as if in a faint.

Leonela and Lothario stood amazed and astounded at the catastrophe, and seeing Camilla stretched on the ground and bathed in her blood they were still uncertain as to the true nature of the act. Lothario, terrified and breathless, ran in haste to pluck out the dagger ; but when he saw how slight the wound was he was relieved of his fears and once more admired the subtlety, coolness, and ready wit of the fair Camilla ; and the better to support the part he had to play he began to utter profuse and doleful lamentations over her body as if she were dead, invoking maledictions not only on himself but also on him who had been the means of placing him in such a position : and knowing that his friend Anselmo heard him he spoke in such a way as to make a listener feel much more pity for him than for Camilla, even though he supposed her dead. Leonela took her up in her arms and laid her on the bed, entreating Lothario to go in quest of some one to attend to her wound in secret, and at the same time asking his advice and opinion as to what they should say to Anselmo about his lady's wound if he should chance to return before it was healed. He replied they might say what they liked, for he was not in a state to give advice that would be of any use ; all he could tell her was to try and stanch the blood, as he was going where he should never more be seen ; and with every appearance of deep grief and sorrow he left the house ; but when he found himself alone, and where there was nobody to see him, he crossed himself unceasingly, lost in wonder at the adroitness of Camilla and the consistent acting of Leonela. He reflected how convinced Anselmo would be that he had a second Portia for a wife, and he looked forward anxiously to meeting him in order to rejoice together over falsehood and truth the most craftily veiled that could possibly be imagined.

Leonela, as he told her, stanched her lady's blood, which was no more than sufficed to support her deception; and washing the wound with a little wine she bound it up to the best of her skill, talking all the time she was tending her in a strain that, even if nothing else had been said before, would have been enough to assure Anselmo that he had in Camilla a model of purity. To Leonela's words Camilla added her own, calling herself cowardly and wanting in spirit, since she had not enough at the time she had most need of it to rid herself of the life she so much loathed. She asked her attendant's advice as to whether or not she ought to inform her beloved husband of all that had happened, but the other bade her say nothing about it, as she would lay upon him the obligation of taking vengeance on Lothario, which he could not do but at great risk to himself; and it was the duty of a true wife not to give her husband provocation to quarrel, but, on the contrary, to remove it as far as possible from him.

Camilla replied that she believed she was right and that she would follow her advice, but at any rate it would be well to consider how she was to explain the wound to Anselmo, for he could not help seeing it; to which Leonela answered that she did not know how to tell a lie even in jest.

'How then can I know, my dear?' said Camilla, 'for I should not dare to forge or keep up a falsehood if my life depended on it. If we can think of no escape from this difficulty, it will be better to tell him the plain truth than that he should find us out in an untrue story.'

'Be not uneasy, señora,' said Leonela; 'between this and to-morrow I will think of what we must say to him, and perhaps the wound being where it is it can be hidden from his sight, and Heaven will be pleased to aid us in a purpose so good and honourable. Compose yourself, señora, and endeavour to calm your excitement lest my lord find you agitated; and leave the rest to my care and God's, who always supports good intentions.'

Anselmo had with the deepest attention listened to and seen played out the tragedy of the death of his honour, which the

performers acted with such wonderfully effective truth that it
seemed as if they had become the realities of the parts they
played. He longed for night and an opportunity of escaping
from the house to go and see his good friend Lothario, and with
him give vent to his joy over the precious pearl he had gained in
having established his wife's purity. Both mistress and maid
took care to give him time and opportunity to get away, and
taking advantage of it he made his escape, and at once went in
quest of Lothario, and it would be impossible to describe how he
embraced him when he found him, and the things he said to him
in the joy of his heart, and the praises he bestowed upon Camilla ;
all which Lothario listened to without being able to show any
pleasure, for he could not forget how deceived his friend was, and
how dishonourably he had wronged him ; and though Anselmo
could see that Lothario was not glad, still he imagined it was only
because he had left Camilla wounded and had been himself the
cause of it ; and so among other things he told him not to be distressed about Camilla's accident, for, as they had agreed to hide it
from him, the wound was evidently trifling ; and that being so, he
had no cause for fear, but should henceforward be of good cheer
and rejoice with him, seeing that by his means and adroitness he
found himself raised to the greatest height of happiness that he
could have ventured to hope for, and desired no better pastime
than making verses in praise of Camilla that would preserve her
name for all time to come. Lothario commended his purpose,
and promised on his own part to aid him in raising a monument
so glorious.

And so Anselmo was left the most charmingly hoodwinked
man there could be in the world. He himself, persuaded he was
conducting the instrument of his glory, led home by the hand
him who had been the utter destruction of his good name ;
whom Camilla received with averted countenance, though with
smiles in her heart. The deception was carried on for some
time, until at the end of a few months Fortune turned her wheel
and the guilt which had been until then so skilfully concealed
was published abroad, and Anselmo paid with his life the
penalty of his ill-advised curiosity.

CHAPTER XXXV.

WHICH TREATS OF THE HEROIC AND PRODIGIOUS BATTLE DON
QUIXOTE HAD WITH CERTAIN SKINS OF RED WINE, AND BRINGS
THE NOVEL OF 'THE ILL-ADVISED CURIOSITY' TO A CLOSE.

THERE remained but little more of the novel to be read,
when Sancho Panza burst forth in wild excitement from
the garret where Don Quixote was lying, shouting, 'Run,
sirs! quick; and help my master, who is in the thick of
the toughest and stiffest battle I ever laid eyes on. By the
living God he has given the giant, the enemy of my lady
the Princess Micomicona, such a slash that he has sliced
his head clean off as if it were a turnip.'

'What are you talking about, brother?' said the curate,
pausing as he was about to read the remainder of the novel.
'Are you in your senses, Sancho? How the devil can it
be as you say, when the giant is two thousand leagues
away?'

Here they heard a loud noise in the chamber, and Don
Quixote shouting out, 'Stand, thief, brigand, villain; now I
have got thee and thy scimitar shall not avail thee!' And
then it seemed as though he were slashing vigorously at
the wall.

'Don't stop to listen,' said Sancho, 'but go in and part
them or help my master: though there is no need of that

now, for no doubt the giant is dead by this time and giving account to God of his past wicked life; for I saw the blood flowing on the ground, and the head cut off and fallen on one side, and it is as big as a large wine-skin.'

'May I die,' said the landlord at this, 'if Don Quixote or Don Devil has not been slashing some of the skins of red wine that stand full at his bed's head, and the spilt wine must be what this good fellow takes for blood;' and so saying he went into the room and the rest after him, and there they found Don Quixote in the strangest costume in the world. He was in his shirt, which was not long enough in front to cover his thighs completely and was six fingers shorter behind; his legs were very long and lean, covered with hair, and anything but clean; on his head he had a little greasy red cap that belonged to the host, round his left arm he had rolled the blanket of the bed, to which Sancho, for reasons best known to himself, owed a grudge, and in his right hand he held his unsheathed sword, with which he was slashing about on all sides, uttering exclamations as if he were actually fighting some giant: and the best of it was his eyes were not open, for he was fast asleep, and dreaming that he was doing battle with the giant. For his imagination was so wrought upon by the adventure he was going to accomplish, that it made him dream he had already reached the kingdom of Micomicon, and was engaged in combat with his enemy; and believing he was laying on to the giant, he had given so many sword cuts to the skins that the whole room was full of wine. On seeing this the landlord was so enraged that he fell on Don Quixote, and with his clenched fist began to pummel him in such a way, that if Cardenio and the curate had not dragged him off, he would have brought the war of the giant to an end. But in spite of all the poor gentleman never woke until the barber brought a great pot of cold water from the well and flung it with one dash all over his body, on which Don Quixote woke up, but not so completely as to understand what was the matter. Dorothea, seeing how short and slight his attire was, would not go in to witness the battle between her champion and her opponent. As for Sancho, he went searching all over the floor for the head of the giant, and not finding it he said, 'I see now that it's all enchantment in this house; for the last time, on this very spot where I am now, I got ever so many thumps and thwacks without knowing who gave them to me, or being able to see anybody; and now this head is not to be seen anywhere about, though I saw it cut off with my own eyes and the blood running from the body as if from a fountain.'

'What blood and fountains are you talking about, enemy of God and his saints?' said the landlord. 'Don't you see, you thief, that the blood and the fountain are only these skins here that have been stabbed and the red wine swimming all over the room?—and I wish I saw the soul of him that stabbed them swimming in hell.'

'I know nothing about that,' said Sancho; 'all I know is it will be my bad luck that through not finding this head my county will melt away like salt in water;'—for Sancho awake was worse than his master asleep, so much had his master's promises addled his wits.

The landlord was beside himself at the coolness of the

squire and the mischievous doings of the master, and swore it should not be like the last time when they went without paying; and that their privileges of chivalry should not hold good this time to let one or other of them off without paying, even to the cost of the plugs that would have to be put to the damaged wine-skins. The curate was holding Don Quixote's hands, who, fancying he had now ended the adventure and was in the presence of the Princess Micomi- cona, knelt before the curate and said, ' Exalted and beau- teous lady, your highness may live from this day forth fearless of any harm this base being could do you; and I too from this day forth am released from the promise I gave you, since by the help of God on high and by the favour of her by whom I live and breathe, I have fulfilled it so successfully.'

'Did not I say so?' said Sancho on hearing this. ' You see I wasn't drunk; there you see my master has already salted the giant; there's no doubt about the bulls;[1] my county is all right!'

Who could have helped laughing at the absurdities of the pair, master and man? And laugh they did, all except the landlord, who cursed himself; but at length the barber, Cardenio, and the curate contrived with no small trouble to get Don Quixote on the bed, and he fell asleep with every appearance of excessive weariness. They left him to sleep, and came out to the gate of the inn to console Sancho Panza on not having found the head of the giant; but much more work had they to appease the landlord, who was furious

---

[1] Prov. 228—expressive probably of popular anxiety on the eve of a bull-fight.

at the sudden death of his wine-skins; and said the landlady, half scolding, half crying, 'At an evil moment and in an unlucky hour he came into my house, this knight-errant— would that I had never set eyes on him, for dear he has cost me; the last time he went off with the overnight score against him for supper, bed, straw, and barley, for himself and his squire and a hack and an ass, saying he was a knight adventurer—God send unlucky adventures to him and all the adventurers in the world—and therefore not bound to pay anything, for it was so settled by the knight-errantry tariff: and then, all because of him, came the other gentleman and carried off my tail, and gives it back more than two quartillos [1] the worse, all stripped of its hair, so that it is no use for my husband's purpose; and then, for a finishing touch to all, to burst my wine-skins and spill my wine! I wish I saw his own blood spilt! But let him not deceive himself, for, by the bones of my father and the shade of my mother, they shall pay me down every quarto; or my name is not what it is, and I am not my father's daughter.' All this and more to the same effect the landlady delivered with great irritation, and her good maid Maritornes backed her up, while the daughter held her peace and smiled from time to time. The curate smoothed matters by promising to make good all losses to the best of his power, not only as regarded the wine-skins but also the wine, and above all the depreciation of the tail which they set such store by. Dorothea comforted Sancho, telling him that she pledged herself, as soon as it should appear certain that his master had

---

[1] Quartillo—the fourth of a real.

decapitated the giant, and she found herself peacefully established in her kingdom, to bestow upon him the best county
there was in it.   With this Sancho consoled himself, and
assured the princess she might rely upon it that he had seen
the head of the giant, and more by token it had a beard that
reached to the girdle, and that if it was not to be seen now it
was because everything that happened in that house went
by enchantment, as he himself had proved the last time he
had lodged there.   Dorothea said she fully believed it, and
that he need not be uneasy, for all would go well and turn
out as he wished.   All therefore being appeased, the curate
was anxious to go on with the novel, as he saw there was but
little more left to read.   Dorothea and the others begged him
to finish it, and he, as he was willing to please them, and enjoyed reading it himself, continued the tale in these words :

The result was, that from the confidence Anselmo felt in the
virtue of Camilla, he lived happy and free from anxiety, and
Camilla purposely looked coldly on Lothario, that Anselmo might
suppose her feelings towards him to be the opposite of what they
were ; and the better to support the position, Lothario begged
to be excused from coming to the house, as the displeasure with
which Camilla regarded his presence was plain to be seen.   But
the befooled Anselmo said he would on no account allow such a
thing, and so in a thousand ways he became the author of his
own dishonour, while he believed he was insuring his happiness.
Meanwhile the satisfaction with which Leonela saw herself
empowered to carry on her amour reached such a height that,
regardless of everything else, she followed her inclinations un-
restrainedly, feeling confident that her mistress would screen her,
and even show her how to manage it safely.   At last one night
Anselmo heard footsteps in Leonela's room, and on trying to
enter to see who it was, he found that the door was held against

him, which made him all the more determined to open it; and exerting his strength he forced it open, and entered the room in time to see a man leaping through the window into the street. He ran quickly to seize him or discover who he was, but he was unable to effect either purpose, for Leonela flung her arms round him crying, 'Be calm, señor; do not give way to passion or follow him who has escaped from this; he belongs to me, and in fact he is my husband.'

Anselmo would not believe it, but blind with rage drew a dagger and threatened to stab Leonela, bidding her tell the truth or he would kill her. She, in her fear, not knowing what she was saying, exclaimed, ' Do not kill me, señor, for I can tell you things more important than any you can imagine.'

' Tell me then at once or thou diest,' said Anselmo.

' It would be impossible for me now,' said Leonela, ' I am so agitated : leave me till to-morrow, and then you shall hear from me what will fill you with astonishment; but rest assured that he who leaped through the window is a young man of this city, who has given me his promise to become my husband.'

Anselmo was appeased with this, and was content to wait the time she asked of him, for he never expected to hear anything against Camilla, so satisfied and sure of her virtue was he ; and so he quitted the room, and left Leonela locked in, telling her she should not come out until she had told him all she had to make known to him. He went at once to see Camilla, and tell her, as he did, all that had passed between him and her handmaid, and the promise she had given him to inform him of matters of serious importance.

There is no need of saying whether Camilla was agitated or not, for so great was her fear and dismay, that, making sure, as she had good reason to do, that Leonela would tell Anselmo all she knew of her faithlessness, she had not the courage to wait and see if her suspicions were confirmed ; and that same night, as soon as she thought that Anselmo was asleep, she packed up the most valuable jewels she had and some money, and without being observed by anybody escaped from the house and betook herself to Lothario's, to whom she related what had occurred, imploring him to convey her to some place of safety or fly with her where they might be safe from Anselmo. The state of perplexity to which Camilla reduced Lothario was such that he was unable to utter a word in reply, still less to decide upon what he should do. At length he resolved to conduct her to a convent of which a sister of his was prioress; Camilla agreed to this, and with the speed which the circumstances demanded, Lothario took her to the convent and left her there, and then himself quitted the city without letting anyone know of his departure.

As soon as daylight came Anselmo, without missing Camilla from his side, rose eager to learn what Leonela had to tell him, and hastened to the room where he had locked her in. He opened the door, entered, but found no Leonela; all he found was some sheets knotted to the window, a plain proof that she had let herself down from it and escaped. He returned, uneasy, to tell Camilla, but not finding her in bed or anywhere in the house he was lost in amazement. He asked the servants of the house about her, but none of them could give him any explanation. As he was going in search of Camilla it happened by chance that he observed her boxes were lying open, and that the greater part of her jewels were gone; and now he became fully aware of his disgrace, and that Leonela was not the cause of his misfortune; and, just as he was, without delaying to dress himself completely, he repaired, sad at heart and dejected, to his friend Lothario to make known his sorrow to him; but when he failed to find him and the servants reported that he had been absent from his house all night and had taken with him all the money he had, he felt as though he were losing his senses; and to make all complete on returning to his own house he found it deserted and empty, not one of all his servants, male or female, remaining in it. He knew not what to think, or say, or do, and his reason seemed to be deserting him little by little. He reviewed his position, and saw himself in a moment left without wife, friend, or servants, abandoned, he felt, by the heaven above him, and more than all robbed of his honour, for in Camilla's disappearance he saw his own ruin. After long reflection he resolved at last to go to his friend's country house where he had been staying when he afforded opportunities for the contrivance of this complication of misfortune. He locked the doors of his house, mounted his horse, and with a broken spirit set out on his journey; but he had hardly gone half-way when, harassed by his reflections, he had to dismount and tie his horse to a tree, at the foot of which he threw himself, giving vent to piteous heartrending sighs; and there he remained till nearly nightfall, when he observed a man approaching on horseback from the city, of whom, after saluting him, he asked what was the news in Florence.

The citizen replied, ' The strangest that have been heard for many a day; for it is reported abroad that Lothario, the great friend of the wealthy Anselmo, who lived at San Giovanni, carried off last night Camilla, the wife of Anselmo, who also has disappeared. All this has been told by a maid-servant of Camilla's, whom the governor found last night lowering herself by a sheet from the windows of Anselmo's house. I know not indeed, precisely, how the affair came to pass; all I know is that the whole city is wondering at the occurrence, for no one could have expected a thing of the kind, seeing the great and intimate friendship that existed between them, so great, they say, that they were called " The two Friends." '

' Is it known at all,' said Anselmo, ' what road Lothario and Camilla took ? '

' Not in the least,' said the citizen, ' though the governor has been very active in searching for them.'

' God speed you, señor,' said Anselmo.

' God be with you,' said the citizen and went his way.

This disastrous intelligence almost robbed Anselmo not only of his senses but of his life. He got up as well as he was able and reached the house of his friend, who as yet knew nothing of his misfortune, but seeing him come pale, worn, and haggard, perceived that he was suffering some heavy affliction. Anselmo at once begged to be allowed to retire to rest, and to be given writing materials. His wish was complied with and he was left lying down and alone, for he desired this, and even that the door should be locked. Finding himself alone he so took to heart the thought of his misfortune that by the signs of death he felt within him he knew well his life was drawing to a close, and therefore he resolved to leave behind him a declaration of the cause of his strange end. He began to write, but before he had put down all he meant to say, his breath failed him and he yielded up his life, a victim to the suffering which his ill-advised curiosity had entailed upon him. The master of the house observing that it was now late and that Anselmo did not call, determined to go in and ascertain if his indisposition was increasing, and found him lying on his face, his body partly in the bed, partly on the writing-table, on which he lay with the written paper open and the pen still in his hand. Having first called to him without receiving any answer, his host approached him, and taking him by the hand, found that it was cold, and saw that he was dead. Greatly surprised and distressed he summoned the household to witness the sad fate which had befallen Anselmo ; and then he read the paper, the handwriting of which he recognised as his, and which contained these words :

' A foolish and ill-advised desire has robbed me of life. If the news of my death should reach the ears of Camilla, let her know that I forgive her, for she was not bound to perform miracles, nor ought I to have required her to perform them ; and since I have been the author of my own dishonour, there is no reason why—'

So far Anselmo had written, and thus it was plain that at this point, before he could finish what he had to say, his life came to an end. The next day his friend sent intelligence of his death to his relatives, who had already ascertained his misfortune, as well as the convent where Camilla lay almost on the point of accompanying her husband on that inevitable journey, not on account of the tidings of his death, but because of those she received of her lover's departure. Although she saw herself a widow, it is said she refused either to quit the convent or take the veil, until, not long afterwards, intelligence reached her that Lothario had been killed in a battle in which M. de Lautrec had been recently engaged with the Great Captain Gonzalo Fernandez de Cordova [1] in the kingdom of Naples, whither her too late repentant lover had repaired. On learning this Camilla took the veil, and shortly afterwards died, worn out by grief and melancholy. This was the end of all three, an end that came of a thoughtless beginning.

'I like this novel,' said the curate; 'but I cannot persuade myself of its truth; and if it has been invented, the author's invention is faulty, for it is impossible to imagine any husband so foolish as to try such a costly experiment as Anselmo's. If it had been represented as occurring between a gallant and his mistress it might pass; but between husband and wife there is something of an impossibility about it. As to the way in which the story is told, however, I have no fault to find.'

---

[1] Lautrec and the Great Captain were not engaged in the same campaigns. The former commanded in Italy in the time of Francis I. and Charles V., several years after the death of the Great Captain.

CHAPTER XXXVI.

WHICH TREATS OF MORE CURIOUS INCIDENTS THAT OCCURRED AT THE INN.

JUST at that instant the landlord, who was standing at the gate of the inn, exclaimed, 'Here comes a fine troop of guests; if they stop here we may say *gaudeamus.*'

'What are they?' said Cardenio.

'Four men,' said the landlord, 'riding *á la jineta,*[1] with lances and bucklers, and all with black veils, and with them there is a woman in white on a side-saddle, whose face is also veiled, and two attendants on foot.'

'Are they very near?' said the curate.

'So near,' answered the landlord, 'that here they come.'

Hearing this Dorothea covered her face, and Cardenio retreated into Don Quixote's room, and they hardly had time to do so before the whole party the host had described entered the inn, and the four that were on horseback, who were of high-bred appearance and bearing, dismounted, and came forward to take down the woman who rode on the side-saddle, and one of them taking her in his arms placed her in a chair that stood at the entrance of the room where Cardenio had hidden himself. All this time neither she

---

[1] I.e. on high saddles with short stirrups.

nor they had removed their veils or spoken a word, only on sitting down on the chair the woman gave a deep sigh and let her arms fall like one that was ill and weak. The attendants on foot then led the horses away to the stable. Observing this the curate, curious to know who these people in such a dress and preserving such silence were, went to where the servants were standing and put the question to one of them, who answered him, ' Faith, sir, I cannot tell you who they are, I only know they seem to be people of distinction, particularly he who advanced to take the lady you saw in his arms ; and I say so because all the rest show him respect, and nothing is done except what he directs and orders.'

' And the lady, who is she ? ' asked the curate.

' That I cannot tell you either,' said the servant, ' for I have not seen her face all the way : I have indeed heard her sigh many times and utter such groans that she seems to be giving up the ghost every time ; but it is no wonder if we do not know more than we have told you, as my comrade and I have only been in their company two days, for having met us on the road they begged and persuaded us to accompany them to Andalusia, promising to pay us well.'

' And have you heard any of them called by his name ? ' asked the curate.

' No, indeed,' replied the servant ; ' they all preserve a marvellous silence on the road, for not a sound is to be heard among them except the poor lady's sighs and sobs, which make us pity her ; and we feel sure that wherever it is she is going, it is against her will, and as far as one can judge from her dress she is a nun or, what is more likely, about to become one; and perhaps it is because taking the vows is not of her own free will, that she is so unhappy as she seems to be.'

'That may well be,' said the curate, and leaving them he returned to where Dorothea was, who, hearing the veiled lady sigh, moved by natural compassion drew near to her and said, 'What are you suffering from, señora? If it be anything that women are accustomed and know how to relieve, I for my part offer you my services with all my heart.'

To this the unhappy lady made no reply; and though Dorothea repeated her offers more earnestly she still kept silence, until the gentleman with the veil, who, the servant said, was obeyed by the rest, approached and said to Dorothea, 'Do not give yourself the trouble, señora, of making any offers to that woman, for it is her way to give no thanks for anything that is done for her; and do not try to make her answer unless you want to hear some lie from her lips.'

'I have never told a lie,' was the immediate reply of her who had been silent until now; 'on the contrary, it is because I am so truthful and so ignorant of lying devices that I am now in this miserable condition; and this I call you yourself to witness, for it is my unstained truth that has made you false and a liar.'

Cardenio heard these words clearly and distinctly, being quite close to the speaker, for there was only the door of Don Quixote's room between them, and the instant he did so, uttering a loud exclamation he cried, 'Good God! what is this I hear ? What voice is this that has reached my ears ? ' Startled at the voice the lady turned her head; and not seeing the speaker she stood up and attempted to enter the room; observing which the gentleman held her back, preventing her from moving a step. In her agitation and sudden movement the silk with which she had covered her face fell off and disclosed a countenance of incomparable and marvellous beauty, but pale and terrified; for she kept turning her eyes, everywhere she .could direct her gaze, with an eagerness that made her look as if she had lost her senses, and so marked that it excited the pity of Dorothea and all who beheld her, though they knew not what caused it. The gentleman grasped her firmly by the shoulders, and being so fully occupied with holding her back, he was unable to put a hand to his veil which was falling off, as it did at length entirely, and Dorothea, who was holding the lady in her arms, raising her eyes saw that he who likewise held her was her husband, Don Fernando. The instant she recognised him, with a prolonged plaintive cry drawn from the depths of her heart, she fell backwards fainting, and but for the barber being close by to catch her in his arms, she would have fallen completely to the ground. The curate at once hastened to uncover her face and throw water on it, and as he did so Don Fernando, for he it was who held the other in his arms, recognised her and stood as if death-stricken by the sight; not, however, relaxing his grasp of Luscinda, for it was she that was struggling to release herself from his hold, having recognised Cardenio by his voice, as he had recognised her. Cardenio also heard Dorothea's cry as she fell fainting, and imagining that it

came from his Luscinda burst forth in terror from the
room, and the first thing he saw was Don Fernando with
Luscinda in his arms. Don Fernando, too, knew Cardenio
at once; and all three, Luscinda, Cardenio, and Dorothea,[1]
stood in silent amazement scarcely knowing what had
happened to them.

They gazed at one another without speaking, Dorothea
at Don Fernando, Don Fernando at Cardenio, Cardenio at
Luscinda, and Luscinda at Cardenio. The first to break
silence was Luscinda, who thus addressed Don Fernando:
'Leave me, señor Don Fernando, for the sake of what you
owe to yourself; if no other reason will induce you, leave
me to cling to the wall of which I am the ivy, to the support
from which neither your importunities, nor your threats,
nor your promises, nor your gifts have been able to detach
me. See how Heaven, by ways strange and hidden from
our sight, has brought me face to face with my true husband; and well you know by dear-bought experience that
death alone will be able to efface him from my memory.
May this plain declaration, then, lead you, as you can do
nothing else, to turn your love into rage, your affection
into resentment, and so to take my life; for if I yield it up
in the presence of my beloved husband I count it well bestowed; it may be by my death he will be convinced that I
kept my faith to him to the last moment of life.'

Meanwhile Dorothea had come to herself, and had
heard Luscinda's words, by means of which she divined who
she was; but seeing that Don Fernando did not yet release

---

[1] Only a few lines back we are told Dorothea had fainted, and a little
farther on how she came to herself.

her or reply to her, summoning up her resolution as well as she could she rose and knelt at his feet, and with a flood of bright and touching tears addressed him thus :

'If, my lord, the beams of that sun that thou holdest eclipsed in thine arms did not dazzle and rob thine eyes of sight thou wouldst have seen by this time that she who kneels at thy feet is, so long as thou wilt have it so, the unhappy and unfortunate Dorothea. I am that lowly peasant girl whom thou in thy goodness or for thy pleasure wouldst raise high enough to call herself thine ; I am she who in the seclusion of innocence led a contented life until at the voice of thy importunity, and thy true and tender passion, as it seemed, she opened the gates of her modesty and surrendered to thee the keys of her liberty ; a gift received by thee but thanklessly, as is clearly shown by my forced retreat to the place where thou dost find me, and by thy appearance under the circumstances in which I see thee. Nevertheless, I would not have thee suppose that I have come here driven by my shame ; it is only grief and sorrow at seeing myself forgotten by thee that have led me. It was thy will to make me thine, and thou didst so follow thy will, that now, even though thou repentest, thou canst not help being mine. Bethink thee, my lord, the unsurpassable affection I bear thee may compensate for the beauty and noble birth for which thou wouldst desert me. Thou canst not be the fair Luscinda's because thou art mine, nor can she be thine because she is Cardenio's ; and it will be easier, remember, to bend thy will to love one who adores thee, than to lead one to love thee who abhors thee now. Thou didst address thyself to my simplicity,

thou didst lay siege to my virtue, thou wert not ignorant of
my station, well dost thou know how I yielded wholly to
thy will; there is no ground or reason for thee to plead
deception, and if it be so, as it is, and if thou art a Christian
as thou art a gentleman, why dost thou by such subterfuges
put off making me as happy at last as thou didst at first?
And if thou wilt not have me for what I am, thy true and
lawful wife, at least take and accept me as thy slave, for so
long as I am thine I will count myself happy and fortunate.
Do not by deserting me let my shame become the talk of
the gossips in the streets; make not the old age of my
parents miserable; for the loyal services they as faithful
vassals have ever rendered thine are not deserving of such
a return; and if thou thinkest it will debase thy blood to
mingle it with mine, reflect that there is little or no nobility
in the world that has not travelled the same road, and that
in illustrious lineages it is not the woman's blood that is of
account; and, moreover, that true nobility consists in virtue,
and if thou art wanting in that, refusing me what in justice
thou owest me, then even I have higher claims to nobility
than thine.   To make an end, señor, these are my last
words to thee: whether thou wilt, or wilt not, I am thy wife;
witness thy words, which must not and ought not to be false,
if thou dost pride thyself on that for want of which thou
scornest me; witness the pledge which thou didst give me,[1]
and witness Heaven, which thou thyself didst call to witness
the promise thou hadst made me; and if all this fail, thy
own conscience will not fail to lift up its silent voice in the

---

[1] The first edition has *firma que hiciste*; but Don Fernando did not
sign any paper, but gave Dorothea a ring.

midst of all thy gaiety, and vindicate the truth of what I say and mar thy highest pleasure and enjoyment.'

All this and more the injured Dorothea delivered with such earnest feeling and such tears that all present, even those who came with Don Fernando, were constrained to join her in them. Don Fernando listened to her without replying, until, ceasing to speak, she gave way to such sobs and sighs that it must have been a heart of brass that was not softened by the sight of so great sorrow. Luscinda stood regarding her with no less compassion for her sufferings than admiration for her intelligence and beauty, and would have gone to her to say some words of comfort to her, but was prevented by Don Fernando's grasp which held her fast. He, overwhelmed with confusion and astonishment, after regarding Dorothea for some moments with a fixed gaze, opened his arms, and, releasing Luscinda, exclaimed, ' Thou hast conquered, fair Dorothea, thou hast conquered, for it is impossible to have the heart to deny the united force of so many truths.'

Luscinda in her feebleness was on the point of falling to the ground when Don Fernando released her, but Cardenio, who stood near, having retreated behind Don Fernando to escape recognition, casting fear aside and regardless of what might happen, ran forward to support her, and said as he clasped her in his arms, 'If Heaven in its compassion is willing to let thee rest at last, mistress of my heart, true, constant, and fair, nowhere canst thou rest more safely than in these arms that now receive thee, and received thee before when fortune permitted me to call thee mine.'

At these words Luscinda looked up at Cardenio, at first
beginning to recognise him by his voice and then satisfying
herself by her eyes that it was he, and hardly knowing what
she did, and heedless of all considerations of decorum, she
flung her arms around his neck and pressing her face
close to his, said, 'Yes, my dear lord, you are the true
master of this your slave, even though adverse fate inter-
pose again, and fresh dangers threaten this life that hangs
on yours.'

A strange sight was this for Don Fernando and those
that stood around, filled with surprise at an incident so unlooked for.   Dorothea fancied that Don Fernando changed
colour and looked as though he meant to take vengeance on
Cardenio, for she observed him put his hand to his sword;
and the instant the idea struck her, with wonderful quickness she clasped him round the knees, and kissing them and
holding him so as to prevent his moving, she said, while her
tears continued to flow, 'What is it thou wouldst do, my
only refuge, in this unforeseen event?   Thou hast thy wife
at thy feet, and she whom thou wouldst have for thy wife
is in the arms of her husband : reflect whether it will be
right for thee, whether it will be possible for thee to undo
what Heaven has done, or whether it will be becoming in
thee to seek to raise her to be thy mate who in spite of
every obstacle, and strong in her truth and constancy, is
before thine eyes, bathing with the tears of love the face
and bosom of her lawful husband.   For God's sake I
entreat of thee, for thine own I implore thee, let not this
open manifestation rouse thy anger; but rather so calm it
as to allow these two lovers to live in peace and quiet with-

out any interference from thee so long as Heaven permits them; and in so doing thou wilt prove the generosity of thy lofty noble spirit, and the world shall see that with thee reason has more influence than passion.'

All the time Dorothea was speaking Cardenio, though he held Luscinda in his arms, never took his eyes off Don Fernando, determined, if he saw him make any hostile movement, to try and defend himself and resist as best he could all who might assail him, though it should cost him his life. But now Don Fernando's friends, as well as the curate and the barber, who had been present all the while, not forgetting the worthy Sancho Panza, ran forward and gathered round Don Fernando, entreating him to have regard for the tears of Dorothea, and not suffer her reasonable hopes to be disappointed, since, as they firmly believed, what she said was but the truth; and bidding him observe that it was not, as it might seem, by accident, but by a special disposition of Providence that they had all met in a place where no one could have expected a meeting. And the curate bade him remember that only death could part Luscinda from Cardenio; that even if some sword were to separate them they would think their death most happy; and that in a case that admitted of no remedy his wisest course was, by conquering and putting a constraint upon himself, to show a generous mind, and of his own accord suffer these two to enjoy the happiness Heaven had granted them. He bade him, too, turn his eyes upon the beauty of Dorothea and he would see that few if any could equal much less excel her; while to that beauty should be added her modesty and the surpassing love she bore him. But

besides all this, he reminded him that if he prided himself
on being a gentleman and a Christian, he could not do otherwise than keep his plighted word; and that in doing so he
would obey God and meet the approval of all sensible
people, who know and recognise it to be the privilege of
beauty, even in one of humble birth, provided virtue accompany it, to be able to raise itself to the level of any
rank, without any slur upon him who places it upon an
equality with himself; and furthermore that when the
potent sway of passion asserts itself, so long as there be no
mixture of sin in it, he is not to be blamed who gives way
to it.

To be brief, they added to these such other forcible
arguments that Don Fernando's manly heart, being after
all nourished by noble blood, was touched, and yielded to
the truth which, even had he wished it, he could not gainsay; and he showed his submission, and acceptance of the
good advice that had been offered to him, by stooping down
and embracing Dorothea, saying to her, ' Rise, dear lady,
it is not right that what I hold in my heart should be kneel-
ing at my feet; and if until now I have shown no sign of
what I own, it may have been by Heaven's decree in
order that, seeing the constancy with which you love me, I
may learn to value you as you deserve. What I entreat of
you is that you reproach me not with my transgression and
grievous wrong-doing; for the same cause and force that
drove me to make you mine impelled me to struggle against
being yours; and to prove this, turn and look at the eyes
of the now happy Luscinda, and you will see in them an
excuse for all my errors : and as she has found and gained

the object of her desires, and I have found in you what
satisfies all my wishes, may she live in peace and contentment as many happy years with her Cardenio, as on my
knees I pray Heaven to allow me to live with my Dorothea ; '
and with these words he once more embraced her and
pressed his face to hers with so much tenderness that he
had to take great heed to keep his tears from completing
the proof of his love and repentance in the sight of all.
Not so Luscinda, and Cardenio, and almost all the others,
for they shed so many tears, some in their own happiness,
some at that of the others, that one would have supposed a
heavy calamity had fallen upon them all.   Even Sancho
Panza was weeping; though afterwards he said he only
wept because he saw that Dorothea was not as he fancied
the queen Micomicona, of whom he expected such great
favours.   Their wonder as well as their weeping lasted
some time, and then Cardenio and Luscinda went and fell
on their knees before Don Fernando, returning him thanks
for the favour he had rendered them in language so
grateful that he knew not how to answer them, and raising
them up embraced them with every mark of affection and
courtesy.

He then asked Dorothea how she had managed to reach
a place so far removed from her own home, and she in a
few fitting words told all that she had previously related
to Cardenio, with which Don Fernando and his companions
were so delighted that they wished the story had been longer ;
so charmingly did Dorothea describe her misadventures.
When she had finished Don Fernando recounted what had
befallen him in the city after he had found in Luscinda's

bosom the paper in which she declared that she was Cardenio's wife, and never could be his. He said he meant to kill her, and would have done so had he not been prevented by her parents, and that he quitted the house full of rage and shame, and resolved to avenge himself when a more convenient opportunity should offer. The next day he learned that Luscinda had disappeared from her father's house, and that no one could tell whither she had gone. Finally, at the end of some months he ascertained that she was in a convent and meant to remain there all the rest of her life, if she were not to share it with Cardenio; and as soon as he had learned this, taking these three gentlemen as his companions, he arrived at the place where she was, but avoided speaking to her, fearing that if it were known he was there stricter precautions would be taken in the convent; and watching a time when the porter's lodge was open he left two to guard the gate, and he and the other entered the convent in quest of Luscinda, whom they found in the cloisters in conversation with one of the nuns, and carrying her off without giving her time to resist, they reached a place with her where they provided themselves with what they required for taking her away; all which they were able to do in complete safety, as the convent was in the country at a considerable distance from the city. He added that when Luscinda found herself in his power she lost all consciousness, and after returning to herself did nothing but weep and sigh without speaking a word; and thus in silence and tears they reached that inn, which for him was reaching heaven where all the mischances of earth are over and at an end.

CHAPTER XXXVII.

IN WHICH IS CONTINUED THE STORY OF THE FAMOUS PRINCESS
MICOMICONA, WITH OTHER DROLL ADVENTURES.

To all this Sancho listened with no little sorrow at heart to
see how his hopes of dignity were fading away and vanish-
ing in smoke, and how the fair princess Micomicona had
turned into Dorothea, and the giant into Don Fernando,
while his master was sleeping tranquilly, totally unconscious
of all that had come to pass. Dorothea was unable to
persuade herself that her present happiness was not all
a dream; Cardenio was in a similar state of mind, and
Luscinda's thoughts ran in the same direction. Don
Fernando gave thanks to Heaven for the favour shown to
him and for having been rescued from the intricate labyrinth in which he had been brought so near the destruction of his good name and of his soul; and in short everybody in the inn was full of contentment and satisfaction
at the happy issue of such a complicated and hopeless
business. The curate as a sensible man made sound reflections upon the whole affair, and congratulated each upon
his good fortune; but the one that was in the highest spirits
and good humour was the landlady, because of the promise
Cardenio and the curate had given her to pay for all the

losses and damage she had sustained through Don Quixote's means. Sancho, as has been already said, was the only one who was distressed, unhappy, and dejected; and so with a long face he went in to his master, who had just awoke, and said to him, 'Sir Rueful Countenance, your worship may as well sleep on as much as you like, without troubling yourself about killing any giant or restoring her kingdom to the princess; for that is all over and settled now.'

'I should think it was,' replied Don Quixote, 'for I have had the most prodigious and stupendous battle with the giant that I ever remember having had all the days of my life; and with one back-stroke—swish!—I brought his head tumbling to the ground, and so much blood gushed forth from him that it ran in rivulets over the earth like water.'

'Like red wine, your worship had better say,' replied Sancho; 'for I would have you know, if you don't know it, that the dead giant is a hacked wine-skin, and the blood four-and-twenty gallons of red wine that it had in its belly, and the cut-off head is the bitch that bore me; and the devil take it all.'

'What art thou talking about, fool?' said Don Quixote; 'art thou in thy senses?'

'Let your worship get up,' said Sancho, 'and you will see the nice business you have made of it, and what we have to pay; and you will see the queen turned into a private lady called Dorothea, and other things that will astonish you, if you understand them.'

'I shall not be surprised at anything of the kind,'

returned Don Quixote; 'for if thou dost remember the last time we were here I told thee that everything that happened here was a matter of enchantment, and it would be no wonder if it were the same now.'

'I could believe all that,' replied Sancho, 'if my blanketing was the same sort of thing also; only it wasn't, but real and genuine; for I saw the landlord, who is here to-day, holding one end of the blanket and jerking me up to the skies very neatly and smartly, and with as much laughter as strength; and when it comes to be a case of knowing people, I hold for my part, simple and sinner as I am, that there is no enchantment about it at all, but a great deal of bruising and plenty of bad luck.'

'Well, well, God will give a remedy,' said Don Quixote; 'hand me my clothes and let me go out, for I want to see these transformations and things thou speakest of.'

Sancho fetched him his clothes; and while he was dressing, the curate gave Don Fernando and the others present an account of Don Quixote's madness and of the stratagem they had made use of to withdraw him from that Peña Pobre where he fancied himself stationed because of his lady's scorn. He described to them also nearly all the adventures that Sancho had mentioned, at which they marvelled and laughed not a little, thinking it, as all did, the strangest form of madness a crazy intellect could be capable of. But now, the curate said, that the lady Dorothea's good fortune prevented her from proceeding with their purpose, it would be necessary to devise or discover some other way of getting him home.

Cardenio proposed to carry out the scheme they had

begun, and suggested that Luscinda would act and support Dorothea's part sufficiently well.

'No,' said Don Fernando, 'that must not be, for I want Dorothea to follow out this idea of hers; and if the worthy gentleman's village is not very far off, I shall be happy if I can do anything for his relief.'

'It is not more than two days' journey from this,' said the curate.

'Even if it were more,' said Don Fernando, 'I would gladly travel so far for the sake of doing so good a work.'

At this moment Don Quixote came out in full panoply, with Mambrino's helmet, all dinted as it was, on his head, his buckler on his arm, and leaning on his staff or pike. The strange figure he presented filled Don Fernando and the rest with amazement as they contemplated his lean yellow face half a league long, his armour of all sorts, and the solemnity of his deportment. They stood silent waiting to see what he would say, and he, fixing his eyes on the fair Dorothea, addressed her with great gravity and composure:

'I am informed, fair lady, by my squire here that your greatness has been annihilated and your being abolished, since, from a queen and lady of high degree as you used to be, you have been turned into a private maiden. If this has been done by the command of the magician king your father, through fear that I should not afford you the aid you need and are entitled to, I may tell you he did not know and does not know half the mass,[1] and was little versed in

---

[1] *No saber de la misa la media,* a familiar mode of describing ignorance.

the annals of chivalry; for, if he had read and gone through them as attentively and deliberately as I have, he would have found at every turn that knights of less renown than mine, have accomplished things more difficult: it is no great matter to kill a whelp of a giant, however arrogant he may be; for it is not many hours since I myself was engaged with one, and—I will not speak of it, that they may not say I am lying; time, however, that reveals all, will tell the tale when we least expect it.'

' You were engaged with a couple of wine-skins, and not a giant,' said the landlord at this; but Don Fernando told him to hold his tongue and on no account interrupt Don Quixote, who continued, ' I say in conclusion, high and dis-inherited lady, that if your father has brought about this metamorphosis in your person for the reason I have mentioned, you ought not to attach any importance to it; for there is no peril on earth through which my sword will not force a way, and with it, before many days are over, I will bring your enemy's head to the ground and place on yours the crown of your kingdom.'

Don Quixote said no more, and waited for the reply of the princess, who, aware of Don Fernando's determination to carry on the deception until Don Quixote had been conveyed to his home, with great ease of manner and gravity made answer, ' Whoever told you, valiant Knight of the Rueful Countenance, that I had undergone any change or transformation did not tell you the truth, for I am the same as I was yesterday. It is true that certain strokes of good fortune, that have given me more than I could have hoped for, have made some alteration in me; but I have

not therefore ceased to be what I was before, or to entertain
the same desire I have had all through of availing myself
of the might of your valiant and invincible arm. And so,
señor, let your goodness reinstate the father that begot me
in your good opinion, and be assured that he was a wise
and prudent man, since by his craft he found out such a
sure and easy way of remedying my misfortune ; for I believe,
señor, that had it not been for you I should never have lit
upon the good fortune I now possess ; and in this I am saying what is perfectly true ; as most of these gentlemen who
are present can fully testify. All that remains is to set out
on our journey to-morrow, for to-day we could not make
much way ; and for the rest of the happy result I am
looking forward to, I trust to God and the valour of your
heart.'

So said the sprightly Dorothea, and on hearing her Don
Quixote turned to Sancho, and said to him, with an angry
air, 'I declare now, little Sancho, thou art the greatest
little villain in Spain. Say, thief and vagabond, hast thou
not just now told me that this princess had been turned
into a maiden called Dorothea, and that the head which I am
persuaded I cut off from a giant was the bitch that bore thee,
and other nonsense that put me in the greatest perplexity
I have ever been in all my life ? I vow ' (and here he looked
to heaven and ground his teeth) 'I have a mind to play the
mischief with thee, in a way that will teach sense for the
future to all lying squires of knights-errant in the world.'

'Let your worship be calm, señor,' returned Sancho,
'for it may well be that I have been mistaken as to the
change of the lady princess Micomicona ; but as to the giant's

head, or at least as to the piercing of the wine-skins, and
the blood being red wine, I make no mistake, as sure as
there is a God; because the wounded skins are there at the
head of your worship's bed, and the red wine has made a
lake of the room ; if not you will see when the eggs come to
be fried ; [1] I mean when his worship the landlord here calls
for all the damages : for the rest, I am heartily glad that
her ladyship the queen is as she was, for it concerns me as
much as anyone.'

'I tell thee again, Sancho, thou art a fool,' said Don
Quixote ; ' forgive me, and that will do.'

' That will do,' said Don Fernando ; 'let us say no more
about it ; and as her ladyship the princess proposes to set
out to-morrow because it is too late to-day, so be it, and we
will pass the night in pleasant conversation, and to-morrow
we will all accompany Señor Don Quixote ; for we wish to
witness the valiant and unparalleled achievements he is
about to perform in the course of this mighty enterprise
which he has undertaken.'

' It is I who shall wait upon and accompany you,' said
Don Quixote ; ' and I am much gratified by the favour that
is bestowed upon me, and the good opinion entertained of
me, which I shall strive to justify or it shall cost me my
life, or even more, if it can possibly cost me more.'

Many were the compliments and expressions of politeness that passed between Don Quixote and Don Fernando ;
but they were brought to an end by a traveller who at this
moment entered the inn, and who seemed from his attire to

---

[1] Prov. 120. The time at which the truth of any statement will be
seen.

be a Christian lately come from the country of the Moors, for he was dressed in a short-skirted coat of blue cloth with half-sleeves and without a collar; his breeches were also of blue cloth, and his cap of the same colour, and he wore yellow buskins and had a Moorish cutlass slung from a baldric across his breast. Behind him, mounted upon an ass, there came a woman dressed in Moorish fashion, with her face veiled and a scarf on her head, and wearing a little brocaded cap, and a mantle that covered her from her shoulders to her feet. The man was of a robust and well-proportioned frame, in age a little over forty, rather swarthy in complexion, with long moustaches and a full beard, and, in short, his appearance was such that if he had been well dressed he would have been taken for a person of quality and good birth. On entering he asked for a room, and when they told him there was none in the inn he seemed distressed, and approaching her who by her dress seemed to be a Moor he took her down from the saddle in his arms. Luscinda, Dorothea, the landlady, her daughter and Maritornes, attracted by the strange, and to them entirely new costume, gathered round her; and Dorothea, who was always kindly, courteous, and quick-witted, perceiving that both she and the man who had brought her were annoyed at not finding a room, said to her, ' Do not be put out, señora, by the discomfort and want of luxuries here, for it is the way of road-side inns to be without them ; still, if you will be pleased to share our lodging with us (pointing to Luscinda) perhaps you will have found worse accommodation in the course of your journey.'

To this the veiled lady made no reply; all she did was

to rise from her seat, crossing her hands upon her bosom, bowing her head and bending her body as a sign that she returned thanks. From her silence they concluded that she must be a Moor and unable to speak a Christian tongue.

At this moment the captive [1] came up, having been until now otherwise engaged, and seeing that they all stood round his companion and that she made no reply to what they addressed to her, he said, 'Ladies, this damsel hardly understands my language and can speak none but that of her own country, for which reason she does not and cannot answer what has been asked of her.'

'Nothing has been asked of her,' returned Luscinda; 'she has only been offered our company for this evening and a share of the quarters we occupy, where she shall be made as comfortable as the circumstances allow, with the good will we are bound to show all strangers that stand in need of it, especially if it be a woman to whom the service is rendered.'

'On her part and my own, señora,' replied the captive, 'I kiss your hands, and I esteem highly, as I ought, the favour you have offered, which, on such an occasion and coming from persons of your appearance, is, it is plain to see, a very great one.'

'Tell me, señor,' said Dorothea, 'is this lady a Christian or a Moor? for her dress and her silence lead us to imagine that she is what we could wish she was not.'

'In dress and outwardly,' said he, 'she is a Moor, but

---

[1] Cervantes forgets that he has not as yet said anything about his captivity.

at heart she is a thoroughly good Christian, for she has the greatest desire to become one.'

'Then she has not been baptised?' returned Luscinda.

'There has been no opportunity for that,' replied the captive, 'since she left Algiers, her native country and home; and up to the present she has not found herself in any such imminent danger of death as to make it necessary to baptise her before she has been instructed in all the ceremonies our holy mother Church ordains; but, please God, ere long she shall be baptised with the solemnity befitting her quality, which is higher than her dress or mine indicates.'

By these words he excited a desire in all who heard him, to know who the Moorish lady and the captive were, but no one liked to ask just then, seeing that it was a fitter moment for helping them to rest themselves than for questioning them about their lives. Dorothea took the Moorish lady by the hand and leading her to a seat beside herself, requested her to remove her veil. She looked at the captive as if to ask him what they meant and what she was to do. He said to her in Arabic that they asked her to take off her veil, and thereupon she removed it and disclosed a countenance so lovely, that to Dorothea she seemed more beautiful than Luscinda, and to Luscinda more beautiful than Dorothea, and all the bystanders felt that if any beauty could compare with theirs it was the Moorish lady's, and there were even those who were inclined to give it somewhat the preference. And as it is the privilege and charm of beauty to win the heart and secure good-will, all forthwith became eager to show kindness and attention to the lovely Moor.

Don Fernando asked the captive what her name was, and he replied that it was Lela Zoraida ; but the instant she heard him, she guessed what the Christian had asked, and said hastily, with some displeasure and energy, 'No, not Zoraida ; Maria, Maria !' giving them to understand that she was called 'Maria' and not 'Zoraida.' These words, and the touching earnestness with which she uttered them, drew more than one tear from some of the listeners, particularly the women, who are by nature tender-hearted and compassionate. Luscinda embraced her affectionately, saying, 'Yes, yes, Maria, Maria,' to which the Moor replied, 'Yes, yes, Maria ; Zoraida macange,'[1] which means 'not Zoraida.'

Night was now approaching, and by the orders of those who accompanied Don Fernando the landlord had taken care and pains to prepare for them the best supper that was in his power. The hour therefore having arrived they all took their seats at a long table like a refectory one, for round or square table there was none in the inn, and the seat of honour at the head of it, though he was for refusing it, they assigned to Don Quixote, who desired the lady Micomicona to place herself by his side, as he was her protector. Luscinda and Zoraida took their places next her, opposite to them were Don Fernando and Cardenio, and next the captive and the other gentlemen, and by the side of the ladies, the curate and the barber. And so they supped in high enjoyment, which was increased when they observed Don Quixote leave off eating, and, moved by an impulse

---

[1] Properly *ma-kan-shy*—the common emphatic negative in popular Arabic, at least in the Barbary States.

like that which made him deliver himself at such length when he supped with the goatherds, begin to address them :

'Verily, gentlemen, if we reflect upon it, great and marvellous are the things they see, who make profession of the order of knight-errantry. Say, what being is there in this world, who entering the gate of this castle at this moment, and seeing us as we are here, would suppose or imagine us to be what we are? Who would say that this lady who is beside me was the great queen that we all know her to be, or that I am that Knight of the Rueful Countenance, trumpeted far and wide by the mouth of Fame? Now, there can be no doubt that this art and calling surpasses all those that mankind has invented, and is the more deserving of being held in honour in proportion as it' is the more exposed to peril. Away with those who assert that letters have the pre-eminence over arms; I will tell them, whosoever they may be, that they know not what they say. For the reason which such persons commonly assign, and upon which they chiefly rest, is, that the labours of the mind are greater than those of the body, and that arms give employment to the body alone; as if the calling were a porter's trade, for which nothing more is required than sturdy strength; or as if, in what we who profess them call arms, there were not included acts of vigour for the execution of which high intelligence is requisite; or as if the soul of the warrior, when he has an army, or the defence of a city under his care, did not exert itself as much by mind as by body. Nay; see whether by bodily strength it be possible to learn or divine the intentions of the enemy, his plans, stratagems, or obstacles, or to ward off impending mischief; for all these are the work of the mind, and in them the body has no share whatever. Since, therefore, arms have need of the mind, as much as letters, let us see now which of the two minds, that of the man of letters [1] or that of the warrior, has most to do; and this will be seen by the end and goal that each seeks to attain; for that purpose is the more estimable which has for its aim the nobler object. The end and goal of letters—I am not speaking now of divine letters, the aim of which is to raise and direct the soul to Heaven; for with an end so infinite no other can be compared—I speak of human letters, the end of which is to establish distributive justice, give to every man that which is his, and see and take care that good laws are observed: an end undoubtedly noble, lofty, and deserving of high praise, but not such as should be given to that sought by arms, which have for their end and object peace, the greatest boon that men can desire in this life. The first good news the world and mankind received was that which the angels announced on the night that was our day, when they sang in the air, " Glory to God in the highest, and peace on earth to men of good will; " and the salutation which the great Master of heaven and earth taught his disciples and chosen followers when they entered any house, was to say, " Peace be on this house; " and many other times he said to them, " My peace I give unto you, my peace I leave you, peace be with you; " a jewel and a precious gift given and left by such a hand; a jewel without which there can be no happiness either on

---

[1] 'Man of letters'—*letrado*, as will be seen, means here specially one devoted to jurisprudence.

earth or in heaven. This peace is the true end of war; and war is only another name for arms. This, then, being admitted, that the end of war is peace, and that so far it has the advantage of the end of letters, let us turn to the bodily labours of the man of letters, and those of him who follows the profession of arms, and see which are the greater.'

Don Quixote delivered his discourse in such a manner and in such correct language, that for the time being he made it impossible for any of his hearers to consider him a madman; on the contrary, as they were mostly gentlemen, to whom arms are an appurtenance by birth, they listened to him with great pleasure as he continued: ' Here, then, I say is what the student has to undergo; first of all poverty; not that all are poor, but to put the case as strongly as possible: and when I have said that he endures poverty, I think nothing more need be said about his hard fortune, for he who is poor has no share of the good things of life. This poverty he suffers from in various ways, hunger, or cold, or nakedness, or all together; but for all that it is not so extreme but that he gets something to eat, though it may be at somewhat unseasonable hours and from the leavings of the rich; for the greatest misery of the student is what they themselves call "going out for soup," [1] and there is always some neighbour's brazier or hearth for them, which, if it does not warm, at least tempers the cold to them, and lastly, they sleep comfortably

---

[1] *Andar á la sopa*—to attend at the convents where soup is given out to the poor. The convent soup, as Quevedo says in the *Gran Tacaño*, was also a great resource of the *picaro* class.

at night under a roof. I will not go into other particulars, as for example want of shirts, and no superabundance of shoes, thin and threadbare garments, and gorging themselves to surfeit in their voracity when good luck has treated them to a banquet of some sort. By this road that I have described, rough and hard, stumbling here, falling there, getting up again to fall again, they reach the rank they desire, and that once attained, we have seen many who have passed these Syrtes and Scyllas and Charybdises, as if borne flying on the wings of favouring fortune ; we have seen them, I say, ruling and governing the world from a chair, their hunger turned into satiety, their cold into comfort, their nakedness into fine raiment, their sleep on a mat into repose in holland and damask, the justly earned reward of their virtue ; but, contrasted and compared with what the warrior undergoes, all they have undergone falls far short of it, as I am now about to show.'

CHAPTER XXXVIII.

WHICH TREATS OF THE CURIOUS DISCOURSE DON QUIXOTE
DELIVERED ON ARMS AND LETTERS.

CONTINUING his discourse Don Quixote said : ' As we began
in the student's case with poverty and its accompaniments,
let us see now if the soldier is richer, and we shall find that
in poverty itself there is no one poorer ; for he is dependent
on his miserable pay, which comes late or never, or else on
what he can plunder, seriously imperilling his life and conscience ; and sometimes his nakedness will be so great that
a slashed doublet serves him for uniform and shirt, and in
the depth of winter he has to defend himself against the
inclemency of the weather in the open field with nothing
better than the breath of his mouth, which I need not say,
coming from an empty place, must come out cold, contrary to the laws of nature. To be sure he looks forward
to the approach of night to make up for all these discom-
forts on the bed that awaits him, which, unless by some fault
of his, never sins by being over narrow, for he can easily
measure out on the ground as many feet as he likes, and
roll himself about in it to his heart's content without any
fear of the sheets slipping away from him. Then, after
all this, suppose the day and hour for taking his degree in
his calling to have come ; suppose the day of battle to have

arrived, when they invest him with the doctor's cap made
of lint, to mend some bullet-hole, perhaps, that has gone
through his temples, or left him with a crippled arm or leg.
Or if this does not happen, and merciful Heaven watches
over him and keeps him safe and sound, it may be he will
be in the same poverty he was in before, and he must go
through more engagements and more battles, and come
victorious out of all before he betters himself; but miracles
of that sort, are seldom seen. For tell me, sirs, if you
have ever reflected upon it, by how much do those who
have gained by war fall short of the number of those
who have perished in it? No doubt you will reply that
there can be no comparison, that the dead cannot be
numbered, while the living who have been rewarded may be
summed up with three figures.[1] All which is the reverse in
the case of men of letters; for by skirts, to say nothing of
sleeves,[2] they all find means of support; so that though the
soldier has more to endure, his reward is much less. But
against all this it may be urged that it is easier to reward
two thousand men of letters than thirty thousand soldiers,
for the former may be remunerated by giving them places,
which must perforce be conferred upon men of their calling,
while the latter can only be recompensed out of the very
property of the master they serve; but this impossibility
only strengthens my argument.

'Putting this, however, aside, for it is a puzzling question
for which it is difficult to find a solution, let us return to
the superiority of arms over letters, a matter still undecided,
so many are the arguments put forward on each side; for

---

[1] I.e. fall short of 1,000.   [2] See Note A, p. 217.

besides those I have mentioned, letters say that without them
arms cannot maintain themselves, for war, too, has its laws
and is governed by them, and laws belong to the domain of
letters and men of letters. To this arms make answer that
without them laws cannot be maintained, for by arms states
are defended, kingdoms preserved, cities protected, roads
made safe, seas cleared of pirates ; and, in short, if it were
not for them, states, kingdoms, monarchies, cities, ways by
sea and land would be exposed to the violence and confusion
which war brings with it, so long as it lasts and is free to
make use of its privileges and powers. And then it is plain
that whatever costs most is valued and deserves to be valued
most. To attain to eminence in letters costs a man time,
watching, hunger, nakedness, headaches, indigestions, and
other things of the sort, some of which I have already
referred to. But for a man to come in the ordinary course
of things to be a good soldier costs him all the student
suffers, and in an incomparably higher degree, for at every
step he runs the risk of losing his life. For what dread of
want or poverty that can reach or harass the student can
compare with what the soldier feels, who finds himself be-
leaguered in some stronghold mounting guard in some
ravelin or cavalier, knows that the enemy is pushing a
mine towards the post where he is stationed, and cannot
under any circumstances retire or fly from the imminent
danger that threatens him ? All he can do is to inform his
captain of what is going on so that he may try to remedy
it by a counter-mine, and then stand his ground in fear
and expectation of the moment when he will fly up to the
clouds without wings and descend into the deep against his

will. And if this seems a trifling risk, let us see whether
it is equalled or surpassed by the encounter of two galleys
stem to stem, in the midst of the open sea, locked and en-
tangled one with the other, when the soldier has no more
standing room than two feet of the plank of the spur; and
yet, though he sees before him threatening him as many
ministers of death as there are cannon of the foe pointed at
him, not a lance length from his body, and sees too that with
the first heedless step he will go down to visit the profundi-
ties of Neptune's bosom, still with dauntless heart, urged on
by honour that nerves him, he makes himself a target for
all that musketry, and struggles to cross that narrow path
to the enemy's ship. And what is still more marvellous,
no sooner has one gone down into the depths he will never
rise from till the end of the world, than another takes his
place; and if he too falls into the sea that waits for him
like an enemy, another and another will succeed him without
a moment's pause between their deaths: courage and daring
the greatest that all the chances of war can show.[1] Happy
the blest ages that knew not the dread fury of those devilish
engines of artillery, whose inventor I am persuaded is in
hell receiving the reward of his diabolical invention, by which
he made it easy for a base and cowardly arm to take the life
of a gallant gentleman; and that, when he knows not how
or whence, in the height of the ardour and enthusiasm that
fire and animate brave hearts, there should come some random bullet, discharged perhaps by one who fled in terror at
the flash when he fired off his accursed machine, which in
an instant puts an end to the projects and cuts off the life of

[1] See Note B, p. 217.

one who deserved to live for ages to come. And thus when I reflect on this, I am almost tempted to say that in my heart I repent of having adopted this profession of knight-errant in so detestable an age as we live in now; for though no peril can make me fear, still it gives me some uneasiness to think that powder and lead may rob me of the opportunity of making myself famous and renowned throughout the known earth by the might of my arm and the edge of my sword. But Heaven's will be done; if I succeed in my attempt I shall be all the more honoured, as I have faced greater dangers than the knights-errant of yore exposed themselves to.'

All this lengthy discourse Don Quixote delivered while the others supped, forgetting to raise a morsel to his lips, though Sancho more than once told him to eat his supper, as he would have time enough afterwards to say all he wanted. It excited fresh pity in those who had heard him to see a man of apparently sound sense, and with rational views on every subject he discussed, so hopelessly wanting in all, when his wretched unlucky chivalry was in question. The curate told him he was quite right in all he had said in favour of arms, and that he himself, though a man of letters and a graduate, was of the same opinion.

They finished their supper, the cloth was removed, and while the hostess, her daughter, and Maritornes were getting Don Quixote of La Mancha's garret ready, in which it was arranged that the women were to be quartered by themselves for the night, Don Fernando begged the captive to tell them the story of his life, for it could not fail to be strange and interesting, to judge by the hints he had let fall on his arrival in company with Zoraida. To this the captive replied that he would very willingly yield to his request, only he feared his tale would not give them as much pleasure as he wished ; nevertheless, not to be wanting in compliance, he would tell it. The curate and the others thanked him and added their entreaties, and he finding himself so pressed said there was no occasion to ask, where a command had such weight, and added, ' If your worships will give me your attention you will hear a true story which, perhaps, fictitious ones constructed with ingenious and studied art cannot come up to.' These words made them settle themselves in their places and preserve a deep silence, and he seeing them waiting on his words in mute expectation, began thus in a pleasant quiet voice.

Note A (page 213).

Clemencin explains this as ' in one way or another.' Another explanation is that by skirts (*faldas*) regular salary is meant, and by sleeves (*mangas*) douceurs, perquisites, and the like.

Note B (page 215).

We have here, no doubt, a personal reminiscence of Lepanto. It was in an affair somewhat of this sort that Cervantes himself received his wounds.

CHAPTER XXXIX.

My family had its origin in a village in the mountains of Leon,[1] and nature had been kinder and more generous to it than fortune ; though in the general poverty of those communities my father passed for being even a rich man ; and he would have been so in reality had he been as clever in preserving his property as he was in spending it. This tendency of his to be liberal and profuse he had acquired from having been a soldier in his youth, for the soldier's life is a school in which the niggard becomes free-handed and the free-handed prodigal ; and if any soldiers are to be found who are misers, they are monsters of rare occurrence. My father went beyond liberality and bordered on prodigality, a disposition by no means advantageous to a married man who has children to succeed to his name and position. My father had three, all sons, and all of sufficient age to make choice of a profession. Finding, then, that he was unable to resist his propensity, he resolved to divest himself of the instrument and cause of his prodigality and lavishness, to divest himself of wealth, without which Alexander himself would have seemed parsimonious ; and so calling us all three aside one day into a room, he addressed us in words somewhat to the following effect :

'My sons, to assure you that I love you, no more need be known or said than that you are my sons ; and to encourage a suspicion that I do not love you, no more is needed than the knowledge that I have no self-control as far as preservation of

[1] See Note A, p. 226.

your patrimony is concerned; therefore, that you may for the future feel sure that I love you like a father, and have no wish to ruin you like a stepfather, I propose to do with you what I have for some time back meditated, and after mature deliberation decided upon. You are now of an age to choose your line of life or at least make choice of a calling that will bring you honour and profit when you are older; and what I have resolved to do is to divide my property into four parts; three I will give to you, to each his portion without making any difference, and the other I will retain to live upon and support myself for whatever remainder of life Heaven may be pleased to grant me. But I wish each of you on taking possession of the share that falls to him to follow one of the paths I shall indicate. In this Spain of ours there is a proverb, to my mind very true—as they all are, being short aphorisms drawn from long practical experience—and the one I refer to says, "The church, or the sea, or the king's house;"[1] as much as to say, in plainer language, whoever wants to flourish and become rich, let him follow the church, or go to sea, adopting commerce as his calling, or go into the king's service in his household, for they say, "Better a king's crumb than a lord's favour."[2] I say so because it is my will and pleasure that one of you should follow letters, another trade, and the third serve the king in the wars, for it is a difficult matter to gain admission to his service in his household, and if war does not bring much wealth it confers great distinction and fame. Eight days hence I will give you your full shares in money, without defrauding you of a farthing, as you will see in the end. Now tell me if you are willing to follow out my idea and advice as I have laid it before you.'

Having called upon me as the eldest to answer, I, after urging him not to strip himself of his property but to spend it all as he pleased, for we were young men able to gain our living, consented to comply with his wishes, and said that mine were to follow the profession of arms and thereby serve God and my king. My second brother having made the same proposal, decided upon

[1] Prov. 121. [2] Prov. 202.

going to the Indies, embarking the portion that fell to him in trade. The youngest, and in my opinion the wisest, said he would rather follow the church, or go to complete his studies at Salamanca. As soon as we had come to an understanding, and made choice of our professions, my father embraced us all, and in the short time he mentioned carried into effect all he had promised; and when he had given to each his share, which as well as I remember was three thousand ducats apiece in cash (for an uncle of ours bought the estate and paid for it down, not to let it go out of the family), we all three on the same day took leave of our good father; and at the same time, as it seemed to me inhuman to leave my father with such scanty means in his old age, I induced him to take two of my three thousand ducats, as the remainder would be enough to provide me with all a soldier needed. My two brothers, moved by my example, gave him each a thousand ducats, so that there was left for my father four thousand ducats in money, besides three thousand, the value of the portion that fell to him which he preferred to retain in land instead of selling it. Finally, as I said, we took leave of him, and of our uncle whom I have mentioned, not without sorrow and tears on both sides, they charging us to let them know whenever an opportunity offered how we fared, whether well or ill. We promised to do so, and when he had embraced us and given us his blessing, one set out for Salamanca, the other for Seville, and I for Alicante, where I had heard there was a Genoese vessel taking in a cargo of wool for Genoa.

It is now some twenty-two years since I left my father's house, and all that time, though I have written several letters, I have had no news whatever of him or of my brothers; my own adventures during that period I will now relate briefly. I embarked at Alicante, reached Genoa after a prosperous voyage, and proceeded thence to Milan, where I provided myself with arms and a few soldier's accoutrements; thence it was my intention to go and take service in Piedmont, but as I was already on the road to Alessandria della Paglia, I learned that the great Duke of Alva was on his way to

Flanders.[1]   I changed my plans, joined him, served under him in the campaigns he made, was present at the deaths of the Counts Egmont and Horn, and was promoted to be ensign under a famous captain of Guadalajara, Diego de Urbina by name.[2] Some time after my arrival in Flanders news came of the league that his Holiness Pope Pius V. of happy memory had made with Venice and Spain against the common enemy, the Turk, who had just then with his fleet taken the famous island of Cyprus, which belonged to the Venetians, a loss deplorable and disastrous. It was known as a fact that the Most Serene Don John of Austria, natural brother of our good king Don Philip, was coming as commander-in-chief of the allied forces, and rumours were abroad of the vast warlike preparations which were being made, all which stirred my heart and filled me with a longing to take part in the campaign which was expected; and though I had reason to believe, and almost certain promises, that on the first opportunity that presented itself I should be promoted to be captain, I preferred to leave all and betake myself, as I did, to Italy ; and it was my good fortune that Don John had just arrived at Genoa, and was going on to Naples to join the Venetian fleet, as he afterwards did at Messina.   I may say, in short, that I took part in that glorious expedition, promoted by this time to be a captain of infantry, to which honourable charge my good luck rather than my merits raised me; and that day—so fortunate for Christendom, because then all the nations of the earth were disabused of the error under which they lay in imagining the Turks to be invincible on sea—on that day, I say, on which the Ottoman pride and arrogance were broken, among all that were there made happy (for the Christians who died that day were happier than those who remained alive and victorious) I alone was miserable ; for, instead of some naval crown that I might have expected had it been in Roman times,

[1] Alva went to Flanders in 1567, so that the present scene would be laid in 1589; but Cervantes paid no attention to chronology.

[2] This was the captain of the company in Diego de Moncada's regiment in which Cervantes first served.

on the night that followed that famous day I found myself with fetters on my feet and manacles on my hands.

It happened in this way : El Uchali,[1] the King of Algiers, a daring and successful corsair, having attacked and taken the leading Maltese galley (only three knights being left alive in it, and they badly wounded), the chief galley of John Andrea,[2] on board of which I and my company were placed, came to its relief, and doing as I was bound to do in such a case, I leaped on board the enemy's galley, which, sheering off from that which had attacked it, prevented my men from following me, and so I found myself alone in the midst of my enemies, who were in such numbers that I was unable to resist ; in short I was taken, covered with wounds ; El Uchali, as you know, sirs, made his escape with his entire squadron, and I was left a prisoner in his power, the only sad being among so many filled with joy, and the only captive among so many free ; for there were fifteen thousand Christians, all at the oar in the Turkish fleet, that regained their longed-for liberty that day.

They carried me to Constantinople, where the Grand Turk, Selim, made my master general at sea for having done his duty in the battle and carried off as evidence of his bravery the standard of the Order of Malta. The following year, which was the year seventy-two, I found myself at Navarino rowing in the leading galley with the three lanterns.[3] There I saw and observed how the opportunity of capturing the whole Turkish fleet in harbour was lost ; for all the marines and janizzaries that belonged to it made sure that they were about to be attacked inside the very harbour, and had their kits and pasamaques, or shoes, ready to flee at once on shore without waiting to be assailed, in so great fear did they stand of our fleet. But Heaven ordered it otherwise, not for any fault or neglect of the general who commanded on our side, but for the sins of Christendom, and because it was God's will and pleasure that we should always have

---

[1] Properly—Aluch Ali.

[2] John Andrea Doria, nephew of the great Andrea Doria.

[3] The distinguishing mark of the admiral's galley.

instruments of punishment to chastise us. As it was, El Uchali took refuge at Modon, which is an island near Navarino, and landing his forces fortified the mouth of the harbour and waited quietly until Don John retired. On this expedition was taken the galley called the Prize, whose captain was a son of the famous corsair Barbarossa. It was taken by the chief Neapolitan galley called the She-wolf, commanded by that thunderbolt of war, that father of his men, that successful and unconquered captain Don Alvaro de Bazan, Marquis of Santa Cruz; and I cannot help telling you what took place at the capture of the Prize.

The son of Barbarossa was so cruel, and treated his slaves so badly, that, when those who were at the oars saw that the She-wolf galley was bearing down upon them and gaining upon them, they all at once dropped their oars and seized their captain who stood on the stage at the end of the gangway shouting to them to row lustily; and passing him on from bench to bench, from the poop to the prow, they so bit him that before he had got much past the mast his soul had already got to hell; so great, as I said, was the cruelty with which he treated them, and the hatred with which they hated him.

We returned to Constantinople, and the following year, seventy-three, it became known that Don John had seized Tunis and taken the kingdom from the Turks, and placed Muley Hamet in possession, putting an end to the hopes which Muley Hamida, the cruelest and bravest Moor in the world, entertained of returning to reign there. The Grand Turk took the loss greatly to heart, and with the cunning which all his race possess, he made peace with the Venetians (who were much more eager for it than he was), and the following year, seventy-four, he attacked the Goletta[1] and the fort which Don John had left half built near Tunis. While all these events were occurring, I was labouring at the oar without any hope of freedom; at least I had no hope of obtaining it by ransom, for I was firmly resolved not to write to my father telling him of my misfortunes. At length the Goletta fell, and the fort fell, before which places there were seventy-five thousand regular

[1] The fort commanding the entrance, the 'gullet,' to the lagoon of Tunis.

Turkish soldiers, and more than four hundred thousand Moors and Arabs from all parts of Africa, and in the train of all this great host such munitions and engines of war, and so many pioneers that with their hands they might have covered the Goletta and the fort with handfuls of earth. The first to fall was the Goletta, until then reckoned impregnable, and it fell, not by any fault of its defenders, who did all that they could and should have done, but because experiment proved how easily entrenchments could be made in the desert sand there; for water used to be found at two palms depth, while the Turks found none at two yards; and so by means of a quantity of sandbags they raised their works so high that they commanded the walls of the fort, sweeping them as if from a cavalier, so that no one was able to make a stand or maintain the defence.

It was a common opinion that our men should not have shut themselves up in the Goletta, but should have waited in the open at the landing-place; but those who say so talk at random and with little knowledge of such matters; for if in the Goletta and in the fort there were barely seven thousand soldiers, how could such a small number, however resolute, sally out and hold their own against numbers like those of the enemy? And how is it possible to help losing a stronghold that is not relieved, above all when surrounded by a host of determined enemies in their own country? But many thought, and I thought so too, that it was a special favour and mercy which Heaven showed to Spain in permitting the destruction of that source and hiding-place of mischief, that devourer, sponge, and moth of countless money, fruitlessly wasted there to no other purpose save preserving the memory of its capture by the invincible Charles V.; as if to make that eternal, as it is and will be, these stones were needed to support it. The fort also fell; but the Turks had to win it inch by inch, for the soldiers who defended it fought so gallantly and stoutly that the number of the enemy killed in twenty-two general assaults exceeded twenty-five thousand. Of three hundred that remained alive not one was taken unwounded, a clear and manifest proof of their gallantry and resolution, and how sturdily they had defended themselves and held their post. A small fort or tower which was in the middle of the lagoon under the command of Don Juan Zanoguera, a Valencian gentleman and a famous soldier, capitulated upon terms. They took prisoner Don Pedro Puertacarrero, commandant of the Goletta, who had done all in his power to defend his fortress, and took the loss of it so much to heart that he died of grief on the way to Constantinople, where they were carrying him a prisoner. They also took the commandant of the fort, Gabrio Cerbellon [1] by name, a Milanese gentleman, a great engineer and a very brave soldier. In these two fortresses perished many persons of note, among whom was Pagano Doria, knight of the Order of St. John, a man of generous disposition, as was shown by his extreme liberality to his brother, the famous John Andrea Doria; and what made his death the more sad was that he was slain by some Arabs to whom, seeing that the fort was now lost, he entrusted himself, and who offered to conduct him in the disguise of a Moor to Tabarca, a small fort or station on the coast held by the Genoese employed in the coral fishery. These Arabs cut off his head and carried it to the commander of the Turkish fleet, who proved on them the truth of our Castilian proverb, that ' though the treason may please, the traitor is hated ; ' [2] for they say he ordered those who brought him the present to be hanged for not having brought him alive.

Among the Christians who were taken in the fort was one named Don Pedro de Aguilar, a native of some place, I know not what, in Andalusia, who had been ensign in the fort, a soldier of great repute and rare intelligence, who had in particular a special gift for what they call poetry. I say so because his fate brought him to my galley and to my bench, and made him a slave to the same master ; and before we left the port this gentleman composed two sonnets by way of epitaphs, one on the Goletta and the other on the fort ; indeed, I may as well repeat them, for I have them by heart, and I think they will be liked rather than disliked.

[1] Or Serbelloni.　　　　　　　　[2] Prov. 230.

The instant the captive mentioned the name of Don Pedro de Aguilar, Don Fernando looked at his companions and they all three smiled; and when he came to speak of the sonnets one of them said, 'Before your worship proceeds any further I entreat you to tell me what became of that Don Pedro de Aguilar you have spoken of.'

'All I know is,' replied the captive, 'that after having been in Constantinople two years, he escaped in the disguise of an Arnaut, in company with a Greek spy; but whether he regained his liberty or not I cannot tell, though I fancy he did, because a year afterwards I saw the Greek at Constantinople, though I was unable to ask him what the result of the journey was.'

'Well then, you are right,' returned the gentleman, 'for that Don Pedro is my brother, and he is now in our village in good health, rich, married, and with three children.'[1]

'Thanks be to God for all the mercies he has shown him,' said the captive; 'for to my mind there is no happiness on earth to compare with recovering lost liberty.'

'And what is more,' said the gentleman, 'I know the sonnets my brother made.'

'Then let your worship repeat them,' said the captive, 'for you will recite them better than I can.'

'With all my heart,' said the gentleman; 'that on the Goletta runs thus.'

[1] The memoirs of this Don Pedro de Aguilar were printed in 1875 by the Sociedad de Bibliofilos Españoles.

Note A (*page* 218).

'Montañas de Burgos' and 'Montañas de Leon' were the names given to the southern slopes of the western continuation of the Pyrenees, the cradle of most of the old Gothic families of Spain, that of Cervantes himself among the number.

CHAPTER XL.

IN WHICH THE STORY OF THE CAPTIVE IS CONTINUED.

SONNET.[1]

'BLEST souls, that, from this mortal husk set free,
  In guerdon of brave deeds beatified,
  Above this lowly orb of ours abide
Made heirs of heaven and immortality,
With noble rage and ardour glowing ye
  Your strength, while strength was yours, in battle plied,
  And with your own blood and the foeman's dyed
The sandy soil and the encircling sea.
It was the ebbing life-blood first that failed
The weary arms; the stout hearts never quailed.
  Though vanquished, yet ye earned the victor's crown:
Though mourned, yet still triumphant was your fall;
For there ye won, between the sword and wall,
  In Heaven glory and on earth renown.'

'That is it exactly, according to my recollection,' said the captive.

'Well then, that on the fort,' said the gentleman, 'if my memory serves me, goes thus:

[1] See Note A, p. 240.

SONNET.

'Up from this wasted soil, this shattered shell,
　　Whose walls and towers here in ruin lie,
　　Three thousand soldier souls took wing on high,
In the bright mansions of the blest to dwell.
The onslaught of the foeman to repel
　　By might of arm all vainly did they try,
　　And when at length 'twas left them but to die,
Wearied and few the last defenders fell.
And this same arid soil hath ever been
A haunt of countless mournful memories,
　　As well in our day as in days of yore.
But never yet to Heaven it sent, I ween,
From its hard bosom purer souls than these,
　　Or braver bodies on its surface bore.'

The sonnets were not disliked, and the captive was rejoiced at the tidings they gave him of his comrade, and continuing his tale, he went on to say:

The Goletta and the fort being thus in their hands, the Turks gave orders to dismantle the Goletta—for the fort was reduced to such a state that there was nothing left to level—and to do the work more quickly and easily they mined it in three places; but nowhere were they able to blow up the part which seemed to be the least strong, that is to say, the old walls, while all that remained standing of the new fortifications that the Fratin [1] had made came to the ground with the greatest ease. Finally the fleet returned victorious and triumphant to Constantinople,

---

[1] Fratin, 'the little friar,' the name by which Jacome Palearo went.

and a few months later died my master, El Uchali, otherwise
Uchali Fartax, which means in Turkish ' the scabby renegade ; '
for that he was; it is the practice with the Turks to name
people from some defect or virtue they may possess ; the reason
being that there are among them only four surnames belonging
to families tracing their descent from the Ottoman house, and
the others, as I have said, take their names and surnames either
from bodily blemishes or moral qualities.   This ' scabby one '
rowed at the oar as a slave of the Grand Signor's for fourteen
years, and when over thirty-four years of age, in resentment at
having been struck by a Turk while at the oar, turned renegade
and renounced his faith in order to be able to revenge himself ;
and such was his valour that, without owing his advancement to
the base ways and means by which most favourites of the Grand
Signor rise to power, he came to be king of Algiers, and afterwards general-on-sea, which is the third place of trust in the
realm.   He was a Calabrian by birth, and a worthy man morally,
and he treated his slaves with great humanity.   He had three
thousand of them, and after his death they were divided, as he
directed by his will, between the Grand Signor (who is heir of all
who die and shares with the children of the deceased) and his
renegades.   I fell to the lot of a Venetian renegade who, when a
cabin-boy on board a ship, had been taken by Uchali and was so
much beloved by him that he became one of his most favoured
youths.   He came to be the most cruel renegade I ever saw : his
name was Hassan Aga,[1] and he grew very rich and became king
of Algiers.   With him I went there from Constantinople, rather
glad to be so near Spain, not that I intended to write to anyone
about my unhappy lot, but to try if fortune would be kinder to
me in Algiers than in Constantinople, where I had attempted in
a thousand ways to escape without ever finding a favourable
time or chance ; but in Algiers I resolved to seek for other
means of effecting the purpose I cherished so dearly ; for the
hope of obtaining my liberty never deserted me ; and when in
my plots and schemes and attempts the result did not answer

[1] This should be Hassan Pacha : Hassan Aga died in 1543.

my expectations, without giving way to despair I immediately began to look out for or conjure up some new hope to support me, however faint or feeble it might be.[1]

In this way I lived on immured in a building or prison called by the Turks a baño,[2] in which they confine the Christian captives, as well those that are the king's as those belonging to private individuals, and also what they call those of the Almacen, which is as much as to say the slaves of the municipality, who serve the city in the public works and other employments ; but captives of this kind recover their liberty with great difficulty, for, as they are public property and have no particular master, there is no one with whom to treat for their ransom, even though they may have the means. To these baños, as I have said, some private individuals of the town are in the habit of bringing their captives, especially when they are to be ransomed ; because there they can keep them in safety and comfort until their ransom arrives. The king's captives also, that are on ransom, do not go out to work with the rest of the crew, unless when their ransom is delayed ; for then, to make them write for it more pressingly, they compel them to work and go for wood, which is no light labour.

I, however, was one of those on ransom, for when it was discovered that I was a captain, although I declared my scanty means and want of fortune, nothing could dissuade them from including me among the gentlemen and those waiting to be ransomed. They put a chain on me, more as a mark of this than to keep me safe, and so I passed my life in that baño with several other gentlemen and persons of quality marked out as held to ransom ; but though at times, or rather almost always, we suffered from hunger and scanty clothing, nothing distressed us so much as hearing and seeing at every turn the unexampled and unheard-of cruelties my master inflicted upon the Christians. Every day he hanged a man, impaled one, cut off the ears of another ; and all with so little provocation, or so entirely without any, that the Turks acknowledged he did it merely for the sake of

---

[1] See Note B, p. 240.   [2] See Note C, p. 240.

doing it, and because he was by nature murderously disposed towards the whole human race. The only one that fared at all well with him was a Spanish soldier, something de Saavedra [1] by name, to whom he never gave a blow himself, or ordered a blow to be given, or addressed a hard word, although he had done things that will dwell in the memory of the people there for many a year, and all to recover his liberty; and for the least of the many things he did we all dreaded that he would be impaled, and he himself was in fear of it more than once ; and only that time does not allow, I could tell you now something of what that soldier did, that would interest and astonish you much more than the narration of my own tale.

To go on with my story; the courtyard of our prison was overlooked by the windows of the house belonging to a wealthy Moor of high position ; and these, as is usual in Moorish houses, were rather loopholes than windows, and besides were covered with thick and close blinds. It so happened, then, that as I was one day on the terrace of our prison with three other comrades, trying, to pass away the time, how far we could leap with our chains, we being alone, for all the other Christians had gone out to work, I chanced to raise my eyes, and from one of these little closed windows I saw a reed appear with a cloth attached to the end of it, and it kept waving to and fro, and moving as if making signs to us to come and take it. We watched it, and one of those who were with me went and stood under the reed to see whether they would let it drop, or what they would do, but as he did so the reed was raised and moved from side to side, as if they meant to say 'no' by a shake of the head. The Christian came back, and it was again lowered, making the same movements as before. Another of my comrades went, and with him the same happened as with the first, and then the third went forward, but with the same result as the first and second. Seeing this I did not like not to try my luck, and as soon as I came under the reed it was dropped and fell inside the baño at my feet. I hastened to untie the cloth, in which I perceived a knot, and in this were ten

[1] See Note D, p. 240.

cianis, which are coins of base gold, current among the Moors, and each worth ten reals of our money.

It is needless to say I rejoiced over this godsend, and my joy was not less than my wonder as I strove to imagine how this good fortune could have come to us, but to me specially ; for the evident unwillingness to drop the reed for any but me showed that it was for me the favour was intended. I took my welcome money, broke the reed, and returned to the terrace, and looking up at the window, I saw a very white hand put out that opened and shut very quickly. From this we gathered or fancied that it must be some woman living in that house that had done us this kindness, and to show that we were grateful for it, we made salaams after the fashion of the Moors, bowing the head, bending the body, and crossing the arms on the breast. Shortly afterwards at the same window a small cross made of reeds was put out and immediately withdrawn. This sign led us to believe that some Christian woman was a captive in the house, and that it was she who had been so good to us ; but the whiteness of the hand and the bracelets we had perceived made us dismiss that idea, though we thought it might be one of the Christian renegades whom their masters very often take as lawful wives, and gladly, for they prefer them to the women of their own nation. In all our conjectures we were wide of the truth ; so from that time forward our sole occupation was watching and gazing at the window where the cross had appeared to us, as if it were our pole-star ; but at least fifteen days passed without our seeing either it or the hand, or any other sign whatever ; and though meanwhile we endeavoured with the utmost pains to ascertain who it was that lived in the house, and whether there were any Christian renegade in it, nobody could ever tell us anything more than that he who lived there was a rich Moor of high position, Hadji Morato by name, formerly alcaide of La Pata,[1] an office of high dignity among them. But when we least thought it was going to rain any more cianis from that quarter, we saw the reed suddenly appear with another cloth tied in a larger knot attached to it, and this at a

_____
[1] La Pata, a fort near Oran.

time when, as on the former occasion, the baño was deserted and unoccupied.

We made trial as before, each of the same three going forward before I did ; but the reed was delivered to none but me, and on my approach it was let drop. I untied the knot and I found forty Spanish gold crowns with a paper written in Arabic, and at the end of the writing there was a large cross drawn. I kissed the cross, took the crowns and returned to the terrace, and we all made our salaams ; again the hand appeared, I made signs that I would read the paper, and then the window was closed. We were all puzzled, though filled with joy at what had taken place ; and as none of us understood Arabic, great was our curiosity to know what the paper contained, and still greater the difficulty of finding some one to read it. At last I resolved to confide in a renegade, a native of Murcia, who professed a very great friendship for me, and had given pledges that bound him to keep any secret I might entrust to him ; for it is the custom with some renegades, when they intend to return to Christian territory, to carry about them certificates from captives of mark testifying, in whatever form they can, that such and such a renegade is a worthy man who has always shown kindness to Christians, and is anxious to escape on the first opportunity that may present itself. Some obtain these testimonials with good intentions, others put them to a cunning use ; for when they go to pillage on Christian territory, if they chance to be cast away, or taken prisoners, they produce their certificates and say that from these papers may be seen the object they came for, which was to remain on Christian ground, and that it was to this end they joined the Turks in their foray. In this way they escape the consequences of the first outburst and make their peace with the Church before it does them any harm, and then when they have the chance they return to Barbary to become what they were before. Others, however, there are who procure these papers and make use of them honestly, and remain on Christian soil. This friend of mine, then, was one of these renegades that I have described ; he had certificates from all our comrades, in which we testified in his favour as strongly as we could ; and if the Moors had found the papers they would have burned him alive.

I knew that he understood Arabic very well, and could not only speak but also write it ; but before I disclosed the whole matter to him, I asked him to read for me this paper which I had found by accident in a hole in my cell. He opened it and remained some time examining it and muttering to himself as he translated it. I asked him if he understood it, and he told me he did perfectly well, and that if I wished him to tell me its meaning word for word, I must give him pen and ink that he might do it more satisfactorily. We at once gave him what he required, and he set about translating it bit by bit, and when he had done he said, ' All that is here in Spanish is what the Moorish paper contains, and you must bear in mind that when it says " Lela Marien " it means " Our Lady the Virgin Mary." ' We read the paper and it ran thus :

' When I was a child my father had a slave who taught me to pray the Christian prayer in my own language, and told me many things about Lela Marien. The Christian died, and I know that she did not go to the fire, but to Allah, because since then I have seen her twice, and she told me to go to the land of the Christians to see Lela Marien, who had great love for me. I know not how to go. I have seen many Christians, but except thyself none has seemed to me to be a gentleman. I am young and beautiful, and have plenty of money to take with me. See if thou canst contrive how we may go, and if thou wilt thou shalt be my husband there, and if thou wilt not it will not distress me, for Lela Marien will find me some one to marry me. I myself have written this : have a care to whom thou givest it to read : trust no Moor, for they are all perfidious. I am greatly troubled on this account, for I would not have thee confide in anyone, because if my father knew it he would at once fling me down a well and cover me with stones. I will put a thread to the reed ; tie the answer to it, and if thou hast no one to write for thee in Arabic, tell it to me by signs, for Lela Marien will make me understand thee. She and Allah and this cross, which I often kiss as the captive bade me, protect thee.'

Judge, sirs, whether we had reason for surprise and joy at the words of this paper; and both one and the other were so great, that the renegade perceived that the paper had not been found by chance, but had been in reality addressed to some one of us, and he begged us, if what he suspected were the truth, to trust him and tell him all, for he would risk his life for our freedom; and so saying he took out from his breast a metal crucifix, and with many tears swore by the God the image represented, in whom, sinful and wicked as he was, he truly and faithfully believed, to be loyal to us and keep secret whatever we chose to reveal to him; for he thought and almost foresaw that by means of her who had written that paper, he and all of us would obtain our liberty, and he himself obtain the object he so much desired, his restoration to the bosom of the Holy Mother Church, from which by his own sin and ignorance he was now severed like a corrupt limb. The renegade said this with so many tears and such signs of repentance, that with one consent we all agreed to tell him the whole truth of the matter, and so we gave him a full account of all, without hiding anything from him. We pointed out to him the window at which the reed appeared, and he by that means took note of the house, and resolved to ascertain with particular care who lived in it. We agreed also that it would be advisable to answer the Moorish lady's letter, and the renegade without a moment's delay took down the words I dictated to him, which were exactly what I shall tell you, for nothing of importance that took place in this affair has escaped my memory, or ever will while life lasts. This, then, was the answer returned to the Moorish lady :

' The true Allah protect thee, Lady, and that blessed Marien who is the true mother of God, and who has put it into thy heart to go to the land of the Christians, because she loves thee. Entreat her that she be pleased to show thee how thou canst execute the command she gives thee, for she will, such is her goodness. On my own part, and on that of all these

Christians who are with me, I promise to do all that we can for thee, even to death. Fail not to write to me and inform me what thou dost mean to do, and I will always answer thee; for the great Allah has given us a Christian captive who can speak and write thy language well, as thou mayest see by this paper; without fear, therefore, thou canst inform us of all thou wouldst. As to what thou sayest, that if thou dost reach the land of the Christians thou wilt be my wife, I give thee my promise upon it as a good Christian; and know that the Christians keep their promises better than the Moors. Allah and Marien his mother watch over thee, my Lady.'

The paper being written and folded I waited two days until the baño was empty as before, and immediately repaired to the usual walk on the terrace to see if there were any sign of the reed, which was not long in making its appearance. As soon as I saw it, although I could not distinguish who put it out, I showed the paper as a sign to attach the thread, but it was already fixed to the reed, and to it I tied the paper; and shortly afterwards our star once more made its appearance with the white flag of peace, the little bundle. It was dropped, and I picked it up, and found in the cloth, in gold and silver coins of all sorts, more than fifty crowns, which fifty times more doubled our joy and strengthened our hope of gaining our liberty. That very night our renegade returned and said he had learned that the Moor we had been told of lived in that house, that his name was Hadji Morato, that he was enormously rich, that he had one only daughter the heiress of all his wealth, and that it was the general opinion throughout the city that she was the most beautiful woman in Barbary, and that several of the viceroys who came there had sought her for a wife, but that she had been always unwilling to marry; and he had learned, moreover, that she had a Christian slave who was now dead; all which agreed with the contents of the paper. We immediately took counsel with the renegade as to what means would have to be adopted in order to carry off the Moorish lady and bring us all to Christian territory; and in the end it was agreed that for the present we should wait for a second communication from Zoraida (for that was the name of her who now desires to be called Maria), because we saw clearly that she and no one else could find a way out of all these difficulties. When we had decided upon this the renegade told us not to be uneasy, for he would lose his life or restore us to liberty. For four days the baño was filled with people, for which reason the reed delayed its appearance for four days, but at the end of that time, when the baño was, as it generally was, empty, it appeared with the cloth so bulky that it promised a happy birth. Reed and cloth came down to me, and I found another paper and a hundred crowns in gold, without any other coin. The renegade was present, and in our cell we gave him the paper to read, which he said was to this effect :

'I cannot think of a plan, señor, for our going to Spain, nor has Lela Marien shown me one, though I have asked her. All that can be done is for me to give you plenty of money in gold from this window. With it ransom yourself and your friends, and let one of you go to the land of the Christians, and there buy a vessel and come back for the others ; and he will find me in my father's garden, which is at the Babazon gate [1] near the sea-shore, where I shall be all this summer with my father and my servants. You can carry me away from there by night without any danger, and bring me to the vessel. And remember thou art to be my husband, else I will pray to Marien to punish thee. If thou canst not trust anyone to go for the vessel, ransom thyself and do thou go, for I know thou wilt return more surely than any other, as thou art a gentleman and a Christian. Endeavour to make thyself acquainted with the garden ; and when I see thee walking yonder I shall know that the baño is empty and I will give thee abundance of money. Allah protect thee, señor.'

These were the words and contents of the second paper, and on hearing them, each declared himself willing to be the ransomed one, and promised to go and return with scrupulous good faith ; and I too made the same offer ; but to all this the renegade objected, saying that he would not on any account consent

---

[1] Babazoun, 'the gate of the sheep,' the south gate of Algiers.

to one being set free before all went together, as experience had taught him how ill those who have been set free keep promises which they made in captivity; for captives of distinction frequently had recourse to this plan, paying the ransom of one who was to go to Valencia or Majorca with money to enable him to arm a bark and return for the others who had ransomed him; but who never came back; for recovered liberty and the dread of losing it again efface from the memory all the obligations in the world. And to prove the truth of what he said, he told us briefly what had happened to a certain Christian gentleman almost at that very time, the strangest case that had ever occurred even there, where astonishing and marvellous things are happening every instant. In short, he ended by saying that what could and ought to be done was to give the money intended for the ransom of one of us Christians to him, so that he might with it buy a vessel there in Algiers under the pretence of becoming a merchant and trading to Tetuan and along the coast; and when master of the vessel, it would be easy for him to hit on some way of getting us all out of the baño and putting us on board; especially if the Moorish lady gave, as she said, money enough to ransom all, because once free it would be the easiest thing in the world for us to embark even in open day; but the greatest difficulty was that the Moors do not allow any renegade to buy or own any craft, unless it be a large vessel for going on roving expeditions, because they are afraid that anyone who buys a small vessel, especially if he be a Spaniard, only wants it for the purpose of escaping to Christian territory. This however he could get over by arranging with a Tagarin Moor to go shares with him in the purchase of the vessel and in the profit on the cargo; and under cover of this he could become master of the vessel, in which case he looked upon all the rest as accomplished. But though to me and my comrades it had seemed a better plan to send to Majorca for the vessel, as the Moorish lady suggested, we did not dare to oppose him, fearing that if we did not do as he said he would denounce us, and place us in danger of losing all our lives if he were to disclose our dealings with Zoraida, for whose life we would have all given our own. We therefore resolved to put ourselves in the hands of God and in the rene-gade's; and at the same time an answer was given to Zoraida, telling her that we would do all she recommended, for she had given as good advice as if Lela Marien had delivered it, and that it depended on her alone whether we were to defer the business or put it in execution at once. I renewed my promise to be her husband; and thus the next day that the baño chanced to be empty she at different times gave us by means of the reed and cloth two thousand gold crowns and a paper in which she said that the next Jumá, that is to say Friday, she was going to her father's garden, but that before she went she would give us more money; and if it were not enough we were to let her know, as she would give us as much as we asked, for her father had so much he would not miss it, and besides she kept all the keys.

We at once gave the renegade five hundred crowns to buy the vessel, and with eight hundred I ransomed myself, giving the money to a Valencian merchant who happened to be in Algiers at the time, and who had me released on his word, pledging it that on the arrival of the first ship from Valencia he would pay my ransom; for if he had given the money at once it would have made the king suspect that my ransom money had been for a long time in Algiers, and that the merchant had for his own advantage kept it secret. In fact my master was so difficult to deal with that I dared not on any account pay down the money at once. The Thursday before the Friday on which the fair Zoraida was to go to the garden she gave us a thousand crowns more, and warned us of her departure, begging me, if I were ransomed, to find out her father's garden at once, and by all means to seek an opportunity of going there to see her. I answered in a few words that I would do so, and that she must remember to com-mend us to Lela Marien with all the prayers the captive had taught her. This having been done, steps were taken to ransom our three comrades, so as to enable them to quit the baño, and lest, seeing me ransomed and themselves not, though the money was forthcoming, they should make a disturbance about it and the devil should prompt them to do something that might injure Zoraida; for though their position might be sufficient to relieve me from this apprehension, nevertheless I was unwilling to run any risk in the matter; and so I had them ransomed in the same way as I was, handing over all the money to the merchant so that he might with safety and confidence give security; without, however, confiding our arrangement and secret to him, which might have been dangerous.

Note A (*page* 227).

Clemencin says the merits of this sonnet are slender, and that the next is no better. He particularly objects to the idea of *souls* dyeing the sea with their *blood*. But Clemencin has no bowels of compassion for the straits of a sonneteer.

Note B (*page* 230).

The story of the captive, it is needless to say, is not the story of Cervantes himself; but it is coloured throughout by his own experiences, and he himself speaks in the person of the captive. In the above passage, for example, we have an expression of the indomitable spirit that supported him, not only in captivity, but in the struggles of his later life.

Note C (*page* 230).

The barrack or building in which slaves were kept. Littré explains it by saying that a 'bath'—*bagne, baño*—was on one occasion used as a place of confinement for Christian slaves at Constantinople. Condé, on the other hand, says the word has nothing to do with *baño*—bath, but is pure Arabic, and means a building coated with plaster or stucco.

Note D (*page* 231).

This 'tal de Saavedra' was of course Cervantes himself. The story of his captivity and adventures had been already written by Haedo, but did not appear in print till 1612. Rodrigo Mendez Silva was so much struck by it that he mentions Cervantes as the most remarkable of the descendants of Nuño Alfonso; but, strange to say, though he wrote in 1648, he does not seem to be aware that he is speaking of the author of *Don Quixote*. Perhaps the good Dryasdust had never heard of such a book.

CHAPTER XLI.

IN WHICH THE CAPTIVE STILL CONTINUES HIS ADVENTURES.

BEFORE fifteen days were over our renegade had already purchased an excellent vessel with room for more than thirty
persons; and to make the transaction safe and lend a colour
to it, he thought it well to make, as he did, a voyage to a place
called Shershel, twenty leagues from Algiers on the Oran side,
where there is an extensive trade in dried figs. Two or three times
he made this voyage in company with the Tagarin already mentioned. The Moors of Aragon are called Tagarins in Barbary,
and those of Granada Mudéjars; but in the Kingdom of Fez they
call the Mudéjars Elches, and they are the people the king
chiefly employs in war. To proceed: every time he passed with
his vessel he anchored in a cove that was not two cross-bow
shots from the garden where Zoraida was waiting; and there the
renegade, together with the two Moorish lads that rowed, used
purposely to station himself, either going through his prayers, or
else practising as a part what he meant to perform in earnest.
And thus he would go to Zoraida's garden and ask for fruit, which
her father gave him, not knowing him; but though, as he afterwards told me, he sought to speak to Zoraida, and tell her who
he was, and that by my orders he was to take her to the land of
the Christians, so that she might feel satisfied and easy, he had
never been able to do so; for the Moorish women do not allow
themselves to be seen by any Moor or Turk, unless their husband
or father bid them: with Christian captives they permit freedom of intercourse and communication, even more than might
be considered proper. But for my part I should have been sorry

if he had spoken to her, for perhaps it might have alarmed her to find her affairs talked of by renegades. But God, who ordered it otherwise, afforded no opportunity for our renegade's well-meant purpose ; and he, seeing how safely he could go to Shershel and return, and anchor when and how and where he liked, and that the Tagarin his partner had no will but his, and that, now I was ransomed, all we wanted was to find some Christians to row, told me to look out for any I should be willing to take with me, over and above those who had been ransomed, and to engage them for the next Friday, which he fixed upon for our departure. On this I spoke to twelve Spaniards, all stout rowers, and such as could most easily leave the city; but it was no easy matter to find so many just then, because there were twenty ships out on a cruise and they had taken all the rowers with them ; and these would not have been found were it not that their master remained at home that summer without going to sea in order to finish a galliot that he had upon the stocks. To these men I said nothing more than that the next Friday in the evening they were to come out stealthily one by one and hang about Hadji Morato's garden, waiting for me there until I came. These directions I gave each one separately, with orders that if they saw any other Christians there they were not to say anything to them except that I had directed them to wait at that spot.

This preliminary having been settled, another still more necessary step had to be taken, which was to let Zoraida know how matters stood that she might be prepared and forewarned, so as not to be taken by surprise if we were suddenly to seize upon her before she thought the Christians' vessel could have returned. I determined, therefore, to go to the garden and try if I could speak to her ; and the day before my departure I went there under the pretence of gathering herbs. The first person I met was her father, who addressed me in the language that all over Barbary and even in Constantinople is the medium between captives and Moors, and is neither Morisco nor Castilian, nor of any other nation, but a mixture of all languages, by means of which we can all understand one another. In this sort of language, I say, he asked me what I wanted in his garden, and to whom I belonged. I replied that I was a slave of the Arnaut Mami [1] (for I knew as a certainty that he was a very great friend of his), and that I wanted some herbs to make a salad. He asked me then whether I were on ransom or not, and what my master demanded for me. While these questions and answers were proceeding, the fair Zoraida, who had already perceived me some time before, came out of the house in the garden, and as Moorish women are by no means particular about letting themselves be seen by Christians, or, as I have said before, at all coy, she had no hesitation in coming to where her father stood with me ; moreover her father, seeing her approaching slowly, called to her to come. It would be beyond my power now to describe to you the great beauty, the high-bred air, the rich brilliant attire of my beloved Zoraida as she presented herself before my eyes. I will content myself with saying that more pearls hung from her fair neck, her ears, and her hair than she had hairs on her head. On her ankles, which as is customary were bare, she had carcajes (for so bracelets or anklets are called in Morisco) of the purest gold, set with so many diamonds that she told me afterwards her father valued them at ten thousand doubloons, and those she had on her wrists were worth as much more. The pearls were in profusion and very fine, for the highest display and adornment of the Moorish women is decking themselves with rich pearls and seed-pearls ; and of these there are therefore more among the Moors than among any other people. Zoraida's father had the reputation of possessing a great number, and the purest in all Algiers, and of possessing also more than two hundred thousand Spanish crowns; and she, who is now mistress of me only, was mistress of all this. Whether thus adorned she would have been beautiful or not, and what she must have been in her prosperity, may be imagined from the beauty remaining to her after so many hardships ; for, as everyone knows, the beauty of some women has its times and its seasons, and is increased or diminished by chance causes ; and

---

[1] See Note A, p. 261.

naturally the emotions of the mind will heighten or impair it, though indeed more frequently they totally destroy it. In a word she presented herself before me that day attired with the utmost splendour, and supremely beautiful; at any rate, she seemed to me the most beautiful object I had ever seen; and when, besides, I thought of all I owed to her I felt as though I had before me some heavenly being come to earth to bring me relief and happiness.

As she approached her father told her in his own language that I was a captive belonging to his friend the Arnaut Mami, and that I had come for salad.

She took up the conversation, and in that mixture of tongues I have spoken of she asked me if I was a gentleman, and why I was not ransomed.

I answered that I was already ransomed, and that by the price it might be seen what value my master set on me, as they had given one thousand five hundred zoltanis [1] for me; to which she replied, ' Hadst thou been my father's, I can tell thee, I would not have let him part with thee for twice as much, for you Christians always tell lies about yourselves and make yourselves out poor to cheat the Moors.'

' That may be, lady,' said I; ' but indeed I dealt truthfully with my master, as I do and mean to do with everybody in the world.'

' And when dost thou go ? ' said Zoraida.

' To-morrow, I think,' said I, ' for there is a vessel here from France which sails to-morrow, and I think I shall go in her.'

' Would it not be better,' said Zoraida, ' to wait for the arrival of ships from Spain and go with them and not with the French who are not your friends ? '

' No,' said I; ' though if there were intelligence that a vessel were now coming from Spain it is true I might, perhaps, wait for it; however, it is more likely I shall depart to-morrow, for the longing I feel to return to my country and to those I love is

---

[1] An Algerine coin equal to about thirty-six reals.

so great that it will not allow me to wait for another opportunity, however more convenient, if it be delayed.'

'No doubt thou art married in thine own country,' said Zoraida, 'and for that reason thou art anxious to go and see thy wife.'

'I am not married,' I replied, 'but I have given my promise to marry on my arrival there.'

'And is the lady beautiful to whom thou hast given it?' said Zoraida.

'So beautiful,' said I, 'that, to describe her worthily and tell thee the truth, she is very like thee.'

At this her father laughed very heartily and said, 'By Allah, Christian, she must be very beautiful if she is like my daughter, who is the most beautiful woman in all this kingdom : only look at her well and thou wilt see I am telling the truth.'

Zoraida's father as the better linguist helped to interpret most of these words and phrases, for though she spoke the bastard language, that, as I have said, is employed there, she expressed her meaning more by signs than by words.

While we were still engaged in this conversation, a Moor came running up, exclaiming that four Turks had leaped over the fence or wall of the garden, and were gathering the fruit, though it was not yet ripe. The old man was alarmed and Zoraida too, for the Moors commonly, and, so to speak, instinctively have a dread of the Turks, but particularly of the soldiers, who are so insolent and domineering to the Moors who are under their power that they treat them worse than if they were their slaves. So her father said to Zoraida, 'Daughter, retire into the house and shut thyself in while I go and speak to these dogs ; and thou, Christian, pick thy herbs, and go in peace, and Allah bring thee safe to thy own country.'

I bowed, and he went away to look for the Turks, leaving me alone with Zoraida, who made as if she were about to retire as her father bade her ; but the moment he was concealed by the trees of the garden, turning to me with her eyes full of tears she said, ' Tameji, cristiano, tameji ? ' that is to say, ' Art thou going, Christian, art thou going ? '

I made answer, ' Yes, lady, but not without thee, come what may : be on the watch for me on the next Jumá, and be not alarmed when thou seest us ; for most surely we shall go to the land of the Christians.'

This I said in such a way that she understood perfectly all that passed between us, and throwing her arm round my neck she began with feeble steps to move towards the house ; but as fate would have it (and it might have been very unfortunate if Heaven had not otherwise ordered it), just as we were moving on in the manner and position I have described, with her arm round my neck, her father, as he returned after having sent away the Turks, saw how we were walking and we perceived that he saw us ; but Zoraida, ready and quick-witted, took care not to remove her arm from my neck, but on the contrary drew closer to me and laid her head on my breast, bending her knees a little and show- ing all the signs and tokens of fainting, while I at the same time made it seem as though I were supporting her against my will. Her father came running up to where we were, and seeing his daughter in this state asked what was the matter with her ; she, however, giving no answer, he said, ' No doubt she has fainted in alarm at the entrance of those dogs,' and taking her from mine he drew her to his own breast, while she sighing, her eyes still wet with tears, said again, ' Ameji, cristiano, ameji '—' Go, Christian, go.' To this her father replied, ' There is no need, daughter, for the Christian to go, for he has done thee no harm, and the Turks have now gone ; feel no alarm, there is nothing to hurt thee, for as I say, the Turks at my request have gone back the way they came.'

' It was they who terrified her, as thou hast said, señor,' said I to her father ; ' but since she tells me to go, I have no wish to displease her : peace be with thee, and with thy leave I will come back to this garden for herbs if need be, for my master says there are nowhere better herbs for salad than here.'

' Come back for any thou hast need of,' replied Hadji Morato ;

' for my daughter does not speak thus because she is displeased with thee or any Christian : she only meant that the Turks should go, not thou ; or that it was time for thee to look for thy herbs.'

With this I at once took my leave of both ; and she, looking as though her heart were breaking, retired with her father. While pretending to look for herbs I made the round of the garden at my ease, and studied carefully all the approaches and outlets, and the fastenings of the house and everything that could be taken advantage of to make our task easy. Having done so I went and gave an account of all that had taken place to the renegade and my comrades, and looked forward with impatience to the hour when, all fear at an end, I should find myself in possession of the prize which fortune held out to me in the fair and lovely Zoraida. The time passed at length, and the appointed day we so longed for arrived ; and, all following out the arrangement and plan which, after careful consideration and many a long discussion, we had decided upon, we succeeded as fully as we could have wished ; for on the Friday following the day upon which I spoke to Zoraida in the garden, the renegade anchored his vessel at nightfall almost opposite the spot where she was. The Christians who were to row were ready and in hiding in different places round about, all waiting for me, anxious and elated, and eager to attack the vessel they had before their eyes ; for they did not know the renegade's plan, but expected that they were to gain their liberty by force of arms and by killing the Moors who were on board the vessel. As soon, then, as I and my comrades made our appearance, all those that were in hiding seeing us came and joined us. It was now the time when the city gates are shut, and there was no one to be seen in all the space outside. When we were collected together we debated whether it would be better first to go for Zoraida, or to make prisoners of the Moorish rowers who rowed in the vessel ; but while we were still uncertain our renegade came up asking us what kept us, as it was now the time, and all the Moors were off their guard and most of them asleep. We told him why we hesitated, but he said it was of more importance first to secure the vessel, which could be done with the greatest ease and without any danger, and then we could go for Zoraida. We all approved of what he said, and so without further delay, guided by him we made for the vessel, and he leaping on board first, drew his cutlass and said in Morisco, 'Let no one stir from this if he does not want it to cost him his life.' By this almost all the Christians were on board, and the Moors, who were fainthearted, hearing their captain speak in this way, were cowed, and without any one of them taking to his arms (and indeed they had few or hardly any) they submitted without saying a word to be bound by the Christians, who quickly secured them, threatening them that if they raised any kind of outcry they would be all put to the sword. This having been accomplished, and half of our party being left to keep guard over them, the rest of us, again taking the renegade as our guide, hastened towards Hadji Morato's garden, and as good luck would have it, on trying the gate it opened as easily as if it had not been locked ; and so, quite quietly and in silence, we reached the house without being perceived by anybody. The lovely Zoraida was watching for us at a window, and as soon as she perceived that there were people there, she asked in a low voice if we were ' Nizarani,' as much as to say or ask if we were Christians. I answered that we were, and begged her to come down. As soon as she recognised me she did not delay an instant, but without answering a word came down immediately, opened the door and presented herself before us all, so beautiful and so richly attired that I cannot attempt to describe her. The moment I saw her I took her hand and kissed it, and the renegade and my two comrades did the same ; and the rest, who knew nothing of the circumstances, did as they saw us do, for it only seemed as if we were returning thanks to her, and recognising her as the giver of our liberty. The renegade asked her in the Morisco language if her father was in the house. She replied that he was and that he was asleep.

'Then it will be necessary to waken him and take him with us,' said the renegade, 'and everything of value in this fair mansion.'

'Nay,' said she, 'my father must not on any account be touched, and there is nothing in the house except what I shall take, and that will be quite enough to enrich and satisfy all of you; wait a little and you shall see,' and so saying she went in again, telling us she would return immediately, and bidding us keep quiet without making any noise.

I asked the renegade what had passed between them, and when he told me, I declared that nothing should be done except in accordance with the wishes of Zoraida, who now came back with a little trunk so full of gold crowns that she could scarcely carry it. Unfortunately her father awoke while this was going on, and hearing a noise in the garden, came to the window, and at once perceiving that all those who were there were Christians, raising a prodigiously loud outcry, he began to call out in Arabic, 'Christians, Christians! thieves, thieves!' by which cries we were all thrown into the greatest fear and embarrassment; but the renegade seeing the danger we were in and how important it was for him to effect his purpose before we were heard, mounted with the utmost quickness to where Hadji Morato was, and with him went some of our party; I, however, did not dare to leave Zoraida, who had fallen almost fainting in my arms. To be brief, those who had gone upstairs acted so promptly that in an instant they came down, carrying Hadji Morato with his hands bound and a napkin tied over his mouth, which prevented him from uttering a word, warning him at the same time that to attempt to speak would cost him his life. When his daughter caught sight of him she covered her eyes so as not to see him, and her father was horror-stricken, not knowing how willingly she had placed herself in our hands. But it was now most essential for us to be on the move, and carefully and quickly we regained the vessel, where those who had remained on board were waiting for us in apprehension of some mishap having befallen us. It was barely two hours after night set in when we were all on board the vessel, where the cords were removed from the hands of Zoraida's father, and the napkin from his mouth; but the renegade once more told him not to utter a word, or they

would take his life. He, when he saw his daughter there, began
to sigh piteously, and still more when he perceived that I held
her closely embraced and that she lay quiet without resisting
or complaining, or showing any reluctance ; nevertheless he
remained silent lest they should carry into effect the repeated
threats the renegade had addressed to him.

Finding herself now on board, and that we were about to give
way with the oars, Zoraida, seeing her father there, and the other
Moors bound, bade the renegade ask me to do her the favour of
releasing the Moors and setting her father at liberty, for she
would rather drown herself in the sea than suffer a father that
had loved her so dearly to be carried away captive before her
eyes and on her account. The renegade repeated this to me,
and I replied that I was very willing to do so ; but he replied
that it was not advisable, because if they were left there they
would at once raise the country and stir up the city, and lead to
the despatch of swift cruisers in pursuit, and our being taken,
by sea or land, without any possibility of escape ; and that all
that could be done was to set them free on the first Christian
ground we reached. On this point we all agreed ; and Zoraida,
to whom it was explained, together with the reasons that prevented us from doing at once what she desired, was satisfied
likewise ; and then in glad silence and with cheerful alacrity
each of our stout rowers took his oar, and commending ourselves
to God with all our hearts, we began to shape our course for the
island of Majorca, the nearest Christian land. Owing, however, to the Tramontana[1] rising a little, and the sea growing
somewhat rough, it was impossible for us to keep a straight
course for Majorca, and we were compelled to coast in the direction of Oran, not without great uneasiness on our part lest we
should be observed from the town of Shershel, which lies on that
coast, not more than sixty miles from Algiers. Moreover we
were afraid of meeting on that course one of the galliots that
usually come with goods from Tetuan ; although each of us for
himself and all of us together felt confident that, if we were to

[1] A wind from the north, so called from coming across the Alps.

meet a merchant galliot, so that it were not a cruiser, not only should we not be lost, but that we should take a vessel in which we could more safely accomplish our voyage. As we pursued our course Zoraida kept her head between my hands so as not to see her father, and I felt that she was praying to Lela Marien to help us.

We might have made about thirty miles when daybreak found us some three musket-shots off the land, which seemed to us deserted, and without anyone to see us. For all that, however, by hard rowing we put out a little to sea, for it was now somewhat calmer, and having gained about two leagues the word was given to row by batches, while we ate something, for the vessel was well provided; but the rowers said it was not a time to take any rest; let food be served out to those who were not rowing, but they would not leave their oars on any account. This was done, but now a stiff breeze began to blow, which obliged us to leave off rowing and make sail at once and steer for Oran, as it was impossible to make any other course. All this was done very promptly, and under sail we ran more than eight miles an hour without any fear, except that of coming across some vessel out on a roving expedition. We gave the Moorish rowers some food, and the renegade comforted them by telling them that they were not held as captives, as we should set them free on the first opportunity.

The same was said to Zoraida's father, who replied, ' Anything else, O Christian, I might hope for or think likely from your generosity and good behaviour, but do not think me so simple as to imagine you will give me my liberty; for you would have never exposed yourselves to the danger of depriving me of it only to restore it to me so generously, especially as you know who I am and the sum you may expect to receive on restoring it; and if you will only name that, I here offer you all you require for myself and for my unhappy daughter there; or else for her alone, for she is the greatest and most precious part of my soul.'

As he said this he began to weep so bitterly that he filled us all with compassion and forced Zoraida to look at him, and when

she saw him weeping she was so moved that she rose from my
feet and ran to throw her arms round him, and pressing her
face to his, they both gave way to such an outburst of tears that
several of us were constrained to keep them company.

But when her father saw her in full dress and with all her
jewels about her, he said to her in his own language, 'What
means this, my daughter ?   Last night, before this terrible
misfortune in which we are plunged befell us, I saw thee in thy
everyday and indoor garments ; and now, without having had
time to attire thyself, and without my bringing thee any joyful
tidings to furnish an occasion for adorning and bedecking thyself,
I see thee arrayed in the finest attire it would be in my power to
give thee when fortune was most kind to us.   Answer me this ;
for it causes me greater anxiety and surprise than even this misfortune itself.'

The renegade interpreted to us what the Moor said to his
daughter ; she, however, returned him no answer.   But when he
observed in one corner of the vessel the little trunk in which she
used to keep her jewels, which he well knew he had left in
Algiers and had not brought to the garden, he was still more
amazed, and asked her how that trunk had come into our hands,
and what there was in it.   To which the renegade, without
waiting for Zoraida to reply, made answer, ' Do not trouble
thyself by asking thy daughter Zoraida so many questions,
señor, for the one answer I will give thee will serve for all ;
I would have thee know that she is a Christian, and that it is
she who has been the file for our chains and our deliverer from
captivity.   She is here of her own free will, as glad, I imagine,
to find herself in this position as he who escapes from darkness
into the light, from death to life, and from suffering to glory.'

'Daughter, is this true, what he says ? ' cried the Moor.

'It is,' replied Zoraida.

'That thou art in truth a Christian,' said the old man, 'and
that thou hast given thy father into the power of his enemies ? '

To which Zoraida made answer, ' A Christian I am, but it is
not I who have placed thee in this position, for it never was my

wish to leave thee or do thee harm, but only to do good to myself.'

'And what good hast thou done thyself, daughter ? ' said he.

'Ask thou that,' said she, 'of Lela Marien, for she can tell thee better than I.'

The Moor had hardly heard these words when with marvellous quickness he flung himself head-foremost into the sea, where no doubt he would have been drowned had not the long and full dress he wore held him up for a little on the surface of the water. Zoraida cried aloud to us to save him, and we all hastened to help, and seizing him by his robe we drew him in half-drowned and insensible, at which Zoraida was in such distress that she wept over him as piteously and bitterly as though he were already dead. We turned him upon his face and he voided a great quantity of water, and at the end of two hours came to himself. Meanwhile, the wind having changed we were compelled to head for the land, and ply our oars to avoid being driven on shore ; but it was our good fortune to make a cove that lies on one side of a small promontory or cape, called by the Moors that of the 'Cava rumia,' which in our language means ' the wicked Christian woman ; ' for it is a tradition among them that La Cava, through whom Spain was lost, lies buried at that spot ; ' cava ' in their language meaning ' wicked woman,' and ' rumia ' ' Christian ; '[1] moreover, they count it unlucky to anchor there when necessity compels them, and they never do so otherwise. For us, however, it was not the resting-place of the wicked woman but a haven of safety for our relief, so much had the sea now got up. We posted a look-out on shore, and never let the oars out of our hands, and ate of the stores the renegade had laid in, imploring God and Our Lady with all our hearts to help and protect us, that we might give a happy ending to a beginning so prosperous. At the entreaty of Zoraida orders were given to set

---

[1] Cervantes gives the popular name by which the spot is known. Properly it is 'Kubba Rumia,' ' the Christian's tomb ; ' that being the name given to the curious circular structure about which there has been so much discussion among French archæologists.

on shore her father and the other Moors who were still bound, for she could not endure, nor could her tender heart bear to see her father in bonds and her fellow-countrymen prisoners before her eyes. We promised her to do this at the moment of departure, for as it was uninhabited we ran no risk in releasing them at that place.

Our prayers were not so far in vain as to be unheard by Heaven, for the wind immediately changed in our favour, and the sea grew calm, inviting us once more to resume our voyage with a good heart. Seeing this we unbound the Moors, and one by one put them on shore, at which they were filled with amazement; but when we came to land Zoraida's father, who had now completely recovered his senses, he said, ' Why is it, think ye, Christians, that this wicked woman is rejoiced at your giving me my liberty? Think ye it is because of the affection she bears me? Nay verily, it is only because of the hindrance my presence offers to the execution of her base designs. And think not that it is her belief that yours is better than ours that has led her to change her religion ; it is only because she knows that immodesty is more freely practised in your country than in ours.' Then turning to Zoraida, while I and another of the Christians held him fast by both arms, lest he should do some mad act, he said to her, ' Infamous girl, misguided maiden, whither in thy blindness and madness art thou going in the hands of these dogs, our natural enemies ? Cursed be the hour when I begot thee ! Cursed the luxury and indulgence in which I reared thee ! ' But seeing that he was not likely soon to cease I made haste to put him on shore, and thence he continued his maledictions and lamentations aloud ; calling on Mohammed to pray to Allah to destroy us, to confound us, to make an end of us ; and when, in consequence of having made sail, we could no longer hear what he said we could see what he did ; how he plucked out his beard and tore his hair and lay writhing on the ground. But once he raised his voice to such a pitch that we were able to hear what he said. ' Come back, dear daughter, come back to shore ; I forgive thee all ; let those men have the money, for it is theirs now, and come back to comfort thy sorrowing father, who will yield up his life on this barren strand if thou dost leave him.'

All this Zoraida heard, and heard with sorrow and tears, and all she could say in answer was, ' Allah grant that Lela Marien, who has made me become a Christian, give thee comfort in thy sorrow, O my father. Allah knows that I could not do otherwise than I have done, and that these Christians owe nothing to my will; for even had I wished not to accompany them, but remain at home, it would have been impossible for me, so eagerly did my soul urge me on to the accomplishment of this purpose, which I feel to be as righteous as to thee, dear father, it seems wicked.'

But neither could her father hear her nor we see him when she said this; and so, while I consoled Zoraida, we turned our attention to our voyage, in which a breeze from the right point so favoured us that we made sure of finding ourselves off the coast of Spain on the morrow by daybreak. But, as good seldom or never comes pure and unmixed, without being attended or followed by some disturbing evil that gives a shock to it, our fortune, or perhaps the curses which the Moor had hurled at his daughter (for whatever kind of father they may come from these are always to be dreaded), brought it about that when we were now in mid-sea, and the night about three hours spent, as we were running with all sail set and oars lashed, for the favouring breeze saved us the trouble of using them, we saw by the light of the moon, which shone brilliantly, a square-rigged vessel in full sail close to us, luffing up and standing across our course, and so close that we had to strike sail to avoid running foul of her, while they too put the helm hard up to let us pass. They came to the side of the ship to ask who we were, whither we were bound, and whence we came, but as they asked this in French our renegade said, ' Let no one answer, for no doubt these are French corsairs who plunder all comers.' Acting on this warning no one answered a word, but after we had gone a little ahead, and the vessel was now lying to lee-ward, suddenly they fired two guns, and apparently both loaded with chain-shot, for with one they cut our mast in half and brought down both it and the sail into the sea, and the other, discharged at the same moment, sent a ball into our vessel amidships, staving her in completely, but without doing any further damage. We, however, finding ourselves sinking began to shout for help and call upon those in the ship to pick us up as we were beginning to fill. They then lay to, and lowering a skiff or boat, as many as a dozen Frenchmen, well armed with match-locks, and their matches burning, got into it and came alongside; and seeing how few we were, and that our vessel was going down, they took us in, telling us that this had come to us through our incivility in not giving them an answer. Our renegade took the trunk containing Zoraida's wealth and dropped it into the sea without anyone perceiving what he did. In short we went on board with the Frenchmen, who, after having ascertained all they wanted to know about us, rifled us of everything we had, as if they had been our bitterest enemies, and from Zoraida they took even the anklets she wore on her feet; but the distress they caused her did not distress me so much as the fear I was in that from robbing her of her rich and precious jewels they would proceed to rob her of the most precious jewel that she valued more than all. The desires, however, of those people do not go beyond money, but of that their covetousness is insatiable, and on this occasion it was carried to such a pitch that they would have taken even the clothes we wore as captives if they had been worth anything to them. It was the advice of some of them to throw us all into the sea wrapped up in a sail; for their purpose was to trade at some of the ports of Spain, giving themselves out as Bretons, and if they brought us alive they would be punished as soon as the robbery was discovered; but the captain (who was the one who had plundered my beloved Zoraida) said he was satisfied with the prize he had got, and that he would not touch at any Spanish port, but pass the Straits of Gibraltar by night, or as best he could, and make for Rochelle, from which he had sailed. So they agreed by common consent to give us the skiff belonging to their ship and all we required for the short voyage that remained to us, and this they did the next day on coming in sight of the Spanish coast, with which, and the joy we felt, all our sufferings and miseries were as completely forgotten as if they had never been endured by us, such is the delight of recovering lost liberty.

It may have been about mid-day when they placed us in the boat, giving us two kegs of water and some biscuit ; and the captain, moved by I know not what compassion, as the lovely Zoraida was about to embark gave her some forty gold crowns, and would not permit his men to take from her those same garments which she has on now. We got into the boat, returning them thanks for their kindness to us, and showing ourselves grateful rather than indignant. They stood out to sea, steering for the straits ; we, without looking to any compass save the land we had before us, set ourselves to row with such energy that by sunset we were so near that we might easily, we thought, land before the night was far advanced. But as the moon did not show that night, and the sky was clouded, and as we knew not whereabouts we were, it did not seem to us a prudent thing to make for the shore, as several of us advised, saying we ought to run ourselves ashore even if it were on rocks and far from any habitation, for in this way we should be relieved from the apprehensions we naturally felt of the prowling vessels of the Tetuan corsairs, who leave Barbary at nightfall and are on the Spanish coast by daybreak, where they commonly take some prize, and then go home to sleep in their own houses. But of the conflicting counsels the one which was adopted was that we should approach gradually, and land where we could if the sea were calm enough to permit us. This was done, and a little before midnight we drew near to the foot of a huge and lofty mountain,[1] not so close to the sea but that it left a narrow space on which to land conveniently. We ran our boat up on the sand, and all sprang out and kissed the ground, and with tears of joyful satisfaction returned thanks to God our Lord for all his incomparable goodness to us on our voyage. We took out of the boat the pro-

[1] The Sierra Tejeda, to the south of Alhama, is apparently that which Cervantes means.

visions it contained, and drew it up on the shore, and then climbed a long way up the mountain, for even there we could not feel easy in our hearts, or thoroughly persuade ourselves that it was Christian soil that was now under our feet.

The dawn came, more slowly, I think, than we could have wished; we completed the ascent in order to see if from the summit any habitation or any shepherds' huts could be discovered, but strain our eyes as we might, neither dwelling, nor human being, nor path nor road could we perceive. However, we determined to push on farther, as it could not but be that ere long we must see some one who could tell us where we were. But what distressed me most was to see Zoraida going on foot over that rough ground; for though I once carried her on my shoulders, she was more wearied by my weariness than rested by the rest; and so she would never again allow me to undergo the exertion, and went on very patiently and cheerfully, while I led her by the hand. We had gone rather less than a quarter of a league when the sound of a little bell fell on our ears, a clear proof that there were flocks hard by, and looking about carefully to see if any were within view, we observed a young shepherd tranquilly and unsuspiciously trimming a stick with his knife at the foot of a cork tree. We called to him, and he, raising his head, sprang nimbly to his feet, for, as we afterwards learned, the first who presented themselves to his sight were the renegade and Zoraida, and seeing them in Moorish dress he imagined that all the Moors of Barbary were upon him; and plunging with marvellous swiftness into the thicket in front of him, he began to raise a prodigious outcry, exclaiming 'The Moors—the Moors have landed! To arms, to arms!' We were all thrown into perplexity by these cries, not knowing what to do; but reflecting that the shouts of the shepherd would raise the country and that the mounted coast-guard would come at once to see what was the matter, we agreed that the renegade must strip off his Turkish garments and put on a captive's jacket or coat which one of our party gave him at once, though he himself was reduced to his shirt; and so commending ourselves to God, we followed the

same road which we saw the shepherd take, expecting every
moment that the coast-guard would be down upon us. Nor did
our expectation deceive us, for two hours had not passed when,
coming out of the brushwood into the open ground, we perceived
some fifty mounted men swiftly approaching us at a hand-gallop.
As soon as we saw them we stood still, waiting for them ; but as
they came close and, instead of the Moors they were in quest of,
saw a set of poor Christians, they were taken aback, and one
of them asked if it could be we who were the cause of the shepherd having raised the call to arms. I said yes, and as I was
about to explain to him what had occurred, and whence we came
and who we were, one of the Christians of our party recognised
the horseman who had put the question to us, and before I could
say anything more he exclaimed, ' Thanks be to God, sirs, for
bringing us to such good quarters ; for, if I do not deceive myself, the ground we stand on is that of Velez Malaga ;[1] unless,
indeed, all my years of captivity have made me unable to recollect
that you, señor, who ask who we are, are Pedro de Bustamente,
my uncle.'

The Christian captive had hardly uttered these words, when
the horseman threw himself off his horse, and ran to embrace
the young man, crying, ' Nephew of my soul and life ! I recognise
thee now ; and long have I mourned thee as dead, I, and my
sister, thy mother, and all thy kin that are still alive, and whom
God has been pleased to preserve that they may enjoy the happiness of seeing thee. We knew long since that thou wert in
Algiers, and from the appearance of thy garments and those of
all this company, I conclude that ye have had a miraculous restoration to liberty.'

' It is true,' replied the young man, ' and by-and-by we will
tell you all.'

As soon as the horsemen understood that we were Christian
captives, they dismounted from their horses, and each offered his
to carry us to the city of Velez Malaga, which was a league and

---

[1] About eighteen miles to the east of Malaga, at a little distance from
the coast.

a half distant. Some of them went to bring the boat to the city, we having told them where we had left it ; others took us up behind them, and Zoraida was placed on the horse of the young man's uncle. The whole town came out to meet us, for they had by this time heard of our arrival from one who had gone on in advance. They were not astonished to see liberated captives or Moorish captives, for people on that coast are well used to see both one and the other ; but they were astonished at the beauty of Zoraida, which was just then heightened, as well by the exertion of travelling as by joy at finding herself on Christian soil, and relieved of all fear of being lost; for this had brought such a glow upon her face, that, unless my affection for her were deceiving me, I would venture to say that there was not a more beautiful creature in the world—at least, that I had ever seen.

We went straight to the church to return thanks to God for the mercies we had received, and when Zoraida entered it she said there were faces there like Lela Marien's. We told her they were her images; and as well as he could the renegade explained to her what they meant, that she might adore them as if each of them were the very same Lela Marien that had spoken to her ; and she, having great intelligence and a quick and clear instinct, understood at once all he said to her about them. Thence they took us away and distributed us all in different houses in the town ; but as for the renegade, Zoraida, and myself, the Christian who came with us brought us to the house of his parents, who had a fair share of the gifts of fortune, and treated us with as much kindness as they did their own son.

We remained six days in Velez, at the end of which the renegade, having informed himself of all that was requisite for him to do, set out for the city of Granada to restore himself to the sacred bosom of the Church through the medium of the Holy Inquisition. The other released captives took their departures, each the way that seemed best to him, and Zoraida and I were left alone, with nothing more than the crowns which the courtesy of the Frenchman had bestowed upon Zoraida, out of which I bought the beast on which she rides; and, I for the present attending her as her father and squire and not as her husband, we are now going to ascertain if my father is living, or if any of my brothers has had better fortune than mine has been; though, as Heaven has made me the companion of Zoraida, I think no other lot could be assigned to me, however happy, that I would rather have. The patience with which she endures the hardships that poverty brings with it, and the eagerness she shows to become a Christian, are such that they fill me with admiration, and bind me to serve her all my life; though the happiness I feel in seeing myself hers, and her mine, is disturbed and marred by not knowing whether I shall find any corner to shelter her in my own country, or whether time and death may not have made such changes in the fortunes and lives of my father and brothers, that I shall hardly find anyone who knows me, if they are not to be found.

I have no more of my story to tell you, gentlemen; whether it be an interesting or a curious one let your better judgments decide; all I can say is I would gladly have told it to you more briefly; although my fear of wearying you has made me leave out more than one circumstance.

Note A (page 243).

The Arnaut Mami was the captor of the *Sol* galley on board of which Cervantes and his brother Rodrigo were returning to Spain. He was noted for his cruelty, and was said to have his house full of noseless and earless Christians.

CHAPTER XLII.

WHICH TREATS OF WHAT FURTHER TOOK PLACE IN THE INN,
AND OF SEVERAL OTHER THINGS WORTH KNOWING.

WITH these words the captive held his peace, and Don
Fernando said to him, 'In truth, captain, the manner in
which you have related this remarkable adventure has been
such as befitted the novelty and strangeness of the matter.
The whole story is curious and uncommon, and abounds
with incidents that fill the hearers with wonder and astonishment; and so great is the pleasure we have found in
listening to it that we should be glad if it were to begin
again, even though to-morrow were to find us still occupied
with the same tale.' And while he said this Cardenio and
the rest of them offered to be of service to him in any way
that lay in their power, and in words and language so
kindly and sincere that the captain was much gratified by
their good-will. In particular Don Fernando offered, if he
would go back with him, to get his brother the marquis to
become godfather at the baptism of Zoraida, and on his
own part to provide him with the means of making his
appearance in his own country with the credit and comfort
he was entitled to. For all this the captive returned thanks
very courteously, but would not accept any of their generous
offers.

By this time night closed in, and as it did, there came up to the inn a coach attended by some men on horseback, who demanded accommodation ; to which the landlady replied that there was not a hand's breadth of the whole inn unoccupied.

'Still, for all that,' said one of those who had entered on horseback, 'room must be found for his lordship the judge here.'

At this name the landlady was taken aback, and said, 'Señor, the fact is I have no beds ; but if his lordship the judge carries one with him, as no doubt he does, let him come in and welcome ; for my husband and I will give up our room to accommodate his worship.'

'Very good, so be it,' said the squire ; but in the meantime a man had got out of the coach whose dress indicated at a glance the office and post he held, for the long robe with ruffled sleeves that he wore showed that he was, as his servant said, a judge of appeal. He led by the hand a young girl in a travelling dress, apparently about sixteen years of age, and of such a high-bred air, so beautiful and so graceful, that all were filled with admiration when she made her appearance, and but for having seen Dorothea, Luscinda, and Zoraida, who were there in the inn, they would have fancied that a beauty like that of this maiden's would have been hard to find. Don Quixote was present at the entrance of the judge with the young lady, and as soon as he saw him he said, 'Your worship may with confidence enter and take your ease in this castle ; for though the accommodation be scanty and poor, there are no quarters so cramped or inconvenient that they cannot make room for

arms and letters ; above all if arms and letters have beauty
for a guide and leader, as letters represented by your worship have in this fair maiden, to whom not only ought
castles to throw themselves open and yield themselves up,
but rocks should rend themselves asunder and mountains
divide and bow themselves down to give her a reception.
Enter, your worship, I say, into this paradise, for here you
will find stars and suns to accompany the heaven your
worship brings with you ; here you will find arms in their
supreme excellence, and beauty in its highest perfection.'

The judge was struck with amazement at the language
of Don Quixote, whom he scrutinized very carefully, no less
astonished by his figure than by his talk ; and before he
could find words to answer him he had a fresh surprise,
when he saw opposite to him Luscinda, Dorothea, and
Zoraida, who, having heard of the new guests and of the
beauty of the young lady, had come to see her and welcome
her ; Don Fernando, Cardenio, and the curate, however,
greeted him in a more intelligible and polished style. In
short, the judge made his entrance in a state of bewilderment, as well with what he saw as what he heard, and the
fair ladies of the inn gave the fair damsel a cordial welcome.
On the whole he could perceive that all who were there
were people of quality ; but with the figure, countenance,
and bearing of Don Quixote he was at his wits' end ; and
all civilities having been exchanged, and the accommodation
of the inn inquired into, it was settled, as it had been
before settled, that all the women should retire to the
garret that has been already mentioned, and that the
men should remain outside as if to guard them ; the

judge, therefore, was very well pleased to allow his daughter, for such the damsel was, to go with the ladies, which she did very willingly; and with part of the host's narrow bed and half of what the judge had brought with him they made a more comfortable arrangement for the night than they had expected.

The captive, whose heart had leaped within him the instant he saw the judge, telling him somehow that this was his brother, asked one of the servants who accompanied him what his name was, and whether he knew from what part of the country he came. The servant replied that he was called the Licentiate Juan Perez de Viedma, and that he had heard it said he came from a village in the mountains of Leon. From this statement, and what he himself had seen, he felt convinced that this was his brother who had adopted letters by his father's advice; and excited and rejoiced, he called Don Fernando and Cardenio and the curate aside, and told them how the matter stood, assuring them that the judge was his brother. The servant had further informed him that he was now going to the Indies with the appointment of judge of the Supreme Court of Mexico; and he had learned, likewise, that the young lady was his daughter, whose mother had died in giving birth to her, and that he was very rich in consequence of the dowry left to him with the daughter. He asked their advice as to what means he should adopt to make himself known, or to ascertain beforehand whether, when he had made himself known, his brother, seeing him so poor, would be ashamed of him, or would receive him with a warm heart.

'Leave it to me to find out that,' said the curate;

'though there is no reason for supposing, captain, that you will not be kindly received, because the worth and wisdom that your brother's bearing shows him to possess do not make it likely that he will prove haughty or insensible, or that he will not know how to estimate the accidents of fortune at their proper value.'

'Still,' said the captain, 'I would not make myself known abruptly, but in some indirect way.'

'I have told you already,' said the curate, 'that I will manage it in a way to satisfy us all.'

By this time supper was ready, and they all took their seats at the table, except the captive, and the ladies, who supped by themselves in their own room.[1] In the middle of supper the curate said, 'I had a comrade of your worship's name, Señor Judge, in Constantinople, where I was a captive for several years, and that same comrade was one of the stoutest soldiers and captains in the whole Spanish infantry; but he had as large a share of misfortune as he had of gallantry and courage.'

'And how was the captain called, señor?' asked the judge.

'He was called Ruy Perez de Viedma,' replied the curate, 'and he was born in a village in the mountains of Leon; and he mentioned a circumstance connected with his father and his brothers which, had it not been told me by so truthful a man as he was, I should have set down as one of those fables the old women tell over the fire in winter; for he said his father had divided his property among his three sons and had addressed words of advice to them

---

[1] Cervantes apparently forgets that they had supped already.

sounder than any of Cato's. But I can say this much, that the choice he made of going to the wars was attended with such success, that by his gallant conduct and courage, and without any help save his own merit, he rose in a few years to be captain of infantry, and to see himself on the high-road and in position to be given the command of a corps before long; but Fortune was against him, for where he might have expected her favour he lost it, and with it his liberty, on that glorious day when so many recovered theirs, at the battle of Lepanto. I lost mine at the Goletta, and after a variety of adventures we found ourselves comrades at Constantinople. Thence he went to Algiers, where he met with one of the most extraordinary adventures that ever befell anyone in the world.'

Here the curate went on to relate briefly his brother's adventure with Zoraida; to all which the judge gave such an attentive hearing as he had never yet given to any cause he heard.[1] The curate, however, only went so far as to describe how the Frenchmen plundered those who were in the boat, and the poverty and distress in which his comrade and the fair Moor were left; of whom he said he had not been able to learn what became of them, or whether they had reached Spain, or been carried to France by the Frenchmen.

The captain, standing a little to one side, was listening to all the curate said, and watching every movement of his brother, who, as soon as he perceived the curate had made

---

[1] If so, the judge's views of the value of evidence were peculiar. How could the curate, for instance, have known that the Frenchmen robbed his friend, if he had never been able to learn whether he reached Spain or had been carried off to France?

an end of his story, gave a deep sigh and said with his eyes
full of tears, ' Oh, señor, if you only knew what news you
have given me and how it comes home to me, making me
show how I feel it with these tears that spring from my
eyes in spite of all my worldly wisdom and self-restraint !
That brave captain that you speak of is my eldest brother,
who, being of a bolder and loftier mind than my other
brother or myself, chose the honourable and worthy calling
of arms, which was one of the three careers our father proposed to us, as your comrade mentioned in that fable you
thought he was telling you. I followed that of letters, in
which God and my own exertions have raised me to the
position in which you see me. My second brother is in
Peru, so wealthy that with what he has sent to my father
and to me he has fully repaid the portion he took with him,
and has even furnished my father's hands with the means
of gratifying his natural generosity, while I too have been
enabled to pursue my studies in a more becoming and
creditable fashion, and so to attain my present standing.
My father is still alive, though dying with anxiety to hear of
his eldest son, and he prays God unceasingly that death
may not close his eyes until he has looked upon those of
his son ; but with regard to him what surprises me is, that
having so much common sense as he had, he should have
neglected to give any intelligence about himself, either in
his troubles and sufferings, or in his prosperity, for if his
father or any of us had known of his condition he need not
have waited for that miracle of the reed to obtain his
ransom ; but what now disquiets me is the uncertainty
whether those Frenchmen may have restored him to liberty,

or murdered him to hide the robbery. All this will make me continue my journey, not with the satisfaction in which I began it, but in the deepest melancholy and sadness. Oh dear brother! that I only knew where thou art now, and I would hasten to seek thee out and deliver thee from thy sufferings, though it were to cost me suffering myself! Oh that I could bring news to our old father that thou art alive, even wert thou in the deepest dungeon of Barbary; for his wealth and my brother's and mine would rescue thee thence! Oh beautiful and generous Zoraida, that I could repay thy goodness to a brother! That I could be present at the new birth of thy soul, and at thy bridal that would give us all such happiness!'

All this and more the judge uttered with such deep emotion at the news he had received of his brother that all who heard him shared in it, showing their sympathy with his sorrow. The curate, seeing, then, how well he had succeeded in carrying out his purpose and the captain's wishes, had no desire to keep them unhappy any longer, so he rose from the table and going into the room where Zoraida was he took her by the hand, Luscinda, Dorothea, and the judge's daughter following her. The captain was waiting to see what the curate would do, when the latter, taking him with the other hand, advanced with both of them to where the judge and the other gentlemen were, and said, 'Let your tears cease to flow, señor judge, and the wish of your heart be gratified as fully as you could desire, for you have before you your worthy brother and your good sister-in-law. He whom you see here is the Captain Viedma, and this is the fair Moor who has been so good to him. The Frenchmen

I told you of have reduced them to the state of poverty you see that you may show the generosity of your kind heart.'

The captain ran to embrace his brother, who placed both hands on his breast so as to have a good look at him, holding him a little way off; but as soon as he had fully recognised him he clasped him in his arms so closely, shedding such tears of heartfelt joy, that most of those present could not but join in them. The words the brothers exchanged, the emotion they showed can scarcely be imagined, I fancy, much less put down in writing. They told each other in a few words the events of their lives; they showed the true affection of brothers in all its strength; then the judge embraced Zoraida, putting all he possessed at her disposal; then he made his daughter embrace her, and the fair Christian and the lovely Moor drew fresh tears from every eye. And there was Don Quixote observing all these strange proceedings attentively without uttering a word, and attributing the whole to chimeras of knight-errantry. Then they agreed that the captain and Zoraida should return with his brother to Seville, and send news to his father of his having been delivered and found, so as to enable him to come and be present at the marriage and baptism of Zoraida, for it was impossible for the judge to put off his journey, as he was informed that in a month from that time the fleet was to sail from Seville for New Spain, and to miss the passage would have been a great inconvenience to him. In short, everybody was well pleased and glad at the captive's good fortune; and as now almost two-thirds of the night were past they resolved to retire to rest for the remainder of it. Don Quixote offered to mount guard over the castle lest they should be attacked by some giant or other malevolent scoundrel, covetous of the great treasure of beauty the castle contained. Those who understood him returned him thanks for this service, and they gave he judge an account of his extraordinary humour, with wa.ch he was not a little amused. Sancho Panza alone was fuming at the lateness of the hour for retiring to rest; and he of all was the one that made himself most comfortable, as he stretched himself on the trappings of his ass, which, as will be told farther on, cost him so dear.

The ladies, then, having retired to their chamber, and the others having disposed themselves with as little discomfort as they could, Don Quixote sallied out of the inn to act as sentinel of the castle as he had promised. It happened, however, that a little before the approach of dawn a voice so musical and sweet reached the ears of the ladies that it forced them all to listen attentively, but especially Dorothea, who had been awake, and by whose side Doña Clara de Viedma, for so the judge's daughter was called, lay sleeping. No one could imagine who it was that sang so sweetly, and the voice was unaccompanied by any instrument. At one moment it seemed to them as if the singer were in the court-yard, at another in the stable; and as they were all attention, wondering, Cardenio came to the door and said, ' Listen, whoever is not asleep, and you will hear a muleteer's voice that enchants as it chants.'

' We are listening to it already, señor,' said Dorothea; on which Cardenio went away; and Dorothea, giving all her attention to it, made out the words of the song to be these:

CHAPTER XLIII.

WHEREIN IS RELATED THE PLEASANT STORY OF THE MULETEER, TOGETHER WITH OTHER STRANGE THINGS THAT CAME TO PASS IN THE INN.

Ah me, Love's mariner am I [1]
  On Love's deep ocean sailing ;
I know not where the haven lies,
  I dare not hope to gain it.

One solitary distant star
  Is all I have to guide me,
A brighter orb than those of old
  That Palinurus [2] lighted.

And vaguely drifting am I borne,
  I know not where it leads me ;
I fix my gaze on it alone,
  Of all beside it heedless.

But over-cautious prudery,
  . And coyness cold and cruel,
When most I need it, these, like clouds,
  Its longed-for light refuse me.

Bright star, [3] goal of my yearning eyes
  As thou above me beamest,
When thou shalt hide thee from my sight
  I 'll know that death is near me.

---

[1] See Note A, p. 285.

[2]   Surgit Palinurus, et . . .
  Sidera cuncta notat tacito labentia cœlo.'—*Æneid* iii.

[3] ' Clara estrella.'

The singer had got so far when it struck Dorothea that it was not fair to let Clara miss hearing such a sweet voice, so, shaking her from side to side, she woke her, saying, 'Forgive me, child, for waking thee, but I do so that thou mayest have the pleasure of hearing the best voice thou hast ever heard, perhaps, in all thy life.' Clara awoke quite drowsy, and not understanding at the moment what Dorothea said, asked her what it was; she repeated what she had said, and Clara became attentive at once; but she had hardly heard two lines, as the singer continued, when a strange trembling seized her, as if she were suffering from a severe attack of quartan ague, and throwing her arms round Dorothea she said, 'Ah, dear lady of my soul and life! why did you wake me? The greatest kindness fortune could do me now would be to close my eyes and ears so as neither to see or hear that unhappy musician.'

'What art thou talking about, child?' said Dorothea. 'Why, they say this singer is a muleteer!'

'Nay, he is the lord of many places,' replied Clara, 'and that one in my heart which he holds so firmly shall never be taken from him, unless he be willing to surrender it.'

Dorothea was amazed at the ardent language of the girl, for it seemed to be far beyond such experience of life as her tender years gave any promise of, so she said to her, 'You speak in such a way that I cannot understand you, Señora Clara; explain yourself more clearly, and tell me what is this you are saying about hearts and places and this musician whose voice has so moved you? But do not tell me anything now; I do not want to lose the pleasure I get from listening to the singer by giving my attention to your transports, for I perceive he is beginning to sing a new strain and a new air.'

'Let him, in Heaven's name,' returned Clara ; and not to hear him she stopped both ears with her hands, at which Dorothea was again surprised ; but turning her attention to the song she found that it ran in this fashion :

> Sweet Hope, my stay,
> That onward to the goal of thy intent
> Dost make thy way,
> Heedless of hindrance or impediment,
> Have thou no fear
> If at each step thou findest death is near.
>
> No victory,
> No joy of triumph doth the faint heart know ;
> Unblest is he
> That a bold front to Fortune dares not show,
> But soul and sense
> In bondage yieldeth up to indolence.
>
> If Love his wares
> Do dearly sell, his right must be confest ;
> What gold compares
> With that whereon his stamp he hath imprest ?
> And all men know
> What costeth little that we rate but low.[1]
>
> Love resolute
> Knows not the word ' impossibility ; '
> And though my suit
> Beset by endless obstacles I see,
> Yet no despair
> Shall hold me bound to earth while heaven is there.

[1] Prov. 190.

Here the voice ceased and Clara's sobs began afresh, all which excited Dorothea's curiosity to know what could be the cause of singing so sweet and weeping so bitter, so she again asked her what it was she was going to say before. On this Clara, afraid that Luscinda might overhear her, winding her arms tightly round Dorothea put her mouth so close to her ear that she could speak safely without fear of being heard by anyone else, and said, ' This singer, dear señora, is the son of a gentleman of Aragon, lord of two villages, who lives opposite my father's house at Madrid ; and though my father had curtains to the windows of his house in winter, and blinds in summer, in some way—I know not how—this gentleman, who was pursuing his studies, saw me —whether in church or elsewhere, I cannot tell—and, in fact, fell in love with me, and gave me to know it from the windows of his house, with so many signs and tears that I was forced to believe him, and even to love him, without knowing what it was he wanted of me. One of the signs he used to make me was to link one hand in the other, to show me he wished to marry me ; and though I should have been glad if that could be, being alone and motherless I knew not whom to open my mind to, and so I left it as it was, showing him no favour, except when my father, and his too, were from home, to raise the curtain or the blind a little and let him see me plainly, at which he would show such delight that he seemed as if he were going mad. Meanwhile the time for my father's departure arrived, which he became aware of, but not from me, for I had never been able to tell him of it. He fell sick, of grief I believe, and so the day we were going away I could not see him to take farewell of

him, were it only with the eyes. But after we had been two
days on the road, on entering the posada of a village a day's
journey from this, I saw him at the inn door in the dress of
a muleteer, and so well disguised, that if I did not carry his
image graven on my heart it would have been impossible
for me to recognise him. But I knew him, and I was surprised, and glad; he watched me, unsuspected by my father,
from whom he always hides himself when he crosses my
path on the road, or in the posadas where we halt; and, as
I know what he is, and reflect that for love of me he makes
this journey on foot in all this hardship, I am ready to die
of sorrow; and where he sets foot there I set my eyes. I
know not with what object he has come; or how he could
have got away from his father, who loves him beyond
measure, having no other heir, and because he deserves it,
as you will perceive when you see him. And moreover, I
can tell you, all that he sings is out of his own head; for I
have heard them say he is a great scholar and poet; and
what is more, every time I see him or hear him sing I
tremble all over, and am terrified lest my father should recognise him and come to know of our loves. I have never
spoken a word to him in my life; and for all that I love him
so that I could not live without him. This, dear señora, is
all I have to tell you about the musician whose voice has
delighted you so much; and from it alone you might easily
perceive he is no muleteer, but a lord of hearts and towns,
as I told you already.'

'Say no more, Doña Clara,' said Dorothea at this, at
the same time kissing her a thousand times over, 'say no
more, I tell you, but wait till day comes; when I trust in God

to arrange this affair of yours so that it may have the happy ending such an innocent beginning deserves.'

' Ah, señora,' said Doña Clara, ' what end can be hoped for when his father is of such lofty position, and so wealthy, that he would think I was not fit to be even a servant to his son, much less wife ? And as to marrying without the knowledge of my father, I would not do it for all the world. I would not ask anything more than that this youth should go back and leave me; perhaps with not seeing him, and the long distance we shall have to travel, the pain I suffer now may become easier; though I daresay the remedy I propose will do me very little good. I don't know how the devil this has come about, or how this love I have for him got in; I such a young girl, and he such a mere boy; for I verily believe we are both of an age, and I am not sixteen yet; for I will be sixteen Michaelmas Day next, my father says.'

Dorothea could not help laughing to hear how like a child Doña Clara spoke. ' Let us go to sleep now, señora,' said she, ' for the little of the night that I fancy is left to us : God will soon send us daylight, and we will set all to rights, or it will go hard with me.'

With this they fell asleep, and deep silence reigned all through the inn. The only persons not asleep were the landlady's daughter and her servant Maritornes, who, knowing the weak point of Don Quixote's humour, and that he was outside the inn mounting guard in armour and on horseback, resolved, the pair of them, to play some trick upon him, or at any rate to amuse themselves for a while by listening to his nonsense. As it so happened there was not a window

in the whole inn that looked outwards except a hole in the
wall of a straw-loft through which they used to throw out
the straw.   At this hole the two demi-damsels posted themselves, and observed Don Quixote on his horse, leaning on
his pike and from time to time sending forth such deep and
doleful sighs, that he seemed to pluck up his soul by the
roots with each of them; and they could hear him, too,
saying in a soft, tender, loving tone, ' Oh my lady Dulcinea
del Toboso, perfection of all beauty, summit and crown of
discretion, treasure house of grace, depositary of virtue,
and, finally, ideal of all that is good, honourable, and delectable in this world!   What is thy grace doing now?
Art thou, perchance, mindful of thy enslaved knight who
of his own free will hath exposed himself to so great perils,
and all to serve thee?   Give me tidings of her, oh luminary
of the three faces![1]   Perhaps at this moment, envious of
hers, thou art regarding her, either as she paces to and fro
some gallery of her sumptuous palaces, or leans over some
balcony, meditating how, whilst preserving her purity and
greatness, she may mitigate the tortures this wretched heart
of mine endures for her sake, what glory should recompense
my sufferings, what repose my toil, and lastly what death
my life, and what reward my services?   And thou, oh sun,
that art now doubtless harnessing thy steeds in haste to rise
betimes and come forth to see my lady; when thou seest
her I entreat of thee to salute her on my behalf: but have
a care, when thou shalt see her and salute her, that thou
kiss not her face; for I shall be more jealous of thee than
thou wert of that light-footed ingrate[2] that made thee sweat

[1] ' Tria virginis ora Dianæ.'---*Æneid* iv. 511.   [2] I.e. Daphne.

and run so on the plains of Thessaly, or on the banks of the Peneus (for I do not exactly recollect where it was thou didst run on that occasion) in thy jealousy and love.'

Don Quixote had got so far in his pathetic speech when the landlady's daughter began to signal[1] to him, saying, ' Señor, come over here, please.'

At these signals and voice Don Quixote turned his head and saw by the light of the moon, which then was in its full splendour, that some one was calling to him from the hole in the wall, which seemed to him to be a window, and what is more, with a gilt grating, as rich castles, such as he believed the inn to be, ought to have ; and it immediately suggested itself to his imagination that, as on the former occasion, the fair damsel, the daughter of the lady of the castle, overcome by love for him, was once more endeavouring to win his affections ; and with this idea, not to show himself discourteous, or ungrateful, he turned Rocinante's head and approached the hole, and as he perceived the two wenches he said, ' I pity you, beauteous lady, that you should have directed your thoughts of love to a quarter from whence it is impossible that such a return can be made to you as is due to your great merit and gentle birth, for which you must not blame this unhappy knight-errant whom love renders incapable of submission to any other than her whom, the first moment his eyes beheld her, he made absolute mistress of his soul. Forgive me, noble lady, and retire to your apartment, and do not, by any further declaration of your passion, compel me to show myself more

---

[1] *Cecear*—to call attention by making a hissing sound such as the Andalusians produce when they have to pronounce *cc*.

ungrateful; and if, of the love you bear me, you should find that there is anything else in my power wherein I can gratify you, provided it be not love itself, demand it of me; for I swear to you by that sweet absent enemy of mine to grant it this instant, though it be that you require of me a lock of Medusa's hair, which was all snakes, or even the very beams of the sun shut up in a vial.'

'My mistress wants nothing of that sort, sir knight,' said Maritornes at this.

'What then, discreet dame, is it that your mistress wants?' replied Don Quixote.

'Only one of your fair hands,' said Maritornes, 'to enable her to vent over it the great passion which has brought her to this loophole, so much to the risk of her honour; for if the lord her father had heard her, the least slice he would cut off her would be her ear.'

'I should like to see that tried,' said Don Quixote; 'but he had better beware of that, if he does not want to meet the most disastrous end that ever father in the world met for having laid hands on the tender limbs of a love-stricken daughter.'

Maritornes felt sure that Don Quixote would present the hand she had asked, and making up her mind what to do, she got down from the hole and went into the stable, where she took the halter of Sancho Panza's ass, and in all haste returned to the hole, just as Don Quixote had planted himself standing on Rocinante's saddle in order to reach the grated window where he supposed the love-lorn damsel to be; and giving her his hand, he said, 'Lady, take this hand, or rather this scourge of the evil-doers of the earth;

take, I say, this hand which no other hand of woman has ever touched, not even hers who has complete possession of my entire body. I present it to you, not that you may kiss it, but that you may observe the contexture of the sinews, the close network of the muscles, the breadth and capacity of the veins, whence you may infer what must be the strength of the arm that has such a hand.'

'That we shall see presently,' said Maritornes, and making a running knot on the halter, she passed it over his wrist and coming down from the hole tied the other end very firmly to the bolt of the door of the straw-loft.

Don Quixote, feeling the roughness of the rope on his wrist, exclaimed, 'Your grace seems to be grating rather than caressing my hand; treat it not so harshly, for it is not to blame for the offence my resolution has given you, nor is it just to wreak all your vengeance on so small a part; remember that one who loves so well should not revenge herself so cruelly.'

But there was nobody now to listen to these words of Don Quixote's, for as soon as Maritornes had tied him she and the other made off, ready to die with laughing, leaving him fastened in such a way that it was impossible for him to release himself.

He was, as has been said, standing on Rocinante, with his arm passed through the hole and his wrist tied to the bolt of the door, and in mighty fear and dread of being left hanging by the arm if Rocinante were to stir one side or the other; so he did not dare to make the least movement, although from the patience and imperturbable disposition of Rocinante, he had good reason to expect that he

would stand without budging for a whole century. Finding
himself fast, then, and that the ladies had retired, he began
to fancy that all this was done by enchantment, as on the
former occasion when in that same castle that enchanted
Moor of a carrier had belaboured him; and he cursed in his
heart his own want of sense and judgment in venturing to
enter the castle again, after having come off so badly the first
time; it being a settled point with knights-errant that when
they have tried an adventure, and have not succeeded in it,
it is a sign that it is not reserved for them but for others,
and that therefore they need not try it again. Nevertheless
he pulled his arm to see if he could release himself, but it
had been made so fast that all his efforts were in vain. It
is true he pulled it gently lest Rocinante should move, but
try as he might to seat himself in the saddle, he had
nothing for it but to stand upright or pull his hand off.
Then it was he wished for the sword of Amadis, against
which no enchantment whatever had any power; then he
cursed his ill fortune; then he magnified the loss the world
would sustain by his absence while he remained there enchanted, for that he believed he was beyond all doubt; then
he once more took to thinking of his beloved Dulcinea del
Toboso; then he called to his worthy squire Sancho Panza,
who, buried in sleep and stretched upon the pack-saddle of his
ass, was oblivious, at that moment, of the mother that bore
him; then he called upon the sages Lirgandeo and Alquife [1]
to come to his aid; then he invoked his good friend Urganda
to succour him; and then, at last, morning found him in such
a state of desperation and perplexity that he was bellowing

' Magicians that figure in 'The Knight of Phœbus.'

like a bull, for he had no hope that day would bring any relief to his suffering, which he believed would last for ever, inas‧much as he was enchanted; and of this he was convinced by seeing that Rocinante never stirred, much or little, and he felt persuaded that he and his horse were to remain in this state, without eating or drinking or sleeping, until the malign influence of the stars was overpast, or until some other more sage enchanter should disenchant him.

But he was very much deceived in this conclusion, for daylight had hardly begun to appear when there came up to the inn four men on horseback, well equipped and accoutred, with firelocks across their saddle-bows. They called out and knocked loudly at the gate of the inn, which was still shut; on seeing which, Don Quixote, even there where he was, did not forget to act as sentinel, and said in a loud and imperious tone, 'Knights, or squires, or what‧ever ye be, ye have no right to knock at the gates of this castle; for it is plain enough that they who are within are either asleep, or else are not in the habit of throwing open the fortress until the sun's rays are spread over the whole surface of the earth. Withdraw to a distance, and wait till it is broad daylight, and then we shall see whether it will be proper or not to open to you.'

'What the devil fortress or castle is this,' said one, ' to make us stand on such ceremony? If you are the innkeeper bid them open to us; we are travellers who only want to feed our horses and go on, for we are in haste.'

'Do you think, gentlemen, that I look like an inn‧keeper?' said Don Quixote.

'I don't know what you look like,' replied the other;

'but I know that you are talking nonsense when you call this inn a castle.'

'A castle it is,' returned Don Quixote, 'nay, more, one of the best in this whole province, and it has within it people who have had the sceptre in the hand and the crown on the head.'

'It would be better if it were the other way,' said the traveller, 'the sceptre on the head and the crown in the hand; but if so, may be there is within some company of players, with whom it is a common thing to have those crowns and sceptres you speak of; for in such a small inn as this, and where such silence is kept, I do not believe any people entitled to crowns and sceptres can have taken up their quarters.'

'You know but little of the world,' returned Don Quixote, 'since you are ignorant of what commonly occurs in knight-errantry.'

But the comrades of the spokesman growing weary of the dialogue with Don Quixote, renewed their knocks with great vehemence, so much so that the host, and not only he but everybody in the inn, awoke, and he got up to ask who knocked. It happened at this moment that one of the horses of the four who were seeking admittance went to smell Rocinante, who melancholy, dejected, and with drooping ears, stood motionless, supporting his sorely stretched master; and as he was, after all, flesh, though he looked as if he were made of wood, he could not help giving way and in return smelling the one who had come to offer him attentions. But he had hardly moved at all when Don Quixote lost his footing; and slipping off the saddle, he would have come to the ground, but for being suspended by the arm, which caused him such agony that he believed either his wrist would be cut through or his arm torn off; and he hung so near the ground that he could just touch it with his feet, which was all the worse for him; for, finding how little was wanted to enable him to plant his feet firmly, he struggled and stretched himself as much as he could to gain a footing; just like those undergoing the torture of the strappado, when they are fixed at 'touch and no touch,' who aggravate their own sufferings by their violent efforts to stretch themselves, deceived by the hope which makes them fancy that with a very little more they will reach the ground.[1]

[1] See Note B, p. 285.

Note A (page 272).

In this translation an attempt has been made to imitate the prevailing rhyme of the Spanish ballad, the double assonant in the second and fourth lines.

Note B (page 285).

There is some inconsistency here. How could Don Quixote fall almost to the ground, if when standing on Rocinante he was tied up so tightly as we are told? Hartzenbusch, *more suo*, has an ingenious explanation, by which he avoids the simpler one, that Cervantes never gave a thought to the matter. The strappado was inflicted by tying the hands of the victim behind his back and then hanging him by the wrists from a crossbeam or bough of a tree. Examples of it may be seen among Callot's sketches. There is something almost ghastly in its introduction here as an illustration which must, as a matter of course be familiar to every reader.

CHAPTER XLIV.

IN WHICH ARE CONTINUED THE UNHEARD-OF ADVENTURES OF
THE INN.

So loud, in fact, were the shouts of Don Quixote, that the landlord opening the gate of the inn in all haste, came out in dismay, and ran to see who was uttering such cries, and those who were outside joined him. Maritornes, who had been by this time roused up by the same outcry, suspecting what it was, ran to the loft and, without anyone seeing her, untied the halter by which Don Quixote was suspended, and down he came to the ground in the sight of the landlord and the travellers, who approaching asked him what was the matter with him that he shouted so. He without replying a word took the rope off his wrist, and rising to his feet leaped upon Rocinante, braced his buckler on his arm, put his lance in rest, and making a considerable circuit of the plain came back at a half-gallop exclaiming, 'Whoever shall say that I have been enchanted with just cause, provided my lady the Princess Micomicona grants me permission to do so, I give him the lie, challenge him and defy him to single combat.'

The newly arrived travellers were amazed at the words of Don Quixote; but the landlord removed their surprise by telling them who he was, and not to mind him as he was out of his senses. They then asked the landlord if by any

chance a youth of about fifteen years of age had come to
that inn, one dressed like a muleteer, and of such and such
an appearance, describing that of Doña Clara's lover. The
landlord replied that there were so many people in the inn he
had not noticed the person they were inquiring for; but one
of them observing the coach in which the judge had come,
said, ' He is here no doubt, for this is the coach he is following : let one of us stay at the gate, and the rest go in to look
for him; or indeed it would be as well if one of us went
round the inn, lest he should escape over the wall of the yard.'
' So be it,' said another; and while two of them went in, one
remained at the gate and the other made the circuit of the
inn; observing all which, the landlord was unable to conjecture for what reason they were taking all these precautions, though he understood they were looking for the youth
whose description they had given him.

It was by this time broad daylight; and for that reason,
as well as in consequence of the noise Don Quixote had
made, everybody was awake and up, but particularly Doña
Clara and Dorothea; for they had been able to sleep but
badly that night, the one from agitation at having her lover
so near her, the other from curiosity to see him. Don
Quixote, when he saw that not one of the four travellers
took any notice of him or replied to his challenge, was
furious and ready to die with indignation and wrath; and
if he could have found in the ordinances of chivalry that
it was lawful for a knight-errant to undertake or engage in
another enterprise, when he had plighted his word and faith
not to involve himself in any until he had made an end of
the one to which he was pledged, he would have attacked

the whole of them, and would have made them return an answer in spite of themselves. But considering that it would not become him, nor be right, to begin any new emprise until he had established Micomicona in her kingdom, he was constrained to hold his peace and wait quietly to see what would be the upshot of the proceedings of those same travellers; one of whom found the youth they were seeking lying asleep by the side of a muleteer, without a thought of anyone coming in search of him, much less finding him.

The man laid hold of him by the arm, saying, 'It becomes you well indeed, Señor Don Luis, to be in the dress you wear, and well the bed in which I find you agrees with the luxury in which your mother reared you.'

The youth rubbed his sleepy eyes and stared for a while at him who held him, but presently recognised him as one of his father's servants, at which he was so taken aback that for some time he could not find or utter a word; while the servant went on to say, 'There is nothing for it now, Señor Don Luis, but to submit quietly and return home, unless it is your wish that my lord, your father, should take his departure for the other world, for nothing else can be the consequence of the grief he is in at your absence.'

'But how did my father know that I had gone this road and in this dress?' said Don Luis.

'It was a student to whom you confided your intentions,' answered the servant, 'that disclosed them, touched with pity at the distress he saw your father suffer on missing you; he therefore despatched four of his servants in quest of you, and here we all are at your service, better pleased than you can imagine that we shall return so soon and restore you to those eyes that so yearn for you.'

'That shall be as I please, or as heaven orders,' returned Don Luis.

'What can you please or heaven order,' said the other, 'except to agree to go back? Anything else is impossible.'

All this conversation between the two was overheard by the muleteer at whose side Don Luis lay, and rising, he went to report what had taken place to Don Fernando, Cardenio, and the others, who had by this time dressed themselves; and told them how the man had addressed the youth as 'Don,' and what words had passed, and how he wanted him to return to his father, which the youth was unwilling to do. With this, and what they already knew of the rare voice that heaven had bestowed upon him, they all felt very anxious to know more particularly who he was, and even to help him if it was attempted to employ force against him; so they hastened to where he was still talking and arguing with his servant. Dorothea at this instant came out of her room, followed by Doña Clara all in a tremor; and calling Cardenio aside, she told him in a few words the story of the musician and Doña Clara, and he at the same time told her what had happened, how his father's servants had come in search of him; but in telling her so, he did not speak low enough but that Doña Clara heard what he said, at which she was so much agitated that had not Dorothea hastened to support her she would have fallen to the ground. Cardenio then bade Dorothea return to her room, as he would endeavour to make the whole matter right, and they did as he desired. All the four who had come in quest of Don Luis had now come into the inn and surrounded him, urging him to return and console his father at once and without a moment's delay. He replied that he could not do so on any account until he had concluded some business in which his life, honour, and heart were at stake. The servants pressed him, saying that most certainly they would not return without him, and that they would take him away whether he liked it or not.

'You shall not do that,' replied Don Luis, 'unless you take me dead; though however you take me, it will be without life.'

By this time most of those in the inn had been attracted by the dispute, but particularly Cardenio, Don Fernando, his companions, the judge, the curate, the barber, and Don Quixote; for he now considered there was no necessity for mounting guard over the castle any longer. Cardenio being already acquainted with the young man's story, asked the men who wanted to take him away, what object they had in seeking to carry off this youth against his will.

'Our object,' said one of the four, 'is to save the life of his father, who is in danger of losing it through this gentleman's disappearance.'

Upon this Don Luis exclaimed, 'There is no need to make my affairs public here; I am free, and I will return if I please; and if not, none of you shall compel me.'

'Reason will compel your worship,' said the man, 'and if it has no power over you, it has power over us, to make us do what we came for, and what it is our duty to do.'

'Let us hear what the whole affair is about,' said the judge at this; but the man, who knew him as a neighbour of theirs, replied, 'Do you not know this gentleman, señor judge? He is the son of your neighbour, who has run away from his father's house in a dress so unbecoming his rank, as your worship may perceive.'

The judge on this looked at him more carefully and recognised him, and embracing him said, 'What folly is this, Señor Don Luis, or what can have been the cause that could have induced you to come here in this way, and in this dress, which so ill becomes your condition?'

Tears came into the eyes of the young man, and he was unable to utter a word in reply to the judge, who told the four servants not to be uneasy, for all would be satisfactorily settled; and then taking Don Luis by the hand, he drew him aside and asked the reason of his having come there.

But while he was questioning him they heard a loud outcry at the gate of the inn, the cause of which was that two of the guests who had passed the night there, seeing everybody busy about finding out what it was the four men wanted, had conceived the idea of going off without paying what they owed; but the landlord, who minded his own affairs more than other people's, caught them going out of the gate and demanded his reckoning, abusing them for their dishonesty with such language that he drove them to reply with their fists, and so they began to lay on him in such a style that the poor man was forced to cry out, and call for help. The landlady and her daughter could see no one more free to give aid than Don Quixote, and to him the daughter said, 'Sir knight, by the virtue God has given you, help my poor father, for there are two wicked men beating him to a mummy.'

To which Don Quixote very deliberately and phlegma-tically replied, ' Fair damsel, at the present moment your request is inopportune, for I am debarred from involving myself in any adventure until I have brought to a happy conclusion one to which my word has pledged me ; but that which I can do for you is what I will now mention : run and tell your father to stand his ground as well as he can in this battle, and on no account to allow himself to be vanquished, while I go and request permission of the Princess Micomicona to enable me to succour him in his distress ; and if she grants it, rest assured I will relieve him from it.'

' Sinner that I am,' exclaimed Maritornes, who stood by ; ' before you have got your permission my master will be in the other world.'

' Give me leave, señora, to obtain the permission I speak of,' returned Don Quixote ; ' and if I get it, it will matter very little if he is in the other world ; for I will rescue him thence in spite of all the same world can do ; or at any rate I will give you such a revenge over those who shall have sent him there that you will be more than mode-rately satisfied ; ' and without saying anything more he went and knelt before Dorothea, requesting her Highness in knightly and errant phrase to be pleased to grant him permission to aid and succour the castellan of that castle, who now stood in grievous jeopardy. The princess granted it graciously, and he at once, bracing his buckler on his arm and drawing his sword, hastened to the inn-gate, where the two guests were still handling the landlord roughly ; but as soon as he reached the spot he stopped short and stood

still, though Maritornes and the landlady asked him why he
hesitated to help their master and husband.

'I hesitate,' said Don Quixote, 'because it is not lawful
for me to draw sword against persons of squirely condition;
but call my squire Sancho to me; for this defence and
vengeance are his affair and business.'

Thus matters stood at the inn-gate, where there was a
very lively exchange of fisticuffs and punches, to the sore
damage of the landlord and to the wrath of Maritornes, the
landlady, and her daughter, who were furious when they saw
the pusillanimity of Don Quixote, and the hard treatment
their master, husband, and father was undergoing. But
let us leave him there; for he will surely find some one to
help him, and if not, let him suffer and hold his tongue
who attempts more than his strength allows him to do;
and let us go back fifty paces to see what Don Luis said in
reply to the judge whom we left questioning him privately
as to his reasons for coming on foot and so meanly dressed.

To which the youth, pressing his hand in a way that
showed his heart was troubled by some great sorrow, and
shedding a flood of tears, made answer: 'Señor, I have no
more to tell you than that from the moment when, through
heaven's will and our being near neighbours, I first saw
Doña Clara, your daughter and my lady, from that instant
I made her the mistress of my will, and if yours, my true
lord and father, offers no impediment, this very day she
shall become my wife. For her I left my father's house,
and for her I assumed this disguise, to follow her whithersoever she may go, as the arrow seeks its mark or the
sailor the pole-star. She knows nothing more of my

passion than what she may have learned from having
sometimes seen from a distance that my eyes were filled
with tears. You know already, señor, the wealth and
noble birth of my parents, and that I am their sole heir;
if this be a sufficient inducement for you to venture to
make me completely happy, accept me at once as your son;
for if my father, influenced by other objects of his own,
should disapprove of this happiness I have sought for
myself, time has more power to alter and change things,
than human will.'

With this the love-smitten youth was silent, while the
judge, after hearing him, was astonished, perplexed, and
surprised, as well at the manner and intelligence with
which Don Luis had confessed the secret of his heart, as at
the position in which he found himself, not knowing what
course to take in a matter so sudden and unexpected. All
the answer, therefore, he gave him was to bid him to make
his mind easy for the present, and arrange with his servants
not to take him back that day, so that there might be time to
consider what was best for all parties. Don Luis kissed his
hands by force, nay, bathed them with his tears, in a way
that would have touched a heart of marble, not to say that
of the judge, who as a shrewd man, had already perceived
how advantageous the marriage would be to his daughter;
though, were it possible, he would have preferred that it
should be brought about with the consent of the father of
Don Luis, who he knew looked for a title for his son.

The guests had by this time made peace with the landlord,
for, by persuasion and Don Quixote's fair words more than
by threats, they had paid him what he demanded, and the

servants of Don Luis were waiting for the end of the conversation with the judge and their master's decision, when the devil, who never sleeps, contrived that the barber, from whom Don Quixote had taken Mambrino's helmet, and Sancho Panza the trappings of his ass in exchange for those of his own, should at this instant enter the inn; which said barber, as he led his ass to the stable, observed Sancho Panza engaged in repairing something or other belonging to the pack-saddle; and the moment he saw it he knew it, and made bold to attack Sancho, exclaiming, 'Ho, sir thief, I have caught you! hand over my basin and my pack-saddle, and all my trappings that you robbed me of.'

Sancho, finding himself so unexpectedly assailed, and hearing the abuse poured upon him, seized the pack-saddle with one hand, and with the other gave the barber a cuff that bathed his teeth in blood. The barber, however, was not so ready to relinquish the prize he had made in the pack-saddle; on the contrary, he raised such an outcry that everyone in the inn came running to know what the noise and quarrel meant. 'Here, in the name of the king and justice!' he cried, 'this thief and highwayman wants to kill me for trying to recover my property.'

'You lie,' said Sancho, 'I am no highwayman; it was in fair war my master Don Quixote won these spoils.'

Don Quixote was standing by at the time, highly pleased to see his squire's stoutness, both offensive and defensive, and from that time forth he reckoned him a man of mettle, and in his heart resolved to dub him a knight on the first opportunity that presented itself, feeling sure that the order of chivalry would be fittingly bestowed upon him.

In the course of the altercation, among other things the barber said, 'Gentlemen, this pack-saddle is mine as surely as I owe God a death, and I know it as well as if I had given birth to it, and here is my ass in the stable who will not let me lie; only try it, and if it does not fit him like a glove, call me a rascal; and what is more, the same day I was robbed of this, they robbed me likewise of a new brass basin, never yet handselled, that would fetch a crown any day.'

At this Don Quixote could not keep himself from answering; and interposing between the two, and separating them, he placed the pack-saddle on the ground, to lie there in sight until the truth was established, and said, 'Your worships may perceive clearly and plainly the error under which this worthy squire lies when he calls that a basin which was, is, and shall be the helmet of Mambrino, which I won from him in fair war, and made myself master of by legitimate and lawful possession. With the pack-saddle I do not concern myself; but I may tell you on that head that my squire Sancho asked my permission to strip off the caparison of this vanquished poltroon's steed, and with it adorn his own; I allowed him, and he took it; and as to its having been changed from a caparison into a pack-saddle, I can give no explanation except the usual one, that such transformations will take place in adventures of chivalry. To confirm all which, run, Sancho my son, and fetch hither the helmet which this good fellow calls a basin.'

'Egad, master,' said Sancho, 'if we have no other proof of our case than what your worship puts forward,

Mambrino's helmet is just as much a basin as this good fellow's caparison is a pack-saddle.'

'Do as I bid thee,' said Don Quixote; 'it cannot be that everything in this castle goes by enchantment.'

Sancho hastened to where the basin was, and brought it back with him, and when Don Quixote saw it, he took hold of it and said, 'Your worships may see with what a face this squire can assert that this is a basin and not the helmet I told you of; and I swear by the order of chivalry I profess, that this helmet is the identical one I took from him, without anything added to or taken from it.'

'There is no doubt of that,' said Sancho, 'for from the time my master won it until now he has only fought one battle in it, when he let loose those unlucky men in chains; and if it had not been for this basin-helmet he would not have come off over well that time, for there was plenty of stone-throwing in that affair.'

CHAPTER XLV.

IN WHICH THE DOUBTFUL QUESTION OF MAMBRINO'S HELMET
AND THE PACK-SADDLE IS FINALLY SETTLED, WITH OTHER
ADVENTURES THAT OCCURRED IN TRUTH AND EARNEST.

'WHAT do you think now, gentlemen,' said the barber, 'of what these gentles say, when they even want to make out that this is not a basin but a helmet?'

'And whoever says the contrary,' said Don Quixote, 'I will let him know he lies if he is a knight, and if he is a squire that he lies again a thousand times.'

Our own barber, who was present at all this, and understood Don Quixote's humour so thoroughly, took it into his head to back up his delusion and carry on the joke for the general amusement; so addressing the other barber he said, 'Señor barber, or whatever you are, you must know that I belong to your profession too, and have had a licence to practise for more than twenty years, and I know the implements of the barber craft, every one of them, perfectly well; and I was likewise a soldier for some time in the days of my youth, and I know also what a helmet is, and a morion, and a headpiece with a visor, and other things pertaining to soldiering, I meant to say to soldiers' arms; and I say—saving better opinions and always with submission to sounder judgments—that this piece we have now before us, which this worthy gentleman has in his hands, not only is no barber's basin, but is as far from being one as white is from black, and truth from falsehood; I say, moreover, that this, although it is a helmet, is not a complete helmet.'

'Certainly not,' said Don Quixote, 'for half of it is wanting, that is to say the beaver.'

'It is quite true,' said the curate, who saw the object of his friend the barber; and Cardenio, Don Fernando and his companions agreed with him, and even the judge, if his thoughts had not been so full of Don Luis's affair, would have helped to carry on the joke; but he was so taken up with the serious matters he had on his mind that he paid little or no attention to these facetious proceedings.

'God bless me!' exclaimed their butt the barber at this; 'is it possible that such an honourable company can say that this is not a basin but a helmet? Why, this is a thing that would astonish a whole university, however wise it might be! That will do; if this basin is a helmet, why, then the pack-saddle must be a horse's caparison, as this gentleman has said.'

'To me it looks like a pack-saddle,' said Don Quixote; but I have already said that with that question I do not concern myself.'

'As to whether it be pack-saddle or caparison,' said the curate, 'it is only for Señor Don Quixote to say; for in these matters of chivalry all these gentlemen and I bow to his authority.'

'By God, gentlemen,' said Don Quixote, 'so many strange things have happened to me in this castle on the two occasions on which I have sojourned in it, that I will

not venture to assert anything positively in reply to any
question touching anything it contains; for it is my belief
that everything that goes on within it goes by enchantment.
The first time, an enchanted Moor that there is in it gave
me sore trouble, nor did Sancho fare well among certain
followers of his ; and last night I was kept hanging by this
arm for nearly two hours, without knowing how or why I
came by such a mishap. So that now, for me to come forward to give an opinion in such a puzzling matter, would be
to risk a rash decision. As regards the assertion that this is
a basin and not a helmet I have already given an answer ;
but as to the question whether this is a pack-saddle or a
caparison I will not venture to give a positive opinion, but
will leave it to your worships' better judgment. Perhaps
as you are not dubbed knights like myself, the enchantments of this place have nothing to do with you, and your
faculties are unfettered, and you can see things in this
castle as they really and truly are, and not as they appear
to me.'

'There can be no question,' said Don Fernando on this,
' but that Señor Don Quixote has spoken very wisely, and
that with us rests the decision of this matter ; and that we
may have surer ground to go on, I will take the votes of
the gentlemen in secret, and declare the result clearly and
fully.'

To those who were in the secret of Don Quixote's humour
all this afforded great amusement ; but to those who knew
nothing about it, it seemed the greatest nonsense in the
world, in particular to the four servants of Don Luis, as
well as to Don Luis himself, and to three other travellers

who had by chance come to the inn, and had the appearance of officers of the Holy Brotherhood, as indeed they were; but the one who above all was at his wits' end, was the barber whose basin, there before his very eyes, had been turned into Mambrino's helmet, and whose pack-saddle he had no doubt whatever was about to become a rich caparison for a horse. All laughed to see Don Fernando going from one to another collecting the votes, and whispering to them to give him their private opinion whether the treasure over which there had been so much fighting was a pack-saddle or a caparison; but after he had taken the votes of those who knew Don Quixote, he said aloud, 'The fact is, my good fellow, that I am tired collecting such a number of opinions, for I find that there is not one of whom I ask what I desire to know, who does not tell me that it is absurd to say that this is the pack-saddle of an ass, and not the caparison of a horse, nay, of a thoroughbred horse; so you must submit, for, in spite of you and your ass, this is a caparison and no pack-saddle, and you have stated and proved your case very badly.'

'May I never share heaven,' said the poor barber, 'if your worships are not all mistaken; and may my soul appear before God as that appears to me a pack-saddle and not a caparison; but, "laws go,"[1]—I say no more; and indeed I am not drunk, for I am fasting, except it be from sin.'

The simple talk of the barber did not afford less amusement than the absurdities of Don Quixote, who now observed, 'There is no more to be done now than for each

[1] See Note A, p. 308.

to take what belongs to him, and to whom God has given it, may St. Peter add his blessing.'

But said one of the four servants, ' Unless, indeed, this is a deliberate joke, I cannot bring myself to believe that men so intelligent as those present are, or seem to be, can venture to declare and assert that this is not a basin, and that not a pack-saddle; but as I perceive that they do assert and declare it, I can only come to the conclusion that there is some mystery in this persistence in what is so opposed to the evidence of experience and truth itself; for I swear by '—and here he rapped out a round oath—' all the people in the world will not make me believe that this is not a barber's basin and that a jackass's pack-saddle.'

' It might easily be a she-ass's,' observed the curate.

' It is all the same,' said the servant; ' that is not the point; but whether it is or is not a pack-saddle, as your worships say.'

On hearing this one of the newly arrived officers of the Brotherhood, who had been listening to the dispute and controversy, unable to restrain his anger and impatience, exclaimed, ' It is a pack-saddle as sure as my father is my father, and whoever has said or will say anything else must be drunk.'

' You lie like a rascally clown,' returned Don Quixote ; and lifting his pike, which he had never let out of his hand, he delivered such a blow at his head that, had not the officer dodged it, it would have stretched him at full length. The pike was shivered in pieces against the ground, and the rest of the officers, seeing their comrade assaulted, raised a shout, calling for help for the Holy Brotherhood. The landlord, who was of the fraternity, ran at once to fetch his staff of office and his sword, and ranged himself on the side of his comrades; the servants of Don Luis clustered round him, lest he should escape from them in the confusion; the barber, seeing the house turned upside down, once more laid hold of his pack-saddle and Sancho did the same; Don Quixote drew his sword and charged the officers; Don Luis cried out to his servants to leave him alone and go and help Don Quixote, and Cardenio and Don Fernando, who were supporting him; the curate was shouting at the top of his voice, the landlady was screaming, her daughter was wailing, Maritornes was weeping, Dorothea was aghast, Luscinda terror-stricken, and Doña Clara in a faint. The barber cudgelled Sancho, and Sancho pommelled the barber; Don Luis gave one of his servants, who ventured to catch him by the arm to keep him from escaping, a cuff that bathed his teeth in blood; the judge took his part; Don Fernando had got one of the officers down and was belabouring him heartily; the landlord raised his voice again calling for help for the Holy Brotherhood; so that the whole inn was nothing but cries, shouts, shrieks, confusion, terror, dismay, mishaps, sword-cuts, fisticuffs, cudgellings, kicks, and bloodshed; and in the midst of all this chaos, complication, and general entanglement, Don Quixote took it into his head that he had been plunged into the thick of the discord of Agramante's camp;[1] and, in a voice that shook the inn like thunder, he cried out, 'Hold all, let all sheathe their swords, let all be calm and attend to me as they value their lives!'

[1] See Note B, p. 308.

All paused at his mighty voice, and he went on to say, ' Did I not tell you, sirs, that this castle was enchanted, and that a legion or so of devils dwelt in it ? In proof whereof I call upon you to behold with your own eyes how the discord of Agramante's camp has come hither, and been transferred into the midst of us. See how they fight, there for the sword, here for the horse, on that side for the eagle, on this for the helmet ; we are all fighting, and all at cross purposes. Come then, you, señor judge, and you, señor curate ; let the one represent King Agramante and the other King Sobrino, and make peace among us ; for by God Almighty it is a sorry business that so many persons of quality as we are should slay one another for such trifling cause.'

The officers, who did not understand Don Quixote's mode of speaking, and found themselves roughly handled by Don Fernando, Cardenio, and their companions, were not to be appeased ; the barber was, however, for both his beard and his pack-saddle were the worse for the struggle ; Sancho like a good servant obeyed the slightest word of his master ; while the four servants of Don Luis kept quiet when they saw how little they gained by not being so. The landlord alone insisted upon it that they must punish the insolence of this madman, who at every turn raised a disturbance in the inn ; but at length the uproar was stilled for the present ; the pack-saddle remained a caparison till the day of judgment, and the basin a helmet and the inn a castle in Don Quixote's imagination.

All having been now pacified and made friends by the persuasion of the judge and the curate, the servants of Don

Luis began again to urge him to return with them at once ; and while he was discussing the matter with them, the judge took counsel with Don Fernando, Cardenio, and the curate as to what he ought to do in the case, telling them how it stood, and what Don Luis had said to him. It was agreed at length that Don Fernando should tell the servants of Don Luis who he was, and that it was his desire that Don Luis should accompany him to Andalusia, where he would receive from the marquis his brother the welcome his quality entitled him to ; for, otherwise, it was easy to see from the determination of Don Luis that he would not return to his father at present, though they tore him to pieces. On learning the rank of Don Fernando and the resolution of Don Luis the four then settled it between themselves that three of them should return to tell his father how matters stood, and that the other should remain to wait upon Don Luis, and not leave him until they came back for him, or his father's orders were known. Thus by the authority of Agramante and the wisdom of King Sobrino all this complication of disputes was arranged ; but the enemy of concord and hater of peace, feeling himself slighted and made a fool of, and seeing how little he had gained after having involved them all in such an elaborate entanglement, resolved to try his hand once more by stirring up fresh quarrels and disturbances.

It came about in this wise : the officers were pacified on learning the rank of those with whom they had been engaged, and withdrew from the contest, considering that whatever the result might be they were likely to get the worst of the battle ; but one of them, the one who had been thrashed and kicked by Don Fernando, recollected that among some warrants he carried for the arrest of certain delinquents, he had one against Don Quixote, whom the Holy Brotherhood had ordered to be arrested for setting the galley slaves free, as Sancho had, with very good reason, apprehended. Suspecting how it was, then, he wished to satisfy himself as to whether Don Quixote's features corresponded; and taking a parchment out of his bosom he lit upon what he was in search of, and setting himself to read it deliberately, for he was not a quick reader, as he made out each word he fixed his eyes on Don Quixote, and went on comparing the description in the warrant with his face, and discovered that beyond all doubt he was the person described in it. As soon as he had satisfied himself, folding up the parchment, he took the warrant in his left hand and with his right seized Don Quixote by the collar so tightly that he did not allow him to breathe, and shouted aloud, ' Help for the Holy Brotherhood ! and that you may see I demand it in earnest, read this warrant which says this highwayman is to be arrested.'

The curate took the warrant and saw that what the officer said was true, and that it agreed with Don Quixote's appearance, who, on his part, when he found himself roughly handled by this rascally clown, worked up to the highest pitch of wrath, and all his joints cracking with rage, with both hands seized the officer by the throat with all his might, so that had he not been helped by his comrades he would have yielded up his life ere Don Quixote released his hold. The landlord, who had perforce to support his brother officers, ran at once to aid them. The landlady, when she saw her husband engaged in a fresh quarrel, lifted up her voice afresh, and its note was immediately caught up by Maritornes and her daughter, calling upon heaven and all present for help; and Sancho, seeing what was going on, exclaimed, ' By the Lord, it is quite true what my master says about the enchantments of this castle, for it is impossible to live an hour in peace in it ! '

Don Fernando parted the officer and Don Quixote, and to their mutual contentment made them relax the grip by which they held, the one the coat collar, the other the throat of his adversary ; for all this, however, the officers did not cease to demand their prisoner and call on them to help, and deliver him over bound into their power, as was required for the service of the King and of the Holy Brotherhood, on whose behalf they again demanded aid and assistance to effect the capture of this robber and footpad of the highways and byways.

Don Quixote smiled when he heard these words, and said very calmly, ' Come now, base, ill-born brood ; call ye it highway robbery to give freedom to those in bondage, to release the captives, to succour the miserable, to raise up the fallen, to relieve the needy ?   Infamous beings, who by your vile grovelling intellects deserve that heaven should not make known to you the virtue that lies in knight-errantry, or show you the sin and ignorance in which ye lie when ye refuse to respect the shadow, not to say the presence, of any knight-errant !   Come now ; band, not of officers, but of thieves ; footpads with the licence of the Holy Brotherhood ; tell me who was the ignoramus who signed a warrant of arrest against such a knight as I am ?   Who

was he that did not know that knights-errant are independent of all jurisdictions, that their law is their sword, their
charter their prowess, and their edicts their will? Who, I
say again, was the fool that knows not that there are no
letters patent of nobility that confer such privileges or
exemptions as a knight-errant acquires the day he is dubbed
a knight, and devotes himself to the arduous calling of
chivalry? What knight-errant ever paid poll-tax, duty,
queen's pin-money, king's dues, toll or ferry? What tailor
ever took payment of him for making his clothes? What
castellan that received him in his castle ever made him pay
his shot?[1] What king did not seat him at his table?
What damsel was not enamoured of him and did not yield
herself up wholly to his will and pleasure? And, lastly,
what knight-errant has there been, is there, or will there
ever be in the world, not bold enough to give, single-handed,
four hundred cudgellings to four hundred officers of the
Holy Brotherhood if they come in his way?'

[1] *Escote*; old French *escot.*

Note A (*page* 301).

Prov. 204. 'Laws go as kings like:' a very old proverb, said to owe its
origin to the summary manner in which Alfonso VI. at Toledo settled the
question as to which of the rival rituals, the French or the Musarabic, was
to be adopted. It was agreed to try them by the test of fire, and the latter
came out victorious, on which the king, who favoured the other, flung it
back into the flames.

Note B (*page* 303).

V. *Orlando Furioso*, canto xxvii. Agramante was the leader of the
Mohammedan kings and princes assembled at the siege of Paris, of whom
Sobrino was one.

CHAPTER XLVI.

OF THE END OF THE NOTABLE ADVENTURE OF THE OFFICERS
OF THE HOLY BROTHERHOOD ; AND OF THE GREAT FEROCITY
OF OUR WORTHY KNIGHT, DON QUIXOTE.

WHILE Don Quixote was talking in this strain, the curate
was endeavouring to persuade the officers that he was
out of his senses, as they might perceive by his deeds and
his words, and that they need not press the matter any
further, for even if they arrested him and carried him off,
they would have to release him by-and-by as a madman ;
to which the holder of the warrant replied that he had
nothing to do with inquiring into Don Quixote's madness,
but only to execute his superior's orders, and that once
taken they might let him go three hundred times if they
liked.

'For all that,' said the curate, 'you must not take him
away this time, nor will he, it is my opinion, let himself be
taken away.'

In short, the curate used such arguments, and Don
Quixote did such mad things, that the officers would have
been more mad than he was if they had not perceived his
want of wits, and so they thought it best to allow themselves
to be pacified, and even to act as peacemakers between the
barber and Sancho Panza, who still continued their alter-

cation with much bitterness. In the end they, as officers
of justice, settled the question by arbitration in such a
manner that both sides were, if not perfectly contented,
at least to some extent satisfied; for they changed the
pack-saddles, but not the girths or head-stalls; and as
to Mambrino's helmet, the curate, under the rose and
without Don Quixote's knowing it, paid eight reals for the
basin, and the barber executed a full receipt and engage-
ment to make no further demand then or thenceforth for
evermore, amen. These two disputes, which were the most
important and gravest, being settled, it only remained for
the servants of Don Luis to consent that three of them
should return while one was left to accompany him whither
Don Fernando desired to take him; and good luck and
better fortune, having already begun to solve difficulties and
remove obstructions in favour of the lovers and warriors
of the inn, were pleased to persevere and bring everything
to a happy issue; for the servants agreed to do as Don
Luis wished; which gave Doña Clara such happiness that
no one could have looked into her face just then without
seeing the joy of her heart. Zoraida, though she did not
fully comprehend all she saw, was grave or gay without
knowing why, as she watched and studied the various coun-
tenances, but particularly her Spaniard's, whom she followed
with her eyes and clung to with her soul. The gift and
compensation which the curate gave the barber had not
escaped the landlord's notice, and he demanded Don Quixote's
reckoning, together with the amount of the damage to his
wine-skins, and the loss of his wine, swearing that neither
Rocinante nor Sancho's ass should leave the inn until he

had been paid to the very last farthing. The curate settled all amicably, and Don Fernando paid; though the judge had also very readily offered to pay the score; and all became so peaceful and quiet that the inn no longer reminded one of the discord of Agramante's camp, as Don Quixote said, but of the peace and tranquillity of the days of Octavianus:[1] for all which it was the universal opinion that their thanks were due to the great zeal and eloquence of the curate, and to the unexampled generosity of Don Fernando.

Finding himself now clear and quit of all quarrels, his squire's as well as his own, Don Quixote considered that it would be advisable to continue the journey he had begun, and bring to a close that great adventure for which he had been called and chosen; and with this high resolve he went and knelt before Dorothea, who, however, would not allow him to utter a word until he had risen; so to obey her he rose, and said, 'It is a common proverb, fair lady, that "diligence is the mother of good fortune,"[2] and experience has often shown in important affairs that the earnestness of the negotiator brings the doubtful case to a successful termination; but in nothing does this truth show itself more plainly than in war, where quickness and activity forestall the devices of the enemy, and win the victory before the foe has time to defend himself. All this I say, exalted and esteemed lady, because it seems to me that for us to remain any longer in this castle now is useless, and may be injurious to us in a way that we shall find out some day; for who knows but that your enemy the giant may have learned by means of secret and diligent spies that I

[1] I.e. Augustus.   [2] Prov. 77.

am going to destroy him, and if the opportunity be given
him he may seize it to fortify himself in some impregnable
castle or stronghold, against which all my efforts and the
might of my indefatigable arm may avail but little ? Therefore, lady, let us, as I say, forestall his schemes by our activity,
and let us depart at once in quest of fair fortune; for your
highness is only kept from enjoying it as fully as you could
desire by my delay in encountering your adversary.'

Don Quixote held his peace and said no more, calmly
awaiting the reply of the beauteous princess, who, with commanding dignity and in a style adapted to Don Quixote's own,
replied to him in these words, 'I give you thanks, sir knight,
for the eagerness you, like a good knight to whom it is a
natural obligation to succour the orphan and the needy, display to afford me aid in my sore trouble ; and heaven grant
that your wishes and mine may be realised, so that you
may see that there are women in this world capable of gratitude; as to my departure, let it be forthwith, for I have
no will but yours ; dispose of me entirely in accordance with
your good pleasure ; for she who has once entrusted to you
the defence of her person, and placed in your hands the
recovery of her dominions, must not think of offering opposition to that which your wisdom may ordain.'

'On, then, in God's name,' said Don Quixote ; 'for, when
a lady humbles herself to me, I will not lose the opportunity
of raising her up and placing her on the throne of her ances-
tors. Let us depart at once, for the common saying that
in delay there is danger,[1] lends spurs to my eagerness to take
the road ; and as neither heaven has created nor hell seen

[1] Prov. 222.

any that can daunt or intimidate me, saddle Rocinante, Sancho, and get ready thy ass and the queen's palfrey, and let us take leave of the castellan and these gentlemen, and go hence this very instant.'

Sancho, who was standing by all the time, said, shaking his head, ' Ah ! master, master, there is more mischief in the village than one hears of,[1] begging all good bodies' pardon.'

' What mischief can there be in any village, or in all the cities of the world, you booby, that can hurt my reputation ? ' said Don Quixote.

' If your worship is angry,' replied Sancho, ' I will hold my tongue and leave unsaid what as a good squire I am bound to say, and what a good servant should tell his master.'

' Say what thou wilt,' returned Don Quixote, ' provided thy words be not meant to work upon my fears; for thou, when thou fearest, art behaving like thyself; but I like myself, when I fear not.'

' It is nothing of the sort, as I am a sinner before God,' said Sancho, ' but that I take it to be sure and certain that this lady, who calls herself queen of the great kingdom of Micomicon, is no more so than my mother ; for, if she was what she says, she would not go rubbing noses with one that is here every instant and behind every door.'

Dorothea turned red at Sancho's words, for the truth was that her husband Don Fernando had now and then, when the others were not looking, gathered from her lips some of the reward his love had earned, and Sancho seeing

---

[1] Prov. 9. Generally mistranslated ' than is dreamt of,' as if it was *sueña* instead of *suena*.

this had considered that such freedom was more like a courtesan than a queen of a great kingdom ; she, however, being unable or not caring to answer him, allowed him to proceed, and he continued, ' This I say, señor, because, if after we have travelled roads and highways, and passed bad nights and worse days, one who is now enjoying himself in this inn is to reap the fruit of our labours, there is no need for me to be in a hurry to saddle Rocinante, put the pad on the ass, or get ready the palfrey ; for it will be better for us to stay quiet, and let every jade mind her spinning,[1] and let us go to dinner.'

Good God, what was the indignation of Don Quixote when he heard the audacious words of his squire! So great was it, that in a voice inarticulate with rage, with a stammering tongue, and eyes that flashed living fire, he exclaimed, ' Rascally clown, boorish, insolent, and ignorant, ill-spoken, foul-mouthed, impudent backbiter and slanderer! Hast thou dared to utter such words in my presence and in that of these illustrious ladies ? Hast thou dared to harbour such gross and shameless thoughts in thy muddled imagination ? Begone from my presence, thou born monster, storehouse of lies, hoard of untruths, garner of knaveries, inventor of scandals, publisher of absurdities, enemy of the respect due to royal personages ! Begone, show thyself no more before me under pain of my wrath ; ' and so saying he knitted his brows, puffed out his cheeks, gazed around him, and stamped on the ground violently with his right foot, showing in every way the rage that was pent up in his heart; and at his words and furious gestures Sancho was so scared and

[1] Prov. 196.

terrified that he would have been glad if the earth had opened that instant and swallowed him, and his only thought was to turn round and make his escape from the angry presence of his master.

But the ready-witted Dorothea, who by this time so well understood Don Quixote's humour, said, to mollify his wrath, ' Be not irritated at the absurdities your good squire has uttered, Sir Knight of the Rueful Countenance, for perhaps he did not utter them without cause, and from his good sense and Christian conscience it is not likely that he would bear false witness against anyone. We may therefore believe, without any hesitation, that since, as you say, sir knight, everything in this castle goes and is brought about by means of enchantment, Sancho, I say, may possibly have seen, through this diabolical medium, what he says he saw so much to the detriment of my modesty.'

' I swear by God Omnipotent,' exclaimed Don Quixote at this, ' your highness has hit the point ; and that some vile illusion must have come before this sinner of a Sancho, that made him see what it would have been impossible to see by any other means than enchantments ; for I know well enough, from the poor fellow's goodness and harmlessness, that he is incapable of bearing false witness against anybody.'

' True, no doubt,' said Don Fernando, ' for which reason, Señor Don Quixote, you ought to forgive him and restore him to the bosom of your favour, *sicut erat in principio*, before illusions of this sort had taken away his senses.'

Don Quixote said he was ready to pardon him, and the curate went for Sancho, who came in very humbly, and falling on his knees begged for the hand of his master, who having presented it to him and allowed him to kiss it, gave him his blessing and said, ' Now, Sancho my son, thou wilt be convinced of the truth of what I have many a time told thee, that everything in this castle is done by means of enchantment.'

' So it is, I believe,' said Sancho, ' except the affair of the blanket, which came to pass in reality by ordinary means.'

' Believe it not,' said Don Quixote, ' for had it been so, I would have avenged thee that instant, or even now; but neither then nor now could I, nor have I seen anyone upon whom to avenge thy wrong.'

They were all eager to know what the affair of the blanket was, and the landlord gave them a minute account of Sancho's flights, at which they laughed not a little, and at which Sancho would have been no less out of countenance had not his master once more assured him it was all enchantment. For all that his simplicity never reached so high a pitch that he could persuade himself it was not the plain and simple truth, without any deception whatever about it, that he had been blanketed by beings of flesh and blood, and not by visionary and imaginary phantoms, as his master believed and protested.

The illustrious company had now been two days in the inn; and as it seemed to them time to depart, they devised a plan so that, without giving Dorothea and Don Fernando the trouble of going back with Don Quixote to his village under pretence of restoring Queen Micomicona, the curate and the barber might carry him away with them as they proposed, and the curate be able to take his madness in hand at home; and in pursuance of their plan they arranged with the owner of an ox-cart who happened to be passing that way to carry him after this fashion. They constructed a kind of cage with wooden bars, large enough to hold Don Quixote comfortably; and then Don Fernando and his companions, the servants of Don Luis, and the officers of the Brotherhood, together with the landlord, by the directions and advice of the curate, covered their faces and disguised themselves, some in one way, some in another, so as to appear to Don Quixote quite different from the persons he had seen in the castle. This done, in profound silence they entered the room where he was asleep, taking his rest after the past frays, and advancing to where he was sleeping tranquilly, not dreaming of anything of the kind happening, they seized him firmly and bound him fast hand and foot, so that, when he awoke startled, he was unable to move, and could only marvel and wonder at the strange figures he saw before him; upon which he at once gave way to the idea which his crazed fancy invariably conjured up before him, and took it into his head that all these shapes were phantoms of the enchanted castle, and that he himself was unquestionably enchanted as he could neither move nor help himself; precisely what the curate, the concoctor of the scheme, expected would happen.[1] Of all that were there Sancho was the only one who was at once in his senses and in his own proper character, and he, though he was within very little of sharing his master's infirmity, did not fail to perceive who all these disguised figures were; but he did not dare to open his lips until he saw what came of this assault and

---

[1] This resembles the scene in the *Morgante Maggiore* (xii. 88), where Orlando is seized and bound by the pagans.

capture of his master; nor did the latter utter a word, waiting to see the upshot of his mishap; which was that, bringing in the cage, they shut him up in it and nailed the bars so firmly that they could not be easily burst open. They then took him on their shoulders, and as they passed out of the room an awful voice—as much so as the barber, not he of the pack-saddle but the other, was able to make it—was heard to say, 'O Knight of the Rueful Countenance, let not this captivity in which thou art placed afflict thee, for this must needs be, for the more speedy accomplishment of the adventure in which thy great heart has engaged thee; the which shall be accomplished when the raging Manchegan lion and the white Tobosan dove shall be linked together, having first humbled their haughty necks to the gentle yoke of matrimony. And from this marvellous union shall come forth to the light of the world brave whelps, that shall rival the ravening claws of their valiant father; and this shall come to pass ere the pursuer of the flying nymph shall in his swift natural course have twice visited the starry signs. And thou, O most noble and obedient squire that ever bore sword at side, beard on face, or nose to smell with, be not dismayed or grieved to see the flower of knight-errantry carried away thus before thy very eyes; for soon, if it so please the Framer of the universe, thou shalt see thyself exalted to such a height that thou shalt not know thyself, and the promises which thy good master has made thee shall not prove false; and I assure thee, on the authority of the sage Mentironiana,[1] that thy wages shall be paid thee, as thou shalt see in due season. Follow then the footsteps

---

[1] A name formed from 'mentir,' to tell lies.

of the valiant enchanted knight, for it is expedient that thou shouldst go to the destination assigned to both of you; and as it is not permitted to me to say more, God be with thee; for I return to that place I wot of; ' and as he brought the prophecy to a close he raised his voice to a high pitch, and then lowered it to such a soft tone, that even those who knew it was all a joke were almost inclined to take what they heard seriously.

Don Quixote was comforted by the prophecy he heard, for he at once comprehended its meaning perfectly, and perceived it was promised to him that he should see himself united in holy and lawful matrimony with his beloved Dulcinea del Toboso, from whose blessed womb should proceed the whelps, his sons, to the eternal glory of La Mancha; and being thoroughly and firmly persuaded of this, he lifted up his voice, and with a deep sigh exclaimed, ' O thou, whoever thou art, who hast foretold me so much good, I implore of thee that on my part thou entreat that sage enchanter who takes charge of my interests, that he leave me not to perish in this captivity in which they are now carrying me away, ere I see fulfilled promises so joyful and incomparable as those which have been now made me; for, let this but come to pass, and I shall glory in the pains of my prison, find comfort in these chains wherewith they bind me, and regard this bed whereon they stretch me, not as a hard battle-field, but as a soft and happy nuptial couch; and touching the consolation of Sancho Panza, my squire, I rely upon his goodness and rectitude that he will not desert me in good or evil fortune; for if, by his ill luck or mine, it may not happen to be in my power to give him the island I have promised, or any equivalent for it, at least his wages shall not be lost; for in my will, which is already made, I have declared the sum that shall be paid to him, measured, not by his many faithful services, but by the means at my disposal.'

Sancho bowed his head very respectfully and kissed both his hands, for, being tied together, he could not kiss one; and then the apparitions lifted the cage upon their shoulders and fixed it upon the ox-cart.

CHAPTER XLVII.

OF THE STRANGE MANNER IN WHICH DON QUIXOTE OF LA MANCHA WAS CARRIED AWAY ENCHANTED, TOGETHER WITH OTHER REMARKABLE INCIDENTS.

WHEN Don Quixote saw himself caged and hoisted on the cart in this way, he said, 'Many grave histories of knights-errant have I read; but never yet have I read, seen, or heard of their carrying off enchanted knights-errant in this fashion, or at the slow pace that these lazy, sluggish animals promise; for they always take them away through the air with marvellous swiftness, enveloped in a dark thick cloud, or on a chariot of fire, or it may be on some hippogriff or other beast of the kind; but to carry me off like this on an ox-cart! By God, it puzzles me! But perhaps the chivalry and enchantments of our day take a different course from that of those in days gone by; and it may be, too, that, as I am a new knight in the world, and the first to revive the already forgotten calling of knight-adventurers, they may have newly invented other kinds of enchantments and other modes of carrying off the enchanted. What thinkest thou of the matter, Sancho my son?'

'I don't know what to think,' answered Sancho, 'not being as well read as your worship in errant writings; but

for all that I venture to say and swear that these apparitions that are about us are not quite Catholic.'

'Catholic!' said Don Quixote. 'Father of me! how
can they be Catholic when they are all devils that have
taken fantastic shapes to come and do this, and bring me to
this condition? And if thou wouldst prove it, touch them,
and feel them, and thou wilt find they have only bodies of
air, and no consistency except in appearance.'

'By God, master,' returned Sancho, 'I have touched
them already; and that devil, that goes about there so
busily, has firm flesh, and another property very different
from what I have heard say devils have, for by all accounts
they all smell of brimstone and other bad smells; but this
one smells of amber half a league off.' Sancho was here
speaking of Don Fernando, who, like a gentleman of his
rank, was very likely perfumed as Sancho said.

'Marvel not at that, Sancho my friend,' said Don
Quixote; 'for let me tell thee devils are crafty; and even if
they do carry odours about with them, they themselves
have no smell, because they are spirits; or, if they have
any smell, they cannot smell of anything sweet, but of
something foul and fetid; and the reason is that as they
carry hell with them wherever they go, and can get no ease
whatever from their torments, and as a sweet smell is a
thing that gives pleasure and enjoyment, it is impossible
that they can smell sweet; if, then, this devil thou speakest
of seems to thee to smell of amber, either thou art deceiving
thyself, or he wants to deceive thee by making thee fancy
he is not a devil.'

Such was the conversation that passed between master

and man ; and Don Fernando and Cardenio, apprehensive of Sancho's making a complete discovery of their scheme, towards which he had already gone some way, resolved to hasten their departure, and calling the landlord aside, they directed him to saddle Rocinante and put the pack-saddle on Sancho's ass, which he did with great alacrity. In the meantime the curate had made an arrangement with the officers that they should bear them company as far as his village, he paying them so much a day. Cardenio hung the buckler on one side of the bow of Rocinante's saddle and the basin on the other, and by signs commanded Sancho to mount his ass and take Rocinante's bridle, and at each side of the cart he placed two officers with their muskets ; [1] but before the cart was put in motion, out came the landlady and her daughter and Maritornes to bid Don Quixote farewell, pretending to weep with grief at his misfortune ; and to them Don Quixote said, ' Weep not, good ladies, for all these mishaps are the lot of those who follow the profession I profess ; and if these reverses did not befall me I should not esteem myself a famous knight-errant ; for such things never happen to knights of little renown and fame, because nobody in the world thinks about them ; to valiant knights they do, for these are envied for their virtue and valour by many princes and other knights who compass the destruction of the worthy by base means. Nevertheless, virtue is of herself so mighty, that, in spite of all the magic that Zoroastes its first inventor knew, she will come victorious out of every trial, and shed her light upon the earth as the sun does upon the heavens. Forgive me, fair

[1] See Note A, p. 334.

ladies, if, through inadvertence, I have in aught offended you; for intentionally and wittingly I have never done so to any; and pray to God that he deliver me from this captivity to which some malevolent enchanter has consigned me; and should I find myself released therefrom, the favours that ye have bestowed upon me in this castle shall be held in memory by me, that I may acknowledge, recognise, and requite them as they deserve.'

While this was passing between the ladies of the castle and Don Quixote, the curate and the barber bade farewell to Don Fernando and his companions, to the captain, his brother, and the ladies, now all made happy, and in particular to Dorothea and Luscinda. They all embraced one another, and promised to let each other know how things went with them, and Don Fernando directed the curate where to write to him, to tell him what became of Don Quixote, assuring him that there was nothing that could give him more pleasure than to hear, and that he too, on his part, would send him word of everything he thought he would like to know, about his marriage, Zoraida's baptism, Don Luis's affair, and Luscinda's return to her home. The curate promised to comply with his request carefully, and they embraced once more, and renewed their promises.

The landlord approached the curate and handed him some papers, saying he had discovered them in the lining of the valise in which the novel of 'The Ill-advised Curiosity' had been found, and that he might take them all away with him as their owner had not since returned; for, as he could not read, he did not want them himself. The curate thanked him, and opening them he saw at the beginning of the manuscript the words, ' Novel of Rinconete and Cortadillo,' by which he perceived that it was a novel, and as that of ' The Ill-advised Curiosity ' had been good he concluded this would be so too, as they were both probably by the same author ; [1] so he kept it, intending to read it when he had an opportunity. He then mounted and his friend the barber did the same, both masked, so as not to be recognised by Don Quixote, and set out following in the rear of the cart. The order of march was this : first went the cart with the owner leading it ; at each side of it marched the officers of the Brotherhood, as has been said, with their muskets ; then followed Sancho Panza on his ass, leading Rocinante by the bridle ; and behind all came the curate and the barber on their mighty mules, with faces covered, as aforesaid, and a grave and serious air, measuring their pace to suit the slow steps of the oxen. Don Quixote was seated in the cage, with his hands tied and his feet stretched out, leaning against the bars as silent and as patient as if he were a stone statue and not a man of flesh. Thus slowly and silently they made, it might be, two leagues, until they reached a valley which the carter thought a convenient place for resting and feeding his oxen, and he said so to the curate, but the barber was of opinion that they ought to push on a little farther, as at the other side of a hill which appeared close by he knew there was a valley that had more grass and much better than the one where they proposed to halt ; and his advice was taken and they continued their journey.

Just at that moment the curate, looking back, saw

[1] See Note B, p. 334.

coming on behind them six or seven mounted men, well found and equipped, who soon overtook them, for they were travelling, not at the sluggish, deliberate pace of oxen, but like men who rode canons' mules, and in haste to take their noontide rest as soon as possible at the inn which was in sight not a league off. The quick travellers came up with the slow, and courteous salutations were exchanged; and one of the new comers, who was, in fact, a canon of Toledo and master of the others who accompanied him, observing the regular order of the procession, the cart, the officers, Sancho, Rocinante, the curate and the barber, and above all Don Quixote caged and confined, could not help asking what was the meaning of carrying the man in that fashion; though, from the badges of the officers, he already concluded that he must be some desperate highwayman or other malefactor whose punishment fell within the jurisdiction of the Holy Brotherhood. One of the officers to whom he had put the question, replied, ' Let the gentleman himself tell you the meaning of his going this way, señor, for we do not know.'

Don Quixote overheard the conversation and said, ' Haply, gentlemen, you are versed and learned in matters of chivalry? Because if you are I will tell you my misfortunes; if not, there is no good in my giving myself the trouble of relating them; ' but here the curate and the barber, seeing that the travellers were engaged in conversation with Don Quixote, came forward, in order to answer in such a way as to save their stratagem from being discovered.

The canon, replying to Don Quixote, said, ' In truth,

brother, I know more about books of chivalry than I do about Villalpando's elements of logic; [1] so if that be all, you may safely tell me what you please.'

'In God's name, then, señor,' replied Don Quixote; 'if that be so, I would have you know that I am held enchanted in this cage by the envy and fraud of wicked enchanters; for virtue is more persecuted by the wicked than loved by the good. I am a knight-errant, and not one of those whose names Fame has never thought of immortalising in her record, but of those who, in defiance and in spite of envy itself, and all the magicians that Persia, or Brahmans that India, or Gymnosophists that Ethiopia ever produced, will place their names in the temple of immortality, to serve as examples and patterns for ages to come, whereby knights-errant may see the footsteps in which they must tread if they would attain the summit and crowning point of honour in arms.'

'What Señor Don Quixote of La Mancha says,' observed the curate, 'is the truth; for he goes enchanted in this cart, not from any fault or sins of his, but because of the malevolence of those to whom virtue is odious and valour hateful. This, señor, is the Knight of the Rueful Countenance, if you have ever heard him named, whose valiant achievements and mighty deeds shall be written on lasting brass and imperishable marble, notwithstanding all the efforts of envy to obscure them and malice to hide them.'

When the canon heard both the prisoner and the man who was at liberty talk in such a strain he was ready to cross himself in his astonishment, and could not make out

[1] See Note C, p. 334.

what had befallen him; and all his attendants were in the same state of amazement.

At this point Sancho Panza, who had drawn near to hear the conversation, said, in order to make everything plain, 'Well, sirs, you may like or dislike what I am going to say, but the fact of the matter is, my master, Don Quixote, is just as much enchanted as my mother. He is in his full senses, he eats and he drinks, and he has his calls like other men and as he had yesterday, before they caged him. And if that's the case, what do they mean by wanting me to believe that he is enchanted? For I have heard many a one say that enchanted people neither eat, nor sleep, nor talk; and my master, if you don't stop him, will talk more than thirty lawyers.' Then turning to the curate he exclaimed, 'Ah, señor curate, señor curate! do you think I don't know you? Do you think I don't guess and see the drift of these new enchantments? Well then, I can tell you I know you, for all your face is covered, and I can tell you I am up to you, however you may hide your tricks. After all, where envy reigns virtue cannot live, and where there is niggardliness there can be no liberality. Ill betide the devil! if it had not been for your worship my master would be married to the Princess Micomicona this minute, and I should be a count at least; for no less was to be expected, as well from the goodness of my master, him of the Rueful Countenance, as from the greatness of my services. But I see now how true it is what they say in these parts, that the wheel of fortune turns faster than a mill-wheel,[1] and that those who were up yesterday are down to-day. I am sorry for

[1] Prov. 209.

my wife and children, for when they might fairly and reasonably expect to see their father return to them a governor or viceroy of some island or kingdom, they will see him come back a horse-boy. I have said all this, señor curate, only to urge your paternity [1] to lay to your conscience your ill-treatment of my master ; and have a care that God does not call you to account in another life for making a prisoner of him in this way, and charge against you all the succours and good deeds that my lord Don Quixote leaves undone while he is shut up.'

' Trim those lamps there ! ' [2] exclaimed the barber at this ; ' so you are of the same fraternity as your master, too, Sancho ? By God, I begin to see that you will have to keep him company in the cage, and be enchanted like him for having caught some of his humour and chivalry. It was an evil hour when you let yourself be got with child by his promises, and that island you long so much for found its way into your head.'

' I am not with child by anyone,' returned Sancho, ' nor am I a man to let myself be got with child, if it was by the King himself. Though I am poor I am an old Christian, and I owe nothing to nobody, and if I long for an island, other people long for worse. Each of us is the son of his own works ; and being a man I may come to be pope, [3] not to say governor of an island, especially as my master may win so many that he will not know whom to give them to. Mind how you talk, master barber ; for shaving is not everything, and there is some difference between Peter and Peter. [4]

---

[1] A title sometimes given to ecclesiastics in lieu of ' Reverence.'
[2] Proverbial phrase — ' Adobadme esos candiles.'
[3] Provs. 112 and 117.　　　　[4] Prov. 178.

I say this because we all know one another, and it will not
do to throw false dice with me ;[1] and as to the enchantment
of my master, God knows the truth ; leave it as it is ; it
will only make it worse to stir it.'

The barber did not care to answer Sancho lest by his
plain speaking he should disclose what the curate and he
himself were trying so hard to conceal ; and under the
same apprehension the curate had asked the canon to ride
on a little in advance, so that he might tell him the mystery
of this man in the cage, and other things that would amuse
him.   The canon agreed, and going on ahead with his
servants, listened with attention to the account of the character, life, madness, and ways of Don Quixote, given him
by the curate, who described to him briefly the beginning
and origin of his craze, and told him the whole story of his
adventures up to his being confined in the cage, together
with the plan they had of taking him home to try if by any
means they could discover a cure for his madness.   The
canon and his servants were surprised anew when they
heard Don Quixote's strange story, and when it was finished
he said, ' To tell the truth, señor curate, I for my part
consider what they call books of chivalry to be mischievous
to the State ; and though, led by idle and false taste, I have
read the beginnings of almost all that have been printed, I
never could manage to read any one of them from beginning to end ; for it seems to me they are all more or less the
same thing ; and one has nothing more in it than another ;
this no more than that.   And in my opinion this sort of
writing and composition is of the same species as the fables

[1] Prov. 69.

they call the Milesian, nonsensical tales that aim solely
at giving amusement and not instruction, exactly the opposite of the apologue fables which amuse and instruct at
the same time.   And though it may be the chief object of
such books to amuse, I do not know how they can succeed,
when they are so full of such monstrous nonsense.   For the
enjoyment the mind feels must come from the beauty and
harmony which it perceives or contemplates in the things
that the eye or the imagination brings before it ; and nothing
that has any ugliness or disproportion about it can give any
pleasure.   What beauty, then, or what proportion of the
parts to the whole, or of the whole to the parts, can there
be in a book or fable where a lad of sixteen cuts down a
giant as tall as a tower and makes two halves of him as if
he was an almond cake ?[1]   And when they want to give us
a picture of a battle, after having told us that there are a
million of combatants on the side of the enemy, let the
hero of the book be opposed to them, and we have perforce
to believe, whether we like it or not, that the said knight
wins the victory by the single might of his strong arm.
And then, what shall we say of the facility with which a
born queen or empress will give herself over into the arms
of some unknown wandering knight ?   What mind, that is
not wholly barbarous and uncultured, can find pleasure in
reading of how a great tower full of knights sails away
across the sea like a ship with a fair wind, and will be to-
night in Lombardy and to-morrow morning in the land of
Prester John of the Indies, or some other that Ptolemy

[1] Alluding to Belianis of Greece, who when only sixteen cut a knight in
two at Persepolis.

never described nor Marco Polo saw ?   And if, in answer to·
this, I am told that the authors of books of the kind write
them as fiction, and therefore are not bound to regard
niceties of truth, I would reply that fiction is all the better·
the more it looks like truth, and gives the more pleasure
the more probability [1] and possibility there is about it.
Plots in fiction should be wedded to the understanding of ·
the reader, and be constructed in such a way that, reconcil-
ing impossibilities, smoothing over difficulties, keeping the
mind on the alert, they may surprise, interest, divert, and
entertain, so that wonder and delight joined may keep·
pace one with the other ; all which he will fail to effect who·
shuns verisimilitude and truth to nature, wherein lies the
perfection of writing.   I have never yet seen any book of·
chivalry that puts together a connected plot complete in all
its numbers, so that the middle agrees with the beginning,.
and the end with the beginning and middle ; on the contrary, they construct them with such a multitude of members
that it seems as though they meant to produce a chimera or·
monster rather than a well-proportioned figure.   And besides all this they are harsh in their style, incredible in
their achievements, licentious in their amours, uncouth
in their courtly speeches, prolix in their battles, silly in
their arguments, absurd in their travels, and, in short,.
wanting in everything like intelligent art ; for which reason
they deserve to be banished from the Christian common--
wealth as a worthless breed.'

The curate listened to him attentively and felt that he·

---

[1] Literally, ' the more of the doubtful,' meaning the more of that which
is not manifestly impossible.

was a man of sound understanding, and that there was
good reason in what he said; so he told him that, being of
the same opinion himself, and bearing a grudge to books of
chivalry, he had burned all Don Quixote's, which were many;
and gave him an account of the scrutiny he had made of
them, and of those he had condemned to the flames and
those he had spared, with which the canon was not a little
amused, adding that though he had said so much in con-
demnation of these books, still he found one good thing in
them, and that was the opportunity they afforded to a gifted
intellect for displaying itself; for they presented a wide and
spacious field over which the pen might range freely, describing shipwrecks, tempests, combats, battles, portraying
a valiant captain with all the qualifications requisite to
make one, showing him sagacious in foreseeing the wiles of
the enemy, eloquent in speech to encourage or restrain his
soldiers, ripe in counsel, rapid in resolve, as bold in biding
his time as in pressing the attack; now picturing some sad
tragic incident, now some joyful and unexpected event;
here a beauteous lady, virtuous, wise, and modest; there a
Christian knight, brave and gentle; here a lawless, barbarous braggart; there a courteous prince, gallant and gracious; setting forth the devotion and loyalty of vassals, the
greatness and generosity of nobles. ' Or again,' said he, ' the
author may show himself to be an astronomer, or a skilled
cosmographer, or musician, or one versed in affairs of state,
and sometimes he will have a chance of coming forward as a
magician if he likes. He can set forth the craftiness of
Ulysses, the piety of Æneas, the valour of Achilles, the
misfortunes of Hector, the treachery of Sinon, the friend-

ship of Euryalus, the generosity of Alexander, the boldness
of Cæsar, the clemency and truth of Trajan, the fidelity of
Zopyrus, the wisdom of Cato, and in short all the faculties that serve to make an illustrious man perfect, now
uniting them in one individual, again distributing them
among many; and if this be done with charm of style and
ingenious invention, aiming at the truth as much as possible,
he will assuredly weave a web of bright and varied threads
that, when finished, will display such perfection and beauty
that it will attain the worthiest object any writing can seek,
which, as I said before, is to give instruction and pleasure
combined; for the unrestricted range of these books enables
the author to show his powers, epic, lyric, tragic, or comic,
and all the moods the sweet and winning arts of poesy and
oratory are capable of; for the epic may be written in prose
just as well as in verse.'

Note A (*page* 323).

Here, for once, Hartzenbusch has overlooked an inconsistency. In
chapter xlv. we were told the officers were *three* in number. Farther on it
will be seen that they carried crossbows, not muskets.

Note B (*page* 325).

Rinconete y Cortadillo is the third of the Novelas Ejemplares published
by Cervantes in 1613. From this we may assume that the *Curioso Impertinente* was written about the same time, i.e. during his residence in Seville.

Note C (*page* 327).

Suma de las Súmulas, Alcala 1557, by Gaspar Carillo de Villalpando, a
theologian who distinguished himself for learning and eloquence at the
Council of Trent.

CHAPTER XLVIII.

IN WHICH THE CANON PURSUES THE SUBJECT OF THE BOOKS
OF CHIVALRY, WITH OTHER MATTERS WORTHY OF HIS WIT.

'IT is as you say, señor canon,' said the curate; 'and for
that reason those who have hitherto written books of the
sort deserve all the more censure for writing without paying
any attention to good taste or to the rules of art, by which
they might guide themselves and become as famous in
prose as the two princes of Greek and Latin poetry are in
verse.'

'I myself, at any rate,' said the canon, 'was once
tempted to write a book of chivalry in which all the points I
have mentioned were to be observed; and if I must own the
truth I have more than a hundred sheets written; and to
try if it came up to my own opinion of it, I showed them
to persons who were fond of this kind of reading, to learned
and intelligent men as well as to ignorant people who cared
for nothing but the pleasure of listening to nonsense, and
from all I obtained flattering approval; nevertheless I proceeded no farther with it, as well because it seemed to me
an occupation inconsistent with my profession, as because
I perceived that the fools are more numerous than the wise;
and, though it is better to be praised by the wise few than

applauded [1] by the foolish many, I have no mind to submit myself to the stupid judgment of the silly public, to whom the reading of such books falls for the most part.

'But what most of all made me hold my hand and even abandon all idea of finishing it was an argument I put to myself taken from the plays that are acted now-a-days, which was in this wise : if those that are now in vogue, as well those that are pure invention as those founded on history, are, all or most of them, downright nonsense and things that have neither head nor tail, and yet the public listens to them with delight, and regards and cries them up as perfection when they are so far from it ; and if the authors who write them, and the players who act them, say that this is what they must be, for the public wants this and will have nothing else ; and that those that go by rule and work out a plot according to the laws of art will only find some half-dozen intelligent people to understand them, while all the rest remain blind to the merit of their composition; and that for themselves it is better to get bread from the many than praise from the few ; then my book will fare the same way, after I have burnt off my eyebrows in trying to observe the principles I have spoken of, and I shall be 'the tailor of El Campillo.' [2] And though I have sometimes endeavoured to convince actors that they are mistaken in this notion they have adopted, and that they would attract more people, and get more credit, by producing plays in accordance with the rules of art, than by absurd ones, they are so thoroughly wedded to their own opinion that no argument or evidence can wean them from it.

[1] See Note A, p. 345.   [2] See Note B, p. 345.

' I remember saying one day to one of these obstinate fellows, " Tell me, do you not recollect that a few years ago, there were three tragedies acted in Spain, written by a famous poet of these kingdoms, which were such that they filled all who heard them with admiration, delight, and interest, the ignorant as well as the wise, the masses as well as the higher orders, and brought in more money to the performers, these three alone, than thirty of the best that have been since produced ? "

' " No doubt," replied the actor in question, " you mean the ' Isabella,' the ' Phyllis,' and the ' Alexandra.' " [1]

' " Those are the ones I mean," said I ; " and see if they did not observe the principles of art, and if, by observing them, they failed to show their superiority and please all the world ; so that the fault does not lie with the public that insists upon nonsense, but with those who don't know how to produce something else. ' The Ingratitude Revenged' was not nonsense, nor was there any in ' The Numantia,' nor any to be found in ' The Merchant Lover,' nor yet in ' The Friendly Fair Foe,' [2] nor in some others that have been written by certain gifted poets, to their own fame and renown, and to the profit of those that brought them out ; " some further remarks I added to these, with which, I think, I left him rather dumbfoundered, but not so satisfied or convinced that I could disabuse him of his error.'

'You have touched upon a subject, señor canon,' observed the curate here, ' that has awakened an old enmity I have against the plays in vogue at the present day, quite

---

[1] By Lupercio Leonardo de Argensola.
[2] See Note C, p. 345.

as strong as that which I bear to the books of chivalry ;
for while the drama, according to Tully, should be the
mirror of human life, the model of manners, and the image
of the truth, those which are presented now-a-days are
mirrors of nonsense, models of folly, and images of lewd-
ness. For what greater nonsense can there be in connection with what we are now discussing than for an infant
to appear in swaddling clothes in the first scene of the first
act, and in the second a grown-up, bearded man ? Or what
greater absurdity can there be than putting before us an
old man as a swashbuckler, a young man as a poltroon, a
lackey using fine language, a page giving sage advice, a
king plying as a porter, a princess who is a kitchen-maid ?
And then what shall I say of their attention to the time in
which the action they represent may or can take place,
save that I have seen a play where the first act began in
Europe, the second in Asia, the third finished in Africa,
and no doubt, had it been in four acts, the fourth would
have ended in America, and so it would have been laid in
all four quarters of the globe ? And if truth to life is the
main thing the drama should keep in view, how is it possible for any average understanding to be satisfied when
the action is supposed to pass in the time of King Pepin
or Charlemagne, and the principal personage in it they
represent to be the Emperor Heraclius who entered Jeru-
salem with the cross and won the Holy Sepulchre, like
Godfrey of Bouillon, there being years innumerable between
the one and the other ? or, if the play is based on fiction
and historical facts are introduced, or bits of what occurred
to different people and at different times mixed up with

it, all, not only without any semblance of probability, but with obvious errors that from every point of view are inexcusable? And the worst of it is, there are ignorant people who say that this is perfection, and that anything beyond this is affected refinement. And then if we turn to sacred dramas—what miracles they invent in them! What apocryphal, ill-devised incidents, attributing to one saint the miracles of another! And even in secular plays they venture to introduce miracles without any reason or object except that they think some such miracle, or transformation as they call it, will come in well to astonish stupid people and draw them to the play. All this tends to the prejudice of the truth and the corruption of history, nay more, to the reproach of the wits of Spain; for foreigners who scrupulously observe the laws of the drama [1] look upon us as barbarous and ignorant, when they see the absurdity and nonsense of the plays we produce. Nor will it be a sufficient excuse to say that the chief object well-ordered governments have in view when they permit plays to be performed in public, is to entertain the people with some harmless amusement occasionally, and keep it from those evil humours which idleness is apt to engender; and that, as this may be attained by any sort of play, good or bad, there is no need to lay down laws, or bind those who write or act them to make them as they ought to be made, since, as I say, the object sought for may be secured by any sort. To this I would reply that the same end would be, beyond all comparison, better attained by means of good plays than by those that are not so; for after listening to an artistic and

---

[1] See Note D, p. 346.

properly constructed play, the hearer will come away en-
livened by the jests, instructed by the serious parts, full of
admiration at the incidents, his wits sharpened by the arguments, warned by the tricks, all the wiser for the examples,
inflamed against vice, and in love with virtue ; for in all
these ways a good play will stimulate the mind of the
hearer be he ever so boorish or dull ; and of all impossibilities the greatest is that a play endowed with all these
qualities will not entertain, satisfy, and please much more
than one wanting in them, like the greater number of those
which are commonly acted now-a-days.   Nor are the poets
who write them to be blamed for this ; for some there are
among them who are perfectly well aware of their faults, and
know thoroughly what they ought to do ; but as plays have
become a saleable commodity, they say, and with truth,
that the actors will not buy them unless they are after this
fashion ; and so the poet tries to adapt himself to the
requirements of the actor who is to pay him for his work.
And that this is the truth may be seen by the countless plays
that a most fertile wit of these kingdoms has written, with
so much brilliancy, so much grace and gaiety, such polished
versification, such choice language, such profound reflections,
and in a word, so rich in eloquence and elevation of style,
that he has filled the world with his fame ; and yet, in
consequence of his desire to suit the taste of the actors,
they have not all, as some of them have, come as near perfection as they ought.[1]   Others write plays with such heedlessness that after they have been acted, the actors have to
fly and abscond, afraid of being punished, as they often

[1] See Note E, p. 346.

have been, for having acted something offensive to some king or other, or insulting to some noble family. All which evils, and many more that I say nothing of, would be removed if there were some intelligent and sensible person at the capital to examine all plays before they were acted, not only those produced in the capital itself, but all that were intended to be acted in Spain; without whose approval, seal, and signature, no local magistracy should allow any play to be acted. In that case actors would take care to send their plays to the capital, and could act them in safety, and those who write them would be more careful and take more pains with their work, standing in awe of having to submit it to the strict examination of one who understood the matter; and so good plays would be produced and the objects they aim at happily attained; as well the amusement of the people, as the credit of the wits of Spain, the interest and safety of the actors, and the saving of trouble in inflicting punishment on them. And if the same or some other person were authorised to examine the newly written books of chivalry, no doubt some would appear with all the perfections you have described, enriching our language with the gracious and precious treasure of eloquence, and driving the old books into obscurity before the light of the new ones that would come out for the harmless entertainment, not merely of the idle but of the very busiest; for the bow cannot be always bent, nor can weak human nature exist without some lawful amusement.'

The canon and the curate had proceeded thus far with their conversation, when the barber, coming forward, joined them, and said to the curate, 'This is the spot, señor licentiate, that I said was a good one for fresh and plentiful pasture for the oxen, while we take our noon-tide rest.'

' And so it seems,' returned the curate, and he told the canon what he proposed to do, on which he too made up his mind to halt with them, attracted by the aspect of the fair valley that lay before their eyes ; and to enjoy it as well as the conversation of the curate, to whom he had begun to take a fancy, and also to learn more particulars about the doings of Don Quixote, he desired some of his servants to go on to the inn, which was not far distant, and fetch from it what eatables there might be for the whole party, as he meant to rest for the afternoon where he was ; to which one of his servants replied that the sumpter mule, which by this time ought to have reached the inn, carried provisions enough to make it unnecessary to get anything from the inn except barley.

' In that case,' said the canon, ' take all the beasts there, and make the sumpter mule come back.'

While this was going on, Sancho, perceiving that he could speak to his master without having the curate and the barber, of whom he had his suspicions, present all the time, approached the cage in which Don Quixote was placed, and said, ' Señor, to ease my conscience I want to tell you the state of the case as to your enchantment, and that is that these two here, with their faces covered, are the curate of our village and the barber ; and I suspect they have hit upon this plan of carrying you off in this fashion, out of pure envy because your worship surpasses them in doing famous deeds ; and if this be the truth it follows that you are not enchanted, but hoodwinked and made a fool of.

And to prove this I want to ask you one thing; and if you answer me as I believe you will answer, you will be able to lay your finger on the trick, and you will see that you are not enchanted but gone wrong in your wits.'

'Ask what thou wilt, Sancho my son,' returned Don Quixote, ' for I will satisfy thee and answer all thou requirest. As to what thou sayest, that these who accompany us yonder are the curate and the barber, our neighbours and acquaintances, it is very possible that they may seem to be those same persons; but that they are so in reality and in fact, believe it not on any account; what thou art to believe and think is that, if they look like them, as thou sayest, it must be that those who have enchanted me have taken this shape and likeness; for it is easy for enchanters to take any form they please, and they may have taken those of our friends in order to make thee think as thou dost, and lead thee into a labyrinth of fancies from which thou wilt find no escape though thou hadst the cord of Theseus; and they may also have done it to make me uncertain in my mind, and unable to conjecture whence this evil comes to me; for if on the one hand thou dost tell me that the barber and curate of our village are here in company with us, and on the other I find myself shut up in a cage, and know in my heart that no power on earth that was not supernatural would have been able to shut me in, what wouldst thou have me say or think, but that my enchantment is of a sort that transcends all I have ever read of in all the histories that deal with knights-errant that have been enchanted ? So thou mayest set thy mind at rest as to the idea that they are what thou sayest, for they are as much so as I am a Turk.

But touching thy desire to ask me something, say on, and I will answer thee, though thou shouldst ask questions from this till to-morrow morning.'

'May Our Lady be good to me!' said Sancho, lifting up his voice; 'and is it possible that your worship is so thick of skull and so short of brains that you cannot see that what I say is the simple truth, and that malice has more to do with your imprisonment and misfortune than enchantment? But as it is so, I will prove plainly to you that you are not enchanted. Now tell me, so may God deliver you from this affliction, and so may you find yourself when you least expect it in the arms of my lady Dulcinea—'

'Leave off conjuring me,' said Don Quixote, 'and ask what thou wouldst know; I have already told thee I will answer with all possible precision.'

'That is what I want,' said Sancho; 'and what I would know, and have you tell me, without adding or leaving out anything, but telling the whole truth as one expects it to be told, and as it is told, by all who profess arms, as your worship professes them, under the title of knights-errant—'

'I tell thee I will not lie in any particular,' said Don Quixote; 'finish thy question; for in truth thou weariest me with all these asseverations, requirements, and precautions, Sancho.'

'Well, I rely on the goodness and truth of my master,' said Sancho; 'and so, because it bears upon what we are talking about, I would ask, speaking with all reverence, whether since your worship has been shut up and, as you think, enchanted in this cage, you have felt any desire or inclination to go anywhere, as the saying is?'

'I do not understand "going anywhere,"' said Don Quixote; 'explain thyself more clearly, Sancho, if thou wouldst have me give an answer to the point.'

'Is it possible,' said Sancho, 'that your worship does not understand "going anywhere"? Why, the schoolboys know that from the time they were babes. Well then, you must know I mean have you had any desire to do what cannot be avoided?'

'Ah! now I understand thee, Sancho,' said Don Quixote; 'yes, often, and even this minute; get me out of this strait, or all will not go right.'

Note A (*page* 336).

In the original it is *burlado*, 'scoffed at,' which makes no sense. Hartzenbusch suggests *vitoreado*, but I think *alabado* is the more likely word and suits the context better.

Note B (*page* 336).

Alluding to the proverb (216) *El sastre del Campillo, que cosia de balde y ponia el hilo*—'The tailor of El Campillo, who stitched for nothing and found thread.' In the original it is 'del *cantillo*,' and the Marquis of Santillana gives the proverb in this form; but in the *Picara Justina*, in Quevedo, and most other authorities it is given as above. 'Cantillo' is unmeaning, while 'Campillo,' or 'El Campillo,' is the name of nearly a score of places in Spain. Anyone versed in proverbial literature will see that this is one of the class of quasi local proverbs to which so many of the Spanish belong, e.g. 'the squire of Guadalajara,' 'the abbot of Zarzuela,' 'the smith of Arganda,' 'the doctors of Valencia,' and that peculiarly humorous one, which ought by right to be Scottish, 'The piper of Bujalance, (who got) one maravedi to strike up and ten to leave off.'

Note C (*page* 337).

La Ingratitud vengada, a comedy by Lope de Vega; *La Numancia*, a tragedy by Cervantes himself, first printed in 1784; *El Mercader amante*, a comedy by Gaspar de Aguilar; and *La Enemiga favorable*, by the licentiate Francisco Tarraga.

Note D (page 339).

The foreigners Cervantes alludes to here could only have been the Italians, who had made some efforts in the direction of dramatic propriety. There was no French stage at the time; and the English certainly did no ' scrupulously observe ' the laws he alludes to.

Note E (page 340).

The fertile wit was, of course, Lope de Vega, at whom, in particular, this criticism is aimed; and Cervantes shows great adroitness in the mode in which he has conducted his attack. There is hardly anything, however, which he says that Lope does not admit with cynical candour in the *Arte nuevo de hacer Comedias*, where he insists upon the right of the public to have nonsense if it prefers it, inasmuch as it pays. This chapter has a peculiar interest, not only as showing the views of Cervantes, but as furnishing an explanation of the bitter feeling with which he was unquestionably regarded by Lope and Lope's school; a feeling that found expression a few years later in the attack made upon him by Avellaneda. Cervantes himself shortly afterwards in his comedies violated nearly all the principles he lays down here, and in the second act of the *Rufian Dichoso* solemnly reads his recantation. Much of what he says here is almost identical with what Sir Philip Sidney had said in the *Apologie for Poetrie*.

CHAPTER XLIX.

WHICH TREATS OF THE SHREWD CONVERSATION WHICH SANCHO
PANZA HELD WITH HIS MASTER DON QUIXOTE.

' AHA, I have caught you,' said Sancho; ' this is what in my
heart and soul I was longing to know. Come now, señor,
can you deny what is commonly said around us, when a
person is out of humour, " I don't know what ails so-and-
so, that he neither eats, nor drinks, nor sleeps, nor gives a
proper answer to any question; one would think he was enchanted " ? From which it is to be gathered that those who
do not eat, or drink, or sleep, or do any of the natural acts
I am speaking of—that such persons are enchanted; but
not those that have the desire your worship has, and drink
when drink is given them, and eat when there is anything
to eat, and answer every question that is asked them.'

' What thou sayest is true, Sancho,' replied Don Quixote;
' but I have already told thee there are many sorts of enchantments, and it may be that in the course of time they
have been changed one for another, and that now it may be
the way with enchanted people to do all that I do, though
they did not do so before; so it is vain to argue or draw
inferences against the usage of the time. I know and feel
that I am enchanted, and that is enough to ease my conscience; for it would weigh heavily on it if I thought that I

was not enchanted, and that in a faint-hearted and cowardly
way I allowed myself to lie in this cage, defrauding multi-
tudes of the succour I might afford to those in need and
distress, who at this very moment may be in sore want of
my aid and protection.'

'Still for all that,' replied Sancho, ' I say that, for your
greater and fuller satisfaction, it would be well if your
worship were to try to get out of this prison (and I promise
to do all in my power to help, and even to take you out of
it), and see if you could once more mount your good Rocinante, who seems to be enchanted too, he is so melancholy
and dejected; and then we might try our chance in looking
for adventures again; and if we have no luck there will be
time enough to go back to the cage; in which, on the faith
of a good and loyal squire, I promise to shut myself up
along with your worship, if so be you are so unfortunate,
or I so stupid, as not to be able to carry out my plan.'

'I am content to do as thou sayest, brother Sancho,'
said Don Quixote, ' and when thou seest an opportunity for
effecting my release I will obey thee absolutely; but thou
wilt see, Sancho, how mistaken thou art in thy conception
of my misfortune.'

The knight-errant and the ill-errant squire kept up their
conversation till they reached the place where the curate, the
canon, and the barber, who had already dismounted, were
waiting for them. The carter at once unyoked the oxen and
left them to roam at large about the pleasant green spot,
the freshness of which seemed to invite, not enchanted
people like Don Quixote, but wide-awake, sensible folk like
his squire, who begged the curate to allow his master to

leave the cage for a little; for if they did not let him out, the prison might not be as clean as the propriety of such a gentleman as his master required. The curate understood him, and said he would very gladly comply with his request, only that he feared his master, finding himself at liberty, would take to his old courses and make off where nobody could ever find him again.

'I will answer for his not running away,' said Sancho.

'And I for everything,' said the canon, 'especially if he gives me his word as a knight not to leave us without our consent.'

Don Quixote, who was listening to all this, said he would give it; and that moreover one who was enchanted as he was could not do as he liked with himself; for he who had enchanted him could prevent his moving from one place for three ages, and if he attempted to escape would bring him back flying; and that being so, they might as well release him, particularly as it would be to the advantage of all; for, if they did not let him out, he protested he would be unable to avoid offending their nostrils unless they kept their distance.

The canon took his hand, tied together as they both were, and on his word and promise they unbound him, and rejoiced beyond measure he was to find himself out of the cage. The first thing he did was to stretch himself all over, and then he went to where Rocinante was standing and giving him a couple of slaps on the haunches said, 'I still trust in God and in his blessed mother, O flower and mirror of steeds, that we shall soon see ourselves, both of us, as we wish to be, thou with thy master on thy back, and I mounted upon thee, following the calling for which God sent me into the world.' And so saying, accompanied by Sancho, he withdrew to a retired spot, from which he came back much relieved and more eager than ever to put his squire's scheme into execution.

The canon gazed at him, wondering at the extraordinary nature of his madness, and that in all his remarks and replies he should show such excellent sense, and only lose his stirrups, as has been already said, when the subject of chivalry was broached. And so, moved by compassion, he said to him, as they all sat on the green grass awaiting the arrival of the provisions, ' Is it possible, gentle sir, that the nauseous and idle reading of books of chivalry can have had such an effect on your worship as to upset your reason so that you fancy yourself enchanted, and the like, all as far from the truth as falsehood itself is ? How can there be any human understanding that can persuade itself there ever was all that infinity of Amadises in the world, or all that multitude of famous knights, all those emperors of Trebizond, all those Felixmartes of Hircania, all those palfreys, and damsels-errant, and serpents, and monsters, and giants, and marvellous adventures, and enchantments of every kind, and battles, and prodigious encounters, splendid costumes, love-sick princesses, squires made counts, droll dwarfs, love-letters, billings and cooings, swashbuckler women,[1] and, in a word, all that nonsense the books of chivalry contain ? For myself, I can only say that when I read them, so long as I do not stop to think that they are

---

[1] E.g. Bradamante, Marfisa, and Antea, in the *Orlando* and *Morgante Maggiore.*

all lies and frivolity, they give me a certain amount of pleasure; but when I come to consider what they are, I fling the very best of them at the wall, and would fling it into the fire if there were one at hand, as richly deserving such punishment as cheats and impostors out of the range of ordinary toleration, and as founders of new sects and modes of life, and teachers that lead the ignorant public to believe and accept as truth all the folly they contain. And such is their audacity, they even dare to unsettle the wits of gentlemen of birth and intelligence, as is shown plainly by the way they have served your worship, when they have brought you to such a pass that you have to be shut up in a cage and carried on an ox-cart as one would carry a lion or a tiger from place to place to make money by showing it. Come, Señor Don Quixote, have some compassion for yourself, return to the bosom of common sense, and make use of the liberal share of it that heaven has been pleased to bestow upon you, employing your abundant gifts of mind in some other reading that may serve to benefit your conscience and add to your honour. And if, still led away by your natural bent, you desire to read books of achievements and of chivalry, read the Book of Judges in the Holy Scriptures, for there you will find grand reality, and deeds as true as they are heroic. Lusitania had a Viriatus, Rome a Cæsar, Carthage a Hannibal, Greece an Alexander, Castile a Count Fernan Gonzalez, Valencia a Cid, Andalusia a Gonzalo Fernandez, Estremadura a Diego García de Paredes, Jerez a Garci Perez de Vargas, Toledo a Garcilaso, Seville a Don Manuel de Leon,[1] to read of whose valiant deeds will enter-

[1] See Note A, p. 356.

tain and instruct the loftiest minds and fill them with delight
and wonder. Here, Señor Don Quixote, will be reading
worthy of your sound understanding; from which you will
rise learned in history, in love with virtue, strengthened in
goodness, improved in manners, brave without rashness,
prudent without cowardice; and all to the honour of God,
your own advantage and the glory of La Mancha, whence,
I am informed, your worship derives your birth and
origin.'

Don Quixote listened with the greatest attention to the
canon's words, and when he found he had finished, after
regarding him for some time, he replied to him, 'It appears
to me, gentle sir, that your worship's discourse is intended
to persuade me that there never were any knights-errant in
the world, and that all the books of chivalry are false, lying,
mischievous and useless to the State, and that I have done
wrong in reading them, and worse in believing them, and
still worse in imitating them, when I undertook to follow
the arduous calling of knight-errantry which they set forth;
for you deny that there ever were Amadises of Gaul or of
Greece, or any other of the knights of whom the books are
full.'

'It is all exactly as you state it,' said the canon; to
which Don Quixote returned, 'You also went on to say that
books of this kind had done me much harm, inasmuch as
they had upset my senses, and shut me up in a cage, and
that it would be better for me to reform and change my
studies, and read other truer books which would afford more
pleasure and instruction.'

'Just so,' said the canon.

'Well then,' returned Don Quixote, 'to my mind it is you who are the one that is out of his wits and enchanted, as you have ventured to utter such blasphemies against a thing so universally acknowledged and accepted as true that whoever denies it, as you do, deserves the same punishment which you say you inflict on the books that irritate you when you read them. For to try to persuade anybody that Amadis, and all the other knights-adventurers with whom the books are filled, never existed, would be like trying to persuade him that the sun does not yield light, or ice cold, or earth nourishment. What wit in the world can persuade another that the story of the Princess Florípes and Guy of Burgundy is not true, or that of Fierabras and the bridge of Mantible, which happened in the time of Charlemagne?[1] For by all that is good it is as true as that it is daylight now; and if it be a lie, it must be a lie too that there was a Hector, or Achilles, or Trojan war, or Twelve Peers of France, or Arthur of England, who still lives changed into a raven, and is unceasingly looked for in his kingdom. One might just as well try to make out that the history of Guarino Mezquino,[2] or of the quest of the Holy Grail, is false, or that the loves of Tristram and the Queen Yseult are apocryphal, as well as those of Guinevere and Lancelot, when there are persons who can almost remember having seen the Dame Quintañona, who was the best cupbearer in Great Britain. And so true is this, that I recollect a grandmother of mine on the father's side, whenever she

---

[1] See Note B, p. 357.

[2] A romance of the Charlemagne series, originally written in Italian, but translated into Spanish in 1527.

saw any dame in a venerable hood, used to say to me, "Grand-
son, that one is like Dame Quintañona;" from which I conclude that she must have known her, or at least had managed
to see some portrait of her. Then who can deny that the
story of Pierres and the fair Magalona [1] is true, when even
to this day may be seen in the king's armoury the pin
with which the valiant Pierres guided the wooden horse
he rode through the air, and it is a trifle bigger than the
pole of a cart? And alongside of the pin is Babieca's
saddle, and at Roncesvalles there is Roland's horn, as large
as a large beam; [2] whence we may infer that there were
Twelve Peers, and a Pierres, and a Cid, and other knights
like them, of the sort people commonly call adventurers.
Or perhaps I shall be told, too, that there was no such
knight-errant as the valiant Lusitanian Juan de Merlo,
who went to Burgundy and in the city of Arras fought
with the famous lord of Charny, Mosen Pierres by name,
and afterwards in the city of Basle with Mosen Enrique
de Remesten, coming out of both encounters covered
with fame and honour; [3] or adventures and challenges
achieved and delivered, also in Burgundy, by the valiant
Spaniards Pedro Barba and Gutierre Quixada (of whose
family I come in the direct male line), when they vanquished
the sons of the Count of San Polo. I shall be told, too, that
Don Fernando de Guevara did not go in quest of adventures

[1] The history of Pierres and Magalona is a Provençal romance written
in the twelfth century by Bernardo Treviez, and translated into Spanish
apparently as early as 1519.

[2] The 'dread horn of Roland,' Olifant, was, in fact, an elephant's tusk.

[3] Juan de Merlo was a Portuguese knight in the reign of John II. of
Castile, whose deeds are celebrated by Juan de Mena in the *Laberinto*
(198, 199).

to Germany, where he engaged in combat with Micer
George, a knight of the house of the Duke of Austria.[1]
I shall be told that the jousts of Suero de Quiñones, him of
the 'Paso,'[2] and the emprise of Mosen Luis de Falces[3]
against the Castilian knight, Don Gonzalo de Guzman, were
mere mockeries; as well as many other achievements of
Christian knights of these and foreign realms, which are
so authentic and true, that, I repeat, he who denies them
must be totally wanting in reason and good sense.'

The canon was amazed to hear the medley of truth and
fiction Don Quixote uttered, and to see how well acquainted
he was with everything relating or belonging to the achievements of his knight-errantry; so he said in reply, 'I cannot
deny, Señor Don Quixote, that there is some truth in what
you say, especially as regards the Spanish knights-errant;
and I am willing to grant too that the Twelve Peers of
France existed, but I am not disposed to believe that they
did all the things that the Archbishop Turpin relates of
them.[4] For the truth of the matter is they were knights
chosen by the kings of France, and called 'Peers' because
they were all equal in worth, rank and prowess (at least if
they were not they ought to have been), and it was a kind
of religious order like those of Santiago and Calatrava in
the present day, in which it is assumed that those who
take it are valiant knights of distinction and good birth;
and just as we say now a Knight of St. John, or of Alcan-

---

[1] Fernando de Guevara was another knight of the time of John II.

[2] See Note C, p. 357.

[3] A knight of Navarre mentioned in the *Cronica of John II.* and in
Zurita's *Annals of Aragon.*

[4] See note on Turpin, chapter vii.

tara, they used to say then a Knight of the Twelve Peers,[1] because twelve equals were chosen for that military order. That there was a Cid, as well as a Bernardo del Carpio, there can be no doubt; but that they did the deeds people say they did, I hold to be very doubtful.[2] In that other matter of the pin of Count Pierres that you speak of, and say is near Babieca's saddle in the Armoury, I confess my sin; for I am either so stupid or so short-sighted, that, though I have seen the saddle, I have never been able to see the pin, in spite of it being as big as your worship says it is.'

'For all that it is there, without any manner of doubt,' said Don Quixote; 'and more by token they say it is inclosed in a sheath of cowhide to keep it from rusting.'

'All that may be,' replied the canon; 'but, by the orders I have received, I do not remember seeing it. However, granting it is there, that is no reason why I am bound to believe the stories of all those Amadises and of all that multitude of knights they tell us about, nor is it reasonable that a man like your worship, so worthy, and with so many good qualities, and endowed with such a good understanding, should allow himself to be persuaded that such wild crazy things as are written in those absurd books of chivalry are really true.'

---

[1] No such title as Knight of the Twelve Peers ever existed.
[2] See Note D, p. 357.

Note A (page 351).

Count Fernan Gonzalez of Castile, the hero of many ballads, flourished in the tenth century; for Gonzalo Fernandez, or Hernandez, and Diego García de Paredes see notes to chapter xxxii.: Garci Perez de Vargas is the hero of more than one ballad, but from the mention of Jerez it may be that Cervantes meant Diego Perez dé Vargas, who, at the siege of Jerez, performed the feat that got him the name of the Pounder. (See chapter viii.) Garcilaso is not the poet but an ancestor of his, known as 'el del Ave Maria,' from having slain at the battle of the Salado a Moor who appeared with a label bearing the words ' Ave Maria ' tied to his horse's tail; an exploit generally said to have been performed at Granada. Don Manuel Ponce de Leon was a knight of the time of Ferdinand and Isabella, who figures in the ballads of the Siege of Granada ; for him see not e to chapter xvii. Part II.

Note B (page 353).

The Princess Florípes was the sister of Fierabras, and wife of Guy of Burgundy, a nephew of Charlemagne. The bridge of Mantible, referred to in the History of Charlemagne, was defended by the giant Galafre supported by the Turks, but carried by Charlemagne with the help of Fierabras. The Estremaduran peasants have given the name to the ruins of the old Roman bridge over the Tagus at Alconétar, north of Caceres.

Note C (page 355).

The ' Paso Honroso ' was one of the most famous feats of chivalry of the Middle Ages. Suero de Quiñones, a knight of Leon, with nine others, undertook in 1434 to hold the bridge of Orbigo, near Astorga, against all comers for thirty days. Each was to break three lances with every gentleman who presented himself. There were 727 encounters and 166 lances broken. An account of it was written by a contemporary, Pero Rodriguez de Lena, secretary of John II., which was afterwards re-edited by Juan de Pineda, and printed at Salamanca in 1588 under the title of *Libro del Paso Honroso*. It is appended to the *Cronica de Alvaro de Luna*, Madrid, 1784.

Note D (page 356).

With regard to the Cid the canon is quite right: there is no historical foundation for three-fourths of the achievements attributed to him by the ballads and cronicas. As to Bernardo del Carpio, there may be, of course, some nucleus of fact round which the legends have clustered, but that is all that can be said for his existence. The saddle of the Cid is not now among the treasures of the Armería at Madrid, if indeed it ever was.

CHAPTER L.

OF THE SHREWD CONTROVERSY WHICH DON QUIXOTE AND THE
CANON HELD, TOGETHER WITH OTHER INCIDENTS.

' A GOOD joke, that ! ' returned Don Quixote. ' Books that
have been printed with the king's licence, and with the
approbation of those to whom they have been submitted,
and read with universal delight, and extolled by great and
small, rich and poor, learned and ignorant, gentle and
simple, in a word by people of every sort, of whatever rank
or condition they may be—that these should be lies ! And
above all when they carry such an appearance of truth with
them ; for they tell us the father, mother, country, kindred,
age, place, and the achievements, step by step, and day
by day, performed by such and such a knight or knights !
Hush, sir ; utter not such blasphemy ; trust me I am advising you now to act as a sensible man should ; only read
them, and you will see the pleasure you will derive from
them. For, come, tell me, can there be anything more delightful than to see, as it were, here now displayed before us
a vast lake of bubbling pitch with a host of snakes and
serpents and lizards, and ferocious and terrible creatures of
all sorts swimming about in it, while from the middle of
the lake there comes a plaintive voice saying : " Knight,
whosoever thou art who beholdest this dread lake, if thou

wouldst win the prize that lies hidden beneath these dusky waves, prove the valour of thy stout heart and cast thyself into the midst of its dark burning waters, else thou shalt not be worthy to see the mighty wonders contained in the seven castles of the seven Fays that lie beneath this black expanse; " and then the knight, almost ere the awful voice has ceased, without stopping to consider, without pausing to reflect upon the danger to which he is exposing himself, without even relieving himself of the weight of his massive armour, commending himself to God and to his lady, plunges into the midst of the boiling lake, and when he little looks for it, or knows what his fate is to be, he finds himself among flowery meadows, with which the Elysian fields are not to be compared. The sky seems more transparent there, and the sun shines with a strange brilliancy, and a delightful grove of green leafy trees presents itself to the eyes and charms the sight with its verdure, while the ear is soothed by the sweet untutored melody of the countless birds of gay plumage that flit to and fro among the interlacing branches. Here he sees a brook whose limpid waters, like liquid crystal, ripple over fine sands and white pebbles that look like sifted gold and purest pearls. There he perceives a cunningly wrought fountain of many-coloured jasper and polished marble; here another of rustic fashion where the little mussel-shells and the spiral white and yellow mansions of the snail disposed in studious disorder, mingled with fragments of glittering crystal and mock emeralds, make up a work of varied aspect, where art, imitating nature, seems to have outdone it. Suddenly there is presented to his sight a strong castle or gorgeous palace with walls of massy

gold, turrets of diamond and gates of jacinth ; in short, so
marvellous is its structure that though the materials of
which it is built are nothing less than diamonds, carbuncles,
rubies, pearls, gold, and emeralds, the workmanship is still
more rare.   And after having seen all this, what can be more
charming than to see how a bevy of damsels comes forth
from the gate of the castle in gay and gorgeous attire, such
that, were I to set myself now to depict it as the histories
describe it to us, I should never have done ; and then how
she who seems to be the first among them all takes the bold
knight who plunged into the boiling lake by the hand, and
without addressing a word to him leads him into the rich
palace or castle, and strips him as naked as when his mother
bore him, and bathes him in lukewarm water, and anoints
him all over with sweet-smelling unguents, and clothes him
in a shirt of the softest sendal, all scented and perfumed,
while another damsel comes and throws over his shoulders
a mantle which is said to be worth at the very least a city,
and even more ?   How charming it is, then, when they tell
us how, after all this, they lead him to another chamber
where he finds the tables set out in such style that he is
filled with amazement and wonder ; to see how they pour
out water for his hands distilled from amber and sweet-
scented flowers ; how they seat him on an ivory chair ; to see
how the damsels wait on him all in profound silence ; how
they bring him such a variety of dainties so temptingly prepared that the appetite is at a loss which to select ; to hear
the music that resounds while he is at table, by whom or
whence produced he knows not.   And then when the repast
is over and the tables removed, for the knight to recline in

the chair, picking his teeth perhaps as usual, and a damsel, much lovelier than any of the others, to enter unexpectedly by the chamber door, and seat herself by his side, and begin to tell him what the castle is, and how she is held enchanted there, and other things that amaze the knight and astonish the readers who are perusing his history. But I will not expatiate any further upon this, as it may be gathered from it that whatever part of whatever history of a knight-errant one reads, it will fill the reader, whoever he be, with delight and wonder; and take my advice, sir, and, as I said before, read these books and you will see how they will banish any melancholy you may feel and raise your spirits should they be depressed. For myself I can say that since I have been a knight-errant I have become valiant, polite, generous, well-bred, magnanimous, courteous, dauntless, gentle, patient, and have learned to bear hardships, imprisonments, and enchantments; and though it be such a short time since I have seen myself shut up in a cage like a madman, I hope by the might of my arm, if heaven aid me and fortune thwart me not, to see myself king of some kingdom where I may be able to show the gratitude and generosity that dwell in my heart; for by my faith, señor, the poor man is incapacitated from showing the virtue of generosity to anyone, though he may possess it in the highest degree; and gratitude that consists of disposition only is a dead thing, just as faith without works is dead. For this reason I should be glad were fortune soon to offer me some opportunity of making myself an emperor, so as to show my heart in doing good to my friends, particularly to this poor Sancho Panza, my squire, who is the best fellow in the world; and

I would gladly give him a county I have promised him this ever so long, only that I am afraid he has not the capacity to govern his realm.'

Sancho partly heard these last words of his master, and said to him, ' Strive hard you, Señor Don Quixote, to give me that county so often promised by you and so long looked for by me, for I promise you there will be no want of capacity in me to govern it ; and even if there is, I have heard say there are men in the world who farm seigniories, paying so much a year, and they themselves taking charge of the government, while the lord, with his legs stretched out, enjoys the revenue they pay him, without troubling himself about anything else. That's what I'll do, and not stand haggling over trifles, but wash my hands at once of the whole business, and enjoy my rents like a duke, and let things go their own way.'

' That, brother Sancho,' said the canon, ' only holds good as far as the enjoyment of the revenue goes ; but the lord of the seigniory must attend to the administration of justice, and here capacity and sound judgment come in, and above all a firm determination to find out the truth ; for if this be wanting in the beginning, the middle and the end will always go wrong ; and God as commonly aids the honest intentions of the simple as he frustrates the evil designs of the crafty.'

' I don't understand those philosophies,' returned Sancho Panza ; ' all I know is I would I had the county as soon as I shall know how to govern it ; for I have as much soul as another, and as much body as anyone, and I shall be as much king of my realm as any other of his ; and being so I should do as I liked, and doing as I liked I should please myself, and pleasing myself I should be content, and when one is content he has nothing more to desire, and when one has nothing more to desire there is an end of it; so let the county come, and God be with you, and let us see one another, as one blind man said to the other.'

'That is not bad philosophy thou art talking, Sancho,' said the canon; 'but for all that there is a good deal to be said on this matter of counties.'

To which Don Quixote returned, 'I know not what more there is to be said;[1] I only guide myself by the example set me by the great Amadis of Gaul, when he made his squire count of the Insula Firme; and so, without any scruples of conscience, I can make a count of Sancho Panza, for he is one of the best squires that ever knight-errant had.'

The canon was astonished at the methodical nonsense (if nonsense be capable of method) that Don Quixote uttered, at the way in which he had described the adventure of the knight of the lake, at the impression that the deliberate lies of the books he read had made upon him, and lastly he marvelled at the simplicity of Sancho, who desired so eagerly to obtain the county his master had promised him.

By this time the canon's servants, who had gone to the inn to fetch the sumpter mule, had returned, and making a carpet and the green grass of the meadow serve as a table, they seated themselves in the shade of some trees

[1] In la Cuesta's third edition of 1608 a passage is inserted here for which there is neither authority or necessity.

and made their repast there, that the carter might not be
deprived of the advantage of the spot, as has been already
said. As they were eating they suddenly heard a loud
noise and the sound of a bell that seemed to come from
among some brambles and thick bushes that were close by,
and the same instant they observed a beautiful goat, spotted
all over black, white, and brown, spring out of the thicket
with a goatherd after it, calling to it and uttering the usual
cries to make it stop or turn back to the fold. The fugitive
goat, scared and frightened, ran towards the company as if
seeking their protection and then stood still, and the goatherd coming up seized it by the horns and began to talk to
it as if it were possessed of reason and understanding : ' Ah
wanderer, wanderer, Spotty, Spotty; how have you gone
limping all this time ? What wolves have frightened you,
my daughter ? Won't you tell me what is the matter, my
beauty ? But what else can it be except that you are a she,
and cannot keep quiet ? A plague on your humours and
the humours of those you take after ! Come back, come
back, my darling ; and if you will not be so happy, at any
rate you will be safe in the fold or with your companions ;
for if you who ought to keep and lead them, go wandering
astray in this fashion, what will become of them ? '

The goatherd's talk amused all who heard it, but especially the canon, who said to him, ' As you live, brother,
take it easy, and be not in such a hurry to drive this goat
back to the fold ; for, being a female, as you say, she will
follow her natural instinct in spite of all you can do to
prevent it. Take this morsel and drink a sup, and that
will soothe your irritation, and in the meantime the goat

will rest herself,' and so saying, he handed him the loins of a cold rabbit on a fork.

The goatherd took it with thanks, and drank and calmed himself, and then said, 'I should be sorry if your worships were to take me for a simpleton for having spoken so seriously as I did to this animal; but the truth is there is a certain mystery in the words I used. I am a clown, but not so much of one but that I know how to behave to men and to beasts.'

'That I can well believe,' said the curate, 'for I know already by experience that the woods breed men of learning, and shepherds' huts harbour philosophers.'

'At all events, señor,' returned the goatherd, 'they shelter men of experience; and that you may see the truth of this and grasp it, though I may seem to put myself forward without being asked, I will, if it will not tire you, gentlemen, and you will give me your attention for a little, tell you a true story which will confirm this gentleman's words (and he pointed to the curate) as well as my own.'

To this Don Quixote replied, 'Seeing that this affair has a certain colour of chivalry about it, I for my part, brother, will hear you most gladly, and so will all these gentlemen, from the high intelligence they possess and their love of curious novelties that interest, charm, and entertain the mind, as I feel quite sure your story will do. So begin, friend, for we are all prepared to listen.'

'I draw my stakes,'[1] said Sancho, 'and will retreat with this pasty to the brook there, where I mean to victual myself for three days; for I have heard my lord, Don

---

[1] The phrase used by a player who wishes to withdraw from a game.

Quixote, say that a knight-errant's squire should eat until he can hold no more, whenever he has the chance, because it often happens them to get by accident into a wood so thick that they cannot find a way out of it for six days; and if the man is not well filled or his alforjas well stored, there he may stay, as very often he does, turned into a dried mummy.'

' Thou art in the right of it, Sancho,' said Don Quixote; ' go where thou wilt and eat all thou canst, for I have had enough, and only want to give my mind its refreshment, as I shall by listening to this good fellow's story.'

' It is what we shall all do,' said the canon; and then begged the goatherd to begin the promised tale.

The goatherd gave the goat which he held by the horns a couple of slaps on the back, saying, ' Lie down here beside me, Spotty, for we have time enough to return to our fold.' The goat seemed to understand him, for as her master seated himself, she stretched herself quietly beside him and looked up in his face to show him she was all attention to what he was going to say, and then in these words he began his story.

CHAPTER LI.

WHICH DEALS WITH WHAT THE GOATHERD TOLD THOSE WHO
WERE CARRYING OFF DON QUIXOTE.

THREE leagues from this valley there' is a village which, though
small, is one of the richest in all this neighbourhood, and in it
there lived a farmer, a very worthy man, and so much respected
that, although to be so is the natural consequence of being rich,
he was even more respected for his virtue than for the wealth he
had acquired. But what made him still more fortunate, as he
said himself, was having a daughter of such exceeding beauty,
rare intelligence, gracefulness, and virtue, that everyone who
knew her and beheld her marvelled at the extraordinary gifts
with which heaven and nature had endowed her. As a child she
was beautiful, she continued to grow in beauty, and at the age of
sixteen she was most lovely. The fame of her beauty began to
spread abroad through all the villages around—but why do I say
the villages around, merely, when it spread to distant cities, and
even made its way into the halls of royalty and reached the ears
of people of every class, who came from all sides to see her as if
to see something rare and curious, or some wonder-working
image ?

Her father watched over her and she watched over herself;
for there are no locks, or guards, or bolts that can protect a young
girl better than her own modesty. The wealth of the father and
the beauty of the daughter led many neighbours as well as
strangers to seek her for a wife; but he, as one might well be who
had the disposal of so rich a jewel, was perplexed and unable to
make up his mind to which of her countless suitors he should

entrust her. I was one among the many who felt a desire so
natural, and, as her father knew who I was, and I was of the same
town, of pure blood, in the bloom of life, and very rich in possessions, I had great hopes of success. There was another of the
same place and qualifications who also sought her, and this made
her father's choice hang in the balance, for he felt that on either
of us his daughter would be well bestowed ; so to escape from
this state of perplexity he resolved to refer the matter to Leandra
(for that is the name of the rich damsel who has reduced me to
misery), reflecting that as we were both equal it would be best to
leave it to his dear daughter to choose according to her inclination—a course that is worthy of imitation by all fathers who
wish to settle their children in life. I do not mean that they
ought to leave them to make a choice of what is contemptible
and bad, but that they should place before them what is good
and then allow them to make a good choice as they please. I do
not know which Leandra chose ; I only know her father put us
both off with the tender age of his daughter and vague words
that neither bound him nor dismissed us. My rival is called
Anselmo and I myself Eugenio—that you may know the names
of the personages that figure in this tragedy, the end of which is
still in suspense, though it is plain to see it must be disastrous.

About this time there arrived in our town one Vicente de la
Roca, the son of a poor peasant of the same town, the said Vicente
having returned from service as a soldier in Italy and divers other
parts. A captain who chanced to pass that way with his company
had carried him off from our village when he was a boy of about
twelve years, and now twelve years later the young man came back
in a soldier's uniform, arrayed in a thousand colours, and all over
glass trinkets and fine steel chains. To-day he would appear in
one gay dress, to-morrow in another ; but all flimsy and gaudy,
of little substance and less worth. The peasant folk, who are
naturally malicious, and when they have nothing to do can be
malice itself, remarked all this, and took note of his finery and
jewellery, piece by piece, and discovered that he had three suits
of different colours, with garters and stockings to match ; but he

made so many arrangements and combinations out of them, that if they had not counted them, anyone would have sworn that he had made a display of more than ten suits of clothes and twenty plumes. Do not look upon all this that I am telling you about the clothes as uncalled for or spun out, for they have a great deal to do with the story. He used to seat himself on a bench under the great poplar in our plaza, and there he would keep us all hanging open-mouthed on the stories he told us of his exploits. There was no country on the face of the globe he had not seen, nor battle he had not been engaged in ; he had killed more Moors than there are in Morocco and Tunis, and fought more single combats, according to his own account, than Garcilaso,[1] Diego García de Paredes and a thousand others he named, and out of all he had come victorious without losing a drop of blood. On the other hand he showed marks of wounds, which, though they could not be made out, he said were gunshot wounds received in divers encounters and actions. Lastly, with monstrous impudence he used to say ' you ' to his equals and even those who knew what he was, and declare that his arm was his father and his deeds his pedigree, and that being a soldier he was as good as the king himself. And to add to these swaggering ways he was a trifle of a musician, and played the guitar with such a flourish that some said he made it speak ; nor did his accomplishments end here, for he was something of a poet too, and on every trifle that happened in the town he made a ballad a league and a half long.

This soldier, then, that I have described, this Vicente de la Roca, this bravo, gallant, musician, poet, was often seen and watched by Leandra from a window of her house which looked out on the plaza. The glitter of his showy attire took her fancy, his ballads bewitched her (for he gave away twenty copies of every one he made), the tales of his exploits which he told about

---

[1] The original editions have ' Gante y Luna,' which are not names of persons known in connection with any feats of the kind described. Garcilaso (*v.* p. 357) is much more likely to be the name mentioned with Diego García de Paredes.

himself came to her ears ; and in short, as the devil no doubt
had arranged it, she fell in love with him before the presumption
of making love to her had suggested itself to him ; and as in
love-affairs none are more easily brought to an issue than those
which have the inclination of the lady for an ally, Leandra and
Vicente came to an understanding without any difficulty ; and
before any of her numerous suitors had any suspicion of her
design, she had already carried it into effect, having left the house
of her dearly beloved father (for mother she had none), and
disappeared from the village with the soldier, who came more
triumphantly out of this enterprise than out of any of the large
number he laid claim to. All the village and all who heard of it
were amazed at the affair ; I was aghast, Anselmo thunderstruck,
her father full of grief, her relations indignant, the authorities
all in a ferment, the officers of the Brotherhood in arms. They
scoured the roads, they searched the woods and all quarters, and
at the end of three days they found the flighty Leandra in a
mountain cave, stript to her shift, and robbed of all the money
and precious jewels she had carried away from home with her.
They brought her back to her unhappy father, and questioned
her as to her misfortune, and she confessed without pressure
that Vicente de la Roca had deceived her, and under promise of
marrying her had induced her to leave her father's house, as he
meant to take her to the richest and most delightful city in the
whole world, which was Naples ; and that she, ill-advised and de-
luded, had believed him, and robbed her father, and handed over
all to him the night she disappeared ; and that he had carried her
away to a rugged mountain and shut her up in the cave where
they had found her. She said, moreover, that the soldier, without robbing her of her honour, had taken from her everything
she had, and made off, leaving her in the cave, a thing that still
further surprised everybody. It was not easy for us to credit the
young man's continence, but she asserted it with such earnestness that it helped to console her distressed father, who thought
nothing of what had been taken since the jewel that once lost
can never be recovered had been left to his daughter. The same

day that Leandra made her appearance her father removed her from our sight and took her away to shut her up in a convent in a town near this, in the hope that time may wear away some of the disgrace she has incurred. Leandra's youth furnished an excuse for her fault, at least with those to whom it was of no consequence whether she was good or bad; but those who knew her shrewdness and intelligence did not attribute her misdemeanour to ignorance but to wantonness and the natural disposition of women, which is for the most part flighty and ill-regulated.

Leandra withdrawn from sight, Anselmo's eyes grew blind, or at any rate found nothing to look at that gave them any pleasure, and mine were in darkness without a ray of light to direct them to anything enjoyable while Leandra was away. Our melancholy grew greater, our patience grew less; we cursed the soldier's finery and railed at the carelessness of Leandra's father. At last Anselmo and I agreed to leave the village and come to this valley; and, he feeding a great flock of sheep of his own, and I a large herd of goats of mine, we pass our life among the trees, giving vent to our sorrows, together singing the fair Leandra's praises, or upbraiding her, or else sighing alone, and to heaven pouring forth our complaints in solitude. Following our example, many more of Leandra's lovers have come to these rude mountains and adopted our mode of life, and they are so numerous that one would fancy the place had been turned into the pastoral Arcadia, so full is it of shepherds and sheep-folds; nor is there a spot in it where the name of the fair Leandra is not heard. Here one curses her and calls her capricious, fickle, and immodest, there another condemns her as frail and frivolous; this pardons and absolves her, that spurns and reviles her; one extols her beauty, another assails her character, and in short, all abuse her, and all adore her, and to such a pitch has this general infatuation gone that there are some who complain of her scorn without ever having exchanged a word with her, and even some that bewail and mourn the raging fever of jealousy, for which she never gave anyone cause, for, as I have already said, her misconduct was known before her passion. There is no nook among the rocks, no brookside, no shade beneath the trees that is not haunted by some shepherd telling his woes to the breezes ; wherever there is an echo it repeats the name of Leandra ; the mountains ring with 'Leandra,' 'Leandra' murmur the brooks, and Leandra keeps us all bewildered and bewitched, hoping without hope and fearing without knowing what we fear. Of all this silly set the one that shows the least and also the most sense is my rival Anselmo, for having so many other things to complain of, he only complains of separation, and to the accompaniment of a rebeck, which he plays admirably, he sings his complaints in verses that show his ingenuity. I follow another easier, and to my mind wiser course, and that is to rail at the frivolity of women, at their inconstancy, their double dealing, their broken promises, their unkept pledges, and in short the want of reflection they show in fixing their affections and inclinations. This, sirs, was the reason of words and expressions I made use of to this goat when I came up just now ; for as she is a female I have a contempt for her, though she is the best in all my fold. This is the story I promised to tell you, and if I have been tedious in telling it, I will not be slow to serve you ; my hut is close by, and I have fresh milk and dainty cheese there, as well as a variety of toothsome fruit, no less pleasing to the eye than to the palate.

CHAPTER LII.

OF THE QUARREL THAT DON QUIXOTE HAD WITH THE GOAT-
HERD, TOGETHER WITH THE RARE ADVENTURE OF THE
PENITENTS, WHICH WITH AN EXPENDITURE OF SWEAT HE
BROUGHT TO A HAPPY CONCLUSION.

THE goatherd's tale gave great satisfaction to all the
hearers, and the canon especially enjoyed it, for he had
remarked with particular attention the manner in which it
had been told, which was as unlike the manner of a clownish goatherd as it was like that of a polished city wit; and
he observed that the curate had been quite right in saying
that the woods bred men of learning. They all offered their
services to Eugenio, but he who showed himself most
liberal in this way was Don Quixote, who said to him,
'Most assuredly, brother goatherd, if I found myself in a
position to attempt any adventure, I would, this very instant,
set out on your behalf, and would rescue Leandra from that
convent (where no doubt she is kept against her will), in
spite of the abbess and all who might try to prevent me,
and would place her in your hands to deal with her according to your will and pleasure, observing, however, the laws
of chivalry which lay down that no violence of any kind is
to be offered to any damsel. But I trust in God our Lord
that the might of one malignant enchanter may not prove

so great but that the power of another better disposed may
prove superior to it, and then I promise you my support
and assistance, as I am bound to do by my profession,
which is none other than to give aid to the weak and needy.'

The goatherd eyed him, and noticing Don Quixote's
sorry appearance and looks, he was filled with wonder, and
asked the barber, who was next him, 'Señor, who is this
man who makes such a figure and talks in such a strain?'

'Who should it be,' said the barber, 'but the famous
Don Quixote of La Mancha, the undoer of injustice, the
righter of wrongs, the protector of damsels, the terror of
giants, and the winner of battles?'

'That,' said the goatherd, 'sounds like what one reads
in the books of the knights-errant, who did all that you say
this man does; though it is my belief that either you are
joking, or else this gentleman has empty lodgings in his
head.'

'You are a great scoundrel,' said Don Quixote, 'and
it is you who are empty and a fool. I am fuller than ever
was the whoreson bitch that bore you;' and passing from
words to deeds, he caught up a loaf that was near him and
sent it full in the goatherd's face, with such force that he
flattened his nose; but the goatherd, who did not understand jokes, and found himself roughly handled in such
good earnest, paying no respect to carpet, table-cloth, or
diners, sprang upon Don Quixote, and seizing him by the
throat with both hands would no doubt have throttled him,
had not Sancho Panza that instant come to the rescue, and
grasping him by the shoulders flung him down on the table,
smashing plates, breaking glasses, and upsetting and scat-

tering everything on it. Don Quixote, finding himself free, strove to get on top of the goatherd, who, with his face covered with blood, and soundly kicked by Sancho, was on all fours feeling about for one of the table-knives to take a bloody revenge with. The canon and the curate, however, prevented him, but the barber so contrived it that he got Don Quixote under him, and rained down upon him such a shower of fisticuffs that the poor knight's face streamed with blood as freely as his own. The canon and the curate were bursting with laughter, the officers were capering with delight, and both the one and the other hissed them on as they do dogs that are worrying one another in a fight.[1] Sancho alone was frantic, for he could not free himself from the grasp of one of the canon's servants, who kept him from going to his master's assistance.

At last, while they were all, with the exception of the two bruisers who were mauling each other, in high glee and enjoyment, they heard a trumpet sound a note so doleful that it made them all look in the direction whence the sound seemed to come. But the one that was most excited by hearing it was Don Quixote, who, though sorely against his will he was under the goatherd, and something more than pretty well pummelled, said to him, 'Brother devil (for it is impossible but that thou must be one since thou hast had might and strength enough to overcome mine), I ask thee to agree to a truce for but one hour, for the solemn note of yonder trumpet that falls on our ears seems to me to summon me to some new adventure.' The goatherd, who was by this time tired of pummelling and being pum-

---

[1] See Note A, p. 388.

melled, released him at once, and Don Quixote rising to his
feet and turning his eyes to the quarter where the sound
had been heard, suddenly saw coming down the slope of a
hill several men clad in white like penitents.

The fact was that the clouds had that year withheld
their moisture from the earth, and in all the villages of the
district they were organising processions, rogations, and
penances, imploring God to open the hands of his mercy
and send them rain; and to this end the people of a village
that was hard by were going in procession to a holy hermitage there was on one side of that valley. Don Quixote,
when he saw the strange garb of the penitents, without
reflecting how often he had seen it before, took it into his
head that this was a case of adventure, and that it fell to
him alone as a knight-errant to engage in it; and he was
all the more confirmed in this notion, by the idea that an
image draped in black they had with them was some illustrious lady that these villains and discourteous thieves were
carrying off by force. As soon as this occurred to him he
ran with all speed to Rocinante who was grazing at large,
and taking the bridle and the buckler from the saddle-bow,
he had him bridled in an instant, and calling to Sancho for
his sword he mounted Rocinante, braced his buckler on his
arm, and in a loud voice exclaimed to those who stood by,
' Now, noble company, ye shall see how important it is that
there should be knights in the world professing the order of
knight-errantry; now, I say, ye shall see, by the deliverance
of that worthy lady who is borne captive there, whether
knights-errant deserve to be held in estimation,' and so
saying he brought his legs to bear on Rocinante—for he had

no spurs—and at a full canter (for in all this veracious history we never read of Rocinante fairly galloping) set off to encounter the penitents, though the curate, the canon, and the barber ran to prevent him. But it was out of their power, nor did he even stop for the shouts of Sancho calling after him, 'Where are you going, Señor Don Quixote? What devils have possessed you to set you on against our Catholic faith? Plague take me! mind, that is a procession of penitents, and the lady they are carrying on that stand there is the blessed image of the immaculate Virgin. Take care what you are doing, señor, for this time it may be safely said you don't know what you are about.' Sancho laboured in vain, for his master was so bent on coming to quarters with these sheeted figures and releasing the lady in black that he did not hear a word; and even had he heard, he would not have turned back if the king had ordered him. He came up with the procession and reined in Rocinante, who was already anxious enough to slacken speed a little, and in a hoarse, excited voice he exclaimed, 'You who hide your faces, perhaps because you are not good subjects, pay attention and listen to what I am about to say to you.' The first to halt were those who were carrying the image, and one of the four ecclesiastics who were chanting the Litany, struck by the strange figure of Don Quixote, the leanness of Rocinante, and the other ludicrous peculiarities he observed, said in reply to him, 'Brother, if you have anything to say to us say it quickly, for these brethren are whipping themselves, and we cannot stop, nor is it reasonable we should stop to hear anything, unless indeed it is short enough to be said in two words.'

'I will say it in one,' replied Don Quixote, 'and it is this; that at once, this very instant, ye release that fair lady whose tears and sad aspect show plainly that ye are carrying her off against her will, and that ye have committed some scandalous outrage against her; and I, who was born into the world to redress all such like wrongs, will not permit you to advance another step until you have restored to her the liberty she pines for and deserves.'

From these words all the hearers concluded that he must be a madman, and began to laugh heartily, and their laughter acted like gunpowder on Don Quixote's fury, for drawing his sword without another word he made a rush at the stand. One of those who supported it, leaving the burden to his comrades, advanced to meet him, flourishing a forked stick that he had for propping up the stand when resting, and with this he caught a mighty cut Don Quixote made at him that severed it in two; but with the portion that remained in his hand he dealt such a thwack on the shoulder of Don Quixote's sword arm (which the buckler could not protect against the clownish assault) that poor Don Quixote came to the ground in a sad plight.

Sancho Panza, who was coming on close behind puffing and blowing, seeing him fall, cried out to his assailant not to strike him again, for he was a poor enchanted knight, who had never harmed anyone all the days of his life; but what checked the clown was, not Sancho's shouting, but seeing that Don Quixote did not stir hand or foot; and so, fancying he had killed him, he hastily hitched up his tunic under his girdle and took to his heels across the country like a deer.

By this time all Don Quixote's companions had come up to where he lay; but the processionists seeing them come running, and with them the officers of the Brotherhood with their crossbows, apprehended mischief, and clustering round the image, raised their hoods, and grasped their scourges, as the priests did their tapers, and awaited the attack, resolved to defend themselves and even to take the offensive against their assailants if they could. Fortune, however, arranged the matter better than they expected, for all Sancho did was to fling himself on his master's body, raising over him the most doleful and laughable lamentation that ever was heard, for he believed he was dead. The curate was known to another curate who walked in the procession, and their recognition of one another set at rest the apprehensions of both parties; the first then told the other in two words who Don Quixote was, and he and the whole troop of penitents went to see if the poor gentleman was dead, and heard Sancho Panza saying, with tears in his eyes, 'Oh flower of chivalry, that with one blow of a stick hast ended the course of thy well-spent life! Oh pride of thy race, honour and glory of all La Mancha, nay, of all the world, that for want of thee will be full of evil-doers, no longer in fear of punishment for their misdeeds! Oh thou, generous above all the Alexanders, since for only eight months of service thou hast given me the best island the sea girds or surrounds![1] Humble with the proud, haughty with the humble, encounterer of dangers, endurer of outrages, enamoured without reason, imitator of the good, scourge of the wicked, enemy of the mean, in short, knight-errant, which is all that can be said!'

[1] See Note B, p. 388.

At the cries and moans of Sancho, Don Quixote came to himself, and the first word he said was, ' He who lives separated from you, sweetest Dulcinea, has greater miseries to endure than these. Aid me, friend Sancho, to mount the enchanted cart, for I am not in a condition to press the saddle of Rocinante, as this shoulder is all knocked to pieces.'

' That I will do with all my heart, señor,' said Sancho ; ' and let us return to our village with these gentlemen, who seek your good, and there we will prepare for making another sally, which may turn out more profitable and creditable to us.'

' Thou art right, Sancho,' returned Don Quixote ; ' it will be wise to let the malign influence of the stars which now prevails pass off.'

The canon, the curate, and the barber told him he would act very wisely in doing as he said ; and so, highly amused at Sancho Panza's simplicities, they placed Don Quixote in the cart as before. The procession once more formed itself in order and proceeded on its road ; the goatherd took his leave of the party ; the officers of the Brotherhood declined to go any farther, and the curate paid them what was due to them ; the canon begged the curate to let him know how Don Quixote did, whether he was cured of his madness or still suffered from it, and then begged leave to continue his journey ; in short, they all separated and went their ways, leaving to themselves the curate and the barber, Don Quixote, Sancho Panza, and the good Rocinante, who regarded everything with as great resignation as his master. The carter yoked his oxen and made Don Quixote comfortable on a truss of hay, and at his usual deliberate pace took the road the curate directed, and at the end of six days they reached Don Quixote's village, and entered it about the middle of the day, which it so happened was a Sunday, and the people were all in the plaza, through which Don Quixote's cart passed. They all flocked to see what was in the cart, and when they recognised their townsman they were filled with amazement, and a boy ran off to bring the news to his housekeeper and his niece that their master and uncle had come back all lean and yellow and stretched on a truss of hay on an ox-cart. It was piteous to hear the cries the two good ladies raised, how they beat their breasts and poured out fresh maledictions on those accursed books of chivalry; all which was renewed when they saw Don Quixote coming in at the gate.

At the news of Don Quixote's arrival Sancho Panza's wife came running, for she by this time knew that her husband had gone away with him as his squire, and on seeing Sancho, the first thing she asked him was if the ass was well. Sancho replied that he was, better than his master was.

'Thanks be to God,' said she, 'for being so good to me; but now tell me, my friend, what have you made by your squirings? What gown have you brought me back? What shoes for your children?'

'I bring nothing of that sort, wife,' said Sancho; 'though I bring other things of more consequence and value.'

'I am very glad of that,' returned his wife; 'show me these things of more value and consequence, my friend; for

I want to see them to cheer my heart that has been so sad and heavy all these ages that you have been away.'

'I will show them to you at home, wife,' said Sancho; 'be content for the present; for if it please God that we should again go on our travels in search of adventures, you will soon see me a count, or governor of an island, and that not one of those everyday ones, but the best that is to be had.'

'Heaven grant it, husband,' said she, 'for indeed we have need of it. But tell me, what's this about islands, for I don't understand it?'

'Honey is not for the mouth of the ass,'[1] returned Sancho; 'all in good time thou shalt see, wife—nay, thou wilt be surprised to hear thyself called "your ladyship" by all thy vassals.'

'What are you talking about, Sancho, with your lady-ships, islands, and vassals?' returned Teresa Panza—for so Sancho's wife was called, though they were not relations, for in La Mancha it is customary for wives to take their husbands' surnames.

'Don't be in such a hurry to know all this, Teresa,' said Sancho; 'it is enough that I am telling you the truth, so shut your mouth. But I may tell you this much by the way, that there is nothing in the world more delightful than to be a person of consideration, squire to a knight-errant, and a seeker of adventures. To be sure most of those one finds do not end as pleasantly as one could wish, for out of a hundred that one meets with, ninety-nine will turn out cross and contrary. I know it by experience, for out of

[1] Prov. 138.

some I came blanketed, and out of others belaboured. Still, for all that, it is a fine thing to be on the look-out for what may happen, crossing mountains, searching woods, climbing rocks, visiting castles, putting up at inns, all at free quarters, and devil take the maravedi to pay.'

While this conversation passed between Sancho Panza and his wife, Don Quixote's housekeeper and niece took him in and undressed him and laid him in his old bed. He eyed them askance, and could not make out where he was. The curate charged his niece to be very careful to make her uncle comfortable and to keep a watch over him lest he should make his escape from them again, telling her what they had been obliged to do to bring him home. On this the pair once more lifted up their voices and renewed their maledictions upon the books of chivalry, and implored heaven to plunge the authors of such lies and nonsense into the midst of the bottomless pit. They were, in short, kept in anxiety and dread lest their uncle and master should give them the slip the moment he found himself somewhat better, and as they feared so it fell out.

But the author of this history, though he has devoted research and industry to the discovery of the deeds achieved by Don Quixote in his third sally, has been unable to obtain any information respecting them, at any rate derived from authentic documents; tradition has merely preserved in the memory of La Mancha the fact that Don Quixote, the third time he sallied forth from his home, betook himself to Saragossa, where he was present at some famous jousts which came off in that city, and that he had adventures there worthy of his valour and high intelligence. Of his

end and death he could learn no particulars, nor would he
have ascertained it or known of it, if good fortune had not
produced an old physician for him who had in his possession a leaden box, which, according to his account, had
been discovered among the crumbling foundations of an
ancient hermitage that was being rebuilt; in which box were
found certain parchment manuscripts in Gothic character,
but in Castilian verse, containing many of his achievements, and setting forth the beauty of Dulcinea, the form
of Rocinante, the fidelity of Sancho Panza, and the burial
of Don Quixote himself, together with sundry epitaphs and
eulogies on his life and character; but all that could be read
and deciphered were those which the trustworthy author of
this new and unparalleled history here presents. And the
said author asks of those that shall read it nothing in return
for the vast toil which it has cost him in examining and
searching the Manchegan archives in order to bring it to
light, save that they give him the same credit that people of
sense [1] give to the books of chivalry that pervade the world
and are so popular; for with this he will consider himself
amply paid and fully satisfied, and will be encouraged to
seek out and produce other histories, if not as truthful, at
least equal in invention and not less entertaining. The
first words written on the parchment found in the leaden
box were these:

[1] See Note C, p. 389.

THE ACADEMICIANS OF ARGAMASILLA,[1]

A VILLAGE OF LA MANCHA,

ON THE LIFE AND DEATH OF DON QUIXOTE OF LA MANCHA,

HOC SCRIPSERUNT.

MONICONGO, ACADEMICIAN OF ARGAMASILLA, ON THE
TOMB OF DON QUIXOTE.

EPITAPH.

The scatterbrain that gave La Mancha more
    Rich spoils than Jason's ; who a point so keen
    Had to his wit, and happier far had been
If his wit's weathercock a blunter bore ;
The arm renowned far as Gaeta's shore,
    Cathay, and all the lands that lie between ;
    The muse discreet and terrible in mien
As ever wrote on brass in days of yore ;
He who surpassed the Amadises all,
    And who as naught the Galaors accounted,
    Supported by his love and gallantry :
Who made the Belianises sing small,
    And sought renown on Rocinante mounted ;
    Here, underneath this cold stone, doth he lie.

PANIAGUADO, ACADEMICIAN OF ARGAMASILLA, IN
LAUDEM DULCINEÆ DEL TOBOSO.

SONNET.

She, whose full features may be here descried,
    High-bosomed, with a bearing of disdain,
    Is Dulcinea, she for whom in vain
The great Don Quixote of La Mancha sighed.
For her, Toboso's queen, from side to side
    He traversed the grim sierra, the champaign
    Of Aranjuez, and Montiel's famous plain :
On Rocinante oft a weary ride.

[1] See Note D, p. 389.

Malignant planets, cruel destiny,
  Pursued them both, the fair Manchegan dame,
And the unconquered star of chivalry.
  Nor youth nor beauty saved her from the claim
Of death ; he paid love's bitter penalty,
  And left the marble to preserve his name.

CAPRICHOSO, A MOST ACUTE ACADEMICIAN OF ARGAMASILLA,
IN PRAISE OF ROCINANTE, STEED OF DON QUIXOTE OF
LA MANCHA.

SONNET.

On that proud throne [1] of diamantine sheen,
  Which the blood-reeking feet of Mars degrade,
The mad Manchegan's banner now hath been
  By him in all its bravery displayed.
  There hath he hung his arms and trenchant blade
Wherewith, achieving deeds till now unseen,
  He slays, lays low, cleaves, hews ; but art hath made
A novel style for our new paladin.
If Amadis be the proud boast of Gaul,
  If by his progeny the fame of Greece
    Through all the regions of the earth be spread,
Great Quixote crowned in grim Bellona's hall
  To-day exalts La Mancha over these,
    And above Greece or Gaul she holds her head.
Nor ends his glory here, for his good steed
Doth Brillador and Bayard far exceed ; [2]
As mettled steeds compared with Rocinante,
The reputation they have won is scanty.

---

[1] See Note E, p. 389.
[2] Brillador was Orlando's horse ; Bayard, Rinaldo's :
      ‘ Quel Brigliador sì bello e sì gagliardo
      Che non ha paragon, fuorche Baiardo.’
                    Orlando Furioso, ix. 60.

Burlador, Academician of Argamasilla, on Sancho Panza.

SONNET.

The worthy Sancho Panza here you see ;
  A great soul once was in that body small,
  Nor was there squire upon this earthly ball
So plain and simple, or of guile so free.
Within an ace of being Count was he,
  And would have been but for the spite and gall
  Of this vile age, mean and illiberal,
That cannot even let a donkey be.
For mounted on an ass (excuse the word),
  By Rocinante's side this gentle squire
    Was wont his wandering master to attend.
Delusive hopes that lure the common herd
  With promises of ease, the heart's desire,
    In shadows, dreams, and smoke ye always end.

Cachidiablo, Academician of Argamasilla, on the Tomb of Don Quixote.

EPITAPH.

The knight lies here below,
  Ill-errant and bruisèd sore,
  Whom Rocinante bore
In his wanderings to and fro.
By the side of the knight is laid
  Stolid man Sancho too,
  Than whom a squire more true
Was not in the esquire trade.

TIQUITOC, ACADEMICIAN OF ARGAMASILLA, ON THE TOMB OF
DULCINEA DEL TOBOSO.

EPITAPH.

Here Dulcinea lies.
Plump was she and robust :
Now she is ashes and dust :
The end of all flesh that dies.
A lady of high degree,
With the port of a lofty dame,
And the great Don Quixote's flame,
And the pride of her village was she.

These were all the verses that could be deciphered; the
rest, the writing being worm-eaten, were handed over to one
of the Academicians to make out their meaning conjectu-
rally. We have been informed that at the cost of many
sleepless nights and much toil he has succeeded, and that
he means to publish them in hopes of Don Quixote's third
sally.

' Forse altro cantera con miglior plectro.' [1]

[1] See Note F, p. 389.

Note A (page 875).

Hartzenbusch, who will never admit an error in taste or judgment in
Cervantes, explains the conduct of the canon and curate on this occasion
by pointing out that it was *after dinner.*

Note B (page 879).

It is commonly said that Sancho, though he would have understood
what ' isla ' meant, had no conception of the meaning of ' insula,' the anti-
quated word for island Don Quixote always uses; but it appears from this
that he understood perfectly what an insula is.

Note C (*page* 384).

One of his grievances against the books of chivalry being that they led astray not merely the silly, thoughtless, and uncritical, but vast numbers of people who ought to know better.

Note D (*page* 385).

Whether or not this is to be held an indication of some grudge on the part of Cervantes against the authorities of the town, it is, at any rate, conclusive that Don Quixote's village, ' the name of which he did not care to call to mind,' was Argamasilla. 'Monicongo' may be translated 'mannikin;' 'Paniaguado' is a sort of parasite hanging about the house of a patron for such scraps as he can pick up; 'Burlador' means a joker, and 'Cachidiablo' a hobgoblin. Except, perhaps, in the sonnet on Sancho Panza, there is not much drollery or humour in these verses, but it would not be fair to criticise them severely, as they are obviously nothing more than a mere outburst of reckless nonsense to finish off with; a sort of flourish or *rubrica* like that commonly appended to a Spanish signature.

Note E (*page* 386).

In the second and third editions *trono*—'throne'—was changed into *tronco*, which Hartzenbusch considers a blundering alteration. I am inclined to think, however, that he is wrong, and that what Cervantes meant was not a diamond-studded throne, but an adamant pillar, a trophy in fact. But it is no great matter; the sonnet was meant for nonsense, and is successful either way.

Note F (*page* 388).

Misquoted from Ariosto, *Orlando Furioso*, xxx. 16:
' Forse altri canterà con miglior plettro.'

Cervantes, it will be seen, leaves it very uncertain whether he means to give a continuation of the adventures of Don Quixote or not, and here almost seems to invite some other historian to undertake the task.

END OF THE SECOND VOLUME.

Spottiswoode & Co., Printers, New-street Square, London.

www.ingramcontent.com/pod-product-compliance
Lightning Source LLC
Chambersburg PA
CBHW020836030726
47496CB00001B/254